SHAWNDIREA

BOOK ONE

AETHEAON CHRONICLES
BOOK ONE

LEONARD D. HILLEY II

SHAWNDIREA

LEONARD HILLEY II

ACKNOWLEDGMENTS

A special thanks to: Carol Ann Murrell, Michelle Lumpkins, and KC Riley-Gyer. Thanks for your encouragement and taking this journey with me.

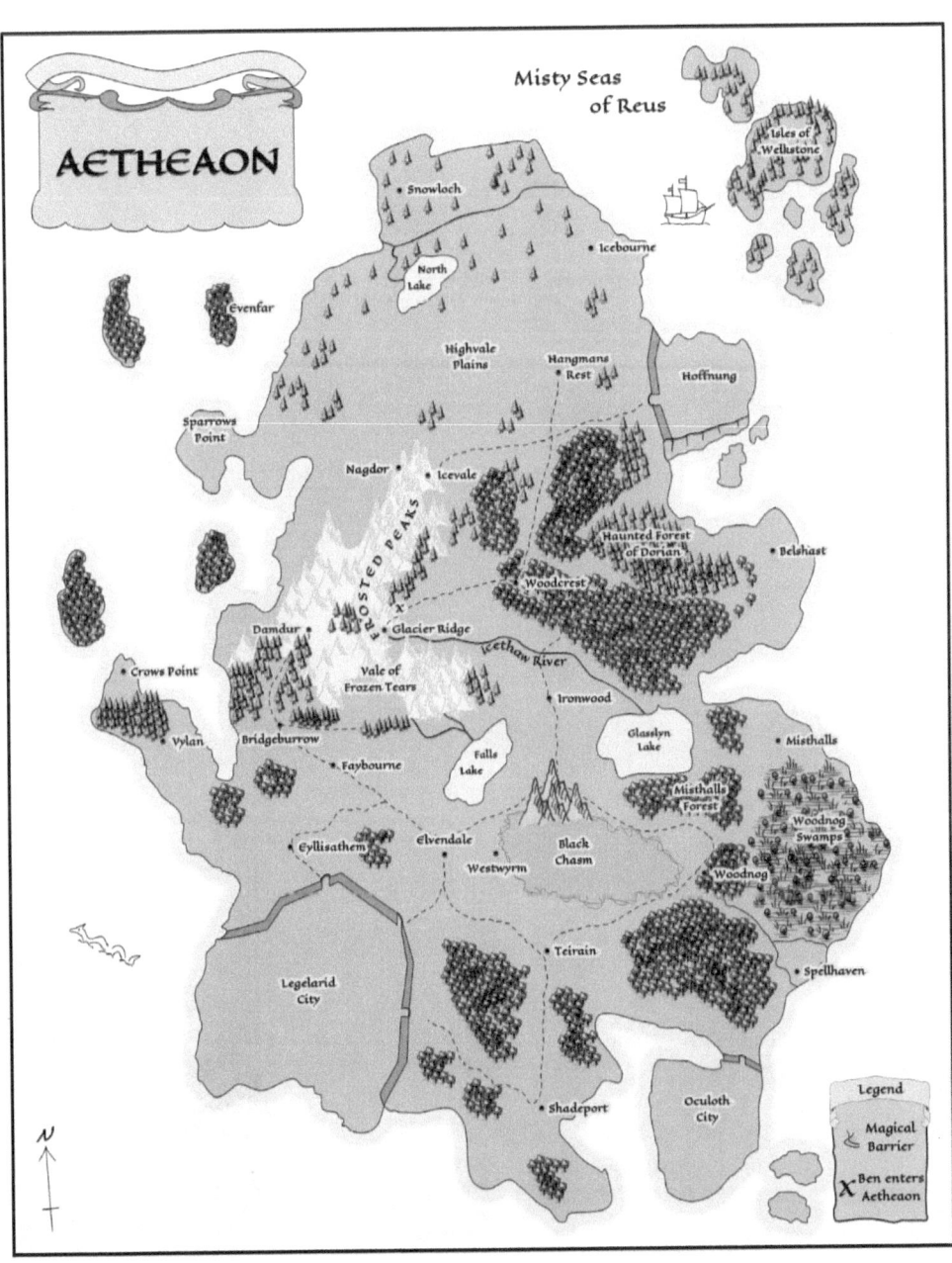

CHAPTER 1

*T*he early autumn sun blazed over the freshly cut hayfield in Cider Knoll, Kentucky. Ben Whytten rested his butterfly net against the rusted, barbed wire fence. He wiped sweat from his brow with the back of his hand. His shirt and blue jeans were soaked with perspiration.

Although late September, the temperature never indicated autumn had begun. Sporting near ninety degrees, summer refused to relinquish its grip. What should've been a pleasant Saturday afternoon was squandered by the sweltering heat.

Ben drank cold water from his canteen. Beads of water dripped down his short, brown beard. He sighed and twisted the canteen cap shut. His piercing brown eyes studied the cloudless sky. No breeze helped combat the hellish, sticky heat.

He combed his sweat-matted hair from his eyes with his fingers. He picked up his butterfly net and trudged across the straw-colored field to a small grove of reddish-orange maples lining a winding stream. The shade was inviting, and he guessed a good ten degrees cooler than the open field. The brittle grass stems crunched beneath his hiking boots.

Collecting butterflies in autumn was better than the spring or summer months because the species' diversity increased. The fall forms of butterflies were brighter and larger. They often fed in greater clusters on the ironweed, milkweed, and clover. Vibrant swallowtails puddled along the creek beds. Plump moth and butterfly larvae were easier to find as they searched for places to spin cocoons or pupate underground before the colder temperatures set in.

"If colder weather ever settles in," Ben thought, *"Hell will have truly frozen over."*

Grasshoppers jumped and took to flight as Ben crossed the field. Their colorful wings buzzed. The grasshoppers glided and drifted downward. Upon landing, they propelled themselves into the air again.

At the shady maple grove, Ben leaned against a thick, tree trunk and closed his eyes. The soothing sounds of nature relaxed him, and he was thankful to be outside, alone. The shallow stream trickled softly. Cicadas hummed. In the distance, a woodpecker rapped the bark of a hollow, dead pine. Weather had stripped away sections of the rough pine bark and revealed the smooth, yellow wood underneath.

His colleague, Dr. Isaac Deiko, had planned to collect insects with Ben this particular Saturday, but at the last minute, he called and cancelled. Deiko needed to set up display tables at a gun show in a neighboring town.

The news didn't disappoint Ben. He'd rather collect butterflies and insects alone. The outdoors was a place where he gathered his thoughts and meditated about life. The forests, bluffs, and meadows comforted him with peace. Leaving the fast-paced, bustling, technological-craving addicts for a calmer, slow-paced life was worth more than millions of dollars. He'd give up all the instant gadgets for the tranquility his grandfather and great-grandfather had experienced working on their farms decades earlier. If such a world existed, he'd go without argument.

Ben kept a serious outlook on life while Dr. Deiko spent more time playing practical jokes on their colleagues and students, which often irritated and infuriated Ben. If Deiko had tagged along, the collecting possibilities would be little or none because Deiko was clumsy-footed and boisterous.

Ben never extended an invitation for Deiko to join him in the first place. In fact, Deiko *invited* himself when he learned about Ben's collecting plans for the weekend. Although Deiko was also a biologist, he sought a discovery to make him famous, whereas Ben loved science and didn't care if anyone other than his students knew he existed. Of course, when final exams rolled around, Ben's students would rather he *didn't* exist. Students joked that Ben took them on field trips from Hell, and his written tests were considered harsher than the rigorous, ten-mile hikes through steep mountainous terrain.

Ben looked across the field and chuckled. He had traipsed hundreds of acres through forests, caves, and fields when he was in middle school. He had done so voluntarily, without any complaint, and yet, today's college students voiced disdain over the least thing. The challenge wasn't getting them to learn; it was separating them from their pacifying need for their cellphones.

His inner frustration brought more heat to his face. He was seconds from rehashing how he wished computers and cellphones weren't so controlling until the soft, bubbling creek caught his attention. The gentle, soft sound of water eased his mind from the classroom tensions and swaddled him within the natural calm. He expelled a long sigh and refocused.

Tall narrow blades of grass covered the sandy banks of a shallow stream. Small, drab, satyr butterflies fluttered lazily from grass blade to grass blade.

Ben shook his head.

After two hours of walking the fields and woods, he'd hoped to capture a few new specimens to add to his collection. But with each species he encountered, he already had at least a half-dozen of those pinned inside glass-top boxes at home. In many ways, he'd have done himself a greater service by staying home.

But regardless of what he deemed bad luck, his career and his life were about to change.

Forever.

He removed his backpack and set it down. Slowly, he sat on the ground and leaned against the tree trunk to rest. He set the canteen to the side of the tree, placed the net handle across his lap, and watched a few minnows dart back and forth in the gentle stream. Water striders skimmed the water's surface like polished skaters on ice.

Drenched in sweet and drained by the heat, Ben sighed when a sudden, cool breeze stirred along the stream. His heavy eyelids coaxed him to surrender and take a nap. Even though the place was comforting and peaceful, he fought the urge to doze. But, if nothing interesting presented itself soon, he'd go home. He dreaded walking across the hot, dry pasture to his SUV.

He unsheathed his hunting knife on his belt and picked up a dead oak twig. He whittled and shaved away the bark.

The extreme heat kept the most brilliant butterflies in hiding. Later in the evening his luck might improve, but he refused to stick around that long. He slid the knife into its sheath and rubbed his tired eyes.

Sunlight filtered through the leafy canopy. Several birds flew low across the stream and through the trees. Seconds later, two yellow butterflies glided to the edge of the far bank and landed. A larger butterfly caught his attention. At first glance, he thought it was a giant swallowtail, but instead, it turned out to be an oversized tiger swallowtail.

Ben's fingers tightened around the net handle. He pushed himself to his feet. Stepping lightly, he headed to the stream to examine the butterflies. Near the bank, a blur of metallic bluish-green streaked past him.

"What the—?" he said.

With incredible speed, the zipping wings caught the breeze and darted up, down, and left to right along the stream's edge. He questioned whether the sweltering heat and his near dehydration were playing tricks on him. The brilliant butterfly left a glittery dust trail behind it.

Ben hurried after the butterfly, which was a prize unlike any in his collection.

Few butterflies in this part of Kentucky had such metallic colorings. The White M Hairstreak was one, but it was small and lethargic. Another butterfly with similar colors was the long-tailed skipper, but the sheen sparkling off the butterfly following the stream was much brighter. Its flight was also more erratic. The skipper stayed near gardens. None would stray this far in the woods since the larvae's food plant was the leaves of various beanstalks.

Ben had discovered a new species. Excitement shot through him.

He hurried along the stream and jumped over a fallen tree. His sudden pursuit had not gone unnoticed. The iridescent creature darted downward and swept through the tiny branches of a shrub. But Ben outpaced it.

The beautifully winged specimen shot through the other side of the bush, and Ben arced the net sharply and captured his prize. The end of the net pulled and stretched while his captive struggled to fight free.

Quickly, Ben clamped his fingers near the end of the net, but by the time he did, the struggling ceased.

He opened the net and looked inside. His eyes widened.

"What the—?" he asked.

At the bottom of the net lie a gorgeous creature, but not what he expected to capture. Her wings were tattered, frayed. Unconscious—he hoped—but he feared she might be dying or already dead. Broken scales and wing fragments covered her nearly nude body.

His excitement of the chase turned to regret and dread.

A faery?

Ben dropped to his knees and gently placed the net on the ground.

He whispered, "What have I done?"

He placed his left hand beside her unmoving form. He nudged her onto his palm with the tip of his finger. She breathed, but her eyes remained closed. Her radiant face was more beautiful than any woman he had ever met.

A vehicle door slammed and echoed near the pasture gate where Ben had parked his SUV.

Ben looked over his shoulder but the vehicle was parked out of view.

"Ben!" Deiko shouted. "Where are you?"

"Dammit." Ben grumbled and whispered, "What the Hell are you doing here?"

He hurried to the tree where he'd set his backpack. He curled his left hand gently around the faery's limp body and reached inside the pack with his right.

"Ben!"

Ben took a wide-mouthed dark plastic bottle, set it between his knees, and unscrewed the hole-punched lid. He hurried. Deiko's lanky figure jogged toward the maple grove. Deiko smiled and waved when their eyes met. His jog turned into a sprint as he approached Ben.

Ben placed the faery inside the jar, turned the lid, and wrapped the jar inside a white cloth before setting it in his pack. No sooner had he zipped the pack shut, Deiko's thundering footsteps stopped beside him.

"Catch something nice, huh?" Deiko asked. He leaned forward and panted. Sweat covered his face.

"No," Ben replied. He looked up without making eye contact with Deiko. "Not much butterfly activity today. I blame the heat."

Deiko smiled broadly and shook his head. Excitement arose in the professor's voice. "But you caught *something*. Something *special*."

Ben shook his head, picked up his pack, and stood. "Look around, Isaac. What do you see?"

Deiko glanced around but then his eyes focused on Ben's backpack again. "I agree. Not much flying around. But *you* caught something."

"What makes you think that?"

"Your eyes indicate you did, even though you claim otherwise. You have an obvious tell. Never play poker unless you learn to suppress your excitement. You'll never win."

Ben's eyes narrowed. He changed the subject. "How was the gun show, Isaac? I thought you'd be there all day."

Deiko shrugged. "That was my plan. Not much going on there, either. Got a couple good deals though. Like this Ruger."

He pulled a handgun from the back of his belt.

"Nice," Ben replied. Carefully, he slipped his pack over his shoulder and walked into the hay field.

"Well?" Deiko tucked the gun behind his belt, stepped in front of Ben, and blocked his path. "Aren't you going to show me?"

Sweat dripped from Deiko's black hair and beaded on his brow. Ben studied the determination set in his colleague's dark eyes and his firm, muscular jaw. Within seconds, Deiko's boyish face hardened into the face of a fierce, murderous villain.

Physically, Deiko had no weight to put behind his facial threat. He was tall and quite bony with slender arms. Although Deiko was probably fifteen years younger, Ben had no doubt if they fought, Deiko would be the one lying on the ground and rubbing his jaw. But, then, Isaac came with a gun. Isaac was armed and Ben's only weapon was a knife. Even those odds weren't in Isaac's favor.

"Show you *what?*" Ben asked.

"Your prize. It must be something nice since you refuse to show me."

"How many times did I tell you I haven't found anything?"

"Wow. Sticking to the lie, eh? Let's play poker sometime," Deiko said. "I'd make a fortune."

Ben shrugged. "Being as I don't play cards, you're probably correct with your assumption."

"Oh, come on, Ben," Deiko said. Hostility loomed in his voice and darkness narrowed his eyes. "Why are you afraid to show me what you found?"

Isaac was a nuisance at times, but he'd never behaved like a demented, spoiled brat. He had his moments, but Dr. Deiko never displayed a quiet, intimidating tone. But out here, away from observers, a deep-seeded violence in the botanist crept its way to the surface. Knowing Deiko lusted for fame, for a discovery beyond what man had ever seen or could fathom, Ben couldn't show Deiko the faery. The second he did, something horrible would happen. To Ben and the lovely faery.

Deiko didn't show the gun as a grand prize from the gun show. He revealed the weapon as a subtle threat. Hunting season was still a few weeks away, and no one needed a gun to collect butterflies. He had shown the gun for a reason—either as a bullying tactic or to exhibit dominance. The crazed lust in Deiko's eyes indicated he'd use it, too.

"The heat's getting to you, Isaac," Ben said. He shook his head and stepped around his colleague.

"Put down the pack," Isaac said.

"What?"

Ben froze when Isaac inserted the magazine into the gun and snapped the gun's chamber back and forth.

"Put down your pack and *show* me what you're hiding inside. Or else."

Ben turned. He stared in Isaac's eyes, and then at the gun.

Isaac shook his head. "Uh-uh. Just set it down."

Ben frowned and lowered his pack to the ground. He held his hands in surrender. "You're making a big mistake."

"So you *did* find something."

"And if I did? You going to kill me for it?" Ben asked.

Isaac chuckled. "Depends on how good a find it is."

"Seriously?"

Isaac didn't reply. He stepped closer to the backpack. He held the gun steadily at Ben, and by the ease with which he carried the weapon, Isaac had a lot of experience using one. Isaac's hand didn't shake or tremble. His cold gaze indicated a side of him Ben had never seen, and he wondered what further words might make Isaac squeeze the trigger.

And over *what*?

Ben thought it odd Isaac was bent on knowing what was inside the backpack. His timing couldn't have been better planned. He'd run into the grove within minutes of the capture. Without being told, Isaac automatically assumed Ben had some spectacular discovery. But how? And why? Then Ben noticed the set of binoculars hanging around Isaac's neck. Had he watched Ben catch the faery?

Isaac tugged at the zipper on the pack with his free hand, but he couldn't unzip it. His building frustration with the zipper troubled Ben. Isaac seemed seconds away from an outburst that might turn deadly.

"Put the gun away," Ben said in a calm, almost apologetic, tone. "I'll show you what's inside the pack."

Isaac peered up unconvinced.

Ben smiled and outstretched his hands while offering a slight shrug. "Look, the old zipper sticks all the time. Almost have to use a combination of tugs to pry it open."

Isaac sighed and regret overshadowed his face. He tucked the gun behind his belt. "I don't know what came over me."

"Yeah, I don't know, either."

"I'm sorry. Just playing around." Isaac half snickered.

"Playing? No. That's not how I view it," Ben said in an even tone.

Ben reached for the pack, but instead of grabbing it, he spun and swiftly planted his boot between Isaac's legs. Isaac's eyes bulged. He clutched himself, bent forward, and collapsed facedown on the ground. Ben grabbed the gun and the backpack.

Ben grinned. "I'm not a fan of guns. I'd rather use my hands and feet. Or knives."

Isaac groaned and writhed in pain.

"Your mother never tell you, you shouldn't play with guns?" Ben turned to walk away.

"The clip was empty. No bullet in the chamber," Isaac said, forcing out the words. He gasped. "You know I pull pranks all the time."

"You're lucky you're not dead. I could've dropped you with my knife in less than a few seconds."

"You knew the gun wasn't loaded?"

"No. It wouldn't have mattered though. I could've hit you with the knife *before* you pulled the trigger."

Isaac rolled to his side. Tears moistened his eyes. "You actually considered doing that?"

"Yes."

"Can I have my gun back at least?"

"I don't want the gun, but what makes you believe *you* deserve it?"

"I bought it."

Ben shrugged. "I'll leave it on your vehicle. But one thing you need to remember."

"What?"

"Never invite yourself to hike or collect insects with me. In fact, never speak to me again. Understood?"

"Sure, no problem," Isaac stuttered between painful gasps.

Ben walked away.

"Then whom do I tell about your winged woman?" he asked. "Faeries exist, huh?"

Ben stopped walking.

"I thought so," Isaac said. He took a couple of deep breaths. "You caught one. My eyes weren't playing tricks on me after all."

"I don't know what you're talking about," Ben said.

"The world will know about her," Isaac said. "Once I get proof, I'll let everyone know."

Ben hurried to his SUV.

"I saw her!" Isaac insisted. "You have her. You can't keep her hidden."

Ben opened the pasture gate. "The heat's making you delirious, Isaac. Find yourself a cool place and rehydrate."

He disassembled the gun and tossed the pieces in Isaac's truck bed.

17

Then he climbed into his SUV. He started the engine, turned on the air conditioner, and unzipped the pack. He took the jar with the faery and placed her so the cooler air could reach her. His guilt was heavy enough. Having injured her with the net, the last thing he wanted was for her to suffocate and die inside the jar.

CHAPTER 2

Ben drove up the steep, winding road to his house at the edge of a bluff. His garage was built into the rocky mountainside. He parked and took the jar with the faery to his study where he kept his vast insect collection.

The walls were built-in, mahogany bookcases. Glass-topped cases covered black Formica tabletops. A microscope and a dozen spreading boards rested on the center table. A stack of *The Journal of the Lepidopterists' Society* journals was neatly placed near his lamp. After flipping on the desk lamp, he opened the jar and looked inside.

The faery was sprawled on the bottom of the jar. She breathed softly but hadn't awakened. Her tattered, metallic wings wilted around her near nude form. Colorful scales covered her breasts, her buttocks, and her pubic area.

Ben gently slid her from the jar and placed her on a thick square of cotton.

Admiring her beauty, and pained by the damage he'd inflicted, he whispered, "I'm so sorry."

Ben took another piece of thick cotton. With a pair of scissors, he cut out a circle and placed the cotton inside a glass gallon jar. He set her inside the jar and covered the jar's opening with cheesecloth. He secured the cloth with a thick rubber band.

He turned his attention to a pinning board where several large Polyphemus moths were spread to dry. In a few more days, he could place them inside another glass-topped box.

Ben left the room to get live crickets to feed his two tarantulas in the divided terrarium. When he returned, he dropped several crickets into each spider's cage. The large tarantulas pounced the crickets and chewed through their soft stomachs while rolling the squishy insects between their large fangs.

"Murderer!"

Ben turned. The faery stood inside the jar with her arms crossed. A rigid frown creased her beautiful face. Catching his gaze, she pressed her hands against the glass and her fingertips glowed green. Her broken, tattered wings hung like ribbons down her back.

He closed the terrarium and faced her.

"Murderer!" she fumed.

"What's your name?" he asked.

Her emerald eyes glared at him with fury. She nodded at the pinned Polyphemus moths. "Did you bother to ask theirs before crucifying them?"

He swallowed hard, not sure how to reply. Never had he considered the insects' points of view. They were, in his mind, specimens for scientific study.

"Look," Ben said. "I'm sorry I hurt you. I truly am. I never imagined anything like you existed."

She crossed her arms and her eyes narrowed even more. Her indignation could maim through her intense glare.

"I'm Ben. Please tell me yours?"

"Shawndirea," she replied in a sour tone.

"A beautiful name."

"Am I next?" she asked.

"For what?"

"To die."

"Why would you think that?"

Shawndirea waved her hand at the pinning boards and insect display boxes. "You killed *them*. And you're holding me prisoner inside a ... a glass bottle. So why would you spare me?"

"I never intended to hurt you."

"Your *intent* was brutal ... nonetheless."

Ben nodded. His eyes saddened. "I agree. I thought you were a butterfly. I never would have imagined you were a—"

"Faery?"

"Yes. I'd never hurt you. I wouldn't have captured you. You're more beautiful than any creature I've ever seen."

"And yet, you kill all these without remorse."

"They're not like you."

She presented a piece of her tattered wing in her hand. With wide eyes, she shrugged. "No?"

Ben sighed. "They're insects. You're much more."

"Am I? So you're saying these butterflies and moths are *less* than I?"

"Of course."

The piece of tattered wing slipped from her fingers. She crossed her arms. "Humans. My mother warned me how cruel and selfish your kind are. All of you think such foolish nonsense. You think all creatures are beneath you. You're more savage than you realize."

Astounded, Ben said, "You actually consider insects equal to yourself?"

"We all have our place."

"I agree, but you're the only faery I've ever seen."

Shawndirea frowned. "So not seeing one doesn't mean I don't exist, does it?"

"I can't deny your existence, but why don't we see more of your kind?"

"Because we choose not to inhabit your realm, and with good reason, as you see." She extended her arms and showed the shredded ribbons of her once glorious wings. A tear trickled and streaked down her cheek.

Ben sighed. "I'm truly sorry. How can I make this up to you?"

"Obviously, *you* can't do anything to reverse my situation."

"Can you?"

"No."

He frowned. "You can't use magic?"

"We can. Just not on ourselves."

"Surely, your wings could be repaired?" he said.

"Not in this realm."

"I could take you to yours."

"I'd suffer greater punishment for bringing a human to my kingdom than the damage you've already inflicted on me."

"Again," Ben said, extending his hands.

She shook her head. "No more apologies."

Ben leaned closer to the jar. He stared into her beautiful, angry eyes. As she studied his, the coldness in hers softened. She looked away, somewhat surprised and startled.

"Are you okay?"

She wiped tears from her brilliant, green eyes.

"I mean, other than the loss of your wings?"

"I'll survive, if that's what you're asking," she replied in a soft, saddened voice.

Ben gave a slight nod. "You ... you won't bleed to death or anything?"

"No."

"Listen, I must take you to your homeland, if you'll show me how."

"No," she replied. "The risks are too great for you and I."

"I'm afraid they're greater for us if you remain here."

Shawndirea faced him at the slight sound of worry in his voice.

"Why?" she asked.

"I'm not the only one who knows about you."

"So?"

Ben shook his head, took the jar in his hands, and held her inches from his face. "You don't understand. The man who knows about you would kill me to possess you."

"Oh, I'm not *that* important." She giggled.

"To him you are."

"Why do you think this?" Her smile faded and she became concerned.

"After he saw me capture you, he pulled a gun on me and demanded I show you to him."

"But you possess me."

Ben shrugged. "His gun was unloaded. Once he finds out where I live, he'll bring a loaded one."

"I doubt he'd be so persistent."

"The unsettling, greedy glint in his eyes indicated to me, he will hunt for you. In his current state of mine, he's capable of torture and murder."

"If he took me, what would he do? You did enough dam—" She shook her head and waved her hands. "Sorry. You apologized. Anyway, what more harm could he do?"

Ben swallowed hard. "Worse than what I've done with these butterflies and moths."

Her eyes widened and her face paled.

"Getting to my realm isn't easy." She sighed. "Dangers and creatures exist unlike anything you've encountered in your realm."

"Maybe so. But I *owe* you."

"You owe me nothing." Her eyes stared questioningly. "*Ben?*"

He smiled. "Yes."

With a slight frown, she shook her head. "Your name doesn't suit you."

"Oh? You've a better one?" He gave a slight grin.

Shawndirea folded her arms and tapped her chin with an index finger. "I'm sure I'll think of one. But in current circumstances, you wouldn't like what I presently *want* to call you."

"Fair enough." Ben chuckled. "When your anger ceases, I'm curious what name you'd pick."

"Oh, the name'll reveal itself. But you don't owe me anything."

"I'll get you home."

"Never make a pledge you cannot keep."

Ben's smile parted his short beard. "I'll get you home."

Nervousness and concern reflected in her deep green eyes. "We shall see."

"I guess I should find you a place for the night. This room probably makes you uncomfortable."

"No, this enclosure's fine."

"Here?"

Shawndirea nodded.

"These dead insects disturbed you earlier. Why would you stay with them?"

She shrugged. "For … spiritual reasons."

With a look of confusion, Ben set the jar down. "You're sure?"

23

She nodded.

"I don't feel right leaving you in a jar," he said.

"It's fine. I'll be okay."

"I don't want you to feel imprisoned."

She shook her head. "With my damaged wings, I'm actually safer *inside* the glass than outside."

"From?"

"Mice, spiders, or whatever else might frequent your home," she said with a wry smile.

"I get it. I don't clean a lot. But the house isn't infested with rodents. Spiders, *maybe*, but no mice or rats."

She laughed.

Ben smiled. "I'll get you first thing in the morning."

"Perfectly fine."

CHAPTER 3

*D*eiko paced his apartment living room floor. From the moment he witnessed Ben capture the faery, Deiko was possessed with a strange, sudden desire to possess her. Never had an urge gnawed inside him in such an overpowering way. He didn't understand, nor could he attempt to explain *why*, he needed her at all costs. He couldn't shake the dark force controlling him.

He ran his fingers through his black hair and uttered a low growl of frustration. He took his cellphone off the end table and scrolled through his contacts. He touched the screen and autodialed the biology department head.

"Dr. Thorsom, this is Isaac."

Thorsom audibly yawned. "Isaac? It's terribly late to call me at home. This best be important."

"Sorry. Could you tell me how to reach Ben?"

"Ben Whytten?"

"Yes."

"At this hour? Why?"

Deiko closed his eyes and bit his upper lip. He sighed. "It's personal."

"Is it urgent?" Thorsom asked with agitation.

"Yes. I believe so."

"Have you tried calling him?"

Deiko replied, "He doesn't have a cellphone. Anyone on campus *knows* that."

"Landline," Thorsom said firmly.

"I tried the number but it's disconnected."

"Then I don't know what else to tell you. I don't have *any* idea where he lives."

"You've gone hiking and fishing with him," Deiko said.

"So?"

"He's never taken you to his house?"

"Never. What business is *that* to you?"

"It seems odd, that's all," Deiko said.

"Ben's a private man. He keeps to himself, except where his teaching priorities demand. I've no idea what he does in his spare time, and I don't care. Take a few lessons from him and stop prying in people's lives."

Veins swelled on Deiko's forehead. Unfamiliar rage surged. Right when he started to yell into the phone, Thorsom disconnected the call.

Deiko growled and made fists.

He wished he'd been on a landline phone, so he could slam the phone down. His rushing anger made him almost throw his expensive smart phone at the wall, but he stopped himself a second before releasing it.

Fuming, he walked to his computer and typed in Ben's name, job description, and college position. He hoped the search engine located an address where he could find Ben.

Very little information surfaced.

Deiko suspected Ben lived under an alias because the Internet notoriously tracked people. Detailed, personal information files were often too easy to find. But Ben's steps seemed to have been erased.

"Why don't you have a trail to follow?" Deiko whispered.

He attempted a couple of updated searches but nothing new surfaced.

He pictured the small iridescent faery Ben had taken from the butterfly net. He wanted the faery. He *needed* the faery. Once he had her, everything he dreamed of achieving fell into place—notoriety, money, and success. He'd be known as the man who unveiled a fictional myth as genuine truth. Television and magazine interviews. Photo ops. Fame would be his. But that wasn't the only reason he wanted her. Something more profound pushed his mind and made her the target of his deepest desires.

Deiko couldn't obtain her until he discovered where Ben lived. He couldn't rest until he claimed her. He tossed his cellphone on the sofa and grabbed the Ruger.

Ben knew more about guns than what he'd disclosed to Deiko. Otherwise, Ben wouldn't have disassembled the gun so quickly. In fact, he'd probably tossed the gun in the truck bed and left.

Once Deiko got home, he cleaned the gun and put it together. The systematic process passed without much thought, almost as if he worked while entranced. When the pieces were in place, he stared at the gleaming metal and smiled. He released the clip and set the magazine on the coffee table. He opened a box of bullets and counted out ten. He held them in his hand until their coldness faded. With methodical movement, he inserted nine bullets. He held the last one between his thumb and index finger, and studied it.

Again, he pictured the faery and the exoticness to own such a creature. The more he thought about her, the less interesting the money and fame became. Of course, he wanted that as well, but owning her seemed more important. A prize. A trophy no one else possessed.

A few moments later, the sharp pain in his bruised scrotum made him wince. Anger boiled inside him. Ben's cheap shot seemed a cowardly thing to do. The severe kick had dropped him hard and hours later, the pain continued radiating. The inflamed area was hot to the touch. He feared he'd suffered a rupture and probably needed to see a physician. He disliked the embarrassment of having a stranger inspect the injury. But if the pain persisted ...

His eyes locked on the brass bullet. Amazing something so small could end a man's life. Quick death if the shot was successful and agonizing otherwise.

For his pain, Deiko wanted Ben to suffer worse agony. He placed the last bullet in the clip and slapped the clip into the Ruger. Had he discovered Ben's whereabouts, he'd end it tonight and take the faery. Now, though, he had to wait until Ben went to campus the next morning and then follow him home later. Until then, Deiko's fury intensified.

CHAPTER 4

Ben turned off his alarm clock five minutes before it was scheduled to awaken him. He slept little through the night. What time he slept, he dreamed about Shawndirea and when he wasn't asleep, he thought about her. Her stunning beauty increased his heartbeat. Throughout the night, he fought his urge to check on her. He didn't want her to feel threatened by his presence.

He thought of different things to tell and ask her. Although she was tiny, she intimidated him. He struggled to find the proper words, as though he was practicing how to ask a gorgeous woman for a first date. He couldn't quite figure out why she made him feel inadequate, except for him having destroyed her wings. His guilt overshadowed him, but his pulse increased with the excitement of seeing her.

Nervousness tensed his stomach.

Her perfect face was forever etched in his mind and captivated him. Even with damaged wings, she held herself with elite regality. He wished he could shrink to her size, but even if he could, he didn't believe she'd ever forgive him. He tried to imagine how beautiful her wings were, as he never beheld their full splendor.

He dressed.

Through the narrow hallway he crept. With apprehension and a bit of excitement, he approached the study door. Never had such a mixture of emotions pulsed through him. Turning the doorknob slightly, he gently eased the door inward. The room buzzed with soft, rasping sounds.

A quick, feathery flutter scraped the door's edge. He opened the door wider and was stunned. His eyes widened and his mouth gaped.

Every butterfly and moth he'd collected were flying around the room. His pinning boards were empty and so were the glass-top boxes of dried specimens. Miraculously, they were alive and flawless. Hundreds of them lofted and glided over the tables.

Shawndirea sat in the jar with a broad, delighted grin. Her smile was the most beautiful one he'd ever seen. Her eyes brightened and her face glowed. The curl of her lips was perfect. His heart raced. Her charm flowed more gracefully than the butterflies and moths drifting around the room. Her smile alone made him cherish his next breath and heartbeat. A world without her radiance was tarnished, dark, and gloomy.

For the first time in his life, he could give his heart and life's devotion to someone else. Although she was a faery, his soul reached for hers. His unexpected desire edged with love and destiny. They'd been brought together for a reason, and it was for more than him taking her home.

Butterflies drifted to the edge of the glass bottle. Each tapped the glass with their antennae and seemed to pay homage to Shawndirea. Each time one tapped the glass, she blew the butterfly a kiss and giggled. The butterfly drifted upward and hovered lazily.

Ben cleared his throat.

Shawndirea turned with a start.

"What have you done?" he asked.

When she looked at his surprised face, she shrugged and crinkled her nose.

Ben marveled. He remembered the time and places for when he'd captured and preserved these winged beauties, especially the rarer ones. Some had been dead for twenty years or more. "*How'd* you do this?"

She smiled. "How else?"

"Magic?" he asked.

"Of course."

Had his collection been destroyed the day before, Ben would've been frantic and possibly gone insane. Such a collection could never be replaced. The exact times and locations where the species had been collected were tagged. While one might replace the specimen, the data records would be different. Some biologists lost their minds when their lifetime collections were destroyed by fire or floods. In Ben's case, hysterical laughter welled inside him, but he didn't feel any loss at all. Only one word explained what had taken place overnight.

Magic.

The warmth of Shawndirea's smile luring the butterflies to her caused him to view the collection in a different light. These creatures were more than trophies for display. Shawndirea recognized their true identities. One day, he hoped to obtain the ability to do the same. She communicated with these glorious insects, and for some odd reason, they *knew* her.

Her constant laughter while greeting each butterfly prevented Ben from looking at the ordeal as a loss. Incredibly, he anxiously awaited for her to reveal other surprises.

The insect pins that had fastened the specimens to the foam inside his insect boxes remained. These pins resembled stainless steel daggers that once pierced the insects' hearts. Their bodies had been dried, brittle, and fragile. Now, they glided, gently and quietly, around the room. They revered Shawndirea.

Ben was ashamed of how selfish he'd been by blindly capturing, killing, and preserving thousands of specimens without considering the depth of his misdeed. Instead of destroying, he now wanted to preserve.

Her sly grin caused him to smile. A few seconds later, he laughed.

"You're not mad?" she asked with a slight, curious frown.

Ben shook his head. "No."

"I'm surprised," she replied.

"Why?"

"Most humans would be furious at losing their *prizes.*"

Ben shrugged. "Perhaps. But I'm not like most humans."

Shawndirea nodded. Her bright eyes peered into his. "I'm beginning to sense that, which aids me in finding you a more suitable name."

He chuckled. "Oh? You haven't come up with one yet?"

She firmly planted her hands on her hips. "Obviously, I've been a bit busy, but it won't take much longer."

Ben waved his hand at the butterflies and moths. "So *this* is why you chose to stay in the room overnight?"

She nodded.

"You indicated your reason was more spiritual."

Shawndirea giggled. "Can you think of anything more spiritual than creatures being resurrected?"

"I suppose not. You didn't free the tarantulas."

Her eyes widened. "Spiders don't respect our kind. Releasing them would place the butterflies and myself into grave danger."

"I understand."

"So," she said. "What will you do with your collection now?"

"Allow me."

Ben walked carefully across the room to the window. Several butter-flies fluttered against the pane trying to escape. Dozens of plump, large moths were attached to the curtains. The cloth was barely visible. He unlocked the window and gently raised the pane. With a quick, solid punch, he knocked the screen out.

"Really?" she said. "You're setting them free?"

Once the outside breeze flowed in the room, the butterflies drifted through the open window by the dozens. The lazy moths clung to the curtains and probably wouldn't stir until after dark.

"What'd you expect?"

"Reclaim them."

With hundreds of butterflies exiting the window, the task would be overwhelming. He viewed the ordeal as nothing less than absolute slaughter, especially after Shawndirea's magic had revived them.

Ben shook his head. "No. I couldn't."

"Even after all the time you invested in obtaining them?"

"No. I could never kill them again."

"If I teleported to my realm—gone in an instant to never be seen again—would you capture them?"

His heart ached more at the thought of her vanishing than releasing his collection to the wild. His throat tightened, and he couldn't speak.

He cleared his throat. "The magical miracle you performed has enlight-ened me. I'll burn my collecting nets. I could never harm them again."

"Good," she said with a nod. "You're more than noble, and I know I can trust you."

"For?"

Shawndirea smiled. "To take me to home."

"I told you I would."

"I know. But now, I trust you'll do everything necessary to protect us."

"The fact I'm keeping you a secret should be enough for you to know I'll protect you. It's also why we leave now before my colleague finds us. His lust for wealth and fame gives us little time though."

Concern furrowed her brow. "He'd actually kill you to obtain me?"

"Yes."

"I doubt I'll ever understand humans."

Ben grinned. "I don't understand my species, either."

He reached inside the jar, and Shawndirea stepped on his palm. He lifted her and let her step on the tabletop. Several remaining butterflies swooped low and politely kissed her cheeks with their tongues. She rubbed the sides of their faces and whispered what Ben assumed were blessings.

Shawndirea raised her arms above her head and outstretched her fingers. She closed her eyes and spoke in a language Ben didn't recog-nize. Green light glowed around her feet and radiated through her body. Seconds later, the light glimmered from her fingertips. The moths on the curtains awakened and lazily flapped their wings. They unlatched their legs from the curtains and clumsily flew out the window.

When the greenish hue surrounding her faded, she drooped like a wilted flower and fell to her knees, exhausted. Her eyes closed, and she curled into a fetal position.

"You okay?" Ben asked.

"I'm fine. Just tired."

"What'd you do?"

"I sent them to the wilderness with my blessings," she said. "They have time to reproduce before the leaves are gone."

"Probably. The abnormally hot temperatures have held steady far longer than normal this year. Winter will be late."

Shawndirea opened her eyes slightly. She met Ben's gaze, smiled weakly, and sighed.

"You're pale. Are you sure you're okay?" he asked.

"Very weak," she whispered before closing her eyes.

Ben rolled a cushioned, desk chair to the edge of the table and sat. "Could I get you something to eat or drink? I've no idea what faeries eat."

"Honey mixed with water. Any fresh fruit will do."

"Rest," he said, rising. "I'll bring you something."

"Thanks."

"Once you regain your strength, you must tell me how to get you home."

"I will."

"I'll be right back."

SHAWNDIREA TRIED to stand but severe dizziness prevented her from doing so. Slightly lifting her head sickened her stomach.

This human surprised her more than any she'd seen before— in this realm, or in hers. Although he'd injured her, his facial expressions and apologies were sincere. He truly felt sorrowful for his actions. She wished he were Fae and *not* human.

Few male Fae suppressed their arrogance long enough to show compassion like Ben. Bringing him to her kingdom wrought possible repercussions from her own race, but with shredded wings, she had few alternatives. Trusting a human with her life was safer than being at the mercy of predators she'd encounter at ground level. Faeries were blessed with wings and meant to fly. They were vulnerable on foot, but lightning fast in flight.

"Most of the time," she whispered while remembering how she'd failed to avoid Ben's swift net.

She hardly remembered being captured after she slammed into the end of the net and thrashed her wings into ribbons. The instant pain tore through her body, and she lost consciousness. Had someone else captured her, she might be dead.

Shawndirea groaned and repositioned herself. She opened her eyes slightly. Several butterflies fluttered out the window. They stretched their wings, caught the morning breeze, and drifted upward. She'd done what she was destined to do. She had given life to those who'd been killed prematurely. Ben capturing her hadn't been a mistake. Fate and destiny had crossed their paths.

Edging closer to sleep, she wondered if their meeting was meant for something deeper. Was he supposed to pass through the Underworld to where her kind and other creatures lived? Could he offer a solution to the dark unrest seeking to control her world and its inhabitants? It certainly appeared so.

BEN HURRIED TO HIS SMALL, drab kitchen. Green wallpaper peeled from the walls. Most of his appliances had somehow outlived their warranties by twenty years. He opened a maple cabinet door above the sink and took out a small bottle of honey. He measured a tablespoon and mixed the honey in a small glass of water. Not certain what ratio she'd prefer, he hoped she found it palatable.

From the old refrigerator, he took a fresh blueberry from a pint cup, grabbed the honey mixture, and hurried to the study.

Shawndirea's chest rose and fell in soft breaths. Her eyes remained closed. Her use of magic had taxed her. At last count, his collection contained over twenty-five hundred butterflies and moths mounted in display boxes. To revive such a number required a massive amount of energy for the faery. To perform the feat, she had to open each insect drawer and sealed glass-topped box, and she did all that *after* suffering her injuries.

Ben set the blueberry on the table and balanced a spoon filled with the honey mixture. He angled the spoon where it wouldn't tip over.

"Here," he said.

Shawndirea's nose twitched slightly. Her eyes opened, and she smiled. She scooted to the spoon, cupped the honey water in her tiny hands, and drank.

"I wasn't sure how much to mix," he said.

"It tastes fine. The sweeter the better though."

Ben turned and took a step toward the door. "I can get more honey."

"No, this is fine. I'm letting you know you don't have to worry about making it *too* sweet."

"Sweet tooth?" he asked with a grin.

"Faeries *thrive* on sugar."

"Noted," Ben said. "How'd you get to our realm?"

Shawndirea sat back and crossed her legs.

"I passed from one plane into this one."

Ben frowned. "How?"

"Sometimes the dimensional walls have weak spots, rifts, where one can pass through. Rifts are rare and difficult to find."

"What about the one you came through? Can't we use it?"

Shawndirea shook her head. "Unfortunately, no. The thin veil somehow reinforced itself after I passed through. It seemed intentional."

"I don't understand."

She pursed her lips. "Someone wants me trapped in your realm."

"Why?"

Shrugging, she said, "It's a long story."

"Have you passed through rifts before?"

Shawndirea nodded. "Only once. Almost didn't return home."

"So why would you return to this realm?"

She shrugged. "Curiosity, I suppose. Other reasons, too. My realm's in unrest."

"Why? What's happening?"

"Darkness is spreading through our lands. Evil has taken root and threatens everything we hold sacred."

"Since the veil you used has sealed shut, how do we find another rift?" he asked.

"Caves are the best places to find a rift."

"We have several caves in this area."

Shawndirea tilted her head and thought. "Do any have deep passages?"

"One on my brother-in-law's property, but it's supposedly haunted."

"Haunted?"

Ben nodded.

"Then we go *there*."

"Why?"

"It's *not* haunted."

"I've been in the cave. You *hear* voices. Shadows move. I've been touched, shoved, and heard my name whispered many times, but I've never seen anyone or anything."

Her eyes brightened. "The passages probably connect to a major rift or pass through one."

"Why would that make a difference?" he asked.

She smiled. "Some sprites like to frighten people. They can move back and forth through the veil to enact mischievousness without being seen. Other creatures are much worse."

"Worse?"

"They abduct humans to enslave or torture to death."

Ben shook his head. "People have vanished in this cave. It's known as Devils Den."

"Not an appropriate name. A devil doesn't cross through a rift like that."

Ben's eyebrows rose.

"Trust me," she said. "I know. There are procedures."

"I'll take your word for it."

"On the other side of the veil, you'll understand a bit more."

"Maybe. But I'm not certain seeing will clear my thoughts about it."

"How much time would it take to get to the cave?" she asked.

Ben shrugged. "About forty-five minutes. But you should rest before we go."

"No. My strength's returning. I'll be refreshed by the time we get to the cave."

CHAPTER 5

*D*eiko parked his car at the far end of the campus parking lot where Ben wouldn't see it when he arrived. He stood and peered through the half-open blinds of his second floor classroom window. Impatiently and with eagerness, he watched Ben's parking spot.

JIM MATHERS, a college student, entered the room and took a seat. "Hi professor. Why are you here so early?"

Deiko said, "Ah. I'm admiring the early morning while I wait for Dr. Whytten to arrive. Most days he's already on campus before now."

"Yeah. He normally arrives before sunrise to check for moths around the lights," Jim replied.

"Well, not today," Deiko replied in a low, slightly agitated, voice. "His vehicle isn't here."

Jim chuckled. "I'd say give him a call, but he swears off cellphones."

"Yes. I'm aware."

"I understand why he doesn't own one though."

Deiko turned and faced Jim. "Oh? Why?"

"His house is on top of a ridge. Probably couldn't get any reception out there anyway."

"You've been to his house?"

Jim shrugged. "Sure. All his Field Botany and Entomology students have. Great place to collect plants and insects. Some hard to find Lobelias grow along that wooded area. We had a great time, a cookout—"

Deiko winced and half limped as he took heavy steps across the room and towered over Jim. "Which ridge does he live on?"

Jim was a husky, young man and more than capable to defend himself under the right circumstances, but Deiko's dark glare startled the young man. The gruffness in Deiko's voice and his sudden closeness took Jim by surprise and caused him to cower in his seat.

Deiko seemed to notice Jim's fear and smiled. An advantage of being in the authoritative role was knowing most students feared striking a professor or a coach because of the difficulty in proving what actually had happened. Without solid proof most colleges allowed leniency for an instructor with no marks on their record. The same held true for outstanding students, but it depended on *whose* story the administration believed.

"Which ridge?" Deiko repeated with a more threatening tone.

For a brief moment, Jim could've sworn the whites of Deiko's eyes had turned black.

Almost stuttering his words, Jim said, "Boykin Ridge. At the very top of the hill. His house is at the dead end."

Deiko turned and walked to the marker board. He took a dry erase marker and wrote: "Today's class is cancelled."

He snapped the cap on the marker and grabbed his satchel off the desk. He glanced at Jim.

Jim didn't seem to know whether to leave or stay.

"You're dismissed," Deiko said evenly. "Unless you want to stick around and let the other students know the message *isn't* a joke."

With raised eyebrows, Jim said, "Whichever you prefer."

Deiko headed to the door. "It doesn't matter to me."

~

A FEW SECONDS after Deiko's footsteps faded down the hallway, Lacy came into the classroom. Jim waved—a bit more nervously than normal —and he pointed at the board. Although he smiled, his face was pale and his eyes, haunted.

"No class?" she asked with overwhelming excitement. Her blue jeans were tattered with holes in the knees. She walked to Jim's seat and lowered her book bag.

Jim gave her a quick nervous glance before quickly looking away. He cleared his throat. "Yes. Odd, huh? I was here when he wrote it."

"Is everything okay?" Lacy asked, standing beside his desk. She flicked her blonde ponytail. Her bright, blue eyes peered into his. "You look upset."

He sighed and straightened in his seat. "Me? Nah, I'm fine."

"No, you're always energetic and chipper. Something happened. You look frightened."

Jim stood and grabbed his backpack. He slung it over his shoulder, ran a hand through his black hair, and shrugged. Gazing at the floor, he walked to the door. "Maybe a little startled, but not *frightened*."

"Why?" she asked. "Did you encounter a road-rager on your way to campus? Or is it something else?"

He explained Deiko's questioning, the professor's bizarre behavior, and how Deiko cancelled the class once he learned where Ben lived.

"I wonder why?" she asked.

"Not sure. He seemed awfully angry."

"You don't think he'd harm Dr. Whytten, do you?"

"I wouldn't think so. I certainly hope not," Jim said. Timidly, he looked both directions down the hall. He feared Deiko suddenly step around the corner. "He was highly agitated. I've never seen him like that. He's such a cutup. Not someone I imagined to have violent tendencies. But his dark eyes—"

"You're right. He usually acts nutty, in a playful way. Not, um, psycho. Should we contact Dr. Whytten and warn him?"

"How? He doesn't have a cellphone. The only way to give him a heads-up would be to go to his house."

Lacy smiled. With an overly cheerful voice, in spite of the circumstances, she said, "Well, we don't have class. Want to drive out and make certain everything's okay? Dr. Whytten needs to know."

"That'd be the best thing to do."

CHAPTER 6

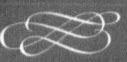

en put on rugged hiking boots, thick jeans, and brought a light jacket. From his previous explorations inside Devils Den, the cave's temperature was much cooler than any cave he'd explored. He tucked a hunting knife inside both jacket pockets. He hooked two knife sheaths to his belt and inserted two sharp throwing knives in them.

Shawndirea apparently feared what they might encounter on the other side of the veil, so he didn't want to take any chances. She could've been teasing him about the dangers to test his bravery, but he doubted it. The more he thought about it, the more her warnings were worth heeding. He shouldn't take her warnings lightly. Crossing into another realm was exciting, but his excitement equaled his apprehension.

Ben was flattered in how she flirted with her eyes, but occasionally she held a fearful gaze when she mentioned returning home. He stared and studied her closely. Her attitude was drastically different than the day before. Her injuries were more than enough reason to despise him and question his motives, but strangely, she'd warmed up to him far quicker than he expected.

Ben was amused that she wanted to give him a new name. The name she'd choose indicated her true feelings—whether she viewed him detestable or respectable.

41

One reason he seldom dated was because of his difficulty in reading a woman's hints on whether she was interested in him or not. He didn't like the pressure of trying to figure out what a woman's smile indicated. Was she flirting, interested, or simply being polite? He preferred direct approaches. Straightforward conversations. Subtle hints left him clueless.

So Ben sidestepped the hope of romance and pursued science. He favored collecting specimens because those answers were readily available in scientific books and journals. He might invest long hours in research, but the information could be found. Guessing what a woman *might* be thinking placed him in awkward situations. If he misread a smile, he set himself up for an embarrassing moment. He'd suffered more than enough of those.

Shawndirea signaled she liked him and perhaps, she was interested in him. But she wasn't human. She was a faery. She wasn't even the same *height*. Was her flirting to torment him? Or, like times past, was he seeing *what* he wanted to see?

Now wasn't the time to mentally wrestle through the dilemma. Getting her home required his devoted attention to detail and the ability to survive any dangerous threats they encountered. Their journey would answer most of his questions, but only if they both survived. They needed to get to Devils Den quickly. The first danger was getting there before they encountered Deiko, provided the clown professor was smart enough to figure out where he lived.

Ben had never given a lot of personal information to Deiko, or anyone else for that matter, and with good reason. The less people knew about him, the easier he maintained his low profile. He never used credit cards. He paid his bills with cash. And he didn't trust phones.

Cellphones had trackers. He refused to buy a vehicle with OnStar, so he kept an older model without all the computer components. He genuinely distrusted people. Using such devices allowed people access into his personal life. People always violated privacy. Always.

No longer was it enough for people to call someone at home. They possessed a *need* to find others wherever they were at any given time of the day. Cyber-stalkers. People were *always* texting or talking to someone. What these people ignored was everything texted was recorded somewhere. Although he wasn't a hermit, he loved his privacy.

In a sense, getting Shawndirea to her realm meant discovering a territory free from the technology he despised. Now that he knew the cave wasn't actually haunted, but possibly led to a different realm, should he enter Devils Den again? What if he were *trapped* on the other side of the veil? In some ways, he liked the idea of never returning, but the uncertainly of the new life he'd live apart from this realm left unanswered questions. He needed those answers to evaluate the situation better. Unfortunately, Shawndirea supplied vague answers.

"There was only one way to find out."

Devils Den.

Ben's sister, Lib, and her husband, John McKnight, owned the property where the mouth of Devils Den surfaced. For years, Ben had tried to map out the passages of Devils Den, but each time he journeyed inside, the pathways were different than those he'd last drawn.

Having drawn the passageways, he knew these alterations weren't memory lapse, but how had they occurred? Something dark and possibly sinister possessed the cave. Shawndirea's suggestion of rifts was the most logical reason.

Ben had not lied about hearing voices in the cave. His name had been whispered several times, but he never found the person or *being* calling his name. *How'd* they know his name?

He wasn't an apprehensive person most of the time, but he feared the possibility of menacing creatures lurking deeper in the dark recesses of the cave. Even with the brightest lights he used, he never found anyone lingering in the cave. With new knowledge, he understood he'd never been alone in the cave. Whatever these creatures were, they didn't want to be seen. The rift concealed them. Unable to see their whereabouts made them even more dangerous.

Discovering these new dangers, Ben wasn't going to enter and explore Devils Den without protection. Knives worked well in tight places. A gun would be too dangerous. One misplaced shot could ricochet and kill him or Shawndirea. And besides, he hated using them.

Older folks in the area feared the cave and begged John and Lib to prohibit anyone from venturing inside. Haunted rumors circulated throughout the community. Church members believed demons hid within the dark passageways and the cave was a portal to hell.

Such conclusions were ridiculous. But superstitions went hand-in-hand with some religious country folks, although they'd never openly admit it.

"Block it up," Old Man Harper kept telling John at the general store. "Seal it shut with cemented blocks to prevent any demons from surfacing. Our world's evil enough."

John laughed off the remarks, but after months of browbeating, he finally told Ben about his plans to block the passageway. Ben convinced John to ignore the old wives' tales, but he expected John to eventually seal the cave's mouth. John never hid his uneasiness and fear too well. He wore his emotions on his face when it came to supernatural stories. Fear creased his wrinkles far more than age ever had.

"But the demons," John said. "Don't you think there's the possibility?"

"Do you?"

John wiped sweat from his brow with a handkerchief. "I don't know. Several people vanished in there. They're documented by the sheriff's department."

"I've been inside countless times, John. I'm still here. I've come back each time."

"I know. Did you see any signs of them?"

Ben shook his head. "Never. I've thoroughly searched the passages multiple times."

"So it's safe leaving it open?"

"If I encountered anything in there, I'd block the cave myself."

"I wonder what became of those who got lost and never found their way out?" John asked.

"Hard to say," Ben replied. "They might've fallen into a drop off or a wild animal. You never know. Maybe they came out a different way, got lost, and died where no one stumbled across their bodies?"

"That's possible."

"Some caverns run for miles underground."

John shook his head. "I can't imagine how horrible it'd be to die lost and alone. Or, how bad it is for the surviving family, not knowing what happened to their loved ones."

"I agree."

John sighed with frustration. "Nearly a dozen church folk came here the other day and begged me to seal the cave. A few got testy with me."

"You don't go to church."

"I know."

Ben shrugged. "It's your property. Don't let others scare you into something you don't *have* to do."

John chuckled. "Everyone at Harper's Grocery calls the cave Devils Den."

Ben smiled. "Not a bad name, actually. Should keep people from trespassing."

"Or attract crazier types out here."

"I never thought about that."

John shook his head. "Devils Den."

Soon after, Devils Den stuck. The elderly men who gathered at Harper's Grocery every morning added more myth to the cave than fact. If a cow died, or unusual weather occurred, they said that another demon escaped from Devils Den.

The expanding tales became so vivid, John refused to enter the cave, and he owned it. Ben was glad John never went inside. He hated lying about things he'd heard in the cave, but John was shaken enough without further things to worry about.

The haunting stories had a different effect for Ben.

The idea of people being afraid to go near the cave thrilled Ben. He could practically keep the place to himself. And in spite of the whispering voices, he kept returning. Nothing bad had ever happened to him while exploring. In many ways, his investigation and mapping the cave paths were like a curious person playing with an Ouija board. Bizarre things might happen, but not enough to deter someone from seeing what happened the next time.

Ben often wondered if the cave actually led to another world. Shawndirea's explanation of rifts excited him and stoked his curiosity. It explained quite a bit, too.

Ben tucked a sharp, silver letter opener behind his belt buckle. He shoved a Swiss Army knife in his front pocket. For some odd reason, this seemed a rather needed necessity.

He grabbed his backpack and went to the kitchen. He poured honey into a half full bottle of water, tightened the lid, and shook it vigorously. From the table, he placed several apples, a blueberry, and hard cheese inside the pack. Sliding open a drawer near the sink, Ben grabbed a flashlight, some extra batteries, matches, a piece of flint, and several candles.

Confident he had enough essentials, he went to his mudroom and took his canteen off a nail. He rinsed and filled it with fresh water.

Once he was certain he wore suitable boots and had ample weapons to protect them, he returned to the study.

Shawndirea sat on the edge of the table and swung her feet back and forth. A black swallowtail glided above her. Her lips moved, but no audible sound came. He smiled. Did she speak in such a high frequency that the insects heard and understood what she said. The butterfly seemed to dance on air and encircled her several times before making a final spiral and drifting to the open window.

"Amazing," Ben said.

Shawndirea turned in surprise and grinned. Her face seemed more beautiful each time he saw her. All worry vanished. He'd fight the most dangerous creature in the world to protect her. He'd even give his life to ensure hers was spared. Was his valor a spell she'd cast? No.

Her energy must've returned. Radiance glowed from her. Her emerald eyes gleamed and twinkled.

"They're drawn to you," he said. "They honor you."

She laughed softly.

"What?"

"You'll understand soon enough."

Ben wondered if she hinted a subtle threat or if she planned to reveal secrets.

CHAPTER 7

*J*im drove slowly through the campus parking lot. He stopped, looked both directions, and pulled out onto the highway.

Lacy texted on her hot pink cellphone. She hit 'send' and a broad smile curled her lips.

"You're one reason Dr. Whytten hates cellphones."

Lacy playfully slapped his arm. "Oh now, you're on your phone all the time."

Jim winced and rubbed his arm. "You over exaggerate."

"Now, Jimmy."

"Jim," he corrected. "I hate being called Jimmy."

"Why?"

"Because it makes me sound like I'm a six-year-old kid."

"Aww," she said. "I bet you were cute then."

He scowled.

"Oh, I don't mean you're *not* cute now." Her face reddened, and she looked out the side window. "I should shut up."

He noticed her embarrassment. This side of her he'd never seen before. Normally she was a bit loud and never at a loss for words, but seeing her shy and a bit awkward made her more down to earth. He liked that she was comfortable enough to let her guard down.

Jim refused to allow their brief silence to escalate.

He cleared his throat. "It's … My father always called me Jimmy or Jimmy Boy when he tossed a softball with me at the park. Then one day he split. He abandoned my mother and me. From then on, I insisted she call me Jim because I was the man of the house."

"I'm sorry."

"Don't be."

She glanced at him. "How old were you when he left?"

"Probably around eight."

"Do you ever see him?"

"No. I don't particularly want to, either. We're actually better off since the deadbeat left."

Apparently noticing the conversation was making him uncomfortable, she changed the subject. "Who do you text after classes? Your girlfriend?"

"No."

"Sorry. I'm being nosy, aren't I?"

"It's okay. I text my mother. I check in on her every few hours."

"Why?"

"She's in hospice care. She has cancer."

Tears formed in Lacy's eyes. She looked away.

"She insists I not drop out of college. She made me swear I wouldn't because she wants me to be successful. After classes, I head straight to her and study for hours."

"That's hard," she replied.

"It was much harder several weeks ago. She was in so much pain," Jim sighed. "Since she's in the last stages of bone cancer, they've given her a morphine pump. She stays too doped up to feel the pain, which is good. But she sleeps all the time and slurs her words when she's awake. I read my notes and books aloud so she knows I'm near. Most of the time she's too incoherent."

Lacy placed her hand atop his and squeezed. He didn't pull away from her touch. The warmth of her fingers made him take a quick breath. He turned his hand slightly, and without hesitation their fingers entwined.

He looked at their hands and met her eyes.

She smiled. "Things will be okay."

Jim's throat tightened. He fought tears. "I don't think she'll live much longer."

"Sometimes we lose people." Lacy squeezed his fingers. "Everyone faces this. Sometimes, though, it's way sooner than it should be. We question, but there's never a good answer. Losing someone hurts, but it happens."

"I know. I've sort of accepted it. The prognosis is too clear to ignore. It sounds bad, but when she dies, she won't suffer anymore."

"I understand." Lacy nodded and wiped her tears with her free hand. "No matter the end result, you're a strong person."

"Thanks. Let's figure out why Deiko's bent on finding Dr. Whytten," Jim said with a shaky voice. "I need this distraction."

"Sure."

"Why would Dr. Deiko suddenly become angry with Dr. Whytten."

"That's the mystery," she replied.

"Solving a mystery is a great way to occupy my mind. Besides, I like puzzles."

Lacy grinned. "Me, too. Of all the professors we have, Dr. Whytten's everyone's favorite. He makes biology fun."

"I know. Do you think Whytten might've pulled a practical joke on Deiko?"

"If he did, Deiko definitely deserved it. Although Deiko's funny at times, his bizarre sense of humor is often more aggravating than amusing."

"Totally agree," Jim said.

They exchanged glances and smiled.

"So who do you text?" Jim asked.

"A couple of my friends."

"On campus?"

"No, from high school. They decided to go to other universities. I miss them."

Jim nodded. "A lot of my friends did the same. My best friend went to a college in Louisiana. Too far away to come in for the weekends."

She looked in his eyes with boldness. "I'm glad I decided to stay in state."

"Me, too."

Several miles from the campus, the roads narrowed. Trees shrouded overhead, and the morning light dimmed. As he drove, they talked. This was the first time they'd ever talked more than polite 'hellos'. Until today, he thought she'd be snobby and stuck on herself. She was too pretty to be interested in a nerd like himself. After being alone with her, his prejudice was proved to be wrong. He wanted to spend a lot more time with her. Her feelings seemed mutual.

So enraptured by their sudden interest for one another, he lowered his guard. He never considered the vast danger they'd soon encounter.

DEIKO TRUDGED HEAVILY across Ben's steep driveway. Gravels crunched beneath his boots. Set with unshakeable determination in his stride, he gripped his Glock tightly. This time his gun wasn't empty. This time he wasn't joking. He intended to take the faery and kill Ben should the need arise. At the very least, Ben would suffer more pain for severely bruising Deiko's groin.

Science had solved many mysteries and myths throughout the centuries, but some things science never explained. Mythical creatures like faeries. For hundreds of years many cultures had seen them, witnessed their magic, and suffered their mischievous pranks. These weren't coincidence or fabrication. Faeries existed, and Deiko sought to claim the discovery for himself.

Through binoculars, Deiko had watched Ben capture one. And if one faery lived there, more must be nearby. But where? Once he obtained her, he'd find out where she came from and much more.

Deiko never thought he'd ever find himself capable of murder. He loved interacting with people and making them laugh. After his confrontation with Ben, something inside Deiko snapped. A dark entity or force sought to control him. When he held the unloaded gun on Ben, a surge of adrenaline and power rushed through Deiko. He'd never felt such control over another person. Such power was invigorating.

For a brief few minutes, he'd thought Ben would give him the faery, or at least, confess he'd caught her. Deiko *might* have considered sharing the discovery spotlight with Ben, had Ben not chosen to be so stubborn.

However, Ben fooled him. At no point did Ben seem fearful of the gun. Even so, Deiko truly thought he had the edge, even with an unloaded gun. When Ben told Deiko with cool smugness that he could've thrown a knife and dropped Deiko before he pulled the trigger, Deiko believed Ben was capable of doing so. He held no doubts Ben could've delivered on his statement.

Had Deiko not tucked the gun away, Ben would've killed him instead of severely bruising Deiko's groin. Deiko winced and wondered if death might've been more favorable.

He loathed Ben. He wanted Ben to suffer. This urge grew and festered. Deiko no longer succumbed to mercy. He sought revenge. Taking the faery was probably the most pain Deiko could inflict on Ben. Death was instant without any agony.

The faery was Ben's prize possession. That's why he chose to keep her a secret, so he could keep her for himself. Taking her would hurt Ben in the worst way. Deiko understood Ben would pursue him, and when he did, Deiko had no choice but to kill him. He didn't know exactly *when* he'd kill Ben. It would be much sooner than later. Probably within minutes after Deiko stole the faery. Deiko nodded with satisfaction and found the timing acceptable.

From near the house, a feathery whispering sound rustled softly. The noise caught his attention and brought him back to reality.

Deiko clicked a round into the gun chamber and headed around the side of Ben's house. One side window was fully opened. Easing closer, he listened for activity inside, but no loud sounds or voices indicated anyone was inside the house. However, the strange whispering continued. He couldn't locate from where the noise radiated.

His heartbeat increased. He held the gun with both hands. Suddenly faced with the possibility of another confrontation, his tightened throat became drier than cotton. Sweat trickled down his back. Taking a deep breath, he braced himself and mentally talked up his confidence. The gun provided less certainty than he'd expected.

Deiko scanned the hillside and down the drive. Nothing moved. He closed his eyes and held his breath. He couldn't wait any longer. The gamble was his to make. Gritting his teeth, he pivoted around quickly and aimed the gun through the open window into the room.

No one.

Somewhat relieved, Deiko lowered the gun.

Even though Ben wasn't waiting for him, shock widened Deiko's eyes. All of Ben's insect boxes on the table were empty.

"What the Hell?" he whispered.

Ben's passion and obsession was collecting butterflies and moths. Nothing on Earth would've caused the man destroy his collection. Ben would probably kill before he allowed anyone to steal them.

Leaning his head partway through the window, he listened for the slightest sound or movement. Nothing stirred inside the room, but the whispering echoes grew louder. More intense.

Above his head the soft quivering noises intensified.

Deiko looked up. Hundreds of butterflies and moths rose in a swirling motion and drifted higher and higher. The slow cloud of wings moved like a delicate, shimmering tornado being summoned by an unseen force.

"What's going on?" he asked.

The butterflies and moths seemed controlled by ... magic. In disbelief, he watched until they floated into the tree canopy and separated outward in different directions. Although his expertise lie outside entomology, he was certain a lot of those butterflies were from tropical rainforests. Their bright metallic blue wings indicated such.

Deiko tucked the gun behind his belt, braced on the windowpane, and pulled himself inside Ben's study. Lying beneath the window, he took deep breaths. His heart pounded. The fast rhythm of his heartbeat thudded in his ears. A sheen of sweat covered him. Sudden fear gripped him. He expected Ben to charge into the room and defend his home. Since Ben didn't fear Deiko, he needed to be extra cautious. Could Deiko fire the gun precisely and fast enough before Ben reached him?

Deiko lie still. He checked every corner of the room, the two doorways, and even in the dim lighting, he assured himself he was alone. No noises stirred in the house other than his labored breathing and his deafening heartbeat ringing in his ears. At the height of his tension, he worried he'd suffer a heart attack before finding Ben and taking the faery.

Satisfied the house was empty, he stood and pulled the gun from the back of his belt. He stepped to the edge of the nearest table. All the insect pins remained in the box bottoms with their paper data labels. The space between the pinheads and the labels indicated the thickness of the insects' bodies. Yet, the dried bodies were gone.

Magic.

The tornado of butterflies and moths outside were a testament. Magic was real. Faeries were real. These couldn't be denied, even by science. And he bore witness to what some might term a miracle. He *must* get possession of the faery. Imagine the fame he'd receive.

Wing scales were scattered along the tabletops like a fine layer of metallic dust. A few large moths remained attached to the curtains. These were nonnative to the country. Rare species like those required permits to import into the country unless they were papered specimens. Living foreign moths were illegal to own without specialized permits.

So why were they on the curtains, alive? These should've been pinned and stored in a box with the rest of his collection. For them to be free in the room risked significant damage to their gorgeous wings. No professional lepidopterist would chance such loss.

On another table set a large gallon jar with a thick wad of cotton in the bottom. A cut blueberry had tiny bite marks. Nearby a spoon filled with dark water was balanced close to the jar. His eyebrows rose from the sudden insight.

"The faery!" Deiko gasped and half cackled mad laughter. "Ben fed you."

Indeed this miracle was done by the faery. She couldn't be far away. The massive resurrection of butterflies and moths had been recent, perhaps during the last hour? Surely no longer than that. Where was she and Ben?

Deiko stepped out of the study and into a dark, long narrow hallway. The aged floorboards creaked with each step he took. Still a bit paranoid Ben might be elsewhere in the house, Deiko tried to step lightly. No matter how softly he stepped, the boards whined beneath his modest weight. At the end of the hall, he paused before stepping into the living room.

A small fireplace was on the far wall. The couch and sofa chairs were cluttered with various scientific journals and magazines. Deiko shook his head. "You really don't have a life, do you, Ben?"

On the mantle above the fireplace were several framed pictures. One was of a couple he assumed were happily married by their smiles and the look in their eyes.

At the base of the picture frame a card was still tucked inside its Hallmark envelope. Curiosity got the best of him, so he pulled out the card and opened it. Neat handwriting frilled beneath the typed message: "Great to have a wonderful brother like you."

It was signed, "Your sister, Lib."

Deiko turned over the envelope and found the McKnights' address neatly written on the front. He smiled.

He took the envelope and hurried through Ben's house. He unlocked the front door and stepped out onto the porch. An oak swing rocked slightly in the breeze. The old chains creaked. A gust of wind tossed a wave of dry leaves in the air. More leaves spiraled from the limbs overhead. Two squirrels played chase around a maple tree.

Caught in the moment, Deiko understood why Ben lived here. He could think of no better place for an entomologist to thrive. Everything Ben loved lived here within reach. He only had a few neighbors nearby, and possibly seldom ever had visitors.

Until today.

The gun weighed heavily in his hand. He looked at the address on the envelope and wondered if this couple could tell him where Ben might've gone. He doubted Ben would actually be at their house, but the possibility existed.

Way below on the driveway entrance at the bottom of the ridge a car slowed. The brakes squealed. A couple seconds later, the motor revved. A vehicle was climbing the winding drive.

Deiko walked to the edge of the porch. From this distance, he had no idea who was approaching. Maybe a neighbor? Perhaps it was Ben, but Deiko's guess was that it wasn't, not unless Ben had ditched his SUV for an older car.

The car increased its speed, so Deiko pulled Ben's front door shut and sprinted across the wide porch, down the steps, and ran across crunching layers of dry orange, yellow, and red leaves to get to his pickup.

The driveway was too narrow for two vehicles to pass one another. He'd have to wait for the oncoming vehicle to reach the top before he could drive downhill.

Instead of waiting for the visitor, Deiko tossed his handgun on the truck seat, climbed inside, and turned around on the paved area outside the garage. While he waited for the car to come into view, he typed the McKnights' address into his GPS locator.

"Twenty-five miles?"

Driving to the McKnights was a great gamble unless Ben had actually gone there. Otherwise, Deiko lost an hour of his time on a feeble hunch.

With an exasperating sigh, he glanced at Ben's house. The old cottage almost blended in the rugged trees and leaves. During the summer, other than seeing a driveway headed up the hillside, most people probably wouldn't expect a house rested at the top of the three-mile, ridge road. The garage held its own camouflaged wonder since it was carved into the side of the narrow ridge.

Deiko parked his truck near the side of the house where it wasn't noticeable until the driver was right on it, so he held the upper hand. He left the engine running, the door open, and stepped out with the gun in his hand.

The car crept up the winding path, much too slow for Deiko's patience.

The front of the car came into view. Not Ben. The driver didn't have a beard and looked much younger.

Deiko raised the gun and aimed. He couldn't leave any witnesses that he'd been at Ben's estate. He squeezed the trigger and fired.

AT THE BASE of the three-mile ridge road, Jim stopped the car and pointed.

He glanced at Lacy. "This is the right place, isn't it?"

She looked at the winding drive that disappeared around a massive tree and shrugged. "I think so."

"Me, too. It looks different."

"Lots of leaves. Everything looks a bit different once fall sets in."

"Ah, look," he said, pointing. A rusted sign for Boykin Ridge Road was slightly covered by an oak branch.

Jim backed the car and then proceeded up the road. Lacy held his hand and had never loosened her hold during the entire drive. With another typical day, overcast by the fact his mother might pass away at any time, Lacy had somehow lessened his pain and lightened his load.

While his mother would succumb to her devastating disease, Jim wouldn't be alone afterwards. He felt certain Lacy would be there for him when the time came. That's what he hoped and what he truly needed.

Jim gently squeezed her hand. She cupped her other hand around the other side of his and surrounded his hand between hers. They smiled at one another. Her radiant eyes sparkled. He had no words. From the look in her eyes, he didn't need any. Nor did she. Uttering words was useless. Words were a total loss. Their mutual expressions and emotions rendered far more value.

He didn't want to break their eye contact, but the road was narrow and the hillside was steep. He reluctantly placed his attention ahead of them. Something large moved at the edge of the road.

Jim hit the brakes.

A doe sprinted from the trees and darted across the road a few feet ahead of them.

"Whoa!" he said, shaking his head. "She came out of nowhere."

"Deer are fast."

"And plentiful."

Lacy nodded. "Yes, when you see one, at least a dozen more are nearby."

He waited a moment before easing off the brake. Satisfied no other deer were in the trees, he drove on.

Approximately one mile up the winding road, a narrow side driveway angled off. A new doublewide trailer set crossways between some massive trees. Flowerbeds encircled the trailer. Orange and yellow marigolds were the size of small shrubs. No cars were parked at the trailer.

"This area certainly has some beautiful places to live," Jim said. "I doubt I'd put a trailer out here, though. I'm impressed someone actually hauled a house trailer up this narrow hillside."

She nodded. "I love it out here. It's always nice when you are away from the overpopulated areas. The only noises are the sounds of nature."

"Those places are getting harder to find."

"I know."

Jim pressed the accelerator. The motor roared and stubbornly climbed the incline.

"One steep hill," he said.

"Yep."

He shook his head. "If this old heap reaches the top, you've seen a miracle."

She laughed softly.

"I'd hate to drive up or down this slope after a winter snow or ice," he said.

Lacy laughed. "You'd slip and slide trying to get to the top, but you'd *ski* down."

"No doubt. Brakes are practically useless on ice."

Embarrassed by his clunker's pulling performance, Jim put the car in third gear. The engine revved and inched forward. They passed the only other driveway that shot off the ridge road. This driveway separated and two small brick houses occupied this section of Boykin Ridge.

Cars were parked in each drive, but no one was outside either home, which made Jim feel a bit more at ease. The way the car's motor whined, he didn't want to further add to his embarrassment of others hearing and witnessing it struggle to pull the hillside.

After he drove another quarter mile, Ben's house came into view. Lacy said, "We're almost to the top."

"Thank God," he whispered.

Coming around the last bend, a harsh TWACK! echoed. Flakes of glass burst inside the car. The back glass exploded. Lacy screamed.

"What was that?" Lacy asked.

"A gunshot!"

Jim looked at Ben's house.

"Get down!" Jim shouted. He pulled her over to him, and put the car in reverse.

"What's going on?" she asked.

"It's Deiko. He has a gun."

"You *see* him?"

"Yeah."

Jim gunned the engine. The car shot backwards. A second bullet lodged in the radiator.

Trying to maneuver the vehicle while looking over his shoulder was impossible. He couldn't take his eyes off the crazed professor. He feared another round exploding through the windshield and killing one of them.

Steam rose from beneath the hood. The punctured water hose sprayed onto the hot engine. The smell of burning antifreeze crept through the air vents.

Jim veered to the left to keep the car on the narrow road. He hoped to control the car long enough to back into a lower driveway, but that was a good distance yet to go.

Jim looked at Deiko. The professor aimed again. Jim panicked and pushed the gas pedal to the floor. The car spun and weaved side to side.

"Stay down," he said, when Lacy tried to lift her head.

The back passenger tire slipped off the road's edge and spun. Jim attempted to slow the car by slamming the brakes, but it was too late. The loss of traction caused the car to dip and leave the road.

Lacy screamed.

"Hang on!" he said, holding her close.

The car tipped over the edge and dropped slowly on a row of saplings. Their thickness held the car for a few seconds before the vehicle's weight splintered them. The bottom of the car scraped rock and tree stumps, which slowed its momentum slightly but didn't prevent the inevitable. Their plummet down the hillside happened quicker than he imagined.

Lacy shrieked. The car bounced and rolled over and over. Then she was quiet. Jim hit his head and everything went silent, black.

~

DEIKO AIMED to fire the third time, but to his surprise, Jim slammed the accelerator. Killing Ben was one thing Deiko had planned to do. Killing a student wasn't something he wanted to do, but the kid had seen him and he'd asked Jim for directions to Ben's house. As much as he liked having Jim as a student, Deiko couldn't let any witnesses escape.

Why had Jim come here? To warn Ben?

He ran after Jim. Rounding the next bend, he aimed and fired, but the car left the roadway. The car struck a small hickory tree, rocked, and teetered over the edge.

Before he could fire again, the car tilted and slid off the embankment. Within a minute, the car rolled and bounced down the side of the ridge. He stepped to the edge of the drive and watched. The car struck a large boulder and came to a dead stop. A cloud of dust puffed over the car and slowly filtered downward.

Deiko checked the time on his watch and waited. On his way up the long winding road, none of Ben's neighbors had been outside their homes. Should any of them be home, he expected the thunderous crash and gunfire to draw them outside. Such a raucous would raise anyone's curiosity.

After five minutes, no one inside the car moved. No neighbors rushed to the side of the ravine to inspect the crash. Confident only he and nature had heard the incidents, he sprinted up the winding hillside and got in his truck. He dropped the truck in neutral and coasted down the sloping, curving driveway. He needed to find Ben. The McKnights' address was the first place he'd look.

He rounded the curve where Jim's car plummeted and stopped. He wasn't for certain, but he thought he saw movement. He grabbed the gun, shut off the truck engine, and watched the crumpled car at the bottom of the ravine. While he waited, he took out the gun clip and inserted more bullets. The best that could happen would be for Ben to drive up the hillside where Deiko waited.

Time would tell.

CHAPTER 8

*B*en drove the back roads. Shawndirea stood on the dashboard and stared through the windshield. Showers of whirling leaves fell from the maples and oaks and skidded across the blacktop.

So many thoughts went through Ben's mind. He looked at Shawndirea. Her radiance glowed. Her beauty was beyond anything he'd ever seen. Looking at her wilted, tattered wings, he winced. He ached at the damage he'd done to her and could never apologize enough. He hoped her wings could be magically repaired once they reached her realm.

She smiled and watched songbirds fly across the road.

Her smile captivated and lured him. He couldn't stop staring at her.

"Lovely countryside, isn't it?" Ben asked.

Shawndirea nodded. "It's beautiful, but pales in comparison to our lush forests. Of course, you don't have near the dangers we do. Don't say you weren't forewarned."

"I won't."

Her eyes focused on the blacktop. She frowned. "I'm not fond of your realm."

"Why not?"

"All the damage humans do. These black scars cut through forests, fields, and cross over waterways. Your roads diminish what might otherwise be spectacular."

Ben nodded. "I won't argue. Our advanced technology troubles me and has for a long time."

She faced him. "You wouldn't say that to impress me, would you?"

He frowned. "Of course not."

She studied his eyes intently for several moments.

"You speak the truth. How much farther?" she asked, changing the subject.

"A few miles. Maybe ten minutes."

"Good. I sense I'm needed."

He frowned. "Even though the veil separates you?"

She nodded. "Our world's connected to yours. A magical barrier doesn't shut off nature's pain. Evil lurks beneath the surface and travels through realms to inflict its damage. Its tendrils reach far."

"Evil exists here, too."

"On a different level."

"How so?" Ben asked.

A thin smile curled her lips. "In your world, most individuals and creatures have a conscious to keep them in check. Of course, some abandon their restraint and do horrendous offenses. In my realm, some creatures are born without a conscious. They exist solely to inflict pain and destroy."

"Like demons?"

"Some are spawned from demons. But sorcery has contaminated the souls of many races in my world. Even my race."

"I'll take you where you need to go."

Shawndirea studied his eyes. She shook her head with sadness. "Perhaps it's best you don't."

"You don't believe I'll succeed?"

She sighed. "I know you'll try. But you don't understand how others will view me bringing a human to our kingdom."

"I won't abandon you after what I did," Ben said.

"In time, I can find another Fae to take me home."

"No," Ben said. "I destroyed your wings, so I must make this right. It's my obligation."

"Fae don't exactly have peaceful terms with humans," she said softly.

"Aren't there humans in your realm?"

"Yes. Thus, the contention. Amongst other things."

Ben frowned. "I don't understand."

"And you won't. Treaties were broken between our races in my realm."

"But I've no part of that."

"No," Shawndirea said. "But they won't care *where* you're from. They'll only see you as a human. To them, *that's* what matters."

Ben smiled. "Then I'll have to prove myself."

"Not a task so easily done."

Ben slowed and turned onto a dirt road.

"We're getting closer," he said. "At the end of the road, we can get to Devils Den."

Ben glanced at the McKnights' farmhouse as he passed. No one was outside, which was good. He didn't want to talk with John at this time. He'd have to hide Shawndirea, and with everything she'd endured, she didn't need to be cramped out of sight.

John didn't mind Ben parking his SUV near the pasture while he explored the cave, which usually lasted a few hours, or a day at most. This time Ben didn't know how long he'd be gone.

Should he leave the SUV parked for days or a few weeks, John would panic, call the authorities, and organize a search party for Ben. Devils Den didn't need the publicity of another person *mysteriously* disappearing inside the cave again. The locals might take matters in their own hands and seal the cave *without* John's permission. Ben needed Devils Den to remain open. It might be his only passageway to return home.

Ben parked the SUV, gathered his jacket, his pack, and extended his palm for Shawndirea. She elegantly stepped onto his hand. He opened the pasture gate, crossed the metal cattle grid, and then closed the gate.

"Where's the cave?" she asked.

Ben pointed. "Through those trees on the other side of the pond."

The sun disappeared behind thick dark clouds. The area darkened. Crows cawed from the pines surrounding Devils Den.

Her vivid eyes scanned the forest line and widened slightly.

"What is it?" he asked.

"Evil surfaces and guards the cave," she said softly.

"Yes. The rumors and superstitious wives tales have stated such," he chuckled.

"No rumors or wives tales," she said with a serious tone. "Yes. It dares us to enter."

"Ahh," Ben said with amusement in his tone.

"That's *not* a good thing."

"We have to enter."

Shawndirea nodded. "We do, but be prepared."

"I am," he said, placing his hand on his knife.

"No. Your weapons are useless against some of these creatures."

"Then how?"

"My magic."

Ben replied, "I don't have the ability."

"I know."

"Are you strong enough?" he asked.

"I have to be."

"You're trying to frighten me."

She smiled. "Fear is sometimes the best respect you can offer."

"It can also get you killed."

"I won't deny that," she said with a firm gaze at the pine thicket. "When an enemy senses fear, they tend to drag out their torture *before* they kill you."

Ben frowned. "How's that good?"

"Gives you an opportunity to counter with an unexpected attack."

"I'll try to remember that."

Ben hurried across the pasture, around the pond's dam, and into the shady forest. The cave mouth was dark, much darker than normal. Cool air seeped out and the coldness radiated farther than it should.

"Wait," Shawndirea said.

"What?" he asked.

"Not sure."

While they watched the cave, several bats fluttered out.

"This place doesn't feel right," Ben said. "Something's different."

"Good. You're senses are awakening to understand what lies beneath your world."

More bats exited and shrieked.

"It taunts us," she said.

Thunder rumbled overhead.

"What's happening?" Ben asked. "The sky was clear before we got here."

"It's a warning for me to stay in your realm."

"Nothing like this has occurred before. I've come and gone freely. Sure, strange things have happened *inside* the cave, but never outside."

"Since you're incapable of using magic, you're not considered a threat. I'm the one he wishes to keep out. I sense his presence."

"His?"

Shawndirea nodded. "A powerful sorcerer has placed his magical hold over this cave. Finding a rift to pass through won't be easy. He'll do everything possible to keep us from reaching the Underworld, my realm. Aetheaon."

"Aetheaon?"

She nodded.

"Why does he want to keep you here?"

She smiled. "I'm weaker on this side of the veil. I cannot help my race when they need me the most."

"What's the urgency?"

"In time, you'll understand."

Thunder bellowed.

"How's he control the weather from the other side?"

"He's powerful, but he doesn't control the weather. He creates a good illusion though."

"No real thunder?" Ben asked, looking at the sky. The rolling black clouds swirled. Lightning flashed. Another grumble of thunder shook. "Looks real to me."

"Real because you believe it's real."

"Do you know who he is?"

She shook her head. "No."

"Will we find out?"

"Let's hope not."

Ben walked to the cave mouth. Cold air funneled out, which felt good considering the sweltering heat, but the cave temperature held an icier touch. Like death. Of all the times he'd entered the cave, this was the first time he was uncomfortable. He feared it might be his last entrance, too.

"I'm ready whenever you are," she said. "*If* you still want to go."

Voices echoed deep inside Devils Den.

The voices Ben had heard before were never quite this angry or so close to the surface. Their undecipherable chattering vibrated off the walls. At other times it sounded like bleating goats. Even more disturbing were the painful moans from what could only be tortured people.

What were they going to encounter? Would he actually see these mischievous imps this time, and would their games no longer be playful? Perhaps now, they played for blood. But that was okay. He might bleed a little, but he was going to attempt to make them suffer and bleed more.

Ben took a deep breath. "Let's go."

CHAPTER 9

*A*fter the long series of rolls, the crumpled car stopped upright. Jim opened his eyes. Lacy's face was covered with blood. Her head was slumped to the side and her eyes were closed. Shock tore through him. He unfastened his seatbelt and reached for her. She was breathing and her pulse was strong. He sighed heavily.

"Lacy," he said, gently rubbing her cheek. "Lacy?"

Blood trickled from a small cut on her scalp. The injury wasn't life threatening, but from his CPR training, he learned any cut on the scalp could bleed profusely. She also had a goose egg bump on the side of her head.

He opened the glove compartment and got the first aid kit. Taking a gauze strip, he applied pressure to the cut to stop the bleeding. As he held it in place, he tried to get his bearings.

He'd lost consciousness after the car rolled a few times. He gazed through the splintered windshield, which looked more like a glass spider web than anything else. The car had stopped in a dry, rocky creek bed.

Jim removed the gauze. The bleeding had stopped on Lacy's head and a soft scab was forming.

"Lacy?" he asked.

He patted her cheek gently.

Lacy's eyes opened. She blinked erratically.

"Are you okay?" he asked.

She looked around, shook her head slightly, and then she gave a slight nod.

"I think so," she said. "Where are we?"

"At the bottom of the ravine," Jim replied.

She offered a confused smile.

Jim looked in her eyes and smiled. "You had me worried."

She noticed the bloody piece of gauze in his hand. "Will I be okay?"

"Just a small cut and a knot on your head. Are you hurting anywhere else? You think any bones were broken?"

She shook her head. "No. I have a bit of a headache."

Their faces were inches apart as they looked in each other's eyes.

Jim said, "Look, I'm so sorry—"

Lacy kissed his lips. Her advance caught him off guard for a moment, but then he kissed her back. When they separated, their faces flushed red.

"The crash wasn't your fault." She hugged his neck tightly.

"Maybe not, but I feel like it is. My driving isn't that great, as you can see."

"We were being shot at. You reacted better than I would've. At least you got us out of his range. Me? I might've driven *up* a tree."

Jim wanted to smile, but he remained serious. "Deiko may still be around. I tried to see where we were, but the only way I can really find out is by getting out of the car."

Lacy shook her head. "No. That's too dangerous."

"He might be headed downhill anyway. I need to check."

"Be careful."

Jim pushed against the passenger door but it was wedged against a large boulder and wouldn't budge.

He groaned. "Let me try my door."

The crumbled door wouldn't budge, either. The side windows were shattered, so his only option was to crawl through a window.

"I'll be back," he said.

"What are you doing?"

"Going to see if he's out there."

Jim cautiously peered through the window. With the distance the car had tumbled and rolled, he was surprised they weren't seriously injured or dead. He scanned the rocky ravine. He couldn't find a clear path safe enough for them to reach the top, not in their bruised and battered condition. But Deiko didn't have an easy way to climb down to them, either.

Jim placed his hands on car's roof and pulled himself through. His feet dropped to the smooth rocks on the dry creek bed. A second later a shot echoed through the small valley. The bullet struck and ricocheted off the hood.

Jim turned and squatted behind the car's trunk. Due to the trees finding Deiko's position was impossible.

"Are you okay?" Lacy asked.

"Yeah. He missed. Otherwise, you'd hear my powerful girly scream. No offense."

"None taken."

He took out his cellphone and shook his head. No bars. He tucked it in his back pocket.

"You have any phone reception?" he asked.

"No. Not here."

"I don't either, but that's normal in this area."

Jim eased to the driver's side window, which was out of Deiko's view, provided the professor was still on Ben's driveway. Crouching low, Jim reached through her window. She eased closer to him.

"You need to climb out this side. He shouldn't see us at this angle."

"Then what?" she asked.

"We follow the creek bed until we find help."

Lacy nodded. "Okay."

She extended her arms to Jim. He remained below the car's top, so Deiko didn't have a clear shot. He helped Lacy out and supported her so she didn't fall face first on the rocks.

Once she was crouched beside him, he pointed. "Stay low. We run for those willows. They should provide a blind to prevent him from getting an easy shot."

"All right."

"If I had my deer rifle and scope, though, we wouldn't *be* running," Jim said with a smile.

"You wouldn't want that on your conscious," she said.

He shrugged. "Maybe not, but right now, I'm a bit pissed. It'd be self-defense, so I'm good with it."

She placed her hand to his cheek and smiled. "I understand."

He took her hand, and on the count of three, they ran to the willow grove. No more shots echoed. Deiko's truck echoed as it wound down the steep drive. Deiko was leaving.

Jim and Lacy hurried along the meandering, dry creek bed and approached a shady forest. Where would they end up if they continued onward? Since they never located Ben, he wondered if Deiko had killed Ben before they arrived.

Still early morning, the sun's intense heat loomed over them. The thick humid air was difficult to breathe.

"Wait." Lacy stopped walking and leaned over. "I'm dizzy and sick to my stomach."

Jim nodded. "Here, lean against me."

She did, and he supported most of her weight while they walked.

The best thing Jim could do until he found out whether Ben was dead or alive was to keep Lacy safe. She was his top priority. He was convinced she liked him as much as he liked her. And if so, theirs was the most unusual first date ever. Nothing like having a car wreck and being shot at to liven things up.

Once they reached the shaded area of the creek bed, Lacy slowed and plopped down on a fallen tree.

"I need to rest," she said. "Everything's spinning. My head's splitting."

"Okay, sure. Hold still. Let me look at your head again."

Jim gently examined the cut on her head. The bleeding had stopped. Dried blood covered her forehead and the left side of her face. The knot was the same size, but her dizziness indicated she might've suffered a concussion.

He ripped a piece of cloth from his shirt and tried to clean off some of her dried blood.

"Wonder what's wrong with Dr. Deiko?" she asked.

"No idea. His eyes were crazy looking."

"You don't think he ... killed Whytten, do you?"

Jim shrugged. "The thought crossed my mind. We'd only know by going to his house to see."

"Then we should," Lacy said. "We should follow the creek until we get to the road. Then we can walk the road to Ben's house."

"His house is three miles straight up the ridge. I'm not certain you're able."

She smiled. "I'm a trooper. I'll be okay."

The uneasiness in her eyes and the uncertainty in her voice indicated she was trying to act tough. She probably suffered from a concussion, so taking their time getting to the road was safer than hurrying in the outrageous heat without water. If she passed out, he'd have to leave her to find help. He didn't want to be in such a situation.

"Maybe our phones will get reception soon. Then we call for help," Jim said. "A ride up the ridge is better than walking. Besides, I didn't see any trails near where the car went off the road."

"A ride would be nice."

"Yes. But if we walk," Jim said, "Deiko should be far away by the time we get to Dr. Whytten's house."

He took her hands into his and smiled. She blushed.

"I'm glad you're okay," he said.

"I'm glad you are, too," she replied. "I'm okay. We should go. At least our day didn't end in tragedy. Let's hope the best for Dr. Whytten."

They walked down the dry creek bed hand in hand.

CHAPTER 10

The harsh intense light from Ben's flashlight shimmered on the wet cave walls. The cold was harsh. Less than fifteen feet inside the cave, he put on his jacket. His breath made little clouds when he exhaled. While he reasoned the abnormal cold was in contrast to the harsh heat outside, this coldness cut deeper and seemed different. The abrupt chill didn't seem like a drop in temperature, but focused on attacking one's psyche and piercing the mind and soul.

Shawndirea sat on his right shoulder.

Moving through the cave tunnel wasn't easy. The atmosphere became thick, heavy, and for some odd reason, he thought he was wading through waist-deep water. His boots seemed to weigh a ton. An invisible force pushed against him. Never had such opposition confronted him inside Devils Den. Shawndirea had not exaggerated about something or someone wanting to keep her from crossing the veil.

In spite of the bright flashlight, their visibility was limited to less than a few feet ahead. The darkness swallowed the light, similar to a black hole in space. The void was empty, quiet, and eerie. Each step forward made him wonder if it might be the last. Voices echoed deeper in the shadows beyond his light's reach. Occasionally, the walls moved and *breathed*.

"It's never been this way before," he whispered.

"It'll get worse," she said.

Ben didn't doubt her prediction, but he wasn't inclined to turn back, either. What he'd encountered many times before was from his side of the veil. He wanted to know what kingdoms lie *beyond* and what creatures he'd discover. Or perhaps, after he gave it more consideration, he wouldn't. But at this particular moment, his curiosity had the better of him.

"This flashlight has a longer range than this," Ben said.

He flashed the light against the wall for a moment. One of the protruding rocks suddenly turned into a hideous face. He stepped back.

"It's not real," Shawndirea said.

"You said that about the thunder."

She frowned. "Don't tell me you still think it was *real?*"

Ben shrugged.

Shawndirea shook her head. "Our journey doesn't look too promising."

"Why?"

"Because you're falling for their simplest illusions."

"Until you," he said, "I didn't know magic existed."

"Again, a reason we shouldn't venture farther."

"You could teach me."

"There's not time."

Ben smiled. He loved the whisper of her voice directly in his ear. Her resonance was the most pleasant sound he'd ever heard. Her soft tone and rich faery accent was alluring.

"Are you indicating I could learn magic?" he asked.

"Anyone can. Some do and never know it. It's best to know your heart's intent before you begin."

"How could someone perform magic and not know they're doing it?"

She whispered, "It depends on how badly someone wants something to occur. Not all intentions are good. Some are pure evil."

Ben replied, "If I even considered learning magic, I don't know what I'd use it for."

"Just remember one thing," she said.

"What?"

"Using magic comes with a cost. There's *always* a price."

"What kind or price?"

Shawndirea said, "Depends on the spell. Dark magic requires sacrifice. Blood or animal. Magic of the light is more complicated."

A low, guttural growl rose farther down the tunnel.

"But now isn't the time to discuss it."

Ben nodded. "Sounds like we have company."

For a moment, he thought the sound might've come from the face on the wall. He shone the light on the rock again. The face was gone.

"See?" she said.

Stepping forward, Ben staggered. The floor shifted and moved. He set his foot firmly on the path. Had all these unusual things occurred when he was alone and without Shawndirea's warning, he'd have thought himself crazy and never returned. The fact she knew strange occurrences would take place didn't make the situation any easier. Exactly what had she *not* warned him about?

Ben crept through the cave corridor and advanced slowly around the next curve. The light radius shrank further. The light retreated, but that wasn't possible.

"How do we find the veil? I can't see three feet ahead."

"It'll be tricky."

"I already assumed such," Ben said. "Every time I've explored this cave, the passageways have never been the same twice."

"The sorcerer has great power."

Ben glanced at Shawndirea. A smoke-like image appeared outside the radius of the light near the moist, cave wall. He turned the light toward it. The image vanished. He'd never seen a ghost, but he was certain one loomed nearby.

"Did you see that?" he asked.

"No. What'd you see?"

"Not quite sure. A ghost?"

Shawndirea shrugged and smiled. "You probably did, which means the veil's nearby."

"How can you be certain?"

"Spirits often wander before they find peace, especially if they died at this particular sorcerer's hand."

"Why'd it vanish?"

She said, "Spirits shun the light."

At the edge of the light, the spectral image drifted. This time Ben didn't turn the light on it because he didn't want to lose sight of it. He trained the flashlight on the opposite wall. Two more lingering spirits joined the first. These were more detailed and wore tattered cloaks and robes. The first didn't have an actual body outline. It was residual and hovered like a long stream of fog on a cold morning.

"Do you see them?"

She shook her head. "No."

"Then why do I?"

"Perhaps you're an empath?"

"Not that I know of. I've been here many times. Never seen a thing."

Shawndirea placed her hand to his cold cheek. "Then your guess is as good as mine."

Ben said, "Then what's your guess?"

"Exactly what I suggested."

He frowned and watched the spirits slink through the corridor. "Why now?"

She whispered, "Maybe my magic has enhanced what you didn't know you had."

Chills shot through him when the formless being crept closer. He turned the light quickly. The spirit screeched and dissolved into nothingness. The other two retreated in slow, bobbing movements.

Seconds later, a low voice said, "Give the faery to me, and you may keep your life and flee."

"Never," Ben said.

"Then you shall die!" it hissed.

Shawndirea looked at him. His eyes were wide and searching. "What do you mean, 'Never?'"

"You didn't hear the threat?" he asked.

"No."

"Something demanded I give you to it, and I'll be allowed to live."

Shawndirea stood on his shoulder and outstretched her hands. "Be alert. Our challenges are about to begin."

She closed her eyes, whispered a chant, and green light glowed at her fingertips. Instinct brought Ben's hand to the hilt of his hunting knife. She thrust her hands forward. A blaze of greenish-blue flames shot across the cave path before them. The two retreating ghosts blazed into small balls of fire before vaporizing. The wet walls shimmered green as her fire rolled through the corridor. After her light faded, she stumbled, and sat on Ben's shoulder.

"You okay?" he asked.

She nodded, closed her eyes, and took a deep breath.

At the curve of the corridor where the green flame ended, large burning eyes glowed. A deep growl reverberated and echoed.

"You dare invade and reveal my presence?" it asked. "Today, you're both mine."

"Illusion?" Ben asked. "Or real?"

"Oh, it's *very* real," she whispered.

"So you *do* see it?"

"Unfortunately, yes."

CHAPTER 11

*D*eiko drove the route to the McKnight farm. His gun was on the seat beside him. At some point, he'd find and kill Jim before Jim contacted the authorities.

Deiko struggled with what he was becoming. His growing obsession to announce his discovery for fame and whatever financial gain he might receive, consumed him. In his overpowering lust for notoriety, murder was no longer an obstacle to achieve his goals. Along with this bent need, a darker force pressed his mind to capture the faery.

He met the reflection of his eyes in the rearview mirror and gasped. His darkened eyes were strange. His reflection frightened him. He didn't recognize himself. He slowed his truck to a stop on the narrow, grassy bank at the edge of the road.

Deiko looked closer in the mirror. His irises were black. The whites of his eyes were ashen gray.

"What the Hell?" His rage and need to find Ben subsided and shock rocked his soul.

He pried his eyelids wider apart with his trembling fingers and peered closer. He was horrified. Little black tendrils, no larger than capillaries, pulsed at the corners of his eyes. Something *was* taking control of him. What exactly, he didn't know. This brief realization made him understand why he was so focused on acquiring the faery.

Deiko had never been a violent person. He enjoyed practical jokes that were often embarrassing and distasteful to others, but he never intentionally set out to inflict deliberate pain. But after seeing the faery, he found himself wanting to hurt, to kill, and to steal. That obsessive drive had turned him into something he didn't truly understand. His mind raced to recall exactly what he was doing, but the gaps in his memory made him uneasy.

Was he ... *possessed?*

And if so, *when* had this occurred? More importantly, why?

Deiko sat back in his seat, rubbed his eyes, and then opened them. About twenty yards ahead was a bridge. Grabbing his gun, he got out and started walking. He didn't understand why, but something inside him insisted he must. So he did.

Midway across the two-lane bridge, he stepped to the edge and looked down at the dry creek bed. Two people walked hand in hand directly toward him.

"Jim?" Deiko whispered through clenched teeth.

As the pair came closer, it *was* Jim. Who was with him? Without thinking, he raised the gun and aimed. His finger tightened on the trigger. He fought the growing urge to kill. His hand shook.

"No," he said, trying to regain control. "I won't do it."

Deiko tried to straighten his trigger finger, but his finger locked in place. The force controlling him squeezed the trigger tighter. He fought to resist and his hand shook violently. Sweat covered his brow.

With his left hand, he grabbed the shaky gun, but even with both hands, he couldn't lower the gun, stop his finger from tightening. He pulled the trigger.

The girl with Jim screamed.

JIM AND LACY walked along the edge of the dry creek bed. He was careful not to walk too fast. Although she walked okay, he didn't want to rush her and add to her fatigue. Her balance was good, she didn't seem confused, but she still needed to see a doctor in spite of her protests.

Layers of dry leaves covered the small, tilted rocks that wobbled when they stepped on them. Twice, he nearly turned his ankle because he kept his focus more on her footing than his own.

"There's the bridge," Lacy said.

"Yeah, I see it."

"One second," she said. She stopped and leaned over to catch her breath. Sweat dripped down her face, and she panted.

Jim stood beside her and rubbed the center of her back. "Perhaps we should sit in the shady trees at the edge of the bank?"

"I'll be okay," she replied.

"You're pale. You need to rest."

He checked his phone. Still no reception.

"Come on," Lacy said. "Let's get to the shade beneath the bridge and then I can rest."

"We're a football field away," he said. "Are you sure?"

She smiled and nodded. "It isn't too far."

"But we got banged up pretty bad in the wreck. You have a nasty knot on your head, and it's extremely hot."

Standing upright, she leaned and kissed him.

"True, but I bet I can beat you to the bridge," she said.

Jim took her hand and smiled. "Maybe next time. Let's just get there without either of us passing out. Okay?"

She pursed her lips. "You know I'd beat you, don't you?"

"Probably. We'll find out at another time, okay?"

"I'll hold you to that."

They walked toward the bridge. An approaching vehicle slowed.

"Listen," he said. "That sounds like Deiko's truck."

The vehicle stopped. They stopped walking.

"You think it's him?" she asked with nervousness in her eyes.

"I hope not. But just in case, let's head to the trees for shelter."

Lacy nodded. Her bright eyes widened with fear. As they turned, she pointed at the man on the bridge. "Is that Deiko?"

The man raised his gun.

"Yes!" Jim grabbed her around the waist. She screamed.

The gun fired. The bullet stuck the rock on the ground and missed Jim's foot by mere inches. He scooped her in his arms and rushed through the tree line where they were safely out of Deiko's sight. Hidden in the trees, Jim lowered her so she could stand.

"You're not hit, are you?" he asked.

"No."

"Good."

"What about you?" she asked.

"He missed."

She sighed with relief and hugged him.

They hid in the trees until Deiko drove away.

Her beautiful eyes were tainted by uncertainty. "What should we do now?"

"We wait a little longer. At least until we're certain he's not coming back. Had we been on the road when he came this way, we'd both be dead."

"I know."

Lacy was clearly rattled.

"I want you safe," Jim said. "We rest for fifteen minutes and if he doesn't return, we'll get on the road and wave someone down for help."

She smiled. He pulled her close and hugged her. She buried her face against his chest. Her body shook and her warm tears dampened his shirt.

"It'll be okay," he whispered. "I promise."

Choking through tears, she said, "I want to believe you, but I'm so scared."

Jim rested his chin on top of her head and listened for traffic. His promise was one he'd keep. He didn't have much left in the world, but what the future held. He wanted Lacy to be a part of his life, so he'd make certain no harm came to her.

CHAPTER 12

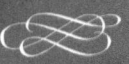

*B*en stared into the shadows. The flashlight's glow didn't reveal anything more than the pair of eyes burning like red-hot coals.

"What'd it mean by you *revealed* him? Is that true?" Ben asked.

"Yes," Shawndirea replied.

"So he was there the entire time, and we couldn't see him?"

She nodded.

"How?"

"Magic," she said with a shrug. "Or he has the ability to move between realms. My guess would be magic."

"So this isn't the sorcerer?" he asked.

She shook her head. "No. It's his pet or minion."

"So that's good?"

"If you mean weaker, then yes. But quite dangerous, all the same."

Ben held his knife at his side. He clenched the hilt firmly, but he didn't recall unsheathing it.

"Human," the creature said. "You don't belong here. This battle isn't yours. Release the faery to me, and I bid you your freedom."

"No way in Hell," Ben replied.

"Hell pales in comparison to what I'll do to you," it said.

The flashlight in Ben's hand went black. He clicked the button on

80

and off several times, but the light never returned. Useless, he tossed the flashlight to the cave floor.

Darkness cloaked them.

"Show yourself!" Shawndirea said.

Laughter bellowed from the darkness. "You've no authority over me, Shawndirea. Don't raise your voice to me."

Ben glanced at her. "He knows you?"

She shrugged. "To whom do I speak?"

The fiery eyes vanished when the creature blinked. A second later, they blazed open and narrowed.

"Gouthan."

"And your master—?" she asked.

"Has demanded I bring you to him." Gouthan chuckled deeply. His laughter rattled like rocks rolling down a hillside.

"His name?"

"Will be revealed once you surrender to me."

Ben said, "No. She stays with me."

"You'd die for her?" Gouthan asked with a hint of amusement.

"Without a second's thought," Ben replied.

"Interesting." More laughter rumbled in Gouthan's throat. "But will she, for you?"

Ben viewed Shawndirea from the corner of his eye. After the damage he'd caused, he wondered her reply. She had no reason to protect him and certainly no reason to die for him.

"Return to your master and let us pass," Shawndirea said, "Or else you'll see the limits I'll go to protect him."

"You're an insolent little imp," Gouthan replied. "I shall end you now."

Shawndirea frowned. Her fury caused her fingertips to glow. To Ben, she whispered, "Be prepared. This may not work the way I plan."

"Nothing seldom does," he replied.

She smiled and winked. "Perhaps our worlds are more alike than most imagine."

"Perhaps."

Green, shimmering orbs encircled her hands. The same light glowed around her feet. She drew her energy from the earth beneath his feet.

Warmth coursed through Ben's body. The two green orbs swelled and grew larger. She closed her eyes. Seconds later, the two orbs joined, intensified, and fired straight ahead through the corridor.

The blast struck the creature. The explosive light revealed the strange beast for several seconds. Its thick massive, black body resembled a cross between a giant cat and a lizard. Its catlike head bore long fangs. Its short-legged, scaleless body stretched like a lizard's but it was furry. No wonder they couldn't see it in the darkness.

Gouthan twisted in the air from the blast, and the light displayed even more of its characteristics. Its scorpion-like tail was long and barbed. Shawndirea's ball of light caught the creature square in the chest and flung it farther down the tunnel.

After the green light vanished, the creature vanished. Ben was uncertain if Shawndirea's hurled magic had hurt Gouthan or shoved him through the veil. Moments later, its vicious growl vibrated the walls.

"You are a fool, faery!"

Before the rattling echo of his voice faded, a blazing orange flame rushed at them. Shawndirea thrust both hands forward. Seconds before the flame reached them, a green barrier shielded them. The flames angrily licked her energy shield but did not pass through and engulf them.

"How good can you throw the knives you carry?" she asked.

Ben grinned. "Very good."

"Good. Once his flame retreats," she said. "Throw the knife hard and aim for his throat."

"I'll try, but I can't see him."

"The receding flame is a direct path to his mouth." She gasped and held the magic shield. "Use the fire line for your guide."

Ben smiled. "Sure."

The flow of Gouthan's flame weakened. His fire slinked backwards and Shawndirea's shield slowly shrank. Whatever spell she'd used not only blocked the flames, it also blocked the heat. The cave became colder than when they first stepped inside.

Shawndirea collapsed on his shoulder. She grabbed the collar of his jacket to prevent sliding off.

"*Now!*" she whispered.

Ben flung the knife hard and fast through the retreating flame. The green shield disappeared, and once again the cave's darkness swallowed them. The blade struck with a solid clack. What had his knife struck? The sound was like metal striking metal, but Gouthan was furry without any armor plating him.

Gouthan growled with a sputtering rattle in his throat. He hissed and spat, but no more flame ignited.

"You hit him," she said.

"Are you certain?"

"He's not dispensing more fire."

Ben nodded. "No threats, either."

"He *was* too talkative," she replied.

"Now what?" he asked. "The flashlight's useless."

"Try it again. Gouthan might've used a spell to thwart light."

Ben grabbed his flashlight off the cave floor. He clicked the button and the light worked.

"I want a closer look at this creature," he said.

"Careful," Shawndirea said. "He's still alive. Although injured, he's not defenseless."

Ben removed another knife. "I understand, but I *want* my blade back."

He aimed the flashlight and walked along the center of the tunnel. Gouthan writhed on the muddy cave floor. He tugged at the deeply lodged blade thrust in its neck. Its long claws prevented it from gaining a solid grasp. Blood oozed from its toothy mouth.

Ben stood in front of Gouthan. Its fiery eyes narrowed.

Ben shone the flashlight across its face and body. The creature was spectacular and intimidating. Scars on this beast's body revealed its body parts had been sewn together from several different creatures. Suture scars were at the neck, the tail, and the clawed bird-like feet.

"What the Hell is it?" Ben asked, setting down his pack.

"The sorcerer created his own creature from different beasts."

"I thought when it shot fire in the darkness that it was a dragon."

Shawndirea cackled with intense laughter.

"What?" Ben asked.

"Dragons are one thing you won't encounter in my realm."

"Really?"

"Yes."

"Did they ever exist?" he asked.

She nodded. "Sure. But no one's seen one for decades."

"That's a shame."

She shrugged. "Perhaps. But when most villages have thatched rooftops, you don't miss dragons too much."

Ben smiled. "I guess not."

Shawndirea stood and peered at Gouthan while Ben held the flashlight on the creature. "Your life is spared provided you name your master."

Gouthan grasped the knife hilt. Blood bubbles frothed from its catlike nose. He hissed and shook his head. Growling, he gnashed his teeth. Ben took a step back. The beast lunged, swung its barbed tail, and narrowly missed him.

Ben hunched and held his knife with his arm outstretched. He had fought another man with a knife before, so his stance prepared him for defense. However, Gouthan wasn't another human. This cunning beast was less predictable.

The long tail circled back. With lightning speed, it snapped forward. A second before the barbed end would've stung him, he rolled. The stinger missed, but he wasn't quick enough to avoid the thick base of its tail. It slammed his side and knocked Ben through the air. He was flung to the right side of the tunnel but managed to turn and brace himself before hitting the wall. The flashlight bounced across the wet floor.

Shawndirea lost her handhold on Ben's jacket collar and dropped to the cavern floor.

Ben grabbed a narrow cave column, swung around, and hit the ground. He rolled and came to his feet with his knife still in his right hand. The flashlight stopped and spun with its light directed at Gouthan. The strange creature moved rapidly across the cave at Shawndirea in spite of its injuries. She ran for Ben's backpack.

Ben rushed Gouthan. His first fear was Gouthan would take her, cross realms, and vanish. *Forever.* He couldn't allow it. Although it sounded premature, his world would be lost without her. He'd never believed in destiny until he met her. Something in his soul let him know they needed one another. His purpose was not only to get her home, but for something far more. Perhaps he'd discover who he really was as well.

Gouthan scuttled through the mud. Blood coated his sharp teeth. It panted heavily. And even though its injury weakened it, he'd reach Shawndirea before Ben.

Ben hurled the knife but his aim was off. Instead of striking a death-blow through the side of its head, the knife lodged in the creature's side. It snarled and turned to face him, swinging its tail madly and wildly at him. The sharp stinger dripped thick drops of poison when it struck the ground beside Ben.

Ben stepped outside its reach. Gouthan reared back its tail again. Ben rushed and kicked the blade wedged in its throat with incredible force. Ben backed away, crouched, and grabbed Shawndirea.

Gouthan's eyes widened. He staggered side to side, trying to maintain balance. It sputtered for air and choked on its own blood. Collapsing forward, its legs twitched. Spasms reverberated throughout its body. Gouthan's breathing ceased.

Blood spilled from its mouth and nose and formed a large dark pool on the cave floor. The barbed tail spasmed. Poison spilled from the sharp tip.

Ben knelt and grabbed the hilt of his hunting knife. With a quick tug, he pulled it from Gouthan's throat. More blood gushed from its throat. Ben found his other blade and pulled it free.

The creature's blazing eyes dimmed and extinguished. Smoke rose from its empty eye sockets. Were they actually coals of fire?

Ben retrieved the flashlight. "Are you okay?"

"Yes."

He looked at Gouthan's corpse. "I thought he'd be stronger and more difficult to kill."

In the flashlight's glow, Shawndirea smiled and her eyes focused on him like someone deeply in love. She looked away.

She said, "You surprise me."

"Why?"

"For most, he'd have been impossible to kill. Most would've died from fear."

Ben frowned. "If the sorcerer created him, why doesn't it have magical powers?"

Shawndirea shrugged. "It's a powerful beast with deadly abilities. Most wizards won't grant their pets access to magic for fear the creature will turn on them. I imagine Gouthan was difficult enough to control as he was."

Ben leaned closer to her. "Do you wish to continue? You look exhausted."

"We best head forward quickly," Shawndirea said.

"Why?"

"Gouthan's master will discover his pet's dead. Sorcerers seek vengeance for lesser offenses."

Ben sighed. "Then we go on. I'm not fond of what possibilities lie in wait. The cave's darkness always holds a spooky atmosphere."

"It won't become easier once we cross the rift."

"At least we'll have light."

"Don't be so certain," she said.

Ben zipped open the backpack, grabbed the plastic bottle of honey mixture, and poured some in the lid.

Shawndirea smiled. "Thanks."

He grabbed an apple and took a huge bite. "Let's take a short break before we find the rift."

CHAPTER 13

*D*eiko turned on a dead end dirt road. According to the GPS, the McKnight farm was where the road ended. He sped far faster than he should. Plumes of dust pillared behind the truck.

Ben's SUV was parked at the end of the road. Deiko parked beside it and looked in the rearview mirror. His eyes were still dark but seemed to be returning to normal. Inside he quaked, fearful of what coerced him to find and steal the faery.

When he fired the gun at Jim and his female companion, he somehow managed enough resistance to miss them by a few feet. After his disobedience, he awakened behind the truck's steering wheel and driving fast. Most of the trip he didn't remember. In fact, he remembered less and less. He wondered why and *what* had occurred during these recent mental blackouts.

A loud tractor approached Deiko's truck and startled him. He opened the door and got out.

"Morning!" John McKnight shouted over the motor. He shut off the tractor and looked down at Deiko. John took the straps of his overalls in his hands and smiled.

"Good morning." Deiko slid his hand behind his back and repositioned his gun to make it less noticeable.

"You here with Ben?" John asked.

Without hesitation, Deiko nodded. "Yeah. I'm a bit late. Where is he?"

John grinned. "He's probably already at the cave."

"Cave?" Deiko frowned and looked across the pasture. "Where?"

John pointed. "Walk down the worn path and past my pond and through those trees. You'll see the mouth of Devils Den easily then."

"Devils Den?"

John nodded. "Yep. Reckon everyone around here knows the name by now. I suppose you're not from 'round here, huh?"

The cave's name startled Deiko. He wanted to get in his truck and leave, but the task wasn't easy to do. Something pressured him to enter the cave to find Ben and the faery. The inner evil force sought complete control. Deiko feared he wasn't strong enough to fight it.

"Well," John said, turning the tractor's ignition key. "I've got a couple of dried out pastures to bush-hog before sunset. You shouldn't have any trouble finding Ben. Since he knows you're coming, he won't venture far inside."

Deiko grinned. "Thanks."

John shifted the tractor in gear and drove through the opened gate.

Deiko waited until the tractor was midway down the field before heading to the pond. When his eyes caught sight of the grove where the cave was hidden, something compelled him to increase his pace.

Grasshoppers jumped and buzzed through the air. His brisk steps crushed brittle, yellowish-tan blades of grass on his way to the trees. Crows angrily burst into flight and the dark shade welcomed Deiko.

His vision darkened when the cave's mouth came in view. Tunnel vision was all he had. Seconds later, his thoughts and vision were no longer his own. He pulled the gun from behind his belt and entered Devils Den.

EXHAUSTION OVERWHELMED Jim and Lacy by the time a truck stopped beside them. One of Ben's neighbors stopped and offered them a ride to Ben's house. They eagerly accepted and climbed in the truck bed. The man waited until they were seated before driving up the winding road to Ben's home.

Jim was thankful the elderly man had stopped when he did. Each step they'd taken along the highway intensified the aches of his scrapes and bruises. Although Lacy hadn't complained, she seemed a few steps from collapsing on the side of the road.

The gentle breeze flowing over them while the man drove was a blessing. Covered in sweat, they said little but held hands, occasionally glancing at one another and exchanging fatigued smiles. Mud and grime coated their clothes, faces, and hair.

Along the way, they checked their phones for service, but nothing had changed. No bars.

The truck slowed and the brakes squealed at the top of the driveway. Stiff and feeling older than the driver, Jim stood and helped Lacy stand. He climbed over the side of the truck bed and landed on the drive. His feet stung, his weak knees buckled slightly, and he winced. He extended his hand, she took it, and he helped her down.

"Much obliged," Jim said. "What do I owe you?"

The old man narrowed his eyes. "Two hundred dollars."

Jim's stomach turned. He didn't have that much money.

"Sir, um," he said, "I don't—"

The old man cut him off with a hysteric laugh and slapped his knee. "Works every time. Nah, I'm happy to help you. Looks like the two of you have been through Hell."

"Close," Jim replied.

"Say your car rolled off the side of this ridge?" he asked.

Lacy nodded.

"I noticed the break in the trees back there. You're lucky to be alive."

"Don't we know it," Lacy replied.

"You sure there's nothing more I can do for you?" he asked.

"No, but thanks. Dr. Whytten can help us ," Jim replied.

"Okay," he said, easing the truck forward and turning around.

They waited until the old man was out of view before staring nervously at Ben's house.

"Should we check the front door to see if it's unlocked?" Lacy asked.

Jim shook his head. "We should probably check the garage first. In case Deiko came back from the other direction."

"Wouldn't we have heard his truck go up the drive?"

"Probably," Jim said. "But I'd rather be certain he's not waiting for us."

Lacy forced a weak smile. "Me, too."

"Look, I'm sorry for bringing you out here. I almost got you killed. Twice."

"No," she said. "Coming to warn Dr. Whytten was *our* idea. Deiko was the one who tried to kill *both* of us. Not just me."

Jim shrugged.

Lacy expressed concern. "You don't think we should've tried to warn Whytten?"

"I should've. Alone."

"What? And let me miss all the excitement?" she said with a cute grin on her grime-covered face.

Jim tried not to smile, but he couldn't help it. This beautiful young lady had chosen to accompany him to Whytten's home. Now, her hair was matted, dirt and grime covered her cheeks, and her tattered knee-less jeans were caked with dirt and blood. She was a complete mess, and no longer the glamorous girl he'd seen on campus each day. She was someone he never thought would give him a second glance. And after all they'd been through—the car crash and the gunfire—she wasn't angry. She didn't blame him, and incredibly, she remained capable of smiling. She wasn't even upset about her appearance.

How could she bounce back so easily? Or, was she suffering from shock, slight hysteria? Extreme trauma or pressure could cause people to react with giddiness. She was a lot stronger than he expected. Maybe she wasn't as pampered like he had assumed.

She brushed the hair from her eyes and stepped closer. "In spite of what's happened today, I'm glad you're the one with me."

Jim hugged her. After a couple minutes, he eased his hold. "Let's make sure Deiko didn't kill Dr. Whytten."

"Okay," Lacy said. "And then what? We don't have phone reception or a car. How do we get home?"

He sighed. "I don't know. We'll figure something out."

They inspected inside and outside of the garage. Nothing seemed out of the ordinary. And better, Deiko's truck wasn't there.

The back door was locked. They circled the far side of the house and walked onto the front porch. He checked the door. It wasn't locked. Once they entered, the house was dark, quiet.

"Might as well check each room," Jim said.

She nodded.

Every room was fairly clean. No sign of Ben. No traces of blood anywhere.

"Apparently Whytten wasn't here when Deiko arrived," Jim said.

"That's good."

After they entered Ben's study, they froze. They exchanged surprised glances. All of the insect collection boxes were empty.

"What happened?" she asked.

"Not sure. But he'd never allow anything to happen to his collection."

"Exactly. It's sacred to him. I remember how excited he was when he showed the class."

"What the—?" Jim said, examining the nearest box. "All the pins are in place. But the butterflies and moths are gone."

"How?"

Baffled, Jim shook his head. "No idea."

They went to the window and a few leaves crunched underfoot. Jim looked outside. "Deiko must've come through the window."

"But Whytten's collection? You think Deiko did that?"

"No. That would've taken too much time, and for what purpose? Pinned butterflies are very brittle. There'd be wing and body fragments all over. You can't unpin them without destroying their wings and bodies. No. If Deiko or anyone had wanted to steal them, they'd have to take the boxes, too."

"Then how?"

"I really don't know," he replied. "Come on. Let's check the other rooms."

Jim flipped a switch on the wall. The hall light came on, so they returned to the living room. The floorboards creaked beneath their footsteps. He turned on a lamp, even though the outside daylight lit the room. Usually a dimly lit room didn't bother Jim, but after Deiko had tried to kill them, he was paranoid, overly cautious, and extremely tired. His adrenaline rush was gone.

He sat on the couch, leaned back, and closed his eyes. Lacy sat beside him and rested her head against his shoulder. Neither said a word, but moments later, sleep overcame them.

CHAPTER 14

Queen Istrell, the Faery Queen of Elvendale, stared over her kingdom from the tallest tree, which was her castle. Rage flowed through her while she searched for her daughter, Shawndirea.

"Where are you?" she asked. "You've been gone for days."

Anger creased her aged brow. With her tiny, balled fists, she glided inside a hollow opening in the massive tree. Luminous mushrooms lit the narrow path, which led deeper into her fortress. Around the next turn of the endless spiraling path, she stopped and stepped softly into a dead-ending path. A rainbow array of tall crystals were attached to the tree. Slid inside a tiny crack of the pulpwood was a black-framed looking glass.

Istrell placed her hands on the crystals as she often did many times over the past few days. The crystals glowed brilliantly. She closed her eyes and drew upon their power, their energy. More energy flowed from the living tree and passed through her feet. The growing sensation brought concurrent heat and chills to her.

The magic magnified. She tilted her head upward. Her mind raced and floated through the tree canopies, through the valleys, dark forests, rivers and lakes, and through the kingdoms beyond hers.

She couldn't locate Shawndirea.

"Where are you, my child?" Pain echoed in her tone. Exhausted, she released the crystals and drooped prostrate on the floor.

Covered in sweat, she shook uncontrollably and sobbed. Sadness broke her heart. Shawndirea was the next heir destined for the throne and was missing. She mustn't be in Aetheaon, but where had she gone?

Istrell didn't sense her spirit. Something blocked their magical bond, which alarmed Istrell even more.

A new darkness had entered the Underworld and passed through to their realm, Aetheaon. Its manifested evil disturbed her more than anything prior to its arrival.

Shawndirea might've been captured. Or, perhaps, she'd been entangled by whatever lurked at the center of their world and had not yet been identified.

Her daughter was often more curious than she should be. She was a stubborn princess, at times, but more suited to keep the kingdom in order than any other royal faery.

Istrell stood, shook her head, and flexed her wings. Her subsiding sadness would soon be replaced with anger yet again. Seldom did she allow her emotions to battle one another, but when Shawndirea's welfare was involved, Istrell lost control. She hoped to be in her sad cycle when Shawndirea finally returned. Otherwise, the harangue she'd unleash on her daughter would be bitter and frightening.

The crystals' power faded and grew cold. She reached to the side of the crystals and took the black mirror from its hiding place. She gazed in the cold mirror. The glass shimmered silver and came to life. The surfaced images were of the darkening region in the center of Aetheaon where the new evil grew.

The Black Chasm.

Smoke and thick fog swirled over this area. Istrell focused harder but the darkness prevented her from seeing what lie beyond. What hid within the darkness, how'd it come to be, and why was it concealing itself. Running her palm across the glass, the images disappeared. The glass grew cold again.

Istrell never looked through the glass for long periods of time. She held the suspicion that while she couldn't see what was within the black smoky region, it could see and identify her whereabouts.

Regaining her strength, Istrell glided to the tree opening and looked out over Elvendale once more. She kept the mirror close, in case she felt the urge to scan the area for Shawndirea.

Should something tragic happen to her daughter, not only would Istrell weep, *all* of Elvendale would weep.

Should Shawndirea not return home soon, Istrell would have to call the High Court together and summon a search party to find and retrieve her. She hoped the length of Shawndirea's absence didn't require such an action. Others in the court might view the loss of her daughter as a sign that someone new should be placed on the throne.

Holding the mirror with both hands, she whispered, "Wherever you are, my child. Please hurry home."

CHAPTER 15

Shawndirea sipped the honey mixture from the plastic lid. Her energy was returning. After she finished, Ben took the lid and sealed the bottle shut. He placed her on his shoulder.

He stood and wiped the blood from his knife against the bottom of his boot. He took the knife and walked to Gouthan's carcass.

"One second," he said.

"What are you doing?" Shawndirea adjusted her seated position on his shoulder.

Ben grinned. "Taking a souvenir."

He reached for Gouthan's ear, and the creature vanished.

"What the Hell?" he said. "Where'd it go?"

"The veil swallowed it."

"Why?"

"To erase any magical evidence that crossed to your side."

"Why not us? Why weren't we taken since we witnessed it?"

Shawndirea smiled. "It doesn't work that way. Imagine what might happen if someone else happened to find its corpse? The realms beyond the Underworld attempt to conceal its existence from those living in the Overlands."

"So what happens if you get stuck on this side of the veil?"

Worry creased Shawndirea's brow. "Let's not speak of such a thing."

He detected her fear. "What happens?"

"At some point, I'll die prematurely," she said softly.

Ben frowned. "Why?"

Shawndirea shifted on his shoulder and released a long sigh. "Magic from the Underworld and beyond must not exist in your world. It creates an unbalance. If I stayed too long, Veil-Watchers will be summoned to find and kill me."

"Veil-Watchers?"

She nodded. "Wraiths."

"Who summons them?"

Shawndirea offered a small shrug. "Once my magic's detected on this side of the rift for several days, they arrive. I don't know what actually summons them, or if anyone summon them at all. But like Gouthan, my body will return to my homeland. One way or another."

"How'd you get past them to cross the veil?"

"They don't stand guard. We can pass freely as long as we don't overextend our stay in your world."

"Then we take you home."

"Thanks," she said, smiling. "It's far more complex than I can explain."

"What about me?" Ben asked.

"What do you mean?"

"What if I stayed in your world?"

She grinned. "You're human. We have many cities occupied by humans. They've been there for hundreds of years."

"So people like me, from the Overlands, have moved from this side of the veil to yours?"

"Of course, but they're generally kept as prisoners or slaves. They never rise to position."

"Why not?"

Shawndirea bit her lower. "They tend to die quickly."

"Rebellion?"

"No," Shawndirea replied. "Most go insane because it's difficult to adapt to a place they never believed existed outside their nightmares. That's why I'm trying to mentally prepare you for what we may encounter when we pass through an Underworld rift into my realm. It's easy for you to say you understand, but you won't. You can't. Not until you've actually seen things you cannot explain."

Ben chuckled. "I have to admit the creature I killed is certainly something I could never explain to someone outside this cave. That's about the best eye-opener an Overlander could encounter."

She gave a cute grin. "True. But, far worse creatures and beings than Gouthan exist. So don't insist you *believe* me until—"

Ben nodded. "Okay. Seeing is believing."

"If you understand the uniqueness of possible dangers I'm stressing, then fine. But for most, seeing is disbelief. Shock causes them freeze and become vulnerable to unexpected attacks. Since there's no logic to what stands before them, they don't act until it's too late. Few humans from the Overlands survive in the Underworld."

Ben slid the hunting knife into its sheath. "Since I've nothing left to take from Gouthan as a souvenir, we'd best head deeper into the cave."

Shawndirea leaned closer to Ben and placed her hand on his cheek. "Wait."

"What is it?"

She held her hands above her head, closed her eyes, and spoke a quick spell in an unfamiliar language. A bright orb of light encircled them. Had Ben not known better, he'd have thought they stood in an open field under the midday sun. The brightness lit up even the darkest crevices in the small cave. On the ceiling amongst the icicle-like stalactites, tiny brown bats chirped and fled from the light's harsh glow. They flew to darker recesses farther down the tunnel.

She smiled. "You get a reward for killing Gouthan."

Puzzled, Ben asked, "What?"

"I've figured out what your name should be."

Ben gave a nervous side-glance. "Oh? What name have you chosen?"

"Roble," she said flatly.

"Roble?"

Shawndirea nodded. "It means noble with great strength."

Roble smiled. "I like it. Much better than I deserve."

"In my realm, that's the name you must give whenever they ask who you are. From this day forward, you're no longer Ben."

"Okay," Roble said. "But I don't understand why."

"Ben's an Overlander name. Using it in my realm betrays you. You don't want anyone to know you aren't of my realm, Aetheaon." Her voice seemed haughty but not in an arrogant way. More like, someone of authority or royalty.

"If you say so."

"No. I *insist*, Roble," she replied.

"As you wish," he said. "Now, let's go."

She laughed. "Since I'm currently at your mercy and cannot fly, I go where you take me. Within *reason*, of course."

Roble smiled. "I'll never put you in harm's way."

When she looked in his eyes, his stomach tightened. Never had he seen a woman look at him with such trust and what he *hoped* indicated her love. It caught him off guard.

He took a quick breath, swallowed hard, and looked away.

"What's wrong?" she asked.

"Nothing."

Shawndirea shook her head.

"What?"

She giggled. "Your eyes give you away."

"Not the first time someone's told me that this week."

"What troubles you about me?" she asked.

"Nothing really *troubles* me. It's just—"

She stood. "Tell me."

Flustered, Roble shrugged. "I'm probably reading too much into your glances."

"In what way?"

"Sorry. But ... I've never been able to read women well."

Her perfect lips formed a sly, flirty grin. "You're afraid to tell me?"

"Not afraid. Just uncertain."

She stepped closer and kissed his cheek. She whispered in his ear, "You never know unless you ask."

Her sultry voice sent chills down his back. Her actions were deliberate. She knew what she was doing.

"Say it!" Shawndirea said sharply and then playfully covered her mouth with her hands.

"Are you flirting with me, or are you attracted to me?" he asked.

She kissed his cheek again and stepped back. "Of course, I'm attracted to you."

"Even after I damaged your wings?"

"I told you to let that go."

"I know, but it bothers me."

Shawndirea sighed. "I wasn't fond of you in the beginning, but you've proven yourself to me. You've shown me your heart's intent. You're noble and strong, which is why you earned the new name."

"But we're not the same race," he said.

"Does that matter?"

Roble laughed and shook his head. "Wouldn't it?"

"Why should it?" she replied evenly.

"Our sizes, for one."

"Phht!" she replied. "Faeries have a great deal of magic. But even magic isn't stronger than love."

Roble turned toward her and held out his hand for her to step on. She did. He brought her even with his face and stared in her eyes. "You're implying you love me?"

"Too soon?"

"I would think."

Shawndirea crossed her arms. Her eyes sparkled from the encircling light's glow. "Your true feelings for me reflect in your eyes. Since I revived and released your collection, you've been unable to hide it."

"I wasn't about to admit it."

"Why not? You still blame yourself for hurting me?"

He nodded.

"I honestly don't hold that against you, Roble."

"I'm glad you don't. But you said faeries and humans are at odds in your realm. Why would you consider falling in love with a human?"

"Love comes without consideration. Besides, you've never met a male Fae. Arrogance is something I detest, and they cannot suppress their loftiness for a second, which is why a majority of female faeries outlive our counterparts. Males foolishly get themselves killed because they *believe* they're invincible."

"Men aren't much different," Roble replied.

Shawndirea pursed her lips. "*You* are different than most men. I don't detect greed or animosity in you. Modesty's perhaps a flaw you've inherited, but even so, you don't lack courage. You stand your ground. You willingly set your life as a sacrifice to protect mine against Gouthan. Few humans in the Underworld would entertain such an detriment."

"I appreciate the compliments."

"No compliments. The truth."

"Thanks all the same."

Shawndirea shrugged. "The first real test was releasing your collection back into the wild. You didn't protest like I expected, which showed me you appreciate living creatures for more than prizes. Had you lost your temper and hurried to catch them all, I'd have seen an ugly side I could never tolerate."

Roble kept her gaze. "What *exactly* were you looking for when you crossed the veil? I don't believe your curiosity enticed you."

She looked away.

"I answered your question. Now, please answer mine," he said.

"You," she replied softly. "I was looking for you. Or someone like you."

"Really?"

Her eyes met his. She nodded.

"A human?"

"More than that. A life companion."

"Why not search in your realm?"

Shawndirea sighed. "I told you why."

"Yes, faery arrogance."

"You'll understand once you encounter a male Fae."

"Okay, maybe so. But how can we be life partners? It simply isn't possible."

"The height, size issue still bothers you?"

Roble shrugged. "It presents some major obstacles."

She smiled. "I can alter my height, but at a cost."

"And that is?"

Her gaze dropped. "I—"

The light encircling them faded. The cave filled with darkness. Shrieks and screeches echoed deeper inside the cavern.

"We must go!" Shawndirea said sternly. "Now!"

"Back outside?"

"No, toward the noise."

Roble frowned. "*Toward*? You're certain?"

"We can't flee now. Our presence has been detected. We must find a rift soon."

Before Roble could reply, Deiko shouted from the cave's opening, "Ben! I know you're in there! Don't make me come in after you!"

Deiko's voice sounded strange, dark, and hate-filled.

Roble looked at Shawndirea and started to reply. She placed her hand on his lips. "Your name's not Ben anymore. Remember?"

"Yes."

She looked concerned. "That's the man?"

Roble nodded. "Yes, that's Deiko."

"Keep moving. Let's hope we find a rift within the next few minutes," she said.

"Why?"

"Because he's being controlled. He's not acting under his own power. Whoever wanted me trapped in the Overlands has decided to use any possible method to kill me. You probably don't understand."

"You mean he's possessed?"

"Has he behaved like himself at all since you found me?"

"No," Roble said. "When he aimed his gun at me, he acted completely different. The Deiko I know acts like a goofball. But, in the field, he became unhinged. Like he had a split personality."

When Deiko received no immediate reply, he shouted, "You're trapped, so you might as well show yourself."

Shawndirea said, "Hurry, Roble."

Roble walked quicker down the tunnel. Shawndirea cast a small wisp of blue light. It floated ahead of them. The wisp wasn't bright enough for Deiko to see from a distance, nor was it too dim for Ben to not see the cave floor. But the light didn't diminish the dangers of the wet, slick floor while he walked.

Rounding the next curve of the cave path, they came to a crossroads. He'd been at this intersection a couple times in the past, but the cross-roads weren't there each time he mapped the pathways. He stopped dead center in the crossroads.

"Which direction?" Roble asked. "I'm open to suggestions."

"I thought you knew the cave."

"It changes, like I told you."

The blue wisp shot straight ahead. Growls and shrieks came from the two side directions the wisp ignored.

"Follow the light," Shawndirea said.

Ben sprinted after the light while she held tightly to his jacket collar beneath his left ear. Her breathing was soft against his skin. He loved having her close, and while he followed the wisp, he wondered what Shawndirea sacrificed for them to remain together. And *why*? Whatever it cost must be precious because her countenance drooped the second he asked and she considered how to reply.

"Even if Deiko wasn't here, we're not alone," she said.

"No need telling me. I heard the other creatures approaching."

"Those are minor to what we're about to encounter."

"Damn," Roble said. "I was hoping we'd get somewhere safer."

"That'll take some time."

"How much time?"

"Could be days," she replied. "*If* we survive."

The blue wisp stopped and hovered about six yards ahead of him. Roble slowed. His boots skidded on the slick cave floor. With his right hand, he found a handhold in the wall and held tightly. His feet slid from beneath him, and he dropped, hard. He stopped inches from running off the edge of the path into a deep abyss. His feet dangled over the ledge.

Roble looked for Shawndirea but couldn't find her. Rolling over, he held himself on hands and knees.

"Are you okay?" he asked, without knowing her location.

Back in the direction from where they'd come, unseen beasts snarled.

"Shawndirea!" Roble shouted. His voice echoed through the fiery fissure below and across the open cavern that spanned somewhat endlessly.

"Shh!" she replied.

"Where are you?" he asked softly.

The blue wisp hovered, turned, and glided to her and floated above her head. She sat with her legs curled beside her. "Here."

Roble crawled to her. "Are you okay?"

In the blue light's glow, she nodded.

"A little shaken but I'm okay."

He held out his hand. She stepped atop his palm.

"Sorry," he said. "I didn't know the path dropped off. The pathway never took me this way before."

Slowly, Roble stood. Using the wisp's blue light as a guide, he returned to the ledge. Below, perhaps several hundred feet, the fiery stream flowed. Occasional bursts of flames shot upward, like tiny exploding gas-filled balloons. The harsh, choking air reeked of rotten eggs. The cave temperature was no longer cold. Heat rose from the yellow-orange fissure. In the glow of the fire small winged creatures zipped back and forth.

"Where are we?" he asked.

Behind them, the pursuing beasts grew closer.

"You tell me!" she said. "It's your cave."

"Not *my* cave. I've never traveled this direction."

Shawndirea smiled. "I tease."

"Normally I'd say that's cute, but we're in a rough spot. Whatever caught our scent at the crossroads is getting closer."

"I know."

Roble stared into the abyss. Jagged rocks lie on this side of the flame-filled stream. He didn't see a clear path leading downward. He opened his mouth to speak but something in the shadows below caught his attention.

Pockets of fire blazed about every fifty yards. At first he thought the little fires were trapped within rock barriers or small outcropping rocks, but then large wings stretched and flapped. Other winged creatures lurked near the edge of the stream. A larger one flapped its wings. Then another. Dozens of these dark beasts huddled around the fires but seldom did they move. They weren't restless, and he hoped they were asleep. As best he could tell, the creatures weren't aware of their arrival. With the snarling beasts coming closer, he and Shawndirea were only minutes from a major confrontation occurred. Either between them and the pursuing monsters or they'd face the winged creatures below. Neither situation looked promising.

"Do you see them?" Roble pointed.

Shawndirea followed the direction of his finger. Several winged creatures stretched their wings.

She leaned close to his ear and whispered, "Back away, slowly."

Roble stepped away from the ledge and eased to the left side of the path.

"What are they?"

"Minions."

Roble frowned. "Like Gouthan?"

She shook her head. "No, closer to demons."

"Really?"

"Yes. The name for the cave isn't wrong. *This* is a den of demons."

"Had I ever seen anything like this, I never would've returned."

She placed her hand against his cheek. "Nor would I."

"You didn't see anything like this?"

"No."

"So they're demons?"

"Or something similar. Underlings are vile creatures usually controlled by a stronger demon."

Roble said, "Did we miss the veil?"

"In a way, I suppose we have. Or, we've been directed to a more dangerous place by whomever seeks to keep me out of Aetheaon."

A loud, hissing flame blazed in the chasm. Shadows danced through the wide cavern. The growling creatures stood at the head of the path and blocked their access to the crossroads. Their green eyes narrowed.

"We don't have any good options," Roble said softly.

"I know."

A man hidden in the shadows on the other side of the path near the overlook said, "Follow me. I can lead you to safety."

Roble turned with a start. He placed his hand on his knife. "Who are you?"

"I'm Forcas."

Shawndirea waved her hand. The blue wisp shot across the path and shimmered brightly, revealing the haggard old man. He stood six foot tall, thin and frail. He leaned on a gnarled staff. His long gray hair flowed into his beard, making it impossible to tell where they met. His tattered, sooty clothes were worn cloth. His wrinkled face cringed tighter as the wisp dipped closer. Other than the staff, the old man didn't appear to have any weapons, but the blue lighting didn't reveal everything.

Forcas shielded his eyes with his right hand. Roble slowly slid his knife from its sheath.

"How can you get us out of here?"

"A hidden path, but you don't have much time."

Shawndirea shook her head. "Don't trust him."

"Why not?" Roble whispered.

"It doesn't *feel* right."

"He's human."

She whispered, "He *appears* to be human. Don't forget how things alter and change down here."

"You mind with the light?" Forcas asked, still blocking its glow with his hand.

"Sorry," Shawndirea said. The wisp's light dimmed but remained bright enough for them to see, should he rush them.

Roble looked at the two green-eyed beasts in the tunnel. They eased closer but stayed outside the blue wisp's radius. They growled and sniffed the air. They were trying to get his scent.

Shawndirea turned and shot a small green ball of fire at them. The fire struck one, it yelped, and both fled in fear.

"How'd you get here?" Roble asked.

Forcas coughed and cleared his throat. He spoke with a deeply strained voice. "I've been here so long I can't remember. I've wandered these passageways for so long that I've given up on ever finding my way out."

"Yet, you offer to get us *safely* away?" Shawndirea said.

The old man shrugged. "Only from the direction I came, which is the path leading down."

"Down there?" Roble pointed. "Where all those creatures wait?"

Forcas nodded and pointed a different direction. "The path goes *away* from them and over the fiery stream."

"Careful," Shawndirea said. "Something's not right about him."

The old man stepped back and turned away. At the side of the tunnel, he descended and used his staff for balance.

"So be it," Forcas said. "Find your own way."

"Wait," Roble said.

Forcas stopped but kept his back to them.

Roble whispered to Shawndirea. "You don't trust him?"

"Not completely."

"But after we get past those underlings, we don't have to continue following."

Forcas cleared his throat. "I don't have an eternity to await your decision."

Shawndirea gave a slight nod. "Fine. Keep your guard up. Never get within an arm's length of him."

"Well?" Forcas asked.

"We'll follow," Roble said.

"Splendid!" he replied. "Haven't had the pleasures of conversation in ages. Other than my own mindless ramblings, that is. I've sorely missed talking to another human."

Shawndirea leaned close to Roble's ear. "Don't trust him. There's something dark about him."

Roble nodded. "I sense it, too. But what else can we do?"

"We watch out for ourselves," she said.

To the old man, Roble said, "You've wandered this cavern for years?"

Forcas stopped walking. "Didn't I say that?"

"Where'd you come from?" Roble asked.

The old man slowly stepped down the path.

"Careful where you step," he said. "So many jagged rocks, holes, and strange creatures waiting for morsels like ourselves to feast on. Don't get snared in the rocks. No. Wouldn't be good. No good at all."

Roble gritted his teeth. "Forcas, *where* are you from? Your home?"

"A place you wouldn't know," he replied.

"Overlands or Underworld?" Shawndirea asked.

"Both, the same, each. Yes. Been many places. Seen many dangers."

"Babbling old fool," Roble whispered.

"Shh!" she said in his ear. "He may hear you."

Roble shrugged. "So?"

"He's far from harmless."

"Seems he suffers more from dementia than anything else."

Shawndirea shook her head. "You've a lot to learn about guise."

"Not quite certain what you mean."

"Many thieves in the Underworld use disguises to lower your guard or guilt you into sympathy to give them coins."

Roble gave an even smile. "Spend more time in my realm, and you'll find much of the same thing."

"Then why taunt him? Those in the Overlands can't bewitch or cripple you with magic."

Forcas took more nimble steps and descended about a dozen steps below them. His pace increased. Roble hurried to get closer. The temperature grew hotter. He wanted to shed his light jacket. Each step he took, the black stairs crackled, crumbled, and powdery ash rose. Not only was the air getting warmer, the smell of sulfur became worse.

Roble shrugged. "That's true. Do you detect he has magical abilities?"

She shook her head. "No. Not magical powers, but something dark."

"Maybe he's the master of Gouthan."

"No. If he were, I'd know it."

The jagged path was dark, steep. One misstep and they'd barrel downward. The rough-hewn steps would slice through their flesh like little razor-tipped pins. Roble struggled to see where to step next. But Forcas moved with ease and seemed to glide down each step. Shawndirea's blue wisp stayed behind Forcas and drifted inches above the path so Roble could see. The old man didn't notice or care. He moved a step at a time.

A burst of yellow flame shot from the meandering fiery stream. The brief explosion lit up the rock stairway. The stairs descended a quarter mile before leveling off, but the bridge Forcas had mentioned wasn't visible.

Forcas muttered jumbled phrases in several different languages. He amused himself, it seemed, by talking aloud and ignoring them.

"How would you know if he's Gouthan's master?" Roble asked.

"The touch of control on Gouthan would be stronger on Forcas, if he were the master. I don't sense such power. I'm certain Gouthan's master seeks to find and make us suffer for killing his pet."

"I've no doubt."

She smiled. "Creating Gouthan required a lot of time, a great deal of magic, and a major blood sacrifice."

"Oh?"

"Yes. Giving life to that creature wasn't easy."

Roble shrugged. "At least he died easily enough."

"We might, too, if we continue following Forcas."

Forcas reached the area where the stairs leveled. The path became smoother. Several dozen stairs remained for Roble to descend. Forcas turned and faced them. He laughed.

"The way you're taking your time, you must want to wander these caverns like me." Forcas turned and continued his stride.

"Wait," Roble said. "Forcas, wait for us."

Forcas stopped and stood with his back to them. Roble hurried down the final jagged steps. Plumes of black ash drifted and formed small, hanging clouds in the acrid air.

Roble stepped off the final step and walked to Forcas. The old man turned. His eyes narrowed. He no longer appeared a frail old man. His face was much younger. His long, twisting beard was now a neat, short mustache and a jet-black goatee. His eyes disturbed Roble the most. A flickering blue glow radiated inside them.

Roble stood still.

Forcas smiled. "There's something we failed to discuss earlier."

"What's that?" Roble placed his hand on the hilt of his hunting knife.

Forcas' eyes flamed red for a second before turning icy white. "My price for leading you to safety. We never discussed that, did we?"

Roble swallowed hard. Shawndirea warned him not to trust Forcas because nothing was exactly as it appeared in the Underworld.

"Did we? Remind me if we did," Forcas said.

"No, we didn't," Roble said. "What's your price?"

"Your lives."

Shawndirea raised her hands.

"I advise you not to, Faery. You've no idea who you're dealing with. I'm more powerful than you, especially inside my domain."

Roble frowned. "Whom are we dealing with?"

"I gave my name," Forcas replied.

"I'm not familiar with it," Roble said.

"Nor I," Shawndirea said.

"It doesn't matter. You won't ever forget it."

Forcas tightened his hands around his staff, lifted it, and then he drove it into the charred floor. The ground split, shook, and a thunderous rumble echoed throughout the dark cavern. The fiery stream bubbled and fissures widened on both sides of it. The stream became a wide river of molten lava. The winged creatures took to flight and shrieked deafening, high-pitched cries.

The thick lava flowed and spiraled. Balls of gas ignited into clouds of evaporating fire. The ground shook. Stalactites dropped like sharp daggers. They burst and shattered all around. Where they struck, holes opened. Streams of smoke billowed from these little cones. The sulfuric air reeked and choked them. Along the walls of the deep cavern, the previously unseen, unlit torches flickered and blazed.

"What the Hell?" Roble said.

Forcas smiled. "Your perception's quite keen."

Roble glanced at Shawndirea. "What's he talking about?"

She shrugged.

Deep rolling laughter echoed from Forcas. His human appearance retreated. A wicked smile crept across his demonic face. He pointed at the flowing lava. "The river below is the River Styx. Welcome to Hell."

CHAPTER 16

*L*acy awakened, curled against Jim on the couch. He was still asleep. Her head throbbed. After glancing around the room, it took a few moments to remember where she was. While he slept, she slid her cellphone from her pocket and checked for reception.

Still nothing.

She shook her head. "I can't believe my silliness."

Lacy dialed 9-1-1. The phone rang through.

"9-1-1. What's your emergency?"

She explained their ordeal, where they were, and they had no means of transportation. She stressed how much she feared Deiko would return to kill them.

"I'm sending out officers now."

"Thanks."

Lacy disconnected the call. She gently shook Jim's shoulder until he awakened. He stared at her with a confused expression.

"Police on their way," she said with a broad smile.

"You got reception?"

She shook her head. "No. I remembered 9-1-1 is accessible without reception."

"Really? I didn't know that, but glad it worked."

"Me, too."

She looked at her filthy hands. "Do you think Dr. Whytten would care if I washed up in his bathroom?"

Jim shrugged. "No. He wouldn't mind."

Lacy smiled. "Good. All this dirt and grime makes my skin crawl. My fingernails are nasty. Be back in a bit."

While she showered, Jim returned to the study where the open insect boxes were. He wanted to make sense of how the butterfly collection disappeared with only the pins left behind. Although he wasn't an entomologist, he understood how brittle dried insects were. Pressing down on the thorax to remove the pin would shatter a specimen.

The open window caught his attention. Before he reached it, a vehicle screeched to a stop in the driveway. Jim moved to the side of the window and pressed his back against the wall. The vehicle didn't sound like Deiko's truck. Before the person exited the vehicle and slammed the door, voices came over a radio transmitter. He sighed with relief. It was a deputy car. The lanky officer headed to the side door.

The officer knocked hard. "Sheriff deputy! We received a 9-1-1 call from this address!"

Jim hurried and opened the door. He noticed the name, "Higgins", on the officer's uniform.

Deputy Higgins asked, "Did you call 9-1-1?"

Jim shook his head. "No. My girlfriend did."

"So, what's the trouble?"

A smile spread across Jim's face after he realized he'd called Lacy his girlfriend. She was his first girlfriend.

"Something amusing here?" Higgins asked.

Jim's smile detracted. "No, sir. Sorry."

Jim stepped outside and explained where Deiko had shot his car, and then he pointed where his car plummeted down the ravine.

Higgins frowned and wrote down the information. After Jim finished, Higgins said, "This man, Dr. Deiko, is your professor?"

Jim nodded. "Yes."

"Any idea why he's bent on killing you?"

"None, sir. He's never acted like he *disliked* me. He always has an odd sense of humor, but he never seemed violent."

The back door opened and Lacy stepped out. Her hair was wet and her makeup was gone. For a moment, she looked startled, but then she offered a modest smile.

The officer glanced from Jim to Lacy. "She was in the car with you?"

"Yes."

Lacy joined them in the driveway. She smelled of soap and shampoo.

Higgins asked, "Do either of you need me to call paramedics?"

Both shook their heads.

"It's surprising the two of you walked away with your lives."

Jim said, "Don't we know it."

"We need a ride though," Lacy said. "I'm certain my mother's getting worried."

Higgins nodded. "Let me call dispatch and give them this information. At least we know who we're looking for. I'll put out an APB. Any idea where he might've gone?"

"No," Jim said. "My guess is he's still looking for Dr. Whytten since there's no sign of him here."

"Okay," Higgins said. "Other officers are on their way. Once they arrive, we'll search the perimeter to make certain Dr. Whytten isn't still here. I'll find someone to take you home."

"Thanks," Lacy said.

FRUSTRATED, Deiko entered the cave, but not exactly willingly. Something forced him to obey and took control over his body. It was an odd sensation to move a certain way, but have no power to object.

The building urgency to find the faery was no longer his own, but whatever possessed him. Several times he fought against this dark power, but he wasn't strong enough to thrust it away or wrestle free of its hold. He seemed outside his body from time to time, watching his body's actions, but he didn't know how to regain control. Now, he wondered how much desire to get the faery was actually his. Whatever controlled him probably knew his desire for fame and wealth. It over-magnified his lust in order to steal the faery.

By granting this entity brief access to his psyche, the being flung open the door and took the reins to enact its own greed and lust.

"Ben!" Deiko shouted against his will.

He walked deeper inside Devils Den. Although he carried a flashlight, the light wasn't on. Oddly enough, he could see, but only through narrow tunnel vision that glowed with a yellowish tint. After a few twists and turns in the darkness, he didn't detect Ben anywhere nearby.

Several more steps and his feet wouldn't budge. His legs seemed to weigh more than he could lift. His arms hung heavy to his side.

"Fool," the voice said in his mind. "You think you're more powerful than I? Your resistance comes at a great price."

Deiko tried to speak, but he was voiceless. In his mind, he asked, "Who are you?"

"Elias."

"Elias who?"

"You have all you need to remember. I'll haunt your dreams. You'll never be the same."

Severe pain ripped through his mind. Everything became darker. Without warning, whatever power controlling him suddenly disappeared.

Coldness rushed through Deiko. He braced against the cave wall and vomited. He staggered several steps in the darkness and collapsed to the chilly, wet floor. Extreme vertigo kept him unsteady.

He clicked the small flashlight on.

"Where am I?" He trembled from the cold.

Rather than trying to stand, he held the flashlight in his mouth and crawled.

"Help," he thought. "I must get help."

Voices echoes from the dark tunnels behind him. Nervousness overtook him. He clawed and pulled himself through the cave following his light. Due to the dizzying sensation, his head lulled to the right, and he crawled sideways. The feeling sickened him. He dry heaved until he nearly collapsed.

Wings fluttered around him. He screamed.

"Leave," Elias whispered in his ear. "Leave and never come back."

Deiko scrambled forward. He crawled so hard that he bruised his knees. He didn't see anyone, but invisible hands smacked him, clawed him, and knocked the flashlight from his mouth. Whispering voices hissed near his ears like irritating mosquitoes. He stopped crawling and pressed his hands against his ears. Screaming, he hoped to drive away the voices, but whenever his screams ceased, their cries continued.

Darkness surrounded him. The shattered flashlight was useless. He pushed himself to his feet and hobbled. Without light he hit the cave wall, spiraled, and smashed his face into the opposite wall. The voices swirled around him.

Deiko placed his right hand against the wall and patted it, using it as a guideline to find the cave opening. His bruised face ached. The clawed cut marks all over his body burned. After ten minutes of running his hand along the wall, light broke through the darkness. He ran to the opening and hurried outside.

He trembled. His hands shook, and he sat against a large rock.

CHAPTER 17

*J*ohn McKnight got off his tractor near Devils Den. When he
reached the cave mouth, he found Deiko sitting on a large
rock. The man trembled worse than a dog that had gotten
the worst end of a raccoon fight. His eyes hollowed from fear.

Deiko didn't notice John's approach. Deiko's face was dark with
swelling bruises. His hands were filthy with mud and grime. A couple of
his fingernails were chipped and split. Strange claw marks covered his
arms and blood oozed from the cuts. Where his face wasn't bruised, his
skin was ashen white.

"What happened?" John asked.

Deiko replied with a short scream. He jumped to his feet and almost
fell.

"Easy, now," John said. "Did you find Ben?"

Deiko's lips quivered. Endless babbling sounds were all he uttered.

John shook his head. "Here. Let me help you."

He gently placed his hand around Deiko's elbow. Deiko stepped beside
him, and John noticed the gun tucked behind Deiko's belt. Slowly, John
placed his hand on the butt of the gun and took it without Deiko noticing.

Deiko mumbled.

"Come with me," John said. "I'd say you're suffering from heatstroke, but you've been inside that cool cave for some time. Your skin's like ice. It's not heatstroke."

Deiko's forehead beaded with sweat. His widened eyes searched erratically, but never focused on any particular object.

John said, "What'd you see in there?"

"Elias," Deiko whispered.

"Come again?" John asked.

Deiko's haunted eyes stared past John. "Elias."

"Let me take you to my house." John said helped Deiko climb on the tractor. "We need to get you to a doctor quickly."

During the short five-minute tractor drive to the McKnight farmhouse, Deiko's behavior didn't change. He babbled endless strings of intangible words. Perhaps the man had a stroke?

John went inside to call 9-1-1 while Lib tended to Deiko on the porch.

When he returned to the porch, the old screen door slammed shut behind him. Lib used a cool, wet cloth to wash the grime off Deiko's face.

"Has he said anything?" John asked.

Lib said, "The only word I understand is, Elias."

John frowned and shook his head. "I don't know anyone by the name."

"Doesn't sound familiar to me, either," she said.

A half hour passed before an ambulance arrived. A few minutes later, Deputy Higgins pulled up and got out of the car. He opened the rear door and let Jim and Lacy out.

"You two stay here for a few minutes," Higgins said.

The rear ambulance doors were open. Deiko sat on the bed while two paramedics examined him.

Higgins approached the ambulance and John came closer.

"Afternoon, John," Higgins said.

"Deputy," John replied.

"Got a call that Isaac Deiko is here."

John nodded. "He's at the back of the ambulance."

"Where'd you find him?"

"He came to see my brother-in-law, Ben. They were going to explore Devils Den."

Higgins frowned. "According to those two teenagers, they said Deiko tried to kill them and he intended to kill Ben as well. We're searching outside Ben's house for a body."

"Ben's truck's here. Deiko arrived well after Ben did."

Higgins sighed. "I guess we can stop searching Ben's house then. Have you seen Ben?"

John shook his head. "No. I found Deiko outside the cave ... in this strange condition. No sign of Ben though. If he went inside the cave, he hasn't come out."

"Has Deiko mentioned anything about Ben, or if he found him?"

"No. The only thing he mentions is Elias."

"Elias?" Higgins frowned.

John nodded.

"Any significance?"

"Doesn't ring a bell for me," John said.

"Thanks, John."

"Don't mention it," he replied.

HIGGINS WENT to the rear of the ambulance, read the name tag of the nearest paramedic, and addressed her, "Patty? How is he?"

"I'm afraid he's not doing well," she replied.

"What's wrong with him?"

"He's delusional."

"Is he still not talking?"

Patty shrugged. "Nothing understandable."

"So questioning him right now isn't a good time?"

"It wouldn't do you much good."

"Any reason for his condition?" Higgins asked.

"Not without taking him in for mental evaluation and testing, I don't know. He appears to be in shock."

"Those two teenagers stated he tried to kill them earlier today."

Patty looked uneasy. "I suppose anything's possible. He's definitely not in a good state of mind."

Higgins motioned Jim and Lacy to come over. They approached slowly, cautiously. Lacy kept her arms crossed and walked a few paces behind Jim.

Higgins motioned toward Deiko. His eyes stared straight ahead. His body trembled. "Is this the man?"

"Yes," they answered.

Lacy stepped closer and stared at Deiko with extreme curiosity. "What's wrong with him?"

Patty offered a slight smile and shrug. "We don't know, honey, but we're taking him for a mental examination. He clearly needs medical attention."

Jim frowned and looked at Higgins. "He didn't act anything like this earlier. He shot at us even after we survived the wreck."

"I've written everything down," Higgins said. "After his mental evaluation, he'll be locked safely away."

Lacy looked at Jim, took his hand in hers, and then she looked at the paramedic. "Do you think his condition might the reason he tried to kill us?"

"Hon, I'm not a doctor, but with the odd things we see from time to time, anything's possible."

"El … El … Elias," Deiko muttered. His glazed eyes stared into nothingness.

"Oh," John said, returning to the ambulance. He held the 9mm by the barrel and extended it to Higgins. "I found this on Deiko when he was outside the cave. I believe it's his."

"Thanks," Higgins said. To Jim and Lacy, he said, "Not much more we can do until he's evaluated by psychiatrists, but I have your report. We need to get you home."

John smiled. "I'll take them home before I head to my insurance office."

Higgins nodded. "Much appreciated."

"Glad to help."

Jim looked at John. "Where's Dr. Whytten?"

John shrugged and shook his head. "We've not seen him."

"Is he in the cave?" Lacy asked.

"That's my guess. He explores it a lot," John replied.

"Deputy," Lacy said. "Shouldn't someone go inside and check for him? Dr. Deiko might've shot and killed Ben."

Deputy Higgins said, "We'll have someone check it out. I assure you."

John glanced at the cave with nervous eyes and then motioned Jim and Lacy to follow him. "Come on, guys. Let's get you two home so your parents won't worry about you."

CHAPTER 18

Roble held Shawndirea in his left hand and pulled his knife with the other.

Forcas vanished.

"Hmm," Roble said, dumbfounded.

"Didn't I *tell* you not to trust him?" she said.

"Yes, you did," Roble said. "I didn't see much alternative at the time."

"I'm not blaming you. Our choices were few."

Roble nodded. "Any suggestions?"

"Watch where you step."

The black volcanic ground had numerous open pockets of bubbling lava. The winged creatures drifted overhead in the sulfuric, smoke-filled air. They were impressively massive creatures, but he didn't want a closer view of them.

Sweat poured from Roble's pores. He wiped his forehead with the back of his hand. He slipped off his light jacket and stuffed it inside his pack.

"It's hot," he said, "But I've always thought Hell to be much hotter. Of course, I've never actually believed such a place existed."

"All religions have a similar belief for eternal damnation."

"So we're damned, I suppose."

She smiled. "Not if we find a rift in the veil."

"I thought we went too far?"

"No. Not necessarily. No one knows the veil's boundaries."

Roble scanned the area around them. Styx flowed slowly. Shadowy creatures burst from the orange lava and were yanked under by what appeared to be massive chains. They cried their agonized protests, but whatever held them captive didn't allow them to break free.

Winged creatures flapped their massive wings. There wasn't a clear path for Roble to follow. After Forcas slammed his staff into the cavern floor, the stairs they'd descended vanished. The expanse encircling them was barren. No large boulders or rocks to hide behind. They were near the center of the massive domed room where Styx cut through.

"So Forcas," Roble said, "was *what* exactly."

She shrugged. "Possibly a demon. I'm not certain. His dark aura makes me believe he is."

The chattering sounds of unseen creatures echoed and chilled Roble. His mind pictured nightmarish beasts lurking within the shadows. Hissing steam rose from fissures around the domed chamber. Occasionally, rocks slides crumbled along the river's edge and splashed into the molten lava.

Hot wind howled and swirled, and seemed purposely directing the dry heat at them. Roble imagined their abandonment in the center of the flaming abyss added great entertainment for the demon's amusement.

Roble said, "You think he'll return?"

"He's probably watching us."

"You think so, too?"

She nodded. "We're part of his game."

"What game?"

"Whatever one he wishes to play."

Roble looked for a path farther away from the river. The closer to the river they walked, the more the temperature increased. The Hellish creatures had an even better chance to see them. Moving to the outskirts might put them in less light and heat, but they'd already been noticed. Several flying gargoyle-like creatures circled overhead.

"Things are about to get heated, if you'll pardon the pun," he said.

"What do you mean?"

Roble nodded at the circling creatures. "We've been located."

She looked at the flying demons, and her eyes widened.

"Perhaps you should slip inside my backpack."

"It's too hot."

"If one of those creatures attacks, you could be get crushed. I can't chance it."

"Put me in your shirt pocket."

"The same may happen," he replied.

"Yes, but at least I could scramble out. I can't if I'm in the pack."

A winged creature shrieked and descended like a hawk.

"It's coming for us. Hurry."

Shawndirea climbed inside his pocket and held fast to the top border. He slung the pack over his left shoulder and sprinted for cover.

Afraid to accidentally step into a lava-filled hole, he kept his attention on the ground ahead. He didn't dare look up or back, even though he didn't know the diving creature's actual location. Its clawed feet grabbed the back of his shirt and lifted him in the air.

"Are you okay?" he asked.

"Fine so far. You?"

Roble gave a slight nod and tried to speak.

He gasped for air, which he regretted because the air reeked worse than rotten eggs. His captor was a black, winged demon. The spaces between its scales were fiery orange, which looked like a cooling, hot coal.

The creature's grip on his shirt tightened the collar around Roble's neck and choked him. He held the knife tightly, but he couldn't reach back enough to strike the demon's foot.

The sharp talons had partially sliced through his shirt and made the material weaker. A slight ripping sound alerted him to the added danger of plummeting into the abyss. Although he wanted freed of the talons' grip, should he fall, he and Shawndirea would fall into the lava river or strike the jagged rocks. Neither outcome would spare them.

Shawndirea turned in his pocket, lifted her hands above her head, and spoke. "Can you breathe?"

Roble shook his head.

His face beamed red and began tinting purple. Veins swelled on his forehead. Death seemed inescapable. Either he'd choke to death or be dropped into the fiery river.

Shawndirea's green fire zapped the creature's chest. Surprise filled its evil black eyes. Its hard brow narrowed in anger and it hissed. The shot didn't do any damage, but surprised the beast enough to release Roble.

"No!" he said.

They fell.

The creature flapped and hovered for several seconds, and then dove after them. Before it recaptured them, another winged demon zipped past and wrapped its claws around Roble's waist. This one's exoskeleton was fiery orange and its scales were outlined in black.

The black Hell-beast grew angry. It growled and lunged into the orange demon in midair. It reared back its head and exposed jagged fangs. They battered one another with their clawed hands. They flogged and snapped. The black winged beast wrapped its wings around its opponent and barrel-rolled.

Roble looked below. Styx was directly below. Roble hated amusement park rides, but this ... This was far worse. He closed his eyes. The beasts spiraled in battle. Neither creature was flying. They were falling. Their wings entangled with one another. Both struggled to get free, and during their attempt to unhook their wings, Roble broke free of the demonic beast's grip. He and Shawndirea began free-falling.

The two falling Hell-beasts growled and bit one another's throat. Their frantic battle to kill one another made them oblivious to their falling destiny.

More than ever, Roble wished he'd never destroyed Shawndirea's wings. If she were able to fly, at least she could fly to safety. Now, each were doomed to fall in the burning river of fire and souls.

She gripped his pocket tightly. Her sad eyes stared into his. She realized their possible fate.

Intense heat encircled them as they fell. They would incinerate well before they hit the river.

The two fighting demons tumbled and struck the lava and ignited in a quick burst of explosive fire. They vanished as fast as they touched the river.

Roble opened his mouth to tell Shawndirea good-bye. His breath was knocked from his lungs by a third winged demon. It grabbed him and swiftly flew over the river. It slowed and hovered above a small ledge on the opposite end of the expanse from where they'd entered with Forcas. On the narrow ledge was a large nest.

"Careful," Shawndirea said. "This one's a female."

The she Hell-beast released Roble gently into the nest. Three large eggs rolled. Roble ran behind an egg to put some distance between them and the demon. Her massive wings folded behind her back. She reached to grab him, but he sliced her boney hand with his blade. Two of her three digits dropped from her hand. She hissed and narrowed her eyes. Yellow fluid flowed from where her long fingers had been.

She gnashed her jagged fangs. Drool dripped from the sides of her mouth. The dribble sizzled on the rocky ledge like acid. Small streams of smoke rose.

"Damn," Roble whispered.

The female demon lunged at him. He darted to the side and swung the blade again. The blade cut through the air with a swish but missed.

A strange gurgling growl rumbled in her throat. Her narrowed eyes loomed with hatred. She paced side-to-side, and studied Roble's movements. Her hesitance indicate she awaited the proper moment to nab him.

Roble stepped back. Rock fragments slid off the ledge. He dropped to a knee to prevent falling off. He gasped. They stood atop a high, narrow perch directly over a large lava pool. Even if he escaped her nest, he had no quick route to flee. Had the pool been water, he'd leap over the edge to the water. But then, he'd have been boiled alive. As it were, he'd have to kill the demon, or she'd have to kill him.

The three eggs vibrated. One cracked. A pointed beak chipped at the hard shell from the inside. Flakes of the shell popped upward. A jagged crack branched down the side of the egg. Inside the shell, two odd shaped feet kicked, and cracked the egg even more. The demon was minutes from breaking free.

Roble pushed the egg, which almost his size and weight. The egg rolled slightly, tipped into a slanted groove, and tumbled over the edge. The she demon's eyes widened. She growled with alarm. Her wings spread, she kicked upward, and dove over the ledge after her hatching egg.

"What now?" Shawndirea asked.

"Not sure." He pressed his back to the cliff wall. He lowered and set his pack against the wall. The loss of the bag's weight helped, but his neck ached from near strangulation when the two demons fought over him and Shawndirea.

Roble panted. The overwhelming heat and undesirable rotten smell sickened him. He took his hunting knife and rammed the sharp serrated blade through one egg and then the other. After he pried apart the shells, he drove the knife through their soft skulls and killed them.

A hot breeze drifted upward and the air pushed Roble against the wall. Shawndirea lowered insdie his pocket.

The she-demon rose over the ledge and planted her feet inside her nest. Her sharp-tipped toenails carved into the rocky surface. Shawndirea crawled from his pocket and scrambled to the rocky ledge to hide.

When the demon noticed the two eggs busted and her dead offspring, she became infuriated. She roared and gnashed her teeth. She set down the egg and rushed him. Without hesitation Roble met her and leapt upward. He drove the blade through her tough exoskeleton and plunged it in her heart.

She flailed her long-fingered hands and smacked him. He held the hilt tightly. She pressed him against the wall, which drove the blade deeper. Her acrid breath gagged him.

The demon's strength weakened. Yellow blood oozed down her chest. Should the she-demon die while pressing him against the wall, he'd died, too. He twisted the blade. Pain tore through her. She pushed away from the wall. Roble refused to let go of the hilt. He had few weapons, and he couldn't afford to lose one. This was his best knife.

She staggered backwards and carried him as she struggled to stand. Due to her height, he dangled two feet above the ledge while gripping the dagger. Roble was unable to brace his feet against the rock to get leverage, so he wrapped his legs through hers and around the back of her knees. He yanked the blade and sliced downward through her chest into her abdomen. Life drained from her.

Roble jerked the blade. It made a sickening wet sound as it slid out. Once the metal was free from her demon flesh, Roble dropped to the ledge with his blade in hand. The demon fell with a heavy thud.

He lowered to his knees with sweat dripping from him. He ached for fresh air, water. Unzipping the pack, he watched the demon. Her shallow breathing stopped. Shawndirea peered from behind broken eggshells and hurried to him.

Roble took the bottle of honey mixture, opened it, and filled the lid. She closed her eyes and drank deep gulps. When she paused, she whispered words he didn't understand, but what he assumed, and hoped, were words of blessings.

He dug through the pack and grabbed the canteen. After opening and turning it up, he nearly spit out the water. It was hot.

"Ehh," he said after forcing down the liquid.

"Make do with it," Shawndirea said. "I am."

"Sorry it's hot."

"Not your fault. It is what it is."

Roble tightened the lid on the canteen and placed it inside the pack. He rolled the last egg over the ledge and watched it fall hundreds of feet until it hit the lava pool. Beyond the lava pool a flash of light shot upward and exploded against the domed ceiling like a bottle rocket. Chips of stalactites showered down.

"What was that?" he asked.

Shawndirea strained to see. "Forcas."

The light flashed again. Roble traced from where it emitted. A dark robed figure stood near the area where the winged demons had snatched them off the ground.

"Come on," Roble said. "Time to find a way out."

Deep laughter bellowed through the cavern.

"Forcas seems pissed," he said.

She shook her head. "Drunk?"

Roble laughed. "No. Angered."

Shawndirea shrugged. "Let his anger consume him. You must get us to the other side of the river."

"Why?"

"Styx divides the realms. He cannot pass."

"But we can?"

She nodded.

"You shall not escape me!" Forcas' voice roared, echoed, and like a small breeze, it whispered past them.

Shawndirea climbed on Roble's shoulder. Roble pushed against the wall. The widest area of the ledge was where the demon had built her nest. On both sides of the nest, the width was only three feet at best. A couple hundred yards away was a lit torch. The path beneath the torch became wider. Unless the flickering light played tricks on him, there were crude steps leading downward.

"It's risky," he said, "But if I reach the torch, we should be safer."

"Look at me," she said softly.

Roble stared into her lovely eyes. They narrowed. He couldn't look away. She whispered words he didn't understand. When she blinked, he shook his head and looked down. He stood on the rough-hewn rock stairs beneath the burning torch on the other side of the lava pool.

"You cast a spell on me?" he asked.

Shawndirea shook her head. "No. I won't ever do that. I promise. I would never marry a man I had bewitched."

Roble's heart raced. He was stunned. *"Marry?"*

"It breaks so many rules of magic," she said.

"Then how'd we get here?"

"I spoke words of encouragement in my language. By speaking to your subconscious, your confidence increased. You did the rest."

"And seconds later, I'm here."

She placed her hand to his cheek and shook her head. "It took a half hour of careful climbing to get here."

"But I was looking into your eyes."

Shawndirea smiled. "The important thing is you got us here safely."

"No magic?"

"None. I vow to you, I'll never cast a spell on you. Never."

"Thanks. I appreciate that."

"If I did, honestly, I couldn't marry you."

Roble smiled. "You want to marry me?"

"It's meant to be. Although, my kingdom won't take the news well."

Roble took the torch and descended the stairs. The light diminished.

"Because of the conflict?"

"That. And my mother."

"Oh?" Roble said. "Why?"

"I'm destined for the throne."

"Royalty. That's nice."

"I'm already known as the Butterfly Queen in my kingdom and throughout the Underworld," she said softly, "Which is why I freed your collection. But I'm also destined for the throne that rules my race."

"Can you have both?"

Shawndirea shrugged. "Anyone can hold multiple titles, but our marriage voids my right to the throne."

"You can't abandon that."

"For the future, *our* future, it's best. Should you prove your worthiness, perhaps the quarrel between our races will end."

Roble frowned. "What started the division?"

Shawndirea looked away. "It's best I don't tell you yet."

"No, you should."

She replied, "*Why* should I?"

"You keep mentioning marriage and bringing me into your kingdom, so I should know why your race hates mine."

She nodded. "You're right. I should, but it's difficult."

Tears formed in her eyes. "My father journeyed with a group of humans and was killed."

"I'm sorry."

She lifted a hand. "He wasn't purposely killed. It was accidental. My mother's the one who declared our species no longer at peace with humans."

"What happened?" Roble walked carefully down the stairs. The torch flickered and barely kept the stairs visible.

"He accepted the task of spying on a group of dark elves outside Kendrick Woods. This renegade group had stolen gold from a Dwarven blacksmith in Hoffnung."

"The elves killed him?"

Shawndirea shook her head. "No. He snuck into their camp while they sat around the campfire. He hid in the brush and found where they kept the gold. He returned to the humans, told them, and they rushed the camp. They got the gold without killing one dark elf."

Roble stopped at the base of the rugged stairwell, held the torch high, and looked around. Although it was quite warm for a cavern, the heat and light slowly dissipated. Unlike the entrance to Devils Den, where the walls were dripping wet, these walls were dry and caked with yellow sulfur.

He held the torch and examined the opening of a small tunnel. It was too small to enter, so he searched the level area until he came to another hidden stairwell that led up.

"Did the dark elves retaliate?"

"No. The humans stripped them of their weapons and boots, and sent them to venture through the woods."

"Harsh."

Shawndirea shook her head. "No. They're thieves. They should've been killed on the spot. They went away. For awhile."

"So how'd your father die?"

"As most humans do when they collect a bounty from a dwarf, they celebrate in the tavern. These men did the same. The blacksmith invited them for drinks. And, of course, they didn't refuse."

Shawndirea sat on Roble's shoulder. The hissing torch flames danced as he ascended the stairs.

"My father drank with them," she said. "It was afterwards, when they left the tavern in the dark of the night that he was killed. By what, we're not certain. He got separated from the humans in the Haunted Forest of Dorlan."

"Haunted?"

She nodded. "Usually no one ventures there. But they needed a shortcut from Hoffnung to Belshast. Halfway through, something grabbed my father and darted into the forest. The men took swords and pursued. They never found the creature, but they found him. All his blood was drained, and his body was shriveled. I'm certain they drained his magic first."

Roble stopped and frowned. "Why would a king join himself with others to pursue a band of thieves?"

"He wasn't king."

"I see."

"This was over a hundred years ago. My mother took the throne about ten years after his death. He never wore the crown, but in his memory, my mother swore the Fae and humans would forever be eternal enemies."

"So this is why your mother will oppose us."

"Yes."

"Did she not believe what happened?"

"The men gave her their explanations, but she refused to accept it as an accident. She insisted they should've taken the long road around the Haunted Forest. Without fully knowing what attacked and killed him, she didn't risk sending scouts to investigate for fear they'd be killed in the same manner."

"Sounds like she believed them," Roble said.

"She does. The problem is she needed closure but she never found it. So, she took her harbored vengeance and blamed the human race."

"Why do you take a different stance?"

"Because one group makes a mistake, it doesn't make all guilty. I talked to two of the men before they died of old age. Each gave the same explanation for what occurred. Both offered regret. Their remorse was real, and they blamed themselves. But they couldn't have saved him."

"I'm sorry."

She smiled.

A quarter of the way up the long stairwell, Shawndirea said, "Stop."

"What is it?"

"Go down."

"Why?"

She pointed. "The veil. It passes there. I sense it."

Roble hurried down the stairs.

At the base of the stairs, she closed her eyes. A frown creased her dainty brow. She pointed again. "Just a bit more over that way."

Roble stepped to where she directed.

Her fingertips glowed. "There."

He turned and took another step.

"Wait. A bit more to the left."

He followed her directions. A massive, flowing wall appeared a few seconds after her fingers touched it. The wall resembled a green tidal wave, but it never crashed forward. It stood like a wall of water.

"How'd it appear?"

She smiled. "Magic detects magic."

"It's good you found it."

"Yes," she said, "But I don't see a rift. No opening to pass through."

Roble wiped the lines of salt from his face where his sweat had dried.

"There must be a place to cross."

"Be patient. We're being too hopeful to expect to find the rift at the exact moment we found the veil."

Roble stared at the veil. The images floating within were distorted. When he caught a glimpse of his own reflection, it resembled what he might see in a funhouse mirror.

"Hurry up the stairs, quick!" She said.

Roble turned and headed upstairs. Midway up, the veil crossed the stairs. He hadn't seen it before, so why was it there now?

"There," she said, pointing. "There's a rift. It's small, but you should still be able to step through."

The veil looked dark and detached. To get through, Roble dropped to his knees and crawled. "Are you certain it's safe?"

"There's never any certainty when you pass through a rift."

He tossed the torch through the veil before he entered the tear on his hands and knees. Immediately the wall swallowed him. The thickness gelled around him and it was like crawling through gelatin. He held his breath until Shawndirea told him to breath.

When he crossed to the other side, he stood and looked around. The veil wall had vanished. Nothing seemed different. Still the same set of stairs and what appeared to be the same hellish cavern.

"It didn't work."

"We won't know yet," she replied.

"When will we?"

She smiled. "Patience. We'll see."

CHAPTER 19

*R*oble and Shawndirea headed up another spiral, rocky path. The heat from the lava river faded. The air chilled to a familiar cave climate, and after being exposed to the extreme heat, Roble failed to acclimate to the comfortable cave temperature he once enjoyed. The farther up the winding cave tunnel they walked, the colder it became. He shivered. He reached inside his pack and took out his jacket. After sliding it over his shoulders and putting it on, Shawndirea returned to his shoulder.

Even a distance from the heat, the glowing lava brightened the cavern, but the light was diminishing. He was glad he'd taken the torch. If not for the demons, sorcerers, and other strange beasts, he'd have taken the time to admire all the marvelous cave formations. Those spectacular natural speleothems were worthy to be studied, photographed, and documented, but not worth sacrificing limb or life for closer examinations.

At the top of the tier, the path ended at a shimmering wall. Roble placed his left hand against it. Ice? He placed the torch in his left hand and removed his knife. He struck the smooth, glassy ice with the blade's tip and the wall chipped, so he stabbed it harder. Pieces of ice fell and shattered at his feet. The ice chips slowly melted.

Using the knife like an ice pick, he jabbed and jabbed until larger pieces of ice broke free. Light filtered through the cracked ice.

Roble pushed his right hand through the icy wall. The outer wall of piled snow crumbled and fell outward. Frigid wind whipped through the opening and cut harshly. He hit and kicked the ice until a large portion of it gave way and fell to the floor. He stepped outside the cave onto the frozen mountainside.

The harsh wind sucked the fiery life from the torch. The torch smoldered for several seconds, and then only a burnt scar remained where the fire once thrived.

Roble whispered, "Building a fire will be difficult now."

Roble pulled his jacket tighter around his neck. The cold wind bit his bare hands and face without mercy. His body involuntarily shivered and his teeth chattered.

"Did you expect us to come out here?" he asked.

"I didn't know what to expect. Like Devils Den's constantly changing pathways, you've no guarantee where a rift might take you."

"But what are the odds we'd end up in a place so cold?" Roble rubbed his hands together and huffed into them.

"Not much different than tossing a golden coin of fate," she replied.

"Seems a bit treacherous a choice." White clouds escaped his mouth as he spoke.

"Oh, fate has crueler outcomes."

Roble grinned. "I suppose. I never expected to go to Hell and back just to get you home."

She giggled. "Neither did I."

"We've gone from one extreme to the other."

Shawndirea hugged herself and snuggled against his coat collar.

"It's brutally cold," he said. "I didn't think I'd need a heavy coat."

"We need shelter."

"We can't return the way we came," Roble said.

She shook her head. "No. I'm not suggesting we do. But neither of us can survive this temperature for long."

The thick forest's twisted trees with forked branches stretched to the gray, overcast sky. Roble took several difficult steps through the knee-deep snow and pointed. "There's a pathway. Something's traveled through here often."

"These tracks," she said, "look more recent."

Tall trees lined both sides of the dark path. Other than the line of thick firs along the forest's edge, most of the trees were bare. Snow caked the sides of the trees, which revealed the storm's direction overnight. Over the valley below, spiraling waves of snow drifted upward to the ridge where he stood. The wind pushed through the forest. Wolves howled from the mountain on the opposite side of the vale. Their cries echoed with driving hunger. They were too far away to be an intrusive threat.

"Where are we in your realm?" Roble asked. Snow crunched beneath his boots as he walked to the forest.

"Most likely Glacier Ridge," she replied.

"How close are we to your home?"

She pursed her lips. Disappointment shadowed her eyes. "About one hundred miles."

The distance shocked him. He never expected he'd have to travel so far on foot. They'd never survive this extreme cold.

Roble leaned forward to make himself a smaller target to the harsh wind cutting at them full force. Stepping under the first intertwined branches that formed a gateway to the icy trees of misery, the severity of their danger became obvious. Even had Shawndirea known they'd arrive in a frozen terrain, he'd never have believed such a forewarning. He foolishly entered Devils Den to find the Underworld based on his masculine curiosity more than crediting the greater risks he might endure once he reached the other side of the veil.

When he thought of a place where faeries lived, he pictured lush green meadows and thick, mossy forests, so he expected such a paradise once they passed through the rift.

She had warned him. *Seeing was believing.* Indeed, rugged experience was the best way to learn, but he never prepared for every possible climate they might encounter. Their deaths would be on his hands. If they both died, which seemed the most probable possibility, his quest and pursuit to discover new creatures, terrains, and a hopeful future away from the Overland technology was doomed. In an odd light, death was more acceptable than returning to his home.

The icy wind blew sharper, howled, and sliced through the leafless branches by boasting its sheer power. He stopped walking. Ahead, a dull creaking sound out-voiced the wind. Pellets of snow and ice rode the wind. They struck and stung his exposed face, nose, and ears. He was thankful he'd not shaved his beard weeks earlier in spite of the abnormal sweltering temperatures in the Overlands.

Uncontrollable shivers ran through his body. He was losing valuable body heat. Shawndirea hid in his jacket pocket, not daring to peek out into the abrasive cold. Her tiny body quivered against his chest. He pulled his thin jacket tighter to block the wind from striking her.

Creeeeaaak! Creeeeaaak!

Roble cupped his hands around his aching, red ears and tried to pinpoint from where this sound came. His nose and ears numbed. Cold ached through him. His lower jaw shook uncontrollably from time to time.

Creeeeaaak!

He massaged his ears, trying to warm them. The action sent a burning sensation through them. Frostbite wasn't far away. Wrapping his arms around himself, he knew Shawndirea was right. Finding shelter was a must, despite his want to discover the source behind the noise.

Creeeeaaak!

Ahead, less than ten yards, a dark figure hung and swayed from a large branch. He didn't have to look again to know it was a man. The dead man's weight sagged the branch. The wind forced the roped noose to cry its announcement of the justice or injustice poorly served.

Roble hurried to the man and looked up. The eyeless man didn't offer a gaze. Pock holes covered his face from vicious pecking. Birds had taken his eyes from their sockets and picked at his flesh before the frigid wind froze the man's flesh.

Blood speckles painted dots of crimson on the snow beneath the man's body. Near the tree, Roble counted three distinct sets of large boot prints in the snow. The footprints were fresh.

No struggling had occurred where the man was hanged. These prints led to the path where massive hoof prints deepened the snow.

Three horses.

Perhaps the riders' trail led to a village. But was this a village he should seek? The hanging corpse might've been a victim they'd robbed and murdered. In which case, he should hope *not* to encounter these men.

Something stirred in the tree limbs above him. When he located them, their appearance caught him off guard.

On a lower branch, three white crows perched. Their feathers were snow white, and their eyes shimmered an icy blue glow. Blood stained their grayish white beaks. They cocked their heads to the side and studied him. As much as he regarded their strangeness to crows he was familiar with, these weren't a species from his realm. They belonged here. He didn't.

Their solid stern gazes indicated they wished him to leave their feast alone. Roble was unable to take his eyes off these fascinating birds. Though flesh-eaters, they were gorgeous. He truly wished he could photograph them to show other scientists these birds' uniqueness, but they weren't unique here. They were probably commonplace.

Shawndirea brought her head up and looked out. "Why aren't you moving?"

He nodded at the hanging man.

"So?" she said. "There's nothing you can do for him."

"I know. Just a puzzle in this world."

"Worrying or trying to solve a puzzle in this horrid weather will be the end of us."

Roble nodded. "I know."

"But," Shawndirea said, "cut him down."

Roble frowned. "Why?"

"Strip him of his clothes. He's dressed for this weather. Besides, your clothes immediately identify you as an Overlander. And depending on whom we encounter, your fate could wind up like his."

Roble didn't like the idea of taking a dead man's clothes, but she was right. The man's overcoat and robe were thick, which would insulate him from the cold winds and building snow and ice. His clothes would draw immediate questions from people in this region. Setting down his pack, he looked around. He drew his knife, studied the limb and the distance up the tree. The massive trunk prevented him from scaling the tree to reach the branch where the rope was tied.

He sighed and shook his head.

"What now?" she asked.

"Trying to figure out how to reach the rope."

She released an aggravated little grunt. "Step back."

Roble took three steps back.

Shawndirea stood inside his pocket. Her shoulders and head were in direct view. She raised her hands, closed her eyes, and a green ball of fire shot from her fingertips. The band of white crows cawed with alarm and took to flight. The fire hit the rope and set it on fire. Soon the rope stretched, the fire grew a bit more, and the rope snapped.

The dead man dropped and hit the ground with a heavy thud. His body bounced and made a sickening, crackling sound, which indicated one of two things. Either he'd been dead a long time while the winter wind froze his corpse, or the plummeting temperature was severely cold enough to freeze flesh within hours. Although he hoped it was the former and the marauders were a safe distance away, he feared those responsible for the hanging lingered nearby in the forest because their tracks were fresh.

"Hurry." Shawndirea hugged herself tighter and snuggled against the pocket lining. "I'm freezing."

Roble unbuttoned the dead man's thick black trench coat. He stared for a moment at the silver medallion fastening the gray cloak in place. He unlatched the medallion, which held the face of a horned dragon skull, and then he tugged the cloak out from the man's stiff carcass. He pulled off the man's leather boots. He pitied the man, and felt somewhat guilty for taking his clothes.

"Sorry about this," he whispered to the dead man.

The tip of the noose smoldered from the remaining small flame. Roble took his knife and cut strips of cloth from the man's cotton undershirt. He placed them on the flame. The fire flickered, rose. While the fire grew, he pried the man's frozen arms out of place so he could remove the coat. He took the cloak and wrapped Shawndirea in the edge of the cloth to keep her out of the cold. After unzipping his jacket, he tossed it on the fire, grabbed the heavy coat, and pulled it on. There wasn't much warmth to gain since the owner was dead, but in time, Roble's own body heat built inside the coat and warmed him.

He removed the man's gray gloves and put them on. Although thin and fitting tight like a second skin, the wind no longer numbed his fingers. His hands became incredibly warm. He untied the man's belt and tugged off his pants. He held them close to the fire until warmth radiated through them.

"Now for the hard part," Roble said, bracing himself for the cold.

He unlaced his hiking boots, loosened them, and kicked them off. He unbuckled his belt, dropped his pants, and tossed them on the fire. Shawndirea peeked from the cloak and smiled. Her eyes widened. In lightning speed, he grabbed the fire-warmed trousers, pulled them to his waist, and tied the belt in place.

Roble took the knife and cut a square of cloth from the bottom of the dark cloak. He cut a small hole in the center and handed the cloth square to Shawndirea. She put her head through the hole and pulled the cloth around her. Taking a loose thread, she used this for a belt to hold the cloth close to her body.

Pulling the cloak around his shoulders, he studied the silver dragon skull medallion. He wondered what the symbol represented before snapping it together to fasten the cloak in place. He pulled the hood over his head to protect his ears. The cloak tightened and whipped around his legs.

Roble exchanged boots and tossed his old ones on the fire. He took his Swiss Army knife and stared at it. Knowing the blades would never burn, he tucked the knife inside the overcoat pocket.

"You realize the fire and smoke will reveal our position?" she asked.

He shrugged. "Maybe so, but it's best I destroy the clothes since none in your realm look like those from the Overlands. Besides, we could use a good fire to heat us before we move farther into the forest."

"True." She nodded.

Roble unzipped his pack, took out the plastic bottle of honey mixture and poured another capful for Shawndirea. While she drank ice formed around the cap and the liquid in the bottle solidified.

"I'm afraid this is the last of it for now."

He stepped closer to the fire. Puddles of water formed from the melting snow. Black smoke rose off the burning rubber soles of his hiking boots. The inviting heat kept him close to the fire. Holding the pack by its handle, he tossed it on the flames. The sides of the pack smoldered, blistered, and finally burst open as the fire ruptured it. All the contents vanished beneath the flame. He worried how they'd find food, especially for her, in this weather.

The cold wind funneled through the trees. Large, wet snowflakes swirled. His beard caught a lot of the passing snow, which slowly built a thin, white layer and made his brown beard look frozen.

A good fifteen minutes passed. He was no longer cold. The weather didn't affect him at all. The clothes had incredible insulation and weighed less than the ones he'd discarded.

With a long branch, he churned the fire to make certain no identifiable traces of clothing remained. He watched the flames settle, and after the clothes turned to ash, the fire lost its power. Smoke pillowed and drifted through the ice-covered trees.

Wolves howled from a great distance across the valley. Their wails were desperate and agitated. Although he loved to hear their cries, he was thankful he wasn't in any threat of confrontation with them. Hunger might be their major motivation.

"That's the best of the fire." Roble marched to the dark path that divided the forest. The wind whipped his cloak behind him while he walked. "Is there a town in Glacier Ridge?"

"Yes, but I wouldn't be so eager to rush to it," she said.

"Why not?"

"Your fate might equal the man's who owned the clothes you now possess."

Roble shook his head. "I'll be careful."

"You're in a different world, Roble. You might have to defend yourself very aggressively."

"I did with Deiko."

She smiled evenly. "Have you ever killed a man?"

He hesitated. "No."

"Understand something. Laws aren't followed by the lawless. When you encounter such people, it's kill or die. Are you capable of killing someone?"

"I hope I never have to."

"Glacier Ridge is where bandits thrive, trade, and murder. You'll face people that will kill you, if you don't kill them first."

"Noted," he replied. "Still we must find shelter, even if we rent a room from a poor family."

Shawndirea shook her head. "I'm afraid such hospitality doesn't exist on this ridge."

Roble frowned. "What do you mean?"

"No peasant family would dare build a home in this frigid climate. Glacier Ridge knows no spring. Nothing except hardy trees grows here. They'd have no means for food, except for game animals. You'd freeze to death before you stalked a deer or rabbit."

"I understand."

"Any fool who built a shack near Glacier Ridge would be robbed and killed by the first bandit who found him," Shawndirea said. "Not a promising risk."

Roble remembered when Deiko pulled his gun on him. He debated throwing his knife and ending Deiko's life. Though he could've easily done so, he didn't. Clearly, it'd have been self-defense. The biggest drawback was afterwards. The headache of dealing with law enforcement and possible court proceedings could entangle him for months, if not years. Proof without witnesses was difficult, regardless of the circumstances. The laws and rules in Aetheaon differed. Shawndirea was right. He didn't have time to debate dangerous situations, which eliminated any reluctance he might have in the Overlands.

He wondered, though, how his mind would cope should he find the need to end a man's life. Deep inside, he truly hoped he never had to find out.

CHAPTER 20

Queen Istrell stared across her kingdom from the highest branch in her tree palace. The sun faded behind the evening clouds, which turned the sky into a lovely array of pastel pinks, purples, and orange.

She wrung her aged hands. Warm tears streaked her cheeks. A gentle rush of magical energy pulsated from the earth. Her eyebrows rose.

"Shawndirea?" she gasped. "I feel your power. Where are you?"

Istrell hurried to the crystals and placed her hands on them. Power surged through her. Shawndirea's face materialized in Istrell's mind. Her daughter's jaw shivered. Frosty clouds exited Shawndirea's nose and mouth. She was freezing to death.

Shawndirea curled inside a dark cloak spread out on the ground with a human standing nearby.

Istrell's attention turned to her daughter. In horror, Istrell's eyes widened. Shawndirea's glorious wings were tattered, destroyed. Tears from her building anger, frustration, and worry streaked Istrell's cheeks.

The human stood over the body of a dead man, and he seemed to be stealing the man's clothes. The man undressed and put on the man's clothes.

Snow spiraled around Shawndirea. She shivered. The man picked up Shawndirea after putting the cloak around his shoulders. He latched the silver pendant to hold the cloak into place. Istrell's stomach became uneasy. She recognized the pendant.

The Dragon Skull Order.

What was this man up to? *Why* did he have Shawndirea?

The man cut material from his cloak and handed it to Shawndirea. After she placed the cloth over her head, the vision of Shawndirea ceased. Istrell could no longer see or feel her daughter's presence. The power from the crystals faded. She grabbed her mirror, but no images appeared.

Istrell's distaste for the human race enraged further. Her husband had died due to reckless humans and now one prevented her daughter from returning to her rightful place in the kingdom. Shawndirea's precious wings. What happened? Istrell's fists tightened.

"I'll find you, my daughter," Istrell vowed. "And when I do, this human shall pay dearly for what he's done."

CHAPTER 21

Shawndirea sat on Roble's shoulder. The square of thin leather from the cloak magically hugged her from neck to feet, detailing the perfection of her body. The black cloth even formed small boots on her feet. Sadly, her tattered wings hung loosely as reminder of her unfortunate capture.

"Did you use magic to transform the cloth into those clothes?" he asked.

Stunned, she examined her clothing and pulled a hood over her head that hid her pointed ears. "No. Not *my* magic. But their instant warmth is welcomed."

Roble stopped walking and took the cloak in his hands. He searched the bottom hem to find where he'd cut away the material he'd handed her. The gap was gone. His eyebrows rose from his sudden surprise.

"What do you make of this?" he asked.

Shawndirea shrugged. "I haven't any idea."

"Magic?"

"Enchanted leather perhaps. It's hard to say."

Roble frowned. "Enchanted by whom?"

"There's no way to know."

Roble flipped the cloak behind him and continued his stride down the path. Fresh falling snow was covering the three sets of hoof prints. In another half hour the prints would be gone.

"What do you know of the humans in Glacier Ridge?" he asked.

"Fae do not venture here. At least none from my kingdom."

Roble slowed his pace. The cold grew even less noticeable the longer he wore the dead man's clothes. "Why not?"

"For one, it's too damn cold. Even if I possessed my wings, I could not fly."

Roble nodded. "Some insects are like that."

She frowned. "I'm *not* an insect!"

He shook his head and grinned. "Of course, you're not. I wasn't implying you were. It was merely a comparison to what I've seen during winter at my home. Sometimes hibernating wasps or bees get exposed from beneath firewood, and they cannot fly. They must generate enough heat for their wings to lift them."

"You *had* to be a scientist," she said.

"So the cold's one reason. What are others?" he asked.

"I get grumpy."

"No comment," Roble said with a smile.

Shawndirea's eyes narrowed, and she crossed her arms. A peevish expression darkened her face.

"Sorry, I didn't mean to anger you."

"Cold weather sours my mood. I'm the Butterfly Queen. Flowers and butterflies aren't viable during winter, so I reside in a valley where the cold never comes. Otherwise, I'd go insane."

"Your homeland never has winter?" he asked.

"No."

"Other than not being able to fly and your grumpiness, why don't Fae venture here?"

"Glacier Ridge is where bandits and assassins gather. If someone wishes to hire an assassin, Glacier Ridge's the best place to find one, provided they're not killed before they make their offer."

"We need a horse."

She nodded. "You need a better weapon."

"I have knives."

She smiled. "Most use swords or crossbows here."

Roble said, "If I have the distance I can stop a man wielding a sword. But even the best swordsman is no match against someone with a crossbow."

Shawndirea cocked her head and nodded slightly. "True. But could you use a sword?"

"Never tried."

"Then you best learn," she said. "Otherwise I'll be without you before long. I simply don't want that."

He smiled. "You doubt my abilities that much?"

"I've witnessed a lot of death in this realm."

"Who'll train me?"

She grinned slyly. "Maybe someone who pities your lack of swordsmanship."

"Oh?"

"It's a major handicap."

"I imagine so."

"In a world where disputes are settled by the blade, you've no idea. Please trust me."

"I trust you," Roble said. "When such opportunity presents itself, I promise to hire someone to train me."

Smoke drifted across the pathway about a quarter mile away. Horses whinnied.

"Get off the road," Shawndirea whispered.

Roble hurried off the path and stepped behind a massive tree. He waited several minutes, watching and waiting for riders to come toward them. No one came.

"Perhaps they're heading the other direction?" he said.

"Perhaps. Proceed slowly but you stay off the main road."

He shook his head. "No. The road's frozen solid. Even with the fresh layer of snow, it's quieter to walk along the road than through frozen briars and deeper snow."

"Be cautious," she said. "Thieves and assassins could be anywhere."

"I know. I'll be careful."

Roble stepped softly along the road to lessen any crunching sounds to give away their position. Laughter echoed off a side path away from the main road. He followed the path for a few hundred feet until he noticed smoke rising from a crackling fire. He leaned against a massive tree and peered around. Three men sat on logs facing the fire. A fourth man sat opposite them. His hands were shackled and his leather armor was similar to the ones Roble wore.

The other three wore brown leather pants. Their heavy fur coats were made from the hides of white wolves and walruses. One man took a long drink from a leather flask, passed it to the man on his right, and he wiped his beard with the back of his hand.

They sat hunched forward, possibly to catch the heat of the fire. One spoke and the other two laughed at whatever he was saying.

"They hold a man prisoner," Roble whispered.

"Or for bounty," Shawndirea replied.

"I really wish you could fly." Roble placed his hands on his knives.

"Not more than I. You're not confronting them, are you?"

"Why not?"

"They're rugged renegades. The man they're holding prisoner was probably in company with the hanged man."

Roble nodded. "That's why I plan to free him."

"What? Why?"

"We could use an ally."

"You've no guarantee he'll side with you and not attempt to kill you."

His eyes studied the men closely while they talked. "I've the feeling he won't."

"Your odds are still three to one."

Roble smiled. "I learned to count years ago."

She frowned. "They learned to fight with swords while *boys*. You're not prepared to combat *one* of them, much less three."

"Where will you feel safest?" he asked.

"What do you mean?"

"My shoulder, in my pocket, or I can place you on this small tree branch," he replied.

"Your shoulder would be best. If necessary I can leap into the snow where you can pick up my frozen carcass, should you survive."

He arched a brow. "Okay?"

Roble stepped away from the tree and to the narrow path leading to the campfire.

"Remember, any hesitation will be your death."

Roble studied the men a few moments longer, took another step, and his foot snapped a branch. The sound echoed and caught the three men's attention. They turned, stood, and drew their blades. The men were massive, in both muscle and their height was over seven-foot. Their long thick beards were woven into neat knots that stopped at their belts.

For possible assassins or thieves, they looked more like Viking warriors. Their stature was unlike anyone Roble had seen in the Overlands. Oddly, he didn't fear them, although they should've intimidated him.

Roble's hands went out to his sides. He tucked his chin to his chest. When he headed their direction, their eyes widened with fear. Their blades lowered momentarily, and then they stood side by side to offer a solid defensive front. The man in the middle stepped forward and pointed the tip of his sword at Roble.

"How?" the center man said. He frowned and squinted, apparently trying to comprehend what he was seeing. "We hanged you."

"There must be a sorcerer," the man to his left said, looking through the trees. "It's sorcery. It has to be. He can't possibly be alive."

"But he is!" the third said. He shifted his sword from hand to hand. "It's his ghost."

The leader turned, grabbed their prisoner by the back of his cloak, and yanked him to his feet.

"Stay back whatever you are," the man said. "Or we kill your comrade!"

Roble's eyes narrowed. The wind whipped his cape behind him as he walked forward and ignored any potential danger. He didn't hesitate his stride and approached without fear. Confidence set in his eyes.

The leader drew his dagger and pressed the sharp, serrated edge against the prisoner's throat. The prisoner closed his eyes and clasped his hands together. He braced himself for the slice of the blade. Or, perhaps he prayed.

"No farther," the leader said. "I swear it!"

The two blades left Roble's hands without notice. The blades sang a near whisper and struck their destined deathblows. One knife blade rammed through the leader's right eye before he could slit the prisoner's throat. The man's left eye widened from the short-lived, instant pain. The serrated blade fell from his hand and landed point down in the snow. The prisoner dove to the ground, crawled through the snow, and rolled over the large log to hide near the tied horses.

The second man clutched the hilt protruding from his throat. He dropped to his knees and fell face forward in the snow. Dark blood spurted from his neck and painted the snow crimson.

The third man glanced at his two dead comrades. He scrambled backwards to make his way to the horses tied to the trees. Roble didn't slow his step. He marched fearlessly.

"Roble!" Shawndirea whispered in his ear sharply.

Roble ignored her.

The man rushed to his saddlebag and fought to retrieve a bow. Roble pulled his last blade, which was too light to be thrown a great distance with much accuracy, so he sprinted through the crunching snow. White puffs of icy clouds drifted from his mouth and nose as he ran.

The large man loaded an arrow and when he turned to face Roble, the small knife struck his shoulder. The man gnashed his teeth, growled, and yanked the tiny blade out. He stared at the blade for a moment. He laughed at the knife, tossed it in the snow, and smiled, pulling back the string.

"Roble!" Shawndirea shouted. "Watch out!"

The words never registered with him. He was in a world all to himself. He stood emotionless and braver than any fool could be.

The arrow went far to the right of Roble's head and sailed into the trees. He never flinched. The man who shot it fell to the ground and growled in pain. The prisoner had kicked the back of his captor's knees, which knocked the massive man off balance and sent him to the ground. The prisoner climbed on the man's chest and battered his face with his cuffed hands until the man's roars stopped.

"You bastard," the prisoner said to his dead captor before spitting on his bruised and bloody face. And for good measure, he swung another heavy blow.

Roble approached, and the prisoner rolled off the dead man. He backed his way through the snow, beneath a horse, and kept pushing to the trees. His fearful eyes were wide and his bluish lips trembled.

"What's wrong?" Roble asked.

"Don't kill me." The prisoner gasped. He settled against the trunk of an enormous tree. His cuffed hands shook, and he held them up in surrender, trembling.

Roble crossed his arms and shook his head. In a gentle tone, he said, "I'm not going to kill you."

"I tried to stop them from hanging you, Bausch," the prisoner said, pleading. "I offered my life for yours. Don't you remember?"

Roble frowned. The man spoke in a delirious manner. His haunted eyes made Roble wonder what torture his captors had done to him.

"Please spare me, Bausch,"

"I'm not Bausch," Roble replied.

"Please. It's me, Lehrling, your friend and trainer since you were a lad. I'm not an old fool. We wear the Dragon Skull pendants. Death occasionally passes us, Bausch. You know that. Perhaps Death spared you and that's the reason for your confusion."

Roble held the silver Dragon Skull clasp between his left forefinger and thumb. He looked at Lehrling. The man was barely five foot six with a plump gut. The lines on his face revealed he smiled more often than he ever frowned. And yet, a hardness around his eyes showed he'd dealt death to enemies in the past. His yellow beard and shoulder length hair was well kempt except for the frozen spittle around his lips where he'd frantically tried to negotiate with the three men to free him. Now he seemed to believe he must beg for his life.

"I'm not Bausch," Roble said. "I wear his clothes since … Well, he had no further need for them."

Lehrling frowned, shook his head, and looked surprised. Sudden recognition calmed him. "I could've sworn you were he. Are you his spirit returned for revenge?"

"No."

"Then who are you?"

"Roble."

"From what land?"

Roble smiled. "No place you would know."

"Perhaps." Lehrling shrugged. "I don't usually travel this far myself."

Roble extended his hand. The man lifted his cuffed hands upward and clasped Roble's hand. Roble pulled the rotund man to his feet.

"Then why did you?" Shawndirea asked, standing on Roble's shoulder.

Lehrling's brow rose. "A faery? The surprises never end. How'd you come to possess her?"

Her piercing green eyes narrowed. "He does *not* possess me."

"My apologies," Lehrling said, lifting his cuffed hands in surrender. The small chain linking his cuffs rattled. "No intention to offend."

"We're on a mutual journey," Roble said. He went from dead man to dead man, and patted them down.

"Oh, I see," Lehrling said softly. "Does your journey consist of robbing a hanged man of his clothes and pilfering through bounty hunters' pockets?"

"This is a brief detour."

Lehrling laughed heartily. "No one detours near Glacier Ridge. It's the end of the mountain trail."

"For most," Shawndirea whispered in Roble's ear.

Roble patted the dead leader's vest, pulled out a small leather pouch, and opened it. It was packed with heavy gold coins. On the dead man's belt, he found a small key ring. He yanked the ring from the belt, examined the keys, and stood.

"We're on the icy plateau overlooking the Vale of Frozen Tears," Lehrling said. "No other path leads down from this ridge into the valley. The only way in is from the other side but getting there's almost a guaranteed death sentence."

Roble took in the information and nodded. "Who were these men and why'd they hold you as their prisoner?"

"They're bounty hunters," Lehrling replied.

Roble studied the dead men. "They're damn near giants."

"Aye. They invaded the ports by sea," Lehrling said. "Hundreds of them. They came at night, killing the port guards without being seen."

Roble said, "That'd be difficult to defend against, I'd guess."

"Of course. But they had help from a traitor in Hoffnung."

"Why do you say that?" Roble asked.

"Because the port's a good thousand feet beneath the city. The city sits atop a rugged cliff. They use lifts to carry supplies and troops up and down. Someone from above had to have been signaled and alerted to their arrival for the lifts to be lowered before sunrise."

"Any idea where they're from?" Shawndirea asked.

"The Isles of Welkstone. They're Vykings."

Roble knelt beside one bounty hunter. He lifted the man's right hand. His massive hands had extra thumbs and unusual tattoos. Their fingernails curved like sharp claws. With their great size and odd hands, he wondered why they sought to use traditional weapons. Up close these men could deal a lot of damage in normal hand to hand combat.

Roble had never thought he'd kill another human, and this occurred far sooner than he imagined. He wanted to feel some remorse, but none came, which worried him. He should feel something for their loss of life. No, he *wanted* to feel, but he didn't. The quickness to attack also alarmed him. He wondered if Deiko's threat had come now rather than when it had, would Roble have killed without question?

In the Overlands, the closest he'd ever come to such violence was when Deiko had pulled the unloaded gun. However, Deiko had kept demanding to see what was in the pack. Roble didn't doubt Deiko would've killed to possess Shawndirea. Should they encounter one another again, Roble could kill Deiko to protect her without second thought.

Roble's skill at throwing knives was exceptional. Studying these three dead men, he marveled at his remarkable accuracy. He didn't remember throwing any knives, which was worrisome. Everything had occurred in a blurred, rapid pace without any recollection. Perhaps that's why remorse didn't register with him. He was alive, and they were dead. What should he feel? Had he actually thought about the confrontation, would he have hesitated and died? Probably.

He tugged his knife from the dead man's throat. The man's lower jaw dropped open and revealed sharp, jagged teeth. Two large fangs were on the top row and two smaller fangs set on the bottom. His tongue was a dark blue, almost black.

Roble pointed at the man's teeth and showed Lehrling the man's strange tattooed hands. "Do you know others who have these traits?"

Lehrling looked closer and shook his head. "No Vyking I've seen has these."

Shawndirea gasped.

"What?" Roble asked.

"The tattoos represent dark, magical sorcery."

"You recognize them, faery?" Lehrling asked.

"Shawndirea's my name."

Lehrling nodded. "My apologies, Shawndirea. From where do you know these?"

She shrugged. "I don't *know* them. I sense the dark force that put them there."

"So demonkin?" Lehrling asked.

"Could be," she replied. "They look similar to Vykings."

Lehrling nodded. "I was thinking the same except for their teeth and extra thumbs."

"That's why I assume they're demonkin and at least half," she said. "Why'd they keep you alive but killed your friend? That seems odd."

"I know."

Catching Lehrling's gaze, Roble said, "So there's a bounty on your head?"

Lehrling smiled. "One for you, too, as long as you wear the armor and pendant."

"Why?"

"We're ... I should say, *I'm* of the Dragon Skull Order. We're the Guardians for Queen Taube of Hoffnung."

"Taube's dead," Shawndirea said. "Her kingdom was overthrown."

Lehrling nodded. "Truth. You're correct. Bausch and I were scouting for her daughter."

"So Lady Dawn lives?" she asked.

"We pray so. Daily. She was never accounted for after Hoffnung was invaded. No one found her body, *but* no one ever saw her leave the city gates."

Roble took the key and unlocked the cuffs. The heavy metal bands dropped and sank in the snow. Lehrling rubbed his wrists and nodded graciously.

Roble walked to the next dead man and pulled his blade from his throat.

"Why take your blades?" Lehrling picked up the dead man's sword. "When you can claim their swords?"

Roble wiped blood from the blade before tucking it in its sheath. "I've never used a sword."

Lehrling's yellow bushy eyebrows rose. "Never?"

Roble shook his head.

"Boys are brought up learning how to use a blade efficiently," Lehrling said. "It's a means for survival. Any father worth a beggar's piece of bread places a sword in his son's hand by the time he's six years of age."

"I guess I'm the exception," Roble replied.

Lehrling frowned. "How have you survived this long? The world's a brutal place."

Roble smiled. "By avoiding fights."

"You're damn good with knives, but you should use a sword."

"He needs training," Shawndirea said.

Lehrling chuckled. "No need telling me. Anyone not trained to use a sword is a fool."

"Can you train him?" she asked. "You mentioned you trained Bausch."

"Aye, but that was years ago. I'm much older and a bit slower."

Shawndirea said, "A modest man is rare these days."

"Me, modest?" he replied, blushing. "I've been called a lot of things, but modest isn't one, especially after I've been drinking."

"If you were slow to use a blade," Shawndirea said, "You'd by no means be journeying across the countryside willing to engage in battle to find Lady Dawn."

"Oh, but to defend her crown, her rightful claim to the throne? I'd die a thousand times if necessary."

She said, "A modest man filled with valor."

Lehrling chuckled and stared at her. His laughter stopped. "My dear one," he said. "What became of your wings?"

Shawndirea's smile faded, and she looked away. "An accident. It's why Roble carries me to my home."

"Aye. Pity, young faery. Is there hope you'll get them back?" he asked.

"Yes."

"That's good."

Lehrling picked up a bastard sword, held it at a downward angle, and admired the blade. "Here, Roble. This was Bausch's blade before they killed him. The blade's sound and well tempered. Lighter weight than most like it, which will aid you in combat."

Roble took the sword. "Thanks."

He maneuvered the blade in his hand and did a couple of practice swings. The weight of the sword felt good in his hand, and he liked the thought of mastering its use. And albeit strange, he felt like he'd used it before.

"Not bad," Lehrling said. "For a man who's never used a sword."

Roble smiled, "Thanks. I guess."

Lehrling shrugged and retrieved the other two swords, their daggers, and their pouches of gold coins.

"I suppose I'm not the only looter among us," Roble said.

"As you said about Bausch's clothes, none of these demon-men will need them. Gold buys ale and hard liquor regardless of the coin's seal."

Lehrling cleared his throat, walked to the log near the fire, and set the weapons against the log before plopping down. Roble joined him, propped his blade against the side of the log, and opened the leather pouch of coins. He examined the gold coins one by one. All were imprinted with the same lettering and a king's image on one side.

"Why do we have bounties on our heads?" Roble asked.

"Lord Waxxon set them on the Dragon Skull Knights because nearly two dozen of us are scouring Aetheaon trying to find Lady Dawn. Should he find and kill her, any legitimate claim to the throne is gone."

"I see." Roble looked at the bust on a gold coin.

Lehrling nodded. "That's Waxxon's ugly face on the coin you're looking at."

"Queen Taube was loved and her charity renowned," Shawndirea said.

"Her daughter was destined for greater," Lehrling added. "Which is why we're scouting to find her."

"Or someone who can help you find her?" Shawndirea asked.

"Not exactly," he replied with a slight shrug. "We hoped by visiting a few taverns along the ridge, we might overhear a drunken rogue reveal he'd found her and was trying to get a ransom."

"Taverns in this area are dangerous," she said. "Competition between hired assassins has led to many deaths."

"Exactly. That's how Waxxon's henchmen found us."

"What if you find her?" Roble asked.

"We return her to power," he replied.

"Two dozen of you? Possibly even less, if any others suffered Bausch's fate."

Sadness claimed Lehrling's eyes. "We'll rally the townspeople and peasants within Hoffnung's boundaries."

Roble shook his head. "That's hardly an army worth storming a city, especially if the troops you're facing are like these dead demonkin warriors."

"Waxxon's ascension to the throne wasn't welcomed. Queen Taube's murder angered the villages, townships, and everyone who knew Her Grace. People will fight to overthrow Waxxon."

"Perhaps," Shawndirea said. "But you'd have a better chance by gathering assistance from the surrounding kingdoms. Since Taube was beloved throughout Aetheaon, others will aid you."

Lehrling nodded. "You're right, but getting to them is difficult."

Roble clasped Lehrling's shoulder firmly. "We have horses. Choose one."

Lehrling shook his head. "No, they're branded with Waxxon's symbol."

"I don't give a damn," Roble said. "I'm not leaving on foot through this miserable, icy forest."

Roble stood, took the sheath and sword Lehrling gave him and fastened it to his belt. The snowflakes became bigger, wetter.

"Very well," Lehrling said. "We keep the horses until we can trade them for different ones."

"That's fine by me."

The horses were large and resembled Clydesdales. Lehrling untied a bay horse.

"No," Roble said, shaking his head. "We should take the other two. Both are white. They'll blend in better with our surroundings."

"What about this one?" Lehrling said. "Should I tether it behind the other?"

"Sure."

"Makes for a better trade."

Roble climbed on the mountain of a horse and adjusted in the saddle. Shawndirea clung to his collar until he was steady.

"Mind if I ask you something?" Lehrling asked.

"Not at all," Roble replied.

"What did you do with Bausch's body?"

Roble sighed. "He's under the tree where I cut him down."

"Before we head southward," Lehrling said, "we should properly set his body to rest."

"The ground's frozen solid."

Lehrling patted an axe tied to the side of the saddle. "Bausch was my friend and the closest to a son I'll ever have. I can't leave him for the birds."

"Okay," Roble said. "It won't be easy to cut the ground with an axe, either."

"I know. His grave will be shallow."

"You should know the crows had access to him before I cut him down."

Lehrling cringed and shook his head. He whispered words Roble believed to be a prayer. Regardless of what words were spoken, prayers weren't enough to protect them from the impending dangers they'd soon face.

CHAPTER 22

*D*eep within the maze of Devils Den, the Dark Chancellor sat on his throne composed from the skulls of his sacrificial victims. His long gray beard flowed down the front of his black robe. He twisted a strand of his beard with a crooked index finger. With his hood pulled over his head, his face was hidden by shadows. His golden eyes glowed while he pondered the various disturbances occurring inside his magical cavern.

His control weakened nearer the depths of the cavern, especially since it continually expanded. With this, he constantly sought to maintain stability but discovered some of his prisoners had gained powers of their own. Unless he reined these prisoners tighter, the possibility of lesser creatures toppling his throne existed. However, he expended a large portion of his energy channeling control over his prisoners.

Sacrificing mortal prisoners no longer granted him sufficient power to subdue those who might eventually challenge him.

Modest fires flickered in each corner of his dark throne room. Darkness soothed him, and cloaked his reptilian, facial features from sporadic or accidental visitors who stumbled before his throne. With little or no light, his strength increased.

A large, tear-shaped amethyst hung at the center of the throne room. The quartz shimmered and glowed. Its sudden, bright light forced the chancellor to shield his eyes with his hand. After the intense purple light vanished, ten aged figures stood before him.

"Ah," the Dark Chancellor said in a hiss-filled voice. "Welcome, Ten Sages of Vylan!"

The eldest, dressed in an elegant crimson robe, stepped forward. In surprise, he turned and looked at the other nine. He acknowledged each of his brothers with a slight nod. He stooped as he walked with the aid of his staff. His fiery-red, feathery hair and beard flowed around his crow-like black beak. His beady eyes stared coldly. In a shrill-pitched cry, he said, "Why have you summoned us, Botis?"

"No time for proper greetings, Staven?" the Dark Chancellor, Botis, asked.

"You called us from our village for what? To cackle? For a conference?"

"You offend me." Botis leaned forward on his throne.

Staven squawked. "My brethren and I maintain the delicate balance in Vylan. Only one of us are to be summoned at a time. Yet, you've summoned us all at once."

"It's an important matter," Botis said, rising to his feet.

"It had best be," Staven replied in a sharp shrill. "What's this matter about?"

"Elias."

"The Overlander? What of him?"

"He's resurrected for the sixth time."

Staven's red eyes narrowed. "You called us here about him? Why? He's no concern of ours. He's a product of *your* dark sorcery. Not ours."

"His power grows," Botis said with a concerned expression.

"Such a fool, Botis, for giving a mortal access to your power. Have you lost control over him?"

Botis hissed. "Not entirely, but his intent for immortality increases with each cycle of his resurrection."

"How long before he attains immortality?" Staven ruffled his feathery hair around his face and neck. He shook his wings beneath his robe.

"After he hibernates in his grave, he'll resurrect for the final time in twenty years. Immortality's within his grasp."

Staven's eyes narrowed. "What about his body's decomposition rate?

After one hundred, twenty years, his decay should've taken a toll on his physical capabilities."

"I had thought so as well. Somehow, he's slowed the rotting process. The only reason I granted him power was because his body should've crumbled to dust well before his fifth resurrection."

"Magic has no guarantees, Botis. Even you know that."

"Yes, which is why I've sought your entire council." Botis' golden eyes brightened.

Staven chuckled with a half laugh, half chirp. "The best hope you have is for his body to deteriorate so he cannot complete the next cycle."

"He's yet to sacrifice an innocent soul. Without that, he's doomed."

Staven nodded. "Perhaps, he'll fail, after all."

"Yes. However, he gained control of a mortal earlier today. But, the man lost track of what Elias sought."

"What?"

The Dark Chancellor smiled grimly. "A faery."

"In the Overlands?" Staven's eyes widened with keen interest.

"Yes."

Staven shook his head and weighed the information. "You realize, had he captured and sacrificed her, you could never rein him under your control?"

"I'm aware. She crossed through my cavern and the veil to return to the Underworld. A human helped her."

"Get control of Elias before he gains immortality," Stark said.

"So can I rely on you and your brothers to help?" Botis asked.

Staven shook his head. "No. This is *your* spell. Elias is *your* minion. *You* must deal with what you've created."

Staven turned and faced the other nine sages. "Come brothers. Vylan awaits."

"I've an alternate solution," Botis said. "Before you leave, at least evaluate and tell me your thoughts on whether it might succeed."

Staven stopped walking and sighed. "What solution?"

"Follow me," he replied.

The Dark Chancellor led the ten sages into the adjoining chamber. At the center of the large room, a solid black staff—held in place by magical, static currents—levitated. Shimmering violet light flowed from the four corners of the ceiling. The staff was a conduit and funneled the humming energy through it and into the floor beneath it.

Staven leaned on his staff and watched the cascading magical energy radiating through the black staff. "What strange magic is this?"

"This staff's carved from a cursed, black tree in Mortel," Botis said.

Staven glanced at Botis in surprise. "Mortel? How's it possible? The darkness in that city is great."

"It wasn't an easy feat," Botis said. "Quite costly."

Staven studied Botis for several moments. Unable to see the chancellor's serpent-like eyes, he said, "I imagine not. The stirring, black mysticism that spawns from Mortel's soil is why we should've never been summoned at once. It leaves our land undefended."

Botis smiled. "You fear Mortel?"

"More a fear of *what* controls it," Staven replied.

Botis hissed with amusement. "Whom, you mean."

"You've met with Tyrann?"

"How do you think I came to possess this staff?"

"He gave it to you?" Staven frowned with skepticism. "At what price?"

"The cost was steep, but acceptable."

The vibrating violet light shimmered. Its droning whine was soothing, coaxing, and drawing.

The other nine raven sages focused on the flowing magic buzzing and humming throughout the chamber. Their eyes glazed a grayish-white. The violet beauty of electrical waves captivated them. Slowly, one by one, they edged closer to the black staff. Staven noticed the power luring his brothers and shrieked warnings, but the sages didn't respond.

"What is this?" Staven turned his red-eyed gaze to Botis. "What sacrifice did you offer to obtain this staff?"

"None," Botis replied. "The cost was heavy, but I found a way to defray the price."

Staven whistled softly. "How? What did Tyrann demand? How heavy a price?"

"Not as heavy a price as you and your brothers will pay."

Staven's nine brothers encircled the staff. He squawked his protest in a high pitch call. He sought to break the hypnotic draw of the magic, but his brethren were deaf to his pleas.

"Stop this, Botis!" Staven pointed a feathered finger.

Botis hissed a long, subtle laugh. "Who's the fool now?"

A great flash of light expelled from the black staff. When the glaring violet light faded, the nine sages around the staff were gone.

Staven shrieked. "Where are my brothers? What did you do to them?"

"The same shall be done to you, Staven." Botis raised his hands.

Staven lifted his magical staff like a shield and shivered behind it. "You've no idea what you've done. Vylan will fall, and it'll be on your head."

Botis laughed and his amusement echoed throughout the chamber. "Vylan's not *my* concern. The Ravenfolk are strong enough to survive without your protection."

"No," Staven said. "They need us. Without us to protect the mountainous forests, they'll have no safe place to nest."

"Again, not *my* concern. No more than Elias is yours."

Staven's beady eyes widened. "Release my brothers, Botis. We'll do whatever you need to stop Elias."

"You will anyway." The Dark Chancellor smiled. "Beirt noier valens."

A strand of violet energy shot out from the staff, looped around Staven's waist, and tugged him to the staff.

Staven fought and resisted. Loose feathers drifted in the static air and fell silently. His staff clattered on the floor. He squawked, fluttered, and protested, but in the end, the magic sapped and pulled him inside the ebony staff. Once the staff possessed the Ten Sages of Vylan, the pulsing magical energy entered the staff and sealed it. The levitating staff dropped and clacked against the chamber floor. The Dark Chancellor walked over and claimed his prize.

He held the staff upward and admired it. Ten sets of beady red eyes blinked through different knotholes, which now housed the sages and contained magical power.

Botis chuckled. "Now, let's take back what once was mine."

CHAPTER 23

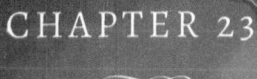

*A*fter they arrived at Bausch's frozen body, Roble took Lehrling's axe and attempted to chop the frozen ground. Ice chips and frozen dirt flicked in the air. The impact jarred Roble's forearms. The sharp axe seemed dull and with each swing, the blade lost its edge. The hardened ground was like striking steel.

Wolves howled in the Vale of Frozen Tears below.

"Something disturbs them," Lehrling said. "Normally, their cries come near dusk, but it's only midday."

Roble buried the axehead into the frozen dirt, pressed his weight against the handle, and broke free a small chunk of earth. He picked up the icy, earthen brick and tossed it aside where a couple hunks of earth lie. He swung the axe again, and its handle cracked. When he tried to pry it loose, it snapped.

Roble growled with agitation.

"Here," Lehrling said, handing a hatchet to him.

Roble took the hatchet and glanced at the solid, gray sky. Heavy, swirling snowflakes dropped. The thick clouds blocked any hint of the sun. Constant twilight hung over the mountainside.

"Midday, you say? How could you possibly know it's midday?" Roble said.

"Trust me. Once the sun sets, the overshadowing darkness would frighten most demons."

"Ah, okay." Roble frowned. "So you really don't know the time?"

"Not exactly, no," Lehrling laughed and clasped Roble's shoulder. "That's why we must leave this forest before the sun sets."

Shawndirea sat beneath the protection of a snow-covered fir branch. "The frigid winds are more dangerous than what lurks in this forest after dark."

"Let's hope so," Lehrling said. "But after what happened to Bausch, we'd best remain cautious."

He looked at his comrade's frozen, eyeless face. Remorse weighted his facial features.

Lehrling swallowed hard and fought tears. "He was like a son to me."

"Did he die honorably?" Roble asked.

A tear edged from Lehrling's right eye. "Yes. He refused to utter a word to those demon-men. He kept his allegiance to Queen Taube and vowed Lady Dawn would assume the throne."

Roble stopped chopping the ground, stood, and looked at Lehrling. "I'm truly sorry for your loss."

"I appreciate that."

After fifteen more minutes of busting the frozen earth, the hole was deep enough for Bausch's body. They covered him with branches, frozen dirt, and snow. Roble extended his hand to Shawndirea. She stepped on his palm, and he placed her on his shoulder.

"I wish I could do more," Roble said. "Not much of a grave."

Lehrling stared into Roble's eyes for a moment, gave a slight nod, and he climbed onto the saddle of a tall steed. "You speak the truth. The grave will have to do. My thanks for giving his body a place to rest."

Roble swung on his horse. "Again, my condolences."

Lehrling gave a weak smile. "He died serving our future queen, Lady Dawn. As will I, should the occasion deem necessary."

"Let's hope it doesn't come to that."

"Should we cross more men riding mounts like these, we'll be forced to fight."

Roble smiled. "That'll be a Hell of a fight."

"You've no idea," Lehrling replied.

Shawndirea whispered in Roble's ear. "Ask him to train you."

"Here? In this weather?"

"No. When we reach a safe place to stay the night."

Roble shook his head. "He can't possibly train me in a few hours what most men spend years mastering."

"I agree," she said. "But he can teach you quick defensive moves that may save your life."

"True. Once we find a place, I'll discuss it with him."

Lehrling frowned. "What's all the whispering about?"

"She insists you train me," Roble replied.

"Sure. I can show you basic tactics, but it takes years of practice to become proficient."

"I'm aware."

The snow fell heavier. They rode along the frozen path dividing the forest. The wolves' howls faded. The trees were gray silhouettes across the white landscape.

Streams of smoky air puffed from the horses' nostrils. The third horse remained tied behind Lehrling's. The leafless trees provided little protection from the windswept snowflakes blowing from the west. In spite of the frigid climate, Roble didn't feel the cold due to Bausch's thin armor.

Lehrling turned in his saddle to look at Roble. "It's odd, but when you approached the three bounty hunters, I could've sworn you were Bausch. I can't believe the resemblance you hold. Could it be you're related?"

"Not possible," Roble replied.

"Where are you from?"

"Again, a place you wouldn't know."

"Entertain me with a name?"

"Cider Knoll," Roble said.

Lehrling frowned and repeated the name softly several times. He forced a frustrated smile. "You're right. I don't know of such a place."

"I told you."

"Trading town?" Lehrling asked.

Roble chuckled. "Far from it."

"Listen," Shawndirea said, interrupting them.

Lehrling pulled back on the reins, and Roble did the same.

Wailing echoed through the woods.

"Go!" she said, pointing ahead.

"Why?" Lehrling asked.

"You don't hear it?" she asked.

Roble and Lehrling shook their heads.

"Hurry!" Shawndirea said. "Or we may be attacked."

Lehrling tapped the flanks of his horse hard. The giant horse reared and bolted forward.

"What is it?" Roble asked. "What's going to attack?"

She frowned and pointed. "Go!"

Roble kicked his horse's side with the heel of his boot. The horse shot forward and galloped to catch Lehrling.

"What are we fleeing from?" Lehrling asked.

"A spirit seeking revenge," she replied. "Possibly Bausch's."

"If it's he, he's no reason to harm us," Lehrling said.

Shawndirea said, "It depends on what he remembers as truth. You're both riding horses of the men responsible for killing him. Roble wears his clothes."

"He knows me, faery," Lehrling said. "Even in the afterlife, he'd know me. I was a second father to him."

She nodded. "I understand. I don't know it's him. These woods are probably littered with corpses since we're near Glacier Ridge. It could be any spirit."

"That's true."

Roble shook his head. "How do you defend yourself against a spirit? Neither Lehrling nor I heard it."

She shrugged. "Death comes for someone is all I can say."

Large snowflakes clung to Roble and Lehrling's beards. Their horses plodded along the dark, wooded trail. Mists of fog and blowing snow suddenly blinded them. They stopped the horses. The horses' eyes widened. They shuffled their feet and stepped backwards and then side-to-side.

"What's going on?" Roble asked.

"Something has frightened them." Lehrling pulled his sword.

Shawndirea's fingertips glowed. "Be prepared. Something has tracked us and seeks to prevent us from going farther."

Roble unsheathed his knife and listened. The horses breathed heavily and whinnied. They reared and stepped backwards. Lehrling struggled to hold his horse steady. He tugged the reins and spoke soft words to his steed to calm it. Roble pulled his horse's reins to the right and circled the horse around.

"What are you doing?" Shawndirea asked.

"Making certain nothing sneaks up from behind," he replied.

From the misty wall, a form moved and floated much like the mist itself. Slowly its form slipped closer. Her facial features became clearer, and her eyes were onyx black. She wore a tattered, white gown and hood.

"Roble," Lehrling said, pointing. "There."

Roble swung the horse around. The ghostly form drifted toward them, and its horrifying eyes stared at them. No emotion appeared on her face, but her haunted eyes were hollowed by sadness, betrayal. She hovered between Roble and Lehrling at the center of the road.

Lehrling's knuckles were white from how tightly he gripped his sword. Although Roble held his knife, he saw no reason to use it. He couldn't defend himself from a spirit, and this one didn't seem hostile.

"What now?" Roble asked.

Lehrling shrugged. "I can guarantee *that's* not Bausch."

"Kind of had the same thought," Roble said.

"My mistake," Shawndirea said.

"What do you mean?" he asked.

"It's not Bausch's spirit. It's a Banshee," she said. "Someone will die."

A cold chill settled over Roble. His stomach knotted. He wasn't certain what Banshees were like in Aetheaon, but the myths and legends he'd heard during his childhood meant that whoever heard the Banshee's cry was the one destined to die. Neither he nor Lehrling had heard the Banshee. However, Shawndirea *had*.

The spirit floated and retreated into the white mist and snow as if she'd never been there. Her interest wasn't in their party.

Roble looked at Lehrling. "How far are we from a town or village?"

Lehrling replied, "In this weather, it's hard to say. All the trees along the path begin to look similar after a time. With this growing fog, it's difficult to predict anything."

"What do you make of the Banshee?"

"Shawndirea's right," he replied. "We don't have an answer for that."

Roble swallowed hard and glanced at Shawndirea. "How is it, you heard the Banshee, but we didn't?"

"I'm Fae," she replied. "The Banshee is a form of faery. It's not the first Banshee I've heard. Near battlegrounds I tune out their cries as they are many. Their stressful laments are burdensome. But here, in the depths of this eerie icy forest, I take the utmost precaution. Too many horrible things have happened to those who ventured here."

"Since you hear them, can't you ask about whom they're forewarning?" Roble asked.

Shawndirea shook her head. "No. Their appearance comes mainly to grieve over a lost loved one they can no longer protect."

"I always understood they were heard by the one doomed to die."

"They deliver a forewarning," she said. "But they're not Death. They never deliver the deathblow. If neither of you heard her, others roam this forest, or we're getting near the hidden trading post at Glacier Ridge. The banshee's tied to someone nearby."

Lehrling coughed and cleared his throat. "We stick to this path."

"We can barely see it," Roble said. "The weather's getting worse, not better."

"Aye," Lehrling replied. "Our pace will be slower, but we must continue on the dark path through the forest. If we leave this road, we'll wander aimlessly through the forest and perhaps freeze to death before we find a place to lodge."

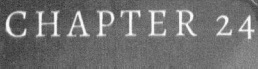

CHAPTER 24

*A*n hour passed. Their horses trudged through the heavy snowfall and nightfall began to settle over Glacier Ridge. The narrow path sloped downward with the thick, dark forest on both sides. Owls hooted on the dusky branches. Their eerie, golden eyes glowed. The cold, whistling breeze howled. Other eyes watched them ride past. Occasionally, wings fluttered and birds sought to hide farther away from the winding path.

Finally, the snowstorm diminished to flurries, but the overcast sky became darker.

"Either the storm's about to drop heavier snow—" Roble said.

"Nightfall's upon us," Lehrling said.

Roble studied the sky. "We've nowhere to stay tonight."

"Without moonlight," Lehrling said, "we'll lose the path. Even the snow will appear dark gray."

Odd sounds came from the forest. They rode down a sharp bend of the path. The horse hooves clopped on the hard icy surface. Had the horses been a smaller breed, they probably would've slid or lost footing, but these massive beasts' hooves chopped deep enough into the ice to keep traction.

The horses' ears backed, their eyes widened, and they snorted.

Shawndirea's nose crinkled. "I smell smoke, food, and ale."

Roble gave her a surprised glance.

"Well," she said, "I do."

Lehrling pulled back the reins and signaled for Roble to stop. Roble did. Lehrling pointed. "Look, light from a lantern."

Roble squinted. At the end of the forest trail, a glowing lantern hung outside a small cottage. After his eyes adjusted, he noticed more lanterns along both sides of the cobblestone street. A rope hung above the street and was strung between buildings on both sides of the road.

If not for the lanterns, they'd have ridden into town before knowing the town was there.

"I think this is Glacier Ridge," Shawndirea said.

"Aye, it is," Lehrling said with a hearty sigh.

Roble studied the buildings. An occasional shadow moved past the lanterns. A couple of robed individuals skittered across the rooftops and disappeared into darker shadows. Roble's hand rested on the hilt of Bausch's sword. His fingers tensed. When he noticed his hold on the sword, he was curious why instinct hadn't reached for his knife instead. He was efficient with knife throwing, but the sword was a new weapon he had yet to test.

"What makes you certain this is Glacier Ridge?" Roble asked.

"Bausch and I encountered the bounty hunters here," Lehrling replied. "Or perhaps I should say, where they *confronted* and took us in custody. More may lie in wait."

Shawndirea placed her hand to Roble's cheek. "Don't be quick to trust anyone in this place. It's a den of thieves and murderers."

"How do you expect to make a fair trade with these horses *here?*" Roble asked Lehrling.

He shrugged. "We may not get the better deal, but we should be able to make a trade."

"Or lose our lives in the process?" Roble asked.

"Nah," Lehrling replied, shaking his head.

"It's a possibility," Shawndirea said.

"I don't see any horses," Roble said.

Lehrling nodded. "If you tied a horse to a post outside, it'd freeze to death or be stolen before you finished your first tankard. A stable master is near the center of town. For a price, we can keep them there."

"How do you know the stable master's trustworthy?"

Lehrling laughed. "Like the faery said. You can't trust anyone here. But he's probably the most honorable."

"Why's that?"

"In his type of business, you'd die quickly if you can't keep track of a man's horse."

"So," Roble said, "did you and Bausch leave your horses there?"

Lehrling grinned. "Yes."

"Then he should still have them, shouldn't he?"

"Aye."

"That's good," Roble said. "Let's go."

"A word of warning," Lehrling said, looking at Shawndirea. "It's best you keep yourself hidden."

"Why?" Roble asked.

Shawndirea nodded. "He's right."

"In this area, a faery is worth our horses' weight in gold," Lehrling said. "For whatever reason, wealth seekers will kill you to get her."

Roble looked at her. "Is this true?"

She nodded.

"Why?"

"Lots of reasons. None are good for the humans, however. Fae don't take kindly to bondage. We take revenge in the most inventive ways."

"Still," Lehrling said. "It's best you hide."

She slid beneath Roble's cloak below his left ear and whispered, "Don't forget I'm here."

"I can't ever forget you," he replied.

Shawndirea smiled and pulled the cloak over herself.

Roble and Lehrling gently tapped their horses' flanks to coax them to move ahead. The horses walked slowly.

"The place looks deserted," Roble said.

"That's the deception of a town where thieves gather. We're being watched from every tavern and inn on both sides of the street. Even at the top of the hill overlooking this place, they're watching. No one enters Glacier Ridge secretly. Not even the best thief."

"Interesting."

"Spies have spies," Lehrling said. "That's how Bausch and I were taken into custody so fast. A few pouches of gold coins handed out here and there for reward will make even the most dishonorable thief loyal for a time. Unless you pay them more than the other pays."

"Loyalty to the highest bidder?"

"So to speak."

Midway through the town, the cobblestone street widened into a large circle. The marketplace was deserted. The vendor tables were empty, either due to the frigid air or because it was late in the evening. The surrounding buildings blocked the harsher winds, but the cold hung heavily. Several metal fire pits atop tripods blazed. Specks of red embers rose in the heat of the flame and darkened once they escaped the fire's hold. The crackling logs should've been inviting for tired, cold travelers, but few people lingered in the street.

Two men dressed in leather armor stood next to a fire and talked. When Lehrling and Roble rode closer, the men ceased talking, placed their hands on the sword hilts, and glared until they rode on past. Secrets were sacred, even among thieves.

Directly ahead, at the far end of the circle, the cobblestone road ended outside the mouth of a massive cavern. No guards were posted, which indicated law and order wasn't something easily enforced. Large burning fires were at each side of the cave mouth. More fires flickered farther down the cave path.

"What's inside the cave?" Roble asked.

"The largest part of this village. Due to the harsh winter climate, the more expensive establishments were built inside the shelter of the ridge. That doesn't mean it's any safer. In fact, it's probably more dangerous."

"And why few people linger outside these buildings?"

"Exactly."

Lehrling nodded at a long building that stood outside the circle to the right of the cavern. A half dozen fire pits were spaced along the side of this building. The wall was divided by dozens of doors.

Lehrling said, "We stable our horses there overnight."

Roble nodded.

Near the center of the stable houses, a forge glowed orange. The clanging racket of a hammer striking metal echoed. Sparks rose from the molten metal as the hammer shaped it. Water hissed and steam rose when the man thrust the crude metal blade into a barrel of cold water.

Roble and Lehrling rode closer. A giant of a man stepped from the open center of the building with a heavy hammer in his hand. He stood seven feet in height, weighed close to four hundred pounds, and other than his slight gut, he was more muscle than fat. The light from the fires revealed his scarred face with hardened, emotionless features. He'd endured many fights, but obviously remained the victor. Sweat dripped down his face, and even in the wintry, bitter cold, the man wore no sleeves. His biceps and forearms were enormous. The man wasn't a stranger to hard work, and his tempered glare was enough to intimidate the most twisted murderer.

The man looked a lot like the men that held Lehrling prisoner, except he didn't have extra thumbs. Since this man offered no smile, Roble wasn't certain about fangs.

Two smaller, young men stood behind him with their hands resting on their swords.

"I'm Riese, the stable master," the mountainous man stated in a gravelly, deep voice. "*What* do you need?"

Lehrling eyed the massive hammer in Riese's huge muscled hand and then gazed at Riese's cold, unblinking eyes. His stare was difficult to hold for any length of time. His eyes resembled shimmering ice.

"We need," Lehrling said, "a place to house our mounts overnight."

The man stepped beside Lehrling's horse. Riese's face was almost even with Lehrling's. "You were here a couple days ago. Were you not?"

"Aye," Lehrling said, swallowing hard.

"You owe me rent for your horses already in my stables."

Sweat beaded Lehrling's brow. "I do."

"I thought you'd abandoned them," Riese said.

"No," Lehrling said. "Wasn't in a position to retrieve them."

"These horses you have now," Riese said, studying the brands on their hindquarters. "These belonged to other men as I recall."

Lehrling glanced at Roble and back to Riese.

Before Lehrling could reply, Riese said with amusement, "Shall I wager they won't be coming here looking for these?"

"Not any more," Roble said.

Riese's attention turned to Roble. He gave a solemn nod. "It doesn't surprise me, but others like them arrived tonight."

"How many?" Lehrling asked.

"Half dozen," Riese said. "I see more of them lately. Can't say I like their presence in my place."

Roble thought the comment odd because Riese was every bit as massive as the ones feeding the ice ravens in the forest. Even though Roble didn't know much about the heritage of different races in Aetheaon, he couldn't help but guess Riese's lineage was the same as the bounty hunters serving Lord Waxxon.

"How about a trade?" Roble said.

Riese frowned. "For these you ride?"

Roble nodded.

"Name your price."

"He owes you stable fees for the other two horses," Roble said. "The tethered one behind him should be more than enough to pay his debt."

Riese walked to the horse behind Lehrling and checked its hooves. He ran his hand across its sides and then checked the horse's teeth.

"She will do nicely, yes," Riese said with a fangless grin. "And you're wanting to get rid of the two you ride?"

"Aye," Lehrling replied.

"What do you ask for those?"

Roble looked at the hammer in the man's hand. "You're a blacksmith?"

Riese gave an odd look because the question was stupid. "Yes."

"What weapons do you have?" Roble asked.

Riese smiled with great pride. "More than you could carry with a dozen of these colossal horses. Any particular weapon you seek?"

"Knives, daggers, and axes," Roble said.

The stable master walked from horse to horse, inspecting each one carefully.

"And the saddles?" he asked.

Lehrling nodded. "Those, too."

"Come," Riese said, resting the massive hammer on his shoulder. "My sons will stable these while I show you some weapons."

"You're not worried about their brands being noticed by the other bounty hunters?" Roble and Lehrling climbed down from their mounts.

Riese laughed heartily. "They won't know they're here. Besides, I can cover their brands with my own. Not difficult for a smith to alter."

"Most horses are smaller," Lehrling said.

Riese shook his head. "Look at me. None of my horses are smaller than these. They'd never survive carrying me."

Roble chuckled. "I suppose not."

Riese led them into his smith. The hot temperature was overbearing from the glowing forge but welcomed. Hanging along the rock wall were numerous swords, daggers, and axes. The steel blades reflected the orange-yellow flames.

Roble found throwing knives atop a thick, wooden table. He held one to check its balance in his hand. He liked the way it felt. After testing a few more, he set three knives aside that he liked better than those he owned.

Riese frowned. "That's it?"

"No," Roble replied. "Still looking."

"May I see your blade?" Riese asked.

Roble shrugged and pulled it from its sheath. He handed it to Riese.

The blacksmith was stunned when he held the blade and eyed it for quality. He gave several sharp swings in the air, listening to the blade's delicate song as it sliced. He checked the hilt and shook his head in disbelief.

"Nice," Riese said. "Odd to find one crafted better than my own. Who forged this?"

Roble looked at Lehrling.

Lehrling replied, "Beren Tiwele of Woodnog."

"An elf?"

Lehrling nodded.

Riese returned the sword to Roble. "Finest quality I've seen. Mind if I test it?"

Concern crossed Roble's brow. "What do you mean?"

Shawndirea whispered, "Watch out."

Riese swung his heavy sword at Roble's head. He ducked and dodged Riese's advancement. Riese pivoted, spun, and with all his strength swung again. Roble brought up his sword to parry the blow, and to his surprise, sparks exploded as the blades clashed. A third of Riese's blade broke loose and hit the floor.

The impact of the battling swords knocked Roble backwards. His hand ached from the violent shockwaves radiating from the sword into his hand. His fingers burned and after a few moments, numbed. Pain radiated up his arm and into his shoulder.

Riese brought his broken blade back and over his head, quickly plunging a downward blow. Roble's blade deflected the blow, and suddenly he became concerned about Shawndirea's insistence about learning how to use a sword effectively. Definitely, *next* on his to-do list.

Roble stared into Riese's eyes. He couldn't read whether this was game or a fight to the death. The man's eyes revealed nothing. No emotion at all. Since Roble had never sparred, he wasn't certain how his reaction should be. Riese seemed bent on drawing blood or dismembering Roble.

Roble braced himself. Riese charged forward with a side sweeping slash. Roble dodged to the side, and Riese continued past. Roble kicked behind Riese's right knee and knocked the massive man off balance and sent him face first on the floor. Riese rolled to get up and found the tip of Lehrling's sword pressed to his throat.

Roble took deep breaths and lowered his blade.

"What is this?" Lehrling asked. His narrowed eyes indicated his anger. "Are you sided with the bounty hunters?"

Riese chuckled, gritted his yellowed teeth, and shook his head. "Never! I wanted to test the metal of his blade. It's truly Elven. That's all I wanted to know."

Lehrling eased back his blade. Riese stood and held out his broken blade. He shook his head. "Look at this. The strongest steel I've ever forged. So heavy and thick. Yours? Light and thin, but stronger than anything I've ever made. Actually, stronger than any I've *seen*."

Lehrling sheathed his blade.

Roble took a deep breath. His heart raced. Riese approached quickly. Roble wasn't certain whether to raise his sword in defense or to sheath it like Lehrling. Lehrling gave a slight nod, and tapped his belt. Roble sheathed the blade.

Riese extended his massive hand to Roble. Roble placed his hand to shake and the blacksmith's hand wrapped and hid his.

He smiled at Roble. "Didn't mean to alarm you."

Roble shook his head. "From the rumors about Glacier Ridge, I wasn't certain if you were going to kill me to get the blade."

"No. I live and thrive here, but never from the misdeeds of thieves and bounty men. I would, however, like to one day be introduced to this Beren Tiwele of Woodnog."

Lehrling nodded. "If ever you're in that region, it'll be my pleasure to introduce you."

"Very well," he said. "Now. Back to business. Surely you need more than those knives."

"An axe," Roble said.

"A battle axe or one to cut wood?" Riese asked.

"To cut wood."

"Since you have a sword like yours, you've no need for a battle axe. Most are too cumbersome and heavy to maneuver unless you're built like me." Riese pounded his thick chest with triumph. "Or, a dwarf."

Riese looked at his weapons on the wall. He took down an axe and handed it to Roble. "Will that do?"

"Yes," Roble said.

On the table where Roble had placed the throwing knives, he noticed smaller daggers that were far too small for a human's hand.

"What are those?" Roble asked.

"The faery blades?" he laughed. "Never had anyone *want* those."

"I'd like a couple of them."

Riese's thick eyebrows rose. "Really?"

Roble nodded.

"Why?"

"Trinkets."

"Ahh. I could see that. Know an enchanter?"

Roble shook his head. "No, but I'm certain to eventually come across one."

"Hopefully on their good side."

Lehrling laughed. "Hopefully."

"What else?" Riese asked. He looked at Lehrling and Roble. They shrugged. "My weapons are superb, but the modest amount you're taking in exchange for the horses isn't sufficient for a trade. You're making me out to be a thief."

"No," Roble said. "We don't have need for any more weapons or those horses. More weapons will weigh us down."

"Then I pay the difference in gold," Riese said and nodded firmly. "I won't cheat anyone."

Lehrling said, "Consider it a gift and of course, payment for my other horses' long stay."

Riese shook his head. "Nay. I won't be indebted to another."

"We don't consider it like that at all," Roble said.

"Perhaps not, but I always will. No, there must be something more."

"Drinks!" Lehrling said. "Buy us a round of drinks in the tavern."

A grin spread across Riese's face. "Now *that* I can do, but that won't compensate the difference in our trade."

Roble gave an even smile. "It's a start."

"Very well," Riese said. "Hobskin's Tavern's where we go. While we drink, I'll find a suitable thing to make this trade more even."

"Honestly," Lehrling said. "It's not necessary."

"I do, or no trade at all."

Roble shrugged. "Then let's get something to drink."

CHAPTER 25

After venturing inside the cavern, they stopped at the third building on the right, which was Hobskin's Tavern. The buildings were constructed from roughly hewed logs. Mortar between the logs looked like frozen clay. Oil lanterns burned smoothly; their wicks shielded by beveled glass. A large guard stood at the tavern door. He hefted a large axe in his massive hands. The smithing quality matched those on Riese's weapon wall. The guard's face was hidden beneath a cloth helm painted to resemble a demon skull. More intimidating was the man's glowing, red eyes behind the mask. He wasn't human. Roble didn't have any idea what his race was.

Riese stared at the guard in his approach. The guard stepped aside and lowered the axe. Riese grinned and pushed the heavy wooden door inward. Lehrling and Roble followed. Stepping inside, the warmth enveloped them.

A large fireplace roared. An iron pot filled with bubbling soup balanced above the flame. Most tavern patrons cowered at the sight of Riese and backed out of his path to let him pass. The closest patrons eyed and sized up Roble and Lehrling and inspected what they carried.

Hanging oil lanterns and several large, candle chandeliers dimly lit the tavern. About two-dozen tables filled the area away from the bar. Strange animals, unlike anything Roble had seen in the Overlands, were mounted and displayed on the walls and above the bar. Mostly humans sat and drank from large tankards at the crude tables. They whispered amongst themselves while curiously eyeing Roble.

Riese looked for an empty table.

Roble wondered if the men detected he was from the Overlands. His uneasiness showed on his face, but to those studying him, his expressions might give them the impression he was an easy target to rob. Knowing confidence often made people second-guess a man's toughness, he narrowed his gaze and straightened his posture.

A wooden sign hung on the wall behind the bar with Hobskin's engraved in the wood. A crude rusted sword was fastened to the wall below the sign. A strange, green hand held the sword's hilt.

"Why's the hand there?" Roble whispered.

Riese replied, "It's a warning to those who befriend hobgoblins. Neither are welcome in Glacier Ridge."

"So they have?"

Riese nodded. "Hobskin's hand holds the sword. I killed him with my hammer. His head's stuck on a pole above the tavern. Thus the tavern took his name. I donated the sword and hand for decoration purposes. Come on, I see a table."

Near a back corner, Riese stopped at an empty table and motioned them to join him. "Here."

Roble eased his back against the wall while Riese did the same at the adjacent seat. Lehrling sat with his back to the crowd.

A few tables over, nearer the kitchen, a large round table was surrounded by six creatures Roble could only describe as being half rat and half human. They were muscular creatures with beady red eyes and pointed noses. Their sharp, yellowed teeth were dangerous weapons like daggers were in a close fight. Their long tails resembled thick ropes and curled behind them and beneath the table.

Their noses twitched when they talked or ate the thick stew from wooden bowls. Their bushy, brown fur shown where they lacked armor. Leather skullcaps covered their heads in between their large round ears. They wore their silver daggers on the outside of their leather armor, but their medium length swords rested on the table near their bowls and mugs. Their wicked, jagged claws were sharp and menacing.

"Don't stare at them long," Lehrling warned.

"Why?"

"Ratkins view it as a threat. They won't waste any time confronting you with their paranoid rants."

"Rough place," Roble said, looking away.

When Riese smiled, his wild wooly beard parted. He gazed around the room with narrowed eyes. If it were an intimidating glance, it frightened onlookers into looking away. All except one. An elf with long, silver hair flowing like silk down his back, didn't flinch. His kept his intent stare set on Roble and no one else.

The elf wore all green. He sipped from a silver mug but never averted his gaze from Roble. His armor was made from large, leathery scales and unlike any other patron's armor. Humans wore leather, chainmail, or black robes.

Loud laughter echoed across the room. A table with four, boisterous dwarves clanked their mugs together before downing their drinks. A large keg sat at the center of their table. Roble watched them momentarily, but his attention returned to the elf who continued to watch him.

Roble stared at him with boldness. He didn't dare break their gaze. He knew the game from the time he had lived in a large city one summer as an intern. Never show weakness or retreat when someone sizes you up. Otherwise, an enemy gained confidence and believed they were stronger.

Lehrling noticed Roble's determined frown. "What's wrong?"

"The elf. He's staring at me."

Lehrling looked over his shoulder.

Riese nodded. "So he is? What of it?"

"Just odd."

"Well," Riese said. "You're at *my* table. If he wants to make something of it, he may find he doesn't like how I deal with those who trouble my guests."

"Perhaps he knows you," Lehrling said.

Roble shook his head. "I've never met an elf."

"*Never*?" Lehrling asked in surprise.

"No."

Riese frowned. "From where do you venture?"

181

"Places you wouldn't know," Roble replied. "Cider Knoll is my home."

Riese nodded. "You're correct. Never heard of it. Is it from another continent or in Aetheaon?"

Roble struggled for a way to explain without letting them know he was from the Overlands. Before he offered an explanation, Lehrling smiled and nodded.

A busty barmaid brought three large mugs of ale to their table. Roble took a gulp of his ale and the bitter taste tightened his throat. He forced the liquid down. The aroma was stronger than any beer he'd ever drank and the alcohol content was much higher. He decided one drink was more than enough in this strange land. Best to keep his senses keen, in case he needed to defend himself.

The barmaid smiled at Roble and Lehrling, did a slight curtsy, and left their table. Her face looked familiar, and for a moment, he struggled to think where he'd seen her before. The question faded when he glanced at Lehrling's pale face. Lehrling recognized her, too. When their eyes met, they read one another's nervousness. Her face was identical to the female spirit in the forest.

"Honey mead," Shawndirea whispered to him.

Her gentle words shook him unexpectedly. Roble tilted his head to the side. "What?"

"I thirst. Order some honey mead."

Roble rose from his seat. "Excuse me."

"Where are you going?" Lehrling asked.

Roble didn't reply. He left the table and deliberately passed the elf on his way to the bar counter. Due to several large seated patrons at the bar, Roble went to the far end of the bar, which was out of view from Lehrling and Riese.

The barkeep turned and frowned. He placed his hand on his dagger at the front of his belt. "Can I help you?"

"Honey mead," Roble said.

The barkeep's brow rose. He turned and faced the large mirror on the wall behind the bar. He poured a flask of honey ale with a strange grin on his face.

"A problem?" Roble asked.

"It's a woman's drink," a voice said behind him.

Roble turned. The silver-haired elf stood directly behind his right shoulder.

The elf chuckled and whispered, "But it's not for you, is it? It's for the faery in your pocket."

"What?" Roble asked.

"Easy," the elf said. "We don't want the others to know she's here."

"What do you want?"

"To talk. Nothing more."

Roble gave a slight nod. "What do you wish to talk about?"

The barkeep returned with a small cup of honey ale and blew a kiss at Roble. Roble frowned and opened his mouth to speak, but the elf tossed a gold coin to the barkeep. "Let it go and take the drink."

Feeling uneasy about the situation, and about taking the honey mead, he grabbed it anyway and left the bar.

"Let's find a table more private," the elf said.

Roble followed him through the other side of the tavern. A set of stairs led upward and the elf took them. Roble stood and hesitated at the bottom for several seconds. Most of the patrons near the stairs were drunk or unconscious. None were watching him like those seated on the other side of the tavern near the entrance.

Roble headed upstairs. When he reached the top, the elf was seated at a table in the darkest corner.

Shawndirea peered from beneath the edge of the cloak.

"Should I seat myself or return to the others," Roble asked.

"See what he wants," she replied.

"How'd he know you were with me?"

"Possibly detected my magic."

Roble pulled back the rugged chair and sat. His hand rested on his dagger.

"Bring her out. Let her drink," he said, extending his hand palm up.

"Who are you?" Roble asked.

"Odlon of Eyllisathem," he said, staring at Roble as though the name held high relevance. "You are?"

"Roble from Cider Knoll."

Odlon studied Roble while he thought about the information. The elf's complexion was perfection. No scars or blemishes flawed the radiance of his fair skin. His emerald-colored eyes almost matched the color of his armor. The silver necklace he wore had a large emerald in the centerpiece, which was surrounded by six smaller emeralds.

Shawndirea crawled from Roble's pocket and jumped to the tabletop. She hurried to the honey mead and sipped it from the cup.

"Gods help us," Odlon said. His eyes widened. "Your wings. What happened to your beautiful wings?"

"Not your concern," she replied.

Odlon propped his elbows on the table, crossed his long fingers together, and rested his chin on the finger-bridge. "Odd you're so far from your homeland, faery."

Shawndirea looked up from the honey mead and frowned. "Again, not your concern."

Odlon grinned and looked at Roble. "Feisty little thing, isn't she?"

"It's the cold weather," Roble replied.

Odlon chuckled. "Did she tell you that? Or is that your theory?"

She glared at Odlon and rested her balled fists on her hips. "What exactly do you want?"

"To talk to Roble."

"About what?" Roble asked.

"Your reason for crossing the Underworld and coming to Aetheaon," Odlon said evenly. "You don't belong here."

"How'd you know?" Roble asked.

A smirk curled Odlon's lips. "You don't have the hardness in your features to survive in this world."

"I've done okay so far."

"Your eyes have more fear and uncertainty than strength," Odlon said.

Shawndirea's eyes narrowed.

"Easy, faery," Odlon said, raising a finger. "I'm being critical, but I have reasons."

"Then, state them," she said.

"I offer my assistance to wherever you wish to travel."

She took her eyes off the elf and returned to drinking the honey mead.

Roble frowned. "Why?"

"Do I need a reason?"

Roble nodded. "Because of the town we're in, yes. A valid reason's worth quite a lot. Who hired you?"

"No one."

"You seem too regal to rub elbows with the dirty thieves occupying this ridge, but the reputation of this region is either to hire or be hired for thievery or as an assassin."

Odlon smiled. "You learn traditions quickly."

"One must in order to survive."

"I like your wisdom. For an Overlander, you might well make the transition to survive where others haven't."

Roble sighed. "I've nothing else in the Overlands."

Odlon stared and marveled with curiosity. "Nothing? Nothing at all?"

"No."

"What do you wish to gain here? Treasures? Become a mercenary? What?"

"Weighing my options."

"The faery plays a big role in whatever you hope to achieve."

Shawndirea lifted her head from the honey mead. The cup was one-third emptier.

"He's mine," she said, slurring her words. She shook her index finger at Odlon. "Just leave him alone. Or else."

Odlon smiled and shook his head. In an elegant tone, he said, "Not quite the answer I expected. Has she bewitched you?"

Roble shook his head. "No."

"None!" she insisted. She staggered and giggled.

"Are you certain?" Odlon asked. "We can get you to a witch to find out."

"I'll never cast a spell on my love." She hiccuped loudly. Embarrassed, she grinned and clamped her hand over her mouth.

Odlon gave an incredulous stare and met Roble's eyes. "Perhaps *you* enchanted her?"

"Me?" Roble scoffed. "I know no magic. Until I found her, I never believed magic existed."

"I find it odd. The two of you share such intense feelings for one another, so *why* are you here?" Odlon asked.

"I volunteered to pass through the Underworld to take her home," Roble said.

"Why?"

"Because her damaged wings are my fault."

Odlon's brow rose. "I see. You injured her, and she's in love with you?"

"It shocks me, too."

"What are your feelings about her?"

"Is it too premature to say I've fallen in love with her?"

Odlon shook his head. "Not if that's how your heart feels. Love has no timeline. Some love occurs at first sight."

"I've never had feelings for anyone else like I do for her. But when I consider the differences in our height and—"

"Trivial," Odlon said. "Where love matters."

"That's what I keepsh telling him." She plopped on the table beside the honey mead flask and giggled.

"You never answered my question, Odlon," Roble asked.

"About why I'm here?"

"Yes."

Even though the small upstairs room was empty, other than themselves, Odlon lowered his voice. "Darkness grows in Aetheaon. Waxxon's men are partly behind it. I'm searching for Lady Dawn to help return her to power."

"As is Lehrling."

"The man seated with you?"

"Yes."

"He believes she's alive, too?"

Roble nodded. "He believes it strong enough to risk his life to venture to Glacier Ridge."

"The Dragon Skull Order?"

"Yes."

"Did they recruit you?" Odlon asked.

"No."

"You wear their pendant and dark, leather armor."

Roble explained how Waxxon's men had killed Bausch. He also told about leaving Devils Den and nearly freezing to death before he found and cut Bausch down from the tree and took his armor.

"Lehrling doesn't protest you becoming one of their knights?"

"He's not said."

"Their number is few. However, members of all races are determined to overthrow Lord Waxxon."

Roble said, "Waxxon's henchmen are not well liked here."

Odlon chuckled. "They're not liked *anywhere*. Vykings are plunderers."

"Vykings?"

Odlon nodded. "Besides, without the proper heir to Hoffnung's throne, anyone assuming power will never be welcome."

"So until Lady Dawn's found, no one plans to overthrow Waxxon?"

"Well, that'd be the ideal time. But something worse than finding Lady Dawn has occurred."

Roble frowned. "What?"

"Waxxon's backed by something dark. A force connected to Mortel. And if that's true, our battle to reclaim Hoffnung must begin there."

"Why?"

"We must destroy the source of his power to prevent him from getting even stronger."

"That'd take an army."

Odlon shrugged. "We have the numbers. We just don't know *what* we'll be fighting once we enter the dark city."

Roble looked confused. "Why wouldn't you know?"

"Not one human, elf, dwarf, or otherwise, has entered and survived to tell what resides there."

"Why not send a group to examine what's there?" Roble asked.

"In my search for Lady Dawn, I've traveled close to Mortel. Darkness hangs over the area. Some have named the place the Black Chasm, which is appropriate, given that evolved from the deepest pit of the valley. I stopped atop a ridge overlooking Mortel. You cannot see through the haze. It's a strange, swirling black and purple mist. It conceals what's within. Every so often lightning shimmers beneath the veil."

Shawndirea's head tilted to the side and her eyes closed. Her body slumped against the flask. She lie unconscious.

Odlon smiled.

"Your armor's interesting," Roble said. "What's it made from?"

"Dragon scales."

"She told me no dragons existed in the Underworld."

Odlon's eyes glanced from the drunken faery to Roble. "She's correct."

"And yet—"

"This was made from the *last* dragon in the Underworld."

Roble admired the armor scale pattern. Seated closer, the detail of the shimmering dragon scale was more vivid than he imagined.

"Who killed it?" Roble asked.

"Me."

"In a sense that's a great victory, but in another, it seems sad no more exist."

Odlon shook his head. "To the contrary, encountering this dragon almost killed me. It ended worse for me than I had expected."

"Were you looking for the dragon?"

"No. But any exploration in Aetheaon has its share of unexpected surprises. No doubt you'll encounter some along your journeys as well."

Roble nodded and sighed. "I have already."

"Oh?"

"Yes. All my life I had heard about the eternal pit of Hell. I regarded it as myth. Never thought I'd actually pass through it on foot."

"River Styx?" Odlon asked.

"Yes."

"Incredible."

Roble laughed. "I didn't find it an appealing place."

"I imagine not." Odlon studied Roble's eyes and his mannerism. "So how long have traveled with the faery?"

"A couple days? I've kind of lost track of time."

"That happens in Glacier Ridge." Odlon eased forward in his seat. "Nice choice of weapon. Elven, is it not?"

Roble nodded. "It is."

"If you carry it, you must know how to use it proficiently. Perhaps you'd like to show me?" Odlon rose to his feet and drew his blade.

CHAPTER 26

*L*ehrling turned in his seat and searched the tavern. "Roble's been gone for quite some time."

"You're worried about him?" Riese asked.

"Wandering off isn't safe. Not here."

Riese turned up his tankard, downed the contents, and slammed it on the wooden table. "He's a man. Not a boy."

Lehrling nervously rubbed his gray beard.

"He's one of the Dragon Skull Order," Riese said. "I assume he's had a lot of specialized training."

"Well, not *officially*, he isn't."

Riese frowned. "He wears the pendant and your light armor."

"He does."

"Is he an imposter?" Riese asked.

"No. He's noble and worthy enough."

Lehrling explained how Roble rescued him from Waxxon's men.

"Ahh," Riese said. "That's why he favors daggers and knives?"

Lehrling nodded. "Yes."

"Few are as good at throwing knives as most are with swords, but if one's talent lies as such, he's a deadly man to challenge."

"I've never seen anyone confront three men as fearlessly as Roble did," Lehrling replied.

"A shame I missed that."

Three men sat at the corner table to Riese's left. They laughed and drank. The thin man in the center was dark skinned with a black beard. His braided ponytail hung down his back. Riese eyed the man until the man became uneasy and looked away.

"Friend?" Lehrling asked with a chuckle.

Riese's eyes narrowed. "Hardly."

"Foe?"

"He's working on it."

"Why?"

"That's Crukas," Riese replied.

"I thought he'd be bigger."

"You know of him, too?"

Lehrling nodded. "Who doesn't? His wanted flyers are everywhere. Most kingdoms know his thievery accomplishments, but no one's ever caught him."

"He's the master of thieves, but I warned him *never* to return here."

"Because of his reputation?"

Riese shrugged. "That, and he's violated the sanctity of Glacier Ridge by not abiding by the rules."

"What'd he do?"

"He recruited three murderers into journeying to Ironwood, the small town north of Woodnog. He promised them a chance to gain great wealth quickly," Riese said while glaring at Crukas. "The only thing he didn't tell them was the wealth was for himself. He turned them into the magistrate for the rewards. They were hanged in the center of Ironwood."

"You think that's why he's returned?" Lehrling asked. "To hire unsuspecting thugs and cash in on their bounties?"

"Could be, but this time, he's the one who'll suffer."

"You have to admit. That's a sly way to make money while eliminating his competition."

"He's cunning, but Glacier Ridge is a retreat for otherwise wanted criminals. If they wish to trade wares they've stolen outside the ridge, they're more than welcome, provided they abide by my rules. But traitorous behavior will be eliminated."

Lehrling looked around the tavern and sighed. No sign of Roble.

"Still worried about Roble?" Riese asked.

"Yes."

"He'll turn up."

"I'm more worried about *how* he might turn up," Lehrling said with worry in his eyes. "If Waxxon's men are here, Roble could find himself in some real danger."

Riese smacked several gold coins on the table and stood. "Then let's go find him."

ODLON RUSHED around the table with his sword drawn. Roble was hardly to his feet and struggled to draw the blade. Odlon brought his blade overhead and swung downward. Roble's hand left the hilt, grabbed a sharp dagger, and flung it. The blade struck the center of Odlon's chest.

Odlon's eyes widened in surprise. He lowered his sword and gazed at the blade. The dagger didn't penetrate the dragon armor, but lodged between two scales. Odlon took a deep breath and tugged the blade free. Roble held a second blade, ready to throw.

Odlon sheathed his sword and held his hands upward. He grinned. "Didn't expect that."

"I thought we were having a friendly chat," Roble said.

Odlon smirked. "Understand, I was testing your reflexes. Great with a dagger, but not so with the sword."

"I know. I've thrown knives and metal stars at targets since I was a child. Never had a sword to practice with."

"I can teach you some tactical moves," Odlon said, handing Roble his knife. "You should hope you don't need the sword before then."

"I'd appreciate it," Roble said. "But why do you wish to help me take Shawndirea home?"

Odlon shrugged. "Perhaps you'll return a favor for me in the future? Besides, you need training."

"Lehrling can train me."

"The old fat man?" Odlon said. "He's slow. I'm nimble and quick. You'll progress quicker from my challenges."

"That's probably true."

"Probably?" Odlon asked with one brow cocked.

"Definitely true."

"Fine. Take your faery and hide her safely before someone sees her. Now's not the time to draw attention to her or yourself."

Roble walked to the table and picked Shawndirea up. He admired her in the dim candlelight. She slept with her mouth slightly open. The shape of her mouth was enticing. He wanted to kiss her perfect lips, but she was so small. He carefully slid her inside his front jacket pocket.

"You said the dragon almost killed you?"

Odlon nodded. "Yes. For the damage and pain he inflicted, I made certain his hide would always be on my body."

"What damage did it do?"

Odlon turned his back to Roble. "Lift my cloak."

After Roble did, Odlon slid his right arm out of the chest piece and revealed the blistered, burnt flesh covering over seventy percent of his back. When the air touched the wound, Odlon winced, closed his eyes, and groaned.

"This looks fresh. When did you kill the dragon?" Roble asked.

"Ten years ago."

Roble's brow rose, and he grimaced. "Ten years? And it still looks blistered?"

"Yes." Odlon pulled the armor over his shoulder and tightened it in place.

Roble pulled out a chair, and Odlon promptly sat. Roble sat on the opposite side of the table.

"Why doesn't it heal?" Roble asked.

"Like I told you earlier, I wasn't looking for this dragon. In fact, I never expected to find one during my lifetime. No one's seen one for years."

"Doesn't mean they're all dead, does it?" Roble asked.

Odlon shrugged. "No reports have been told since my encounter. I ventured inside a cave to gather a rare herb my sister needed for a potion. I found the herb in plentiful supply and while I harvested it, I walked through a narrow passageway that opened into a grand cavern.

"The dragon apparently heard my approach. Perhaps he thought I came to steal treasure, but I never saw any gold or silver. No treasure at all. Just a large crop of these herbs and other rare plants alchemists covet."

Roble nodded. "Perhaps the dragon protected the herbs."

"Never thought about that, but I suppose the herbs were his treasure."

"Who would need such plants?"

"Wizards, witches, and perhaps healing priests," Odlon replied.

"Would a dragon protect herbs for someone?"

"Possibly. While picking the herbs I never noticed the dragon until I smelled the brimstone. When I turned, it craned its long serpent-like neck and faced me. Without warning the green drake opened his mouth and tried to snap me with its jagged teeth. I rolled and pulled the lance from off my back. When it lunged at me, I threw the lance. The point went directly through its eye about four feet deep.

"I turned and ran through the corridor. It rose and roared, and thrashed its head side to side. It struck the side of the cavern and drove the lance even deeper. It growled and hissed. A wall of flames spread from its mouth and followed me down the corridor. The licking fire ignited my leather armor and consumed it. I dropped to the cold, hard floor and rolled over, batting the flames with my hand. The dragon dropped forward and cursed me moments before its death."

"A curse?" Roble asked.

"That my burns never healed."

Roble said, "There must be a way to reverse it."

"My sister has tried every healing spell she knows. Nothing has altered it. Wearing the dragon's hide and scales is the only thing that stops the constant pain."

"Did you ever return to the cavern to see what other herbs grow there?"

Odlon replied, "I did."

"You never know," Roble said. "The cure to his curse might be hidden there."

"Sadly, no. When my sister and I returned to harvest more herbs, they were all wilted or dead."

Roble frowned. "Dead?"

Odlon nodded.

"I don't know anything about dragons since I'm an Overlander," Roble said. "But could this have been a magical dragon? Did something like that exist?"

Odlon thought for several moments. A barmaid brought him another mug of wine. He took a long drink. "So much lore is no longer taught. But, to answer your question, dragons have always held magical abilities. Like any race that practices magic, one's only as good as they research and practice."

"Are you certain yours was the last dragon?" Roble asked.

"No one's ever entirely sure," Odlon replied. "When I brought out this dragon's head with enough hide and scales to craft my armor and shield, the residents of my city were shocked to learn one had lived so close. We changed the name of our city to Eyllisathem, which means "Land of Dragons."

"To honor the dragon?" Roble asked.

"No," Odlon replied. "To strike fear in travelers venturing to our city. The dragon's head, which is only a skull now, rests atop a tall pole right at the gates."

"Dragon skull." Roble rubbed the pendant between two fingers.

Odlon nodded. "Perhaps the gods have crossed our paths. It's not mere coincidence you passed through the Underworld, wear the clothes of the Dragon Skull Order, and have teamed with one of their knights."

"This battle isn't mine. The only reason I came to Aetheaon is to ensure Shawndirea returns home safely."

"Maybe your intention, but trust me, the gods make no mistakes. They occasionally amuse themselves by drawing people into unusual situations to see how they squirm when put to ultimate tests."

Roble glanced at Shawndirea in his pocket. "You think she's a test?"

"What do you think?"

"I'm not certain anymore."

Odlon smiled evenly. "Fae occasionally cross into the Overlands merely out of curiosity, but has she ever given you a reason why she did?"

"To find me."

Odlon rose from his chair and frowned. "She actually phrased it like that?"

"Yes, *exactly* word for word."

"See?"

"She meant as a husband to end the animosity between the human race and the Fae."

Odlon shook his head. His long silver hair gleamed in the faint candlelight. "What inspired her for such a quest?"

"Arrogance of male Fae."

Odlon laughed. "She has a valid point, but still, plenty of humans live here. And yet, she chose to seek one from the Overlands."

"So?"

"She was struck with a lust to hunt for someone outside the Underworld. The gods, or at least a mischievous one, decided to sour any thought of her settling for a husband unless he came from the Overlands."

"I'm hardly one equipped for the conflicts and explorations you and Lehrling talk about." Roble placed his hand on the sword. "I'm not a swordsman. I'm great at throwing knives but not skilled enough to defend myself with a sword. Certainly, not efficient like someone who's grown up in this realm."

Odlon studied Roble's face for several moments. He stood and slowly walked around Roble, and sized him up. "You're framed to be an agile, strong fighter. With the proper training from Lehrling or myself, you'll be feared on the battlefield."

"I never came to be a warrior or soldier."

Odlon cocked his head. "Did you think the Underworld consisted of numerous luxuries, sitting in meadows, or lying beside cascading rivers? These lands are crude, violent, and dangerous. You fight or you die. It's that simple. Once you take Shawndirea home, what do you expect will happen?"

"I'm not certain."

"Do you expect an open arm welcome?"

"No," Roble said. "Shawndirea said her mother wouldn't approve of me."

"*None* of the Fae will accept her choice, no matter how noble and upstanding a human you are. Understand what she sacrifices once she's home and she announces her decision."

"I know."

Odlon frowned and anger rose in his voice. "You've absolutely no idea what's at stake for her."

"The decision, her choice, remains *hers*," Roble said. "If she chooses me, I'll accept their decision for myself, but I'll try to sway her *not* to be with me."

"You cannot sway her decision. She's smitten by you. Her heart cannot be changed. But understand this."

Roble nodded. "Okay?"

"Even after she's safely home, her kingdom isn't."

"Why?"

"Because the forces controlling Lord Waxxon are a danger to every continent in Aetheaon and throughout all its kingdoms. The darkness spawned in Mortel intensifies. It grows and festers and will spread until everything falls beneath its black veil. Waxxon's only the beginning. His henchmen roam the lands. Their numbers are immense."

Heavy footsteps thudded up the stairs.

"Roble!" Lehrling said.

Lehrling and Riese stepped into the small, dim room. Lehrling glanced at Odlon and then met Roble's eyes. "Is everything okay?"

"Everything's fine," Roble replied.

"This is the elf that kept staring at you?"

Roble nodded. "Lehrling, this is Odlon. He's also looking for Lady Dawn."

Lehrling gave a slight nod of recognition but couldn't suppress his concerned expression. "What interest is Lady Dawn to you?"

"The same as yours. To see her take her rightful claim to her family's throne."

"I appreciate your desire to see her seated where she belongs, but why's it matter to you?"

Odlon smiled. "It's not I, nor the elves in general. Most kingdoms in

Aetheaon, regardless of their race, support her being found and Hoff-nung under the proper ruler. Lord Waxxon leaves a distaste in the mouth of all."

Riese stooped because the ceiling was too low. He held his hammer tightly and eyed Odlon with suspicion.

Lehrling said, "What does he want?"

"He's offered to travel with us," Roble replied.

Riese said, "Where are you from, Odlon?"

"Eyllisathem."

"The Land of Dragons?" Riese asked. His thick eyebrows rose with interest. He stepped closer and examined Odlon's armor. "Are you the one that killed the dragon?"

"Yes."

Riese opened his mouth to speak, but the main entrance door of Hobskin's Tavern swung open and slammed hard against the wall downstairs. Two barmaids screamed. The clamorous drinkers became less noisy. The barkeep shouted an obscenity filled threat but stopped mid-sentence.

The bartender yelled, "You've no jurisdiction here!"

Riese turned and headed for the stairs. "Seems we've unwelcome company."

Lehrling pulled his sword and followed.

Odlon drew his sword and pushed past Roble. "Keep out of harm's way, Overlander. I'll help you take Shawndirea home, and we'll see the aftermath. If I'm correct in my assumption, you'll help me inspect Mortel."

Roble followed Odlon down the crude staircase. Five of Waxxon's henchmen stood to block the exit. Their leader held his jagged sword to the barkeep's throat.

Riese stepped forward and held the hammer at his side. "What is it you seek?"

The leader turned to face Riese and the blade pressed to the barkeep's throat lowered. "Who are you?"

"The one to take your life unless you leave."

The leader stood a couple inches taller than Riese, so he appeared amused by the threat. "At least give your name so I'll know who to haunt in the afterlife."

Riese laughed heartily. "*I'll* haunt you *in* your afterlife. The thought of my face will be your torture."

Recognition set in the leader's eyes. "You're the stable master? You dare threaten Baron Tierman?"

"As the barkeep said, 'you've no jurisdiction here.'"

The leader approached Riese. "Glacier Ridge has no true laws I know of. A place where chaos rules over order."

"If you planned to toss your threats, you should've brought more than six. There are dozens of us," Riese said. "You may strike fear in peasants, townsfolk, and maidens, but you might rethink where you are. These are the worst of the worst and we fear no one."

Roble glanced around the tavern. Dwarves, humans, and other races stared at the henchmen with narrowed gazes and angered brows. None were happy to have their drinking disrupted. Their hands went to their weapons. Apparently Riese noticed the same. Friction and tension increased amongst the alcohol-induced patrons.

"Aye!" two dwarves said in agreement. They pounded their axe heads together and hunched forward, ready to charge into a brawl.

The leader of Waxxon's men glanced nervously around the tavern. "Don't think I only brought five men. More are searching the ridge for the Dragon Skull Order."

"I checked your horses in," Riese said. "No others came with you."

The five henchmen near the door pulled their swords and braced themselves for attack. Two men held leashed, furless dogs. Their red scaly skin was covered with small thorn-like bones. Grabbing one with bare hands would be impossible without shredding skin and flesh to the bone. They growled and exposed rows of sharp, pointed teeth.

Tierman's eyes widened when he looked past Riese and noticed Lehrling and Roble.

"Release the two Dragon Skull Knights in our custody, and we'll leave peacefully." Tierman pointed.

Riese grinned at Roble. Lehrling gave a half smile.

Riese frowned at Tierman. In a thunderous voice, he said, "You dare infringe on my patrons like you've authority over us?"

Chairs scooted from tables. Half drunken people stood with

weapons drawn. Tierman turned and looked around. Uneasiness settled on his face.

Roble realized no governmental body was set over Glacier Ridge. Riese was the leader and had the ability to set a battle cry whenever the need for action arose.

Riese shook his hammer in the air and looked at the tavern customers. "Are you going to stand for this kind of interruption?"

"No!" the patrons shouted in near unison.

Crukas slunk into a corner where the shadows were darker. He slid barbed fist weapons on his knuckles. Seconds later, Crukas was gone.

Riese roared. "Show these men their rightful place!"

And with that, Riese rushed Tierman and swung his massive hammer hard before the baron braced himself for the assault. The head of the hammer clanged against Tierman's chest piece and sent him toppling backwards. Tierman hit the floor hard, slid, and winced. He toppled several heavy stools, and they crashed atop him. He lie on his back and hardly moved for several seconds.

The table of dwarves rushed the two men nearest them and yanked them to the ground. They pummeled them with their thick fists and smashed their faces with their silver tankards.

The two hellish beasts broke free of their leashes and sprinted into the frenzied crowd. The Ratkin grabbed their daggers and swords, and decapitated the hellhounds. Afterwards, the Ratkin knelt and drank the blood.

Tierman rolled when Riese swung his heavy hammer downward at the baron's head. The hammer cracked the floorboards. A layer of dust puffed in the air. Chairs and tables rattled as the vibrations traveled through the floor.

Crouched, Tierman spun around with his sword, but Riese moved faster. The head of his hammer caught the sword's blade. Sparks flew as metal struck metal. The hammer blow knocked Tierman's sword arm back and tilted him off balance. Riese shoved his shoulder into Tierman with enough force to knock the man into the air. He landed on his back several inches from Roble's feet. Roble stared at the baron and shook his head.

Tierman's eyes filled with pain. He clutched his chest where the shape of the hammer dented his chest piece. Riese rushed forward and brought the hammer up over his head with both hands. Tierman flung his hands over his face and closed his eyes tightly, anticipating the deathblow.

"No, wait!" Roble shouted over the raucous brawl.

Riese paused, held the hammer overhead, and frowned. "You want me to spare this dog? Why?"

"Answers," Roble replied.

"He plots to kill you and the other Dragon Skull Knights."

"He had *hoped*, but he's in no position to do anything." Roble pointed at the maddened crowd. The other five henchmen lie on the floor in pools of blood. The crowd fought amongst themselves for the dead henchmen's armor, weapons, and any valuables they discovered in their pockets.

Riese shrugged. "Then why let him live?"

"He's a baron, which means he has a lot of information about Lord Waxxon's plans and strategies. He probably knows where the sentries are positioned."

"You cannot trust anything he tells you," Riese said.

"I'd wager he's more trustworthy than most of those men and women over there."

Riese lowered the hammer and shook his head with disappointment. "He's yours at your own danger."

Lehrling looked at Roble with uncertainty. "You want him kept alive?"

"For now."

Riese turned to leave.

"Wait," Roble said. "I need you to help."

"With what?" Riese asked with a gruff, soured voice.

"We need a place to question him. The tavern isn't exactly a good one. If he refuses to talk, do whatever's necessary to *make* him talk."

Riese grinned and his bushy eyebrows rose with interest. He looked at Odlon. "Check him for daggers, hidden knives, and escort him to the stables. I'll get answers for you."

Riese headed out the tavern door. Lehrling helped Roble get Tierman to his feet while the drunken patrons scuffled and bickered over the loot they'd gathered from the dead bounty hunters. Odlon pressed the tip of his sword to the baron's back. Roble stood. Shawndirea awakened and stood in his pocket and looked around.

A Ratkin noticed her. His eyes narrowed when she made eye contact. It tapped its comrade's shoulder and pointed. Although very tipsy, she ducked inside Roble's pocket.

Roble, Odlon, and Lehrling exited the warmth of the tavern and entered the frozen Hell of Glacier Ridge with their prisoner.

CHAPTER 27

*R*iese's sons pumped the bellows to increase the forge's temperature. The baron's ankles were tied to the legs of a heavy wooden chair. His hands were tied tightly behind his back. He winced and wheezed each time he breathed. The shrewd harsh winter wind had not alleviated his hampered breathing and entering the forge's immense heat added further pain and complications.

Dried blood caked Tierman's nose and mouth. Riese had violently dented the baron's chestpiece with the hammer. Roble was certain the baron's ribs were broken, and Tierman probably suffered worse internal damage as well. A rib might've punctured a lung.

In the blazing, roaring fire, Riese turned the end of a branding iron in the flames until the metal dragonhead glowed orange. He held the glowing dragon tip inches from the baron's cheek. Although the baron swallowed hard, his eyes held indignation, not fear.

"Since you despise dragons," Riese said, "I chose this iron especially for you."

"You dare inflict such pain on one of your brethren?" Tierman asked.

"You're not my brother."

The baron shook his head. "You're every bit a Vyking. Why deny it?"

"Where are you from?" Riese asked.

"Hoffnung."

Riese shook his head. "No, you arrived at Hoffnung to conspire with Lord Waxxon. I know my former homeland. I've never ventured to Hoffnung."

Riese moved the searing branding iron closer to Tierman's face. The heat formed a red outline on the man's flesh even though the metal had not touched him. The baron tightened his jaw and braced for the pain.

"Name your actual homeland *before* you sided with Lord Waxxon."

Baron Tierman's eyes narrowed. He looked from the brand to Riese's eyes. "Do it. I won't tell you anything."

Riese lowered the brand and pressed it to the wooden seat between Tierman's legs. Tierman took a sharp breath and held it. Smoke rose where the fire singed the wood. His leather leggings smoked, too.

Tierman released a nervous breath and glanced at the burnt impression of the dragonhead in the wood. Tiny flames licked upward.

Riese took the brand and positioned it closer to Tierman's right cheek. "Last chance."

Tierman closed his eyes. Sweat beaded his brow. He coughed. Fresh blood coated his teeth and spilled on his wiry beard. "Do it! I've little life left. It's obvious I'm dying, so I refuse to tell you anything."

Riese pressed the brand against Tierman's cheek. His jaw clenched. His head shook. His flesh blistered and bubbled beneath the dragon brand. When Riese didn't pull the branding iron away, Tierman finally screamed. Blood-spittle frothed from his mouth.

Odlon turned and walked out of view of the fiery interrogation.

Roble winced and looked away. Although Roble wanted Riese to make the baron talk, he never imagined Riese would go to such lengths of torture, so early, and he certainly didn't expect Riese to enjoy making the baron suffer.

Riese lowered the brand and placed it in the fire. He grabbed Tierman's hair and pulled tightly. He peered in Tierman's wide eyes. "The next brand will be worse. Where's your homeland?"

Sweat covered Tierman's face. He panted and quaked. The smell of urine drifted from the chair.

Still holding Tierman's hair, Riese took the branding iron from the fire. Riese aimed the bright orange dragon at Tierman's right eye.

"The Isles of Welkstone in the Misty Seas of Reus," Tierman said.

Riese released Tierman's hair and gave a slight nod. "Where's that?"

"You don't know?" Tierman asked.

"No."

Tierman frowned in disbelief and slight confusion. The burn on his face puffed, burst and bled. "You lie. Your lineage is the same as mine."

"Never heard of these isles. Never been there."

Roble seemed surprised at Tierman's insistence but agreed with the baron. With Riese's physical characteristics, how could Riese deny he wasn't a Vyking?

Tierman coughed and leaned forward. He vomited a pool of blood between his legs. After he finished, Riese grabbed his hair and yanked his head back. Tierman's eyes lulled in their sockets. His tongue hung from his mouth. The baron stopped breathing.

With disappointment, Riese said, "He's dead."

Roble examined the pool of blood and shook his head. "His lung was probably punctured by a broken rib."

Riese shoved the branding iron into a bucket of cool water and walked away. Steam rose.

"It's late," Lehrling said to Roble.

"I know."

"I've rooms above the stables," Riese said. "If you'd like a safer place to stay the night."

Roble nodded. "That'd be great. We'll consider the trade even."

Riese shook his head. "That doesn't even our trade."

Roble smiled. "You can't put a decent price on a good night's sleep. And safety in Glacier Ridge is priceless."

"Very well. Looks like I have gained six more horses besides yours now." Riese smiled.

"Eliminating visitors is a quick way to add to your profits," Roble said, jokingly.

Riese's eyes narrowed. "I don't add to my wealth in such a manner."

"I wasn't implying you did," Roble said.

Riese held a hardened gaze at Roble for a half minute before bursting into roaring laughter. "Occasions arise from time to time though. Since I'm the only stable master, their losses are my gains."

Roble looked at Lehrling and Odlon. All were uncertain of whether to laugh along with Riese or not.

Riese pointed. "Those stairs to the right lead to the rooms. I've no other tenants tonight, so help yourself to any room you find to your comfort."

Lehrling nodded. "Thanks for your kindness."

Odlon followed Lehrling's lead. "You're too gracious."

Riese crossed his arms. "After my sons dispose of the baron's body, they'll lock down the forge and stables for the night. The surrounding walls are thick steel."

"Good to know," Roble said to Lehrling.

"Aye."

Odlon joined them at the foot of the stairs. Riese's sons carried Tierman's body out the front of the forge. Although the outside temperature was well below zero, the heat from the forge would keep them warm through the night. Perhaps too warm, Roble thought, wiping sweat from his forehead.

Lehrling struck a match against the wall and lit the lantern in a room with two bunks. The room smelled of stale hay and mildew. Once the lantern flame grew, Roble helped Shawndirea onto the small table beside the lantern.

The mattresses were thin layers of hay atop hard wooden slats. A woolen blanket covered the hay. Roble didn't realize how tired he was from the journey through Devils Den to Glacier Ridge. Once he sprawled on the rough bed, he dozed off.

WHEN ROBLE AWAKENED several hours later, the room was pitch black. Lehrling's snoring rose abruptly from the cot across the room. He listened for other noises, almost afraid to move. He hoped his eyes adjusted to the darkness, but they never did. The room was much colder than he expected. How could the forge cool so quickly? The rising heat should've kept them comfortable throughout the night. He rubbed his hands together.

"Roble?" Shawndirea whispered.

"Yes?"

"Good," she said. "You're awake."

"Is something wrong?"

"Strange sounds awakened me earlier."

"You sure Lehrling's boisterous snoring didn't wake you?"

"No." She patted her way across the bed to him. When she reached him, she curled in a fetal position on the crude pillow near his face. "Definitely not. This was a gnawing sound. Like something trying to gnaw through the walls or the ceiling."

"I don't hear anything," Roble said.

"It stopped."

"When?"

"A few hours ago."

Roble sighed. "Perhaps the wind was blowing against the wooden shingles."

"I don't think so."

"You remember the harsh wind we weathered through the frozen forest."

"Of course, but this was different."

"I didn't realize you liked to drink so much," Roble said.

"Normally, I don't. But honey mead, after our long journey, was something I couldn't resist. I was parched and exhausted. Clearly not in my best frame of mind."

Roble smiled. "I was afraid to drink much. I needed to keep my senses keen."

"I'm sorry," she whispered. She ran her fingers through his short beard.

"For what?"

"I should've done the same. I couldn't help you when you needed it."

"Odlon, Lehrling, and Riese took care of matters."

"But still," she whispered. "You're here because of me."

"I've no regrets being here. Dangers arise but seeing this new world and even this frozen wilderness with strange races I never imagined existed, I cannot wait to see what I encounter next. I've always loved exploring."

"This room smells odd," she said softly.

"Mildewed hay," he replied.

"Possibly. Or vermin nest in the walls."

Roble said, "Rats and mice are usually a problem in stables and barns. Anywhere there is feed and hay."

Shawndirea's right fingertips glowed green and seconds later, a ball of green light illuminated on the palm of her hand. She smiled at him in the faint green glow. He stared at her beauty, the gentle curl of her lips, and the brightness in her eyes. In the light of the small orb something else caught his attention. Five sets of silver eyes reflected in the dark corner across the room. Before he could grab a knife, a burlap bag covered Shawndirea and her light vanished.

She screamed.

"I have her!" a raspy voice said.

The door flung open and Odlon entered with a lit lantern. He set the lantern down and drew his sword.

Four Ratkins rushed Roble while her captor leapt and reached for the extended hand of a Ratkin perched on the overhead beam. The one pulled the other to the beam. Both scaled out to the rooftop. Nimble footsteps rushed across the roof. Shawndirea's next scream was muffled and farther away.

Roble kicked the closest Ratkin in the gut. It pivoted backwards and was impaled with Odlon's drawn blade. Roble tried to stand, but three Ratkins lunged at him. They snarled and bore jagged teeth.

Lehrling rolled over and rubbed his eyes. The snarling, growling beasts had awakened him. He shook his head and his eyes widened.

"What nightmare's this?" Lehrling swung his feet off the edge of the bed, and he grabbed his sword.

Odlon placed his foot against the skewered Ratkin's back and freed his blade from its corpse. He hurried across the room to rescue Roble from two Ratkins climbing on top of him.

Twisted, yellow teeth gnashed and bit at Roble. He fought to prevent their bites, fearful of what diseases these unusual beasts carried. He clutched one's throat so tightly its eyes bulged and its tongue stiffened in its wide-open mouth. Their breath smelled of rotten fish and garbage. Roble suppressed his urge to vomit. Why'd they want Shawndirea? How could he find and rescue her?

Anger and desperation rose inside him. He squeezed the Ratkin's throat even harder. The choking sound gurgling in its throat stopped after he cracked and snapped bones in its neck. He shoved its dead body away, kicked another Ratkin, and grabbed the third one with both hands. The creature's wild eyes gleamed and narrowed. It lifted Roble in the air. Its strength was incredible. Given that it was a foot shorter than he, he didn't expect such power in its thin arms.

The creature shoved Roble hard and seemed ready to slam him against the wall, but its eyes widened and it gasped. It lowered Roble with shaking arms. Life faded from its gaze, and its long pointed fingers released him. Roble pushed the Ratkin away. Lehrling's sword stuck partway through the beast's gut.

Lehrling smiled.

"Thanks," Roble said.

"Any time."

The fourth Ratkin's head plopped and rolled across the hardwood floor beside Odlon's lantern. Its headless body collapsed to the floor. Odlon stood with blood dripping from his sword.

"These Ratkin were at the tavern," Odlon said.

"I remember them," Roble replied. He nodded at the hole in the ceiling. "Help me up there."

"You're going after them?" Odlon asked.

"Of course. They have Shawndirea."

Lehrling gasped. "Gods have mercy."

"Gods might, but when I catch them, I won't," Roble said.

Lehrling cupped his hands together and leaned forward for Roble to place his foot. Once Roble balanced, Lehrling heaved him upward. Roble grabbed the beam and climbed to the hole. The opening was narrow, but once his shoulders squeezed through, he pulled himself to the roof.

CHAPTER 28

The frigid, cold wind blasted its way across the rooftops and stung Roble's face. He squinted to protect his eyes from the sharp sheet. He was amazed how little the cold affected the rest of his body. Bausch's dark, lightweight armor was better insulated than anything Roble owned in the Overlands.

In the vast darkness, nothing scurried along the rooftops. At least, nothing near him moved. Without a visible moon, the unrelenting, dense, dark clouds loomed overhead. Visibility was less than ten feet. The howling wind drown out any other sounds. Those who'd taken Shawndirea might not fare any better in the eerie darkness.

Thinking of Shawndirea, his heart ached. Where'd they take her? *What* did they *want* her for?

Light rose behind him. Odlon pushed the lantern through the opening. Roble grabbed the lantern and helped Odlon to the roof.

Roble whispered, "They're gone."

"We'll find them."

"Not in this darkness. By dawn, they could be anywhere."

In the lantern's glow, Odlon's piercing eyes peered into Roble's. Determination and confidence rose in the elf's voice. "We'll find her, my friend."

Roble shook his head. "I doubt it."

"Don't accept defeat before you begin." Odlon clasped Roble's shoulder. "You're definitely new to our realm. The Ratkin *won't* stick to the rooftops. They're like rats. They travel through sewers or underground tunnels."

"But, with this town being full of thieves, won't they sell her to the highest bidder?"

Odlon shook his head. "No. Too many others would kill the Ratkin to take her. The brawl you witnessed earlier was tame compared to what thieves would do to get Shawndirea. Only two Ratkin survived. They want to leave Glacier Ridge unseen."

"How'd they know she was with me?"

Odlon knelt and slid partway into the roof's gnawed hole. He looked at Roble and shrugged. "Not sure. These Ratkins have black fur, so none are mages. Any white or cream colored Ratkin are usually mages and might've detected her magic. They probably saw her during all the chaos in the tavern."

"But she was unconscious and hidden in my pocket."

"Not when she was upstairs on the table with us."

"That's true," Roble said.

Odlon slowly dropped through the hole.

"Where are you going?" Roble asked. He pointed. "They went that direction."

"I told you. They'll seek underground tunnels, which means, we need to awaken Riese."

"Why?"

"Because he knows where the sewers are," Odlon said.

Roble dropped through the roof and landed near the four dead Ratkin. He rolled the largest one over. Anger pulsed through Roble. These were dead, but when, or if, he found the two that had taken Shawndirea, he'd torture them before he killed them.

He looked at the pillow where she'd rested beside him only minutes earlier. His heart ached. A part of him was gone. He longed for her sweet whispers in his ear, to see her radiant face, and to ensure she got home safely. And yet, his greater disappointment was knowing he'd failed to keep her safe.

Odlon placed his hand around Roble's elbow and turned him. "Now's not the time to wallow in self-pity or blame yourself. None of us expected this. To find her, we must act fast before they put too much distance between us."

"Accepting the blame is difficult *not* to do."

"Maybe so," Odlon said. "But if you wish to survive in Aetheaon, never display your emotions on your face. At the tavern, your uncertainty made you appear nervous and worried. You never want thieves to see vulnerability. They thrive on weakness. The meaner you look, the less trouble you'll face."

Roble nodded. "I understand. The same's true from where I come, but not an issue I needed to worry about."

"You're not in the Overlands anymore. This realm's much different. Few have a conscience, and those who do? They *never* show it."

"Provided Riese shows us where to enter the sewers, I've no idea how to search for her."

"Take heart," Odlon said. "You're not searching alone. Lehrling and I will accompany you. First, let's search what these filthy beasts' possessed. We could find helpful information to let us know where they're headed."

Roble checked the belt of the largest Ratkin. On the front of its belt was a rolled map, two small pouches of gold, and a scroll. He took a crooked dagger and a strange spiked hand weapon similar to brass knuckles. On the back of its belt was a pouch filled with silver trinkets. In its vest pocket was an iron key. Finding what it opened would take a lifetime of searching, so he considered tossing the key.

Odlon and Lehrling rummaged through the pockets of the other Ratkins. Roble hid the key in his hand and tucked it inside his pocket.

Odlon stripped two Ratkins of their gold pouches while Lehrling searched the last one.

Odlon stood and counted the oddly shaped gold coins. "We have a decent amount to hire others to help us find the beasts."

"No," Lehrling said. "Hiring strangers puts Shawndirea at risk of being taken by whomever finds the Ratkins."

"I agree," Roble said. "Too many fighting over her could easily get her killed."

"Very well," Odlon said. "Then we best find Riese and search the underground tunnels."

Roble entered the hallway. Once they descended the stairs, Riese stood near the forge sharpening a sword. He rubbed a whetstone across the blade's edge. His thick eyebrows rose. "Up early?"

"Ratkin came through the roof," Odlon said.

Riese set the blade and stone on a table. His face flushed red. "What?"

Lehrling nodded. "We killed four of them."

"Bloody rat filth!" he roared. His eyes narrowed and his jaw tightened. "There's nothing here they should want. The walls are steel."

"The roof isn't," Odlon said. "They gnawed and cut their way through the thatch. Then they attacked Roble."

Roble looked at Odlon and shook his head. He didn't believe they should tell Riese about Shawndirea.

"Did you kill them all?" Riese asked.

"No," Odlon said. "Two escaped across the roof. We wish to pursue them."

"Why? What'd they take?" Riese asked.

Odlon opened his mouth, but Roble cut him off. "What they stole from me is something I value greatly but care not to divulge exactly what."

Riese cocked a brow. "Why's that?"

"Personal reasons."

Riese studied Roble for a couple minutes. "I can respect that."

Odlon said, "Are there tunnels beneath the town's taverns where they may have fled?"

"The only tunnel entrance is inside Hobskin's Tavern, but it's locked at this hour," Riese said.

Roble stared at him intently. "But you have a key, don't you?"

"What makes you think that?" he asked with a suspicious glint in his eyes.

"Because you're the official authority in Glacier Ridge, whether you boast it or not," Roble said. "No one questions you and all hail your commands. That was evident in the tavern. The patrons charged Waxxon's men at your word. You're the only order in this town."

Riese smiled, crossed his massive arms, and shook his head. "I rule because I allow thieves in this town without question or judgment, provided they don't rob my people or the marketplace. To my knowledge, this is the only township where thieves and murderers have refuge and delivered bounties are worthless. That's why Waxxon's men died quickly. Had they not made demands and wished to sit and drink with others at the tavern, they'd be alive."

Lehrling coughed, cleared his throat, and looked at Riese. "What happened with Bausch and myself then? He died at the hands of Waxxon's previous bounty hunters. They'd have killed me, if not for Roble."

Anger creased Riese's brow. "Where'd they capture you? It wasn't in the tavern or at my stables."

"No," Lehrling said. "We crossed through the marketplace after we left the stables and were looking for an inn. Bausch insisted we get a room at the inn near the town's entrance."

"Myrtle's Inn?"

Lehrling nodded. "Waxxon's men approached us outside the inn."

Riese frowned. "I remember them stabling their horses for the night. One returned and took them less than an hour later."

"Yes," Lehrling said. His eyes weighed with fear. "He came for the horses while his comrades took our weapons. They held us at blade point until he returned with the horses."

"Then what?" Riese asked.

"They shackled us, tied us to their saddles, and led us to the icy forest."

Riese shook his head. "Had I known, they'd have been killed. I don't tolerate such activity here. Due to the cold, few people stay outside, so no one reported it to me."

Roble frowned. "What about the Ratkin? Do your rules prohibit us from finding and exterminating them?"

"No. They broke the rules. Find and kill them. Few Ratkin venture this far north. Most live near the sea or along wide rivers where they loot unloading cargo ships or wagons carrying wares. They travel light and don't ride horses. That's why I wasn't aware of their arrival until I entered Hobskin's Tavern. Since they came to eat and drink, I figured they weren't a threat or would harm anyone else. Apparently, I was wrong."

Lehrling said, "They did quite a bit of damage to your roof."

"My sons will patch the roof at daybreak after we place a steel barrier in the ceiling."

Roble studied Riese's hands. He didn't have extra thumbs, nor had the baron or Waxxon's other men.

"Might I ask something?" Roble asked.

Riese nodded.

"The men that took Lehrling and killed Bausch had extra thumbs. None of the bounty hunters serving Waxxon do. Why's that?"

Riese snarled. "They're the sons of King Obed and his demon wife, Xaeeria. Some of her physical characteristics are evident with her children. Her children are powerful, except when they're too far from her magic to shield them."

"Like here?" Roble asked.

"Yes."

Odlon admired the weapons along the wall. From the worktable, he picked up a crossbow. He held it and checked the sights.

"You like that?" Riese asked.

Odlon nodded.

"Take it. That is, if you plan to kill those worthless Ratkins with it."

"Thanks." Odlon smiled. He grabbed the quiver of bolts off the table and positioned it over his shoulder.

Riese walked to the other side of the forge and into a small, side room. He returned with four unlit torches. Ropes saturated with pitch were tied around the torch heads. He handed each of them a torch and kept one for himself.

"At this hour," Riese said. "Light a torch and keep it handy, especially if you plan to comb the sewers beneath the cellar."

"Why not a lantern?" Roble asked.

"Torches also make good weapons," Lehrling said. "Lanterns, when shattered, tend to gush fire wherever the oil splashes. If the oil splashes on you, you'll be engulfed in flames."

Riese placed the tip of his torch to the open forge. It blazed and crackled. Roble, Lehrling, and Odlon lit their torches, too.

"Let's go." Riese walked to the locked double gate. He turned a steel key in the lock and lifted a heavy metal bar from its hold. He pulled the door inward enough for them to exit. Once they were outside, Riese shoved the door shut.

The sharp night wind didn't diminish its harshness. Their torches flickered in the breeze, but the heavy coldness hampered any heat the flames offered. Their heavy footsteps crunched the icy, hard snow. Roble stared past the torch and his mind raced. He worried Shawndirea might already be dead. If so, what then?

He pictured the full detail of her face. Every dimple. Every delicate curve. The radiance in her eyes, and how she'd captured his heart with her smile. A lump formed in his throat. He refused to shed a tear. To do so meant he'd lost her forever. He wouldn't accept that unless he found her lifeless body. And then, his life mission would be to kill every Ratkin he encountered, city-by-city, town-by-town. He'd hunt them relentlessly until he wiped their species out or they killed him.

Heated anger stirred through his soul. A sudden thought stopped him dead in his tracks. His stomach ached.

Lehrling stopped walking. "What is it?"

"The banshee," Roble replied.

"Oh," Lehrling said.

Riese stopped, turned, and faced them. "What banshee?"

Roble explained what they'd seen in the forest. The ghostly female figure had loomed out from the white fog.

"What are you saying? You heard her?" Riese asked.

"No," Roble replied.

Riese held his torch and its light washed over Lehrling's nervous round face.

Riese asked, "Did you hear her?"

"No."

Riese shrugged. "What importance is the banshee then? She didn't sing of *your* death."

"I know," Roble replied softly. "Not ours, but Shawndirea's."

"Who?"

Roble explained. "She's only one who heard the banshee."

Riese's jaw tightened. "You should've mentioned this sooner. Come on."

"Why?" Roble asked.

"No time to explain, but if you hope to find her alive, we can't waste time out here."

Riese increased his pace to a near jog while Odlon, Roble, and Lehrling hurried behind the near giant. They stopped outside Hobskin's Tavern, only to find the door open. Wood had been partially gnawed away near the keyhole. The gnawed wood was enough to allow them to pry the door open.

"Bloody Ratkin," Riese said.

Riese opened the door and went to a door behind the bar. The door opened to the storage room where barrels of ale and hard liquors were stored. "Keep your torches held high, but don't burn the tavern down."

At the far end of the storage room, a set of stairs led downward. At the foot of the stairs, a large wooden door stood ajar. Cold air drifted through the opening. The area around the lock was solid steel. Nothing could gnaw its way inside.

"They picked the lock?" Roble asked.

An even grin parted Riese's beard. "No lock's safe in a town that welcomes thieves."

"Perhaps you should *change* those rules," Roble said.

"They're not stealing from *me*," Riese said. "They're trying to escape."

"They stole from me."

"When you find them, kill them."

"I plan to," Roble replied. As soon as he spoke those words, he caught the coldness in his voice and his lack of hesitation in stating such a harsh vow. He'd never been a violent person, and yet, since his arrival into Aetheaon where strange creatures and races lived, he'd already shed blood and taken lives. This primal way of living was unlike how he'd been raised. The laws were different. Survival was different. And whether or not he liked it, he was adapting to the hardness of life in this realm, much faster than he expected.

Riese placed his huge hand at the side of the door. He looked at Odlon. "Elf, when I open this door, be ready to fire."

Odlon nodded and readied the crossbow.

Riese heaved the door inward, but the passageway was empty.

Roble stepped around Riese and lit the narrow tunnel with his torch. Nothing stirred. He looked at Riese. "Where does this lead?"

"Beneath most of the town. It's where waste is dumped from the houses, taverns, and inns."

"Does it lead outside Glacier Ridge?" Lehrling asked.

Riese shrugged. "I've never ventured through them, so I don't know. Someone or something picked the lock, so your best hope to find them is to search it out."

The walls, carved from thick permafrost, were coated with layers of blue ice. Slender icicles hung from the ceiling. The floor was semi-frozen slush formed from discarded water and waste. The farther they walked, the worse the rotten stench became.

CHAPTER 29

*J*ohn McKnight drove his pickup and parked beside Ben's SUV at the end of the dirt road. He shut off the engine and stared across the pasture at Devils Den. Ben had not emerged overnight. The officers, who entered the cave to search for Ben, found no trace of him, either.

John unlocked the gate and drove closer to the cave. Although he feared what might reside in the cave, he worried Ben might be injured and needed help.

At the cave mouth, he shouted, "Ben!"

His voice echoed several times through the cave without an answer ever returning.

"What's with him?" John said aloud. He placed his hands against the cold cave wall. "Why does he spend so much time in this cave?"

"Don't you think it's time you sealed this cave?" Deputy Higgins asked.

John turned with a start. "I didn't hear you pull up."

"I came to have another quick inspection of this cave. Still no sign of Ben, eh?"

"No."

"I hope he exits soon."

John looked at Higgins. "Why? Is he in some kind of trouble?"

"No. No trouble. Too many in this community believe it's hazardous for this old cave to remain open. I was at Old Man Harper's store earlier, and most everyone agrees this cave is a passageway to Hell."

"Do you?" John asked.

Higgins wiped his sweaty brow with a handkerchief. "Doesn't matter what I believe. It's what's best for the people that matters most."

"What's on my property is *mine*," John said evenly. "I won't have a bunch of ninnies and wives' tale worriers telling me what to do with my cave."

"I don't disagree with you, but Mr. Harper said you seem uncomfortable with the old cave, too."

John nodded. "I won't lie. The cave makes me uneasy, but Ben has gone inside numerous times. He insists there aren't any dangers inside."

"And yet, he's not resurfaced."

"I know."

"Has Ben ever been gone this long before?"

"Actually, he's camped several days inside. With him inside, I certainly won't seal the cave."

Higgins said, "I understand. But Mr. Harper insists evil exits this cave."

"What does he mean by that?"

"Some strange occurrences have happened near your farm."

"Like what?" John asked.

"We're not quite certain, but several of your neighbors filed reports detailing their sightings of what appears to be a walking corpse."

"Surely you don't believe *that?*" John grinned.

"I can't vouch for what they saw. They're all teetotalers and church-goers. They swear they've seen something."

"When?"

"Last night."

John wiped sweat from his forehead. "How is this associate to the cave?"

"Two of them are your neighbors, the Ridgeways," Higgins said, pointing at the dark wooded section of John's property. "Whatever they saw entered your pasture. They watched it by moonlight. It headed to the swampy section of your tree line over there."

John's face paled. He swallowed hard. "Nothing except tall pines and hemlocks grows on that section of my property. No grasses or small trees. Even briars won't grow there."

"You've never seen or heard anything unusual?" Higgins asked.

John stared at the trees in silence for several seconds. "No, sir. That's why I don't view the cave as a problem."

"As a favor, would you mind riding with me to your neighbors' house and tell them you've not seen anything?"

John glanced at his watch and shrugged. "How long will that take? I need to get to my insurance office in an hour."

"Shouldn't take more than fifteen minutes."

"Sure, if you think it will help."

"I appreciate it. Dr. Deiko hasn't improved any, either."

"Really? He looked delirious from the heat."

"Premeditated attempts to commit murder aren't usually the result of heat stroke."

"That's true."

Higgins scratched the back of his neck. "The doctors informed me Deiko only repeats one word over and over. Elias."

"Elias?" John frowned. "I don't know anyone by that name."

"I've had others research it. They cannot find any records of anyone in this area with Elias as a first or last name. No one at the university has that name, either. The university hasn't heard anything from Ben since the other day, either."

"He only has the SUV," John said. "He's still in the cave."

From the dark grove of pines, a flock of crows squawked and burst into flight, which startled John and Higgins.

"Reckon what scared them?" Higgins asked.

"I've no idea. Let's go, if you want me to talk to the Ridgeways before I leave for work."

John got in his pickup and Higgins followed him out of the pasture in his patrol car. John parked beside Ben's SUV and got in the passenger side of the patrol car. They neared John's mailbox, he asked Higgins to stop. John's son, Jack, and his friend, Donnie, were carrying their fishing poles and tackle boxes.

"You boys keep an eye out for Ben," John said.

Jack squinted with the morning sun striking his face. "He's still in the cave?"

"Yes," John said.

Higgins leaned toward the open window. "If you see or hear him, call 911. Dispatch will let me know, okay."

"Sure," Jack said.

"Catch a big one," John said.

Jack and Donnie smiled. "We'll try."

"And beware of boogiemen," Higgins said.

"What?" Jack asked.

"You two stay away from the cave," John said.

Donnie snickered and looked at Jack. "We're not afraid of that ol' cave."

"Well," Higgins said, "to be on the safe side, don't go inside it right now."

"Nah, we're too interested in catching a lunker," Jack said.

"Be back in a bit," John said.

ELIAS JACKSON STOOD beneath the shadow of a large Canadian hemlock branch. He watched Higgins and John talk outside Devils Den. His aged body ached. He needed to sacrifice a pure hearted person before the moon began to wane at midnight.

Deiko had failed him and exerting mind control over another individual had drained Elias even more. Had Deiko captured the faery, there was no end to what power Elias gained by sacrificing a rare, magical creature.

In his pursuit for immortality, Elias summoned Loa's dark power, and to his surprise, the Dark Chancellor had appeared. The chancellor offered to grant his wish provided Elias, in turn, resurrected and offered a blood sacrifice every twenty years, as homage to his dark master. The toughest feat was successfully performing this seven times.

Elias wasn't a fool. After his third resurrection, he realized the sacrifices were increasing the chancellor's power, but Elias' body suffered further decay. Completing the requirements was impossible. His rotting body would become dust well before he reached one hundred, forty years.

Though dormant, he suffered decay. To minimize the rot, he shunned daylight and lurked during the darkness of night. If anyone witnessed him, they'd speculate he was a walking corpse. Even though magic had allowed him to live well beyond his years, he wasn't immortal.

Weapons could kill him and end his quest for eternal life. Despite one hundred twenty years of dormancy, his body was in better condition than he expected. Part of his success came from his knowledge of black magic as a Bokor Voodoo priest from Haiti. So instead of offering sole sacrifices to the chancellor, Elias made extra sacrifices strictly for himself to revert his aging process, which allowed his body to rejuvenate while dormant, rather than decay.

The stench of partial decay emitted from his body. He detested smelling rancid during the extreme summer heat, but nothing alleviated it. The longer he roamed in the sweltering heat, the worse his odor became. Flies and other carrion insects pestered him.

A crow dropped from the top of a dead pine and dug its claws into his shoulder. Elias swatted it with a strong backhand. It squawked in terror and alarmed dozens of perched crows in the neighboring trees to burst into flight and add their frightened cries to his. The crows circled and drifted farther into the dark swampy forest.

After Higgins and John left the front of the cave and departed in their vehicles, Elias edged along the tree line and hobbled for the coolness of Devils Den. Once inside, he welcomed the decreased temperature. He pressed his body to the cold, wet cave wall and clung to it. For two days, he painstakingly made his way to the cave and now inside, he could hide and rest in partial comfort. When the night came, he'd find a suitable sacrifice.

But he never expected a sacrifice would come to him.

JACK AND DONNIE set their tackle boxes on the bank of Miller's Pond. They cast their lines and reeled in their rooster tail lures. The spinning blades caught the early morning sunlight. The gleam usually attracted the attention of hungry bass or large bream, but not today.

The overwhelming heat, even at the early morning hour, deterred fish from attacking artificial or live bait. The frustrating thing for the twelve-year-old boys was seeing huge largemouth bass lying near the bottom of the clear pond. No matter what they used to entice them, the bass refused to strike.

"Unbelievable," Donnie said.

Cicadas hummed in the trees surrounding Devils Den. Dragonflies darted and skimmed above the still pond.

Jack shook his head. "I've not caught anything in days. I was hoping the early morning would be better."

Sweat beaded above Donnie's upper lip. He ran his tongue across it. "It's already scorching."

"Another hundred degree day, I bet. Might as well return to the farm and play a game inside."

"Or we could go inside the cave," Donnie said.

"Nah. You heard what my dad and Deputy Higgins said. We'd best not go inside."

"Why not? Isn't your uncle inside?"

"He went inside early yesterday, but I don't know why he's never come out."

Donnie stared across the pond and squinted against the beaming sun. "What if he's in trouble? We might hear him calling for help or something?"

The windless morning made the sun feel even hotter. Jack had been inside the cave a couple of times with his father and once with his uncle, Ben. The cave temperature was much cooler and definitely would be far more pleasant than standing on the bank hoping the stubborn fish would bite.

"I guess it wouldn't hurt to go right inside the entrance to see if we hear him," Jack said.

"All right!" Donnie set his fishing pole on the ground beside his tackle box. "If we find him, we'll be heroes."

Jack shook his head. "We're *not* going far inside the cave. Just inside the entrance, okay?"

"Why? Are you afraid of the boogieman?"

"No, but if we go in without my father and he finds out ... Nah, it's not worth the whopping I'd get. Besides, I didn't bring a flashlight."

"Me, either."

They left their fishing gear at the pond and walked across the pasture until they got to the trees. As they neared the entrance, the cool air blew past. With the wind came the rotten odor of something dead.

"Eww," Donnie said.

Jack pulled his shirt collar over his nose. "Yeah, I smell it, too."

"What is it?"

"Probably a raccoon or something crawled in and died."

"Cool. Let's find it."

Jack said, "No. We stay where there's light."

"What are you afraid of?"

"Nothing."

"Then, come on, just a little farther," Donnie said, taking several more steps.

"Donnie, wait!"

Donnie darted deeper into the cave where Jack couldn't see him. Jack hesitated. Then Donnie screamed. The loud scream frightened Jack, but what scared him more was when Donnie's scream muffled and went quiet.

A lump rose in Jack's throat. He took a couple of cautious steps deeper into the cave. Donnie's muffled cries indicated someone had covered his friend's mouth. Donnie was in trouble. Jack took another step, and the light faded. Two more steps, and he'd be standing in pitch black. No light.

"Donnie? You okay?" He hoped Donnie answered. He hoped this was a mean prank. If it were, he'd wrestle Donnie to the ground and pin him until he apologized when they returned outside.

Jack took a few more steps. The decayed smell became stronger. Heavy rasping breathing paralyzed Jack with fear.

Donnie struggled with something in the dark. Apparently he pulled partially free of its hold. He yelled, "Run, Jack! Go get help!"

Before Jack could move, an arm reached out, grabbed him, and spun him around. The arm wrapped around his throat. Jack pulled forward to run. With his sudden adrenaline-filled strength, Jack dragged their attacker out of the dark shadows and into the faint light.

The black, slimy arm tugged him. Pieces of flesh were missing on the arm. Still in its hold, Jack spun enough to see the black man's face. Most of the man's skin was missing and his facial muscles were visible. The man's yellow eyes bulged and for a moment, Jack forgot to breathe. When he came to his senses and realized what was happening, he saw Donnie's terrified face. Shock overcame his friend, who stood wide-eyed and silent, and was too fearful to fight this hideous living corpse.

Jack shoved and kicked the man. "Let him go!"

The man, who by all reasonable means to Jack should be dead, was powerfully strong. Jack fought to get free, but the man's grip was unbelievable. He reached for the man's throat, and in the faint light, he grabbed the man's necklace, which resembled finger bones linked together to encircle his neck. He pulled and the bone necklace dropped from the man's throat. Where the necklace circled the man's neck was a deep scar. Had the man been strangled or hanged? Either way, *how* was he still alive?

When the necklace hit the ground, the man's eyes widened. He clutched his throat and gasped for air. His strength decreased enough for Jack to break free. Donnie jerked and tried to try to escape, too.

"Come on, Donnie! Run!"

The corpselike man yanked his necklace off the cave floor and his strength returned. He pulled Donnie close to his chest and pointed his long finger at Jack. "You're next!"

Terrified, Jack turned and sprinted out of the cave. He ran all the way home. Once inside the house, his mother, Lib, tried to console him. She kept asking what was wrong. But Jack was too afraid to speak. Shock consumed him. He shook uncontrollably.

"Where's Donnie?" his mother asked.

"It got him," he eventually said.

"What?"

"Some man in the cave. He took Donnie."

Lib hurried to the phone and called 9-1-1. They relayed the message to Higgins who said he was returning.

When Higgins and John arrived, they rushed inside the cave with flashlights but never found Donnie or any trace he'd been there. When nightfall came, Jack kept his bedroom light on and his hunting knife beside his pillow. For some reason, he expected the man was coming for him. Regardless of how sleepy he became, his inner fears prevented him from closing his eyes until sunrise.

CHAPTER 30

*B*otis, the Dark Chancellor, sat on his throne of skulls with his ebony staff in hand. The large crystal across the room glowed to life. Soon the violet color turned crimson red. A magical line seeped from the crystal, crossed the floor, and crept up the staff. Botis tilted his head and closed his eyes as the power from Elias' blood sacrifice flowed through the staff. Warmth and energy radiated up his arm and throughout his body.

Botis grinned. Soon Elias would return to his grave and not emerge for another twenty years. By that time, Botis was certain to find a way to prevent Elias from completing his quest for immortality.

~

ROBLE HELD his torch at a forty-five degree angle to keep the flaming tar from dripping on his hand. With his torch, he lit the sconces every twenty feet or so while they walked through the rough permafrost tunnel. The floor was littered with broken crates and empty wooden kegs. Dead mice were scattered through the debris. Their throats had been slit.

Riese left them at the door to inspect the tavern and make certain nothing had been stolen. They sloshed through the half frozen, sewer mush and Odlon kept the crossbow ready. Lehrling coughed a couple times and spit a wad of green, bloody phlegm on the nasty brownish ice. He leaned against the cold wall to catch his breath.

"You okay?" Roble asked him.

He nodded and wheezed. "Yeah, the putrid smell's getting to me."

"The sooner we check out the tunnel, the quicker we leave," Odlon said, motioning them forward.

Roble lit another sconce and glanced up. About twelve feet overhead was another grate. They were beneath another building. Four sconces blazed behind them. By his estimate, they'd probably crossed beneath the street to the other buildings. And if so, no set of stairs led upward. Only Hobskin's Tavern had an exit leading to the streets.

"It's a dead end," Roble said. His heart sank. He feared Shawndirea was lost to him forever.

"It's not a dead end." Odlon pointed at a busted keg tilted against the wall. Sewer sludge dripped and drained beneath it.

Roble pulled the keg from the blocked hole. Warmer air flowed from the opening. Roughly hewn steps, covered with a thin layer of sticky sludge, descended.

Lehrling gagged. "Surely we're not wading through that muck?"

"You two don't," Roble said. "I'll go alone. I won't rest until I find her."

Odlon shook his head. "No. You're not entering alone. If you die and she's rescued, how will she feel?"

"I'm not saying I *won't* go," Lehrling said. "I'll go if you believe those Ratkin are in there."

"I honestly don't know," Roble said. "But rats kill mice and we walked past a trail of freshly killed mice."

Roble lowered his torch to check the opening. Red beady eyes reflected in the light. Seconds later, they were gone.

"Rats," Odlon said.

"The Ratkin could be in there," Lehrling said. "Rats are loyal to the Ratkin."

Roble lowered to his knees. "I hope this is where they've gone."

Odlon and Roble easily slid through the narrow opening, but Lehrling had a difficult time maneuvering on his knees and squeezing his gut through. Once through the hole, they stood and descended the slick stairs.

The sewer tunnel was narrow. At the bottom of the stairs, they stood inside a larger room. Although cool, the air was much warmer than where they'd been moments earlier. The water was deeper. No ice. Large rats swam through the water emitting frightened squeaks. Roble and Odlon held their torches to better view the flooded room. It seemed endless.

Rapid footsteps sloshed through the water.

"There!" Odlon pointed. He fired a bolt but missed.

Two figures sloshed and disappeared outside the light's radius.

"That has to be them," Lehrling said.

"Good." Roble pulled his knife. "I'll skin them both."

SHAWNDIREA TOSSED BACK and forth in the burlap sack while the running Ratkin carried her. She didn't know where she was or who had captured her. She wondered where Roble was.

His warm smile when she had lain beside him had been wonderful. He was destined to be with her. She was comfortable beside him. Gazing in his eyes, their love for one another was mutual. But then, sudden alarm and panic separated them. Who else had been in the room? They took her before he could protect her or himself.

Was he still alive? Her heart and mind ached. She needed to see him, to be with him. Her boldness and determination heightened. When she returned to her homeland, she'd renounce her right to the throne and wed Roble. The longer her captors held her, the less chance she'd experience those things.

She gagged. The smell of wet vermin was terribly strong. She'd use her magic except the abrupt jarring inside the sack didn't allow her the necessary concentration to focus her magic. She grabbed fistfuls of the bag material to steady herself and prevent any further bruising.

Water sloshed beneath her. The strong scent of sewer water sickened her worse than the vermin smell. She pressed her nose against the cloth wall surrounding her, and desperately hoped it lessened the odor. It didn't.

"Keep moving!" a harsh voice shouted.

"I am. I am," replied the one carrying her.

"They sees us!"

"How much farther?"

"Not far. Not far."

"We has her," the one carrying her said. "Great reward for this one, yes?"

"If alive, yes. Not if she's dead."

Tears filled Shawndirea's eyes. "Where are you, Roble?"

THE ONLY LIGHT inside the dark, open room came from the light radius of their torches. Small chunks of earth dropped from the ceiling and splashed in the water. Roble focused on the watery path ahead. Little groups of brown rats squeaked and ran from where he stepped.

"Where are we?" Roble asked.

"Sewers," Lehrling replied.

"No mistaking that," Roble replied. "But sewers beneath where? The temperature's grown warmer. No ice. If I gambled a guess, I'd say the overhead ground is about to cave in."

"Could be under the mountain," Odlon replied. "Deep enough and insulated enough to keep the frigid temperature out."

"Maybe." Roble walked through the ankle deep water.

"Why?" Lehrling asked. "What are you thinking?"

"Passed through Styx to get to Glacier Ridge. Surely we're not heading there?"

Odlon chuckled. "Doubtful."

The splashing footsteps dashed across the center of the room. The immense darkness prevented them from seeing their exact position.

"This could be a large enclosed room with only one way in and out," Odlon said.

"True," Roble said softly.

"In which case," Odlon said, "One of us should remain near the small doorway."

"I'll gladly go," Lehrling said, gagging.

"If they head your direction, call out to us."

"I will."

Odlon and Roble walked side-by-side. They headed toward the splashing footsteps. The walls seemed to be closer together. The room wasn't as big as Roble estimated. Whispering echoed in the shadows whenever the rapid splashing ceased. Then the whisperers took to running again.

"I think you're right," Roble said.

"About?"

"No other way out."

Odlon smiled. "Be prepared. Ratkin are known to attack swiftly, especially when they become desperate."

Roble moved his torch to his left hand and pulled his dagger.

"I should inform you," Odlon said. "The Ratkin are carriers of diseases and plagues. Avoid getting clawed or bitten."

Roble remembered their jagged teeth when they had snarled and tried to bite him. They didn't need steel weapons with those teeth. If they were plague-carriers as well, they were even more dangerous.

"Why would they take Shawndirea?" Roble asked.

"She possesses magic. She's powerful."

"Shouldn't they fear her then?"

"Possibly. But if she's inside a bag, she's no threat to them," Odlon said. "A lot of races will drain a faery of her power in order to gain favors for themselves."

"How?"

"A sorcerer can place a spell to tap a faery's magic. Some drain the blood and drink it."

Roble swallowed hard. His stomach became uneasy.

"But with these Ratkins, that's not the situation," Odlon said. "Since they abducted her in a thief's sanctuary, they want to sell her for gold."

"So they won't kill her?" Roble asked.

Odlon shook his head. "Not here. Not with us this close."

"They won't kill her to gain power?"

Odlon chuckled. "They don't have time to perform a ritual. Besides, none of them are mages. Since they're hiding inside this sewer, and it's obvious they are, they're trapped. No, they're trying to escape Glacier Ridge. As a last desperate move, they might offer her in exchange for their lives being spared."

"They'll die."

Roble sloshed forward with his torch ahead of them and watched the brownish water.

"Watch out!" Odlon shouted and pushed Roble to the wall.

In the torchlight, yellow teeth gnashed. A Ratkin leapt from the side of the wall. Roble's right shoulder struck the wall, and the lunging Ratkin ripped at Odlon. Odlon pressed his flaming torch against the Ratkin's throat and set its fur on fire. The beast howled in pain and buried its face in the nasty water to extinguish the flame. The stench of burnt hair rose with the smoke.

"Where'd it go?" Roble searched the tunnel with his torch.

"He swam off. He's injured, but he's not dead."

"Not yet, anyway."

"He doesn't have Shawndirea," Odlon said.

"How could you tell?"

"He didn't have any packs or bags with him. Most likely he's trying to distract and frighten us so his companion can escape with her."

Roble hurried into deeper water.

Odlon grabbed his arm. "Careful. You don't know how deep the water is."

"I can swim."

"Ratkin are better swimmers." Odlon held his torch over the water. "See?"

Dozens of rats swam through the water toward them.

"So? Those are regular rats, not Ratkin."

"These rats hold allegiance to the Ratkin. Often they do whatever the Ratkin request, and in this case, it's to attack."

The small, swimming rat swarm treaded the water and squeaked. They swam and gnashed their sharp teeth. Roble positioned his torch between him and the rats. The blazing torch singed a few rats. The rats parted and circled farther into the darkness. Their red eyes reflected in the torch's flame.

"Roble!" Lehrling shouted. "Over here!"

Odlon glanced at Roble. "Hurry."

Roble and Odlon sloshed through the water to reach the small opening Lehrling guarded. The water slowed their progress, but two shadowy figures struggled with Lehrling and knocked his torch in the water. The light vanished.

Roble moved faster than he thought possible, but when they reached the door, Lehrling lie on the slimy steps and partially through the door. Frantically, Lehrling tugged a Ratkin's leg.

The hairy Ratkin snarled and angrily jabbed at Lehrling's gloved hand.

"Let go!" it shrieked.

Once Roble reached shallower water, he ran to the opening. Lehrling gasped and groaned, but held the creature tighter.

"Hurry," Lehrling said.

Roble drew the sword, and although not proficient with it, he swung it hard and fast. The blade sliced an inch above Lehrling's hand and chopped the Ratkin's foot off. The sudden release sent Lehrling forward. Roble pushed around the heavy man and squeezed through the small opening.

The lit sconces flickered enough to brighten the room.

A pool of blood surrounded the severed foot. A heavy trail of dark blood lined the semi-frozen sludge on the permafrost floor. The Ratkin hobbled and turned to see Roble approach. Its voice rose in a strange shrill.

"No!" It said. "Let me free!"

Roble rushed across the cold floor, tossed his torch to the frozen floor, and flung a dagger. The knife buried into its right shoulder with enough force to spin the Ratkin forward and off balance. It dropped facedown, but turned and spun enough to catch itself with its left elbow.

In terror, its eyes widened. Blood streamed from its footless leg. Roble stood over the Ratkin and placed the tip of the sword to its throat.

"Where's the faery?" Roble asked.

"I not have," it said. It's long tongue hung from the side of its nasty, yellow-toothed mouth.

Roble glanced back. Odlon pulled Lehrling through the small hole. He faced the Ratkin again and pressed the blade harder against its throat. The Ratkin was losing a lot of blood. The other one was nowhere in sight. Roble wasn't certain the beast would live much longer. He needed to know where its partner had gone or where it planned to go.

Roble stepped on its bloody stump with enough force to stop the flowing blood. The abrupt pain forced the Ratkin to scream, but with the sword's tip pressed to its throat, it couldn't attack.

"Where is she?" Roble asked.

"Dirf has her."

Odlon and Lehrling stood beside Roble.

Lehrling said, "Both of them ran past me. I could only grab him."

Odlon aimed the crossbow at the Ratkin's good leg. "Where's Dirf?"

In a half chuckle, half pain-filled gasp, it said, "Gone. Gone."

"Where's he going?" Roble asked.

The Ratkin snarled. "I not telling."

Roble twisted his foot back and forth on its bloody stump.

It howled out. "That hurts!"

"It's supposed to." Roble pressed harder.

"I not tell!"

"You think more of your comrade than he does you," Odlon said.

The Ratkin turned and its rat-like ears twitched. "What you mean?"

"He's not concerned about your pain and suffering. He's not inter-ested in helping you at all. And yet, you're willing to let him escape and reap great wealth without you?"

"So?" it said. "Look at me. I no good to run anymore. Gold not do me good. Cannot buy new foot."

Roble pressed the side of the sword blade against the Ratkin's throat, trapping it against the wall. He grabbed a loose strand of its sleeve and ripped it off the soiled shirt. He handed it to Lehrling.

"Tie that around his leg tight enough to stop the bleeding," Roble said.

"Why?"

"Because I don't want him bleeding to death."

The Ratkin's eyes brightened with hope. "You save me to find Dirf?"

"No."

Curiosity overcame the Ratkin's expressions as it studied Roble. "You're bandaging my wound."

Roble's eyes narrowed and he smiled. "Oh, you're going to die. You need to decide whether it's going to be instant or *painfully* long."

The Ratkin's eyes grew wider with fear. Roble took the sword hilt in his left hand and drew another dagger with his left. The shining steel blade flashed in the glow of Odlon and Lehrling's torches.

Roble slowly moved the dagger to the Ratkin. Its whiskers twitched. It tried to crawl out of reach, but it was pressed against the wall.

"I doubt rat pelt is worth much," Roble said.

The Ratkin swallowed hard. His breathing increased.

"Where is she?" Roble asked again.

The Ratkin hesitated.

"Remember," Roble said, "Quick death or torture. Your only choices."

"He go to Icevale," he said. "Make it quick, please?"

Roble looked at Odlon questioningly.

Odlon smiled. "The valley north of Glacier Ridge. Not far."

Roble stepped back from the Ratkin.

Odlon said, "Allow me."

The elf fired a quick shot through its heart. Its body sagged in death.

"Let's get our horses," Lehrling said. "It's time we get to a better climate. I've had enough of Glacier Ridge for a lifetime."

Odlon nodded.

"How do we know the Ratkin was telling the truth?" Roble asked.

"We don't," Lehrling said. "But it's the best we'd get out of him anyway."

"Why's that?"

"Can you ever truly trust a thief?" Lehrling asked.

"Good point," Roble replied.

Odlon shrugged. "Sometimes you're left without a choice."

They headed to the steel door. Riese was lying facedown on the stairs. Roble hurried to Riese and turned him over. He was breathing regularly but unconscious. He couldn't see how the escaping Ratkin could've possibly beaten Riese in a one-on-one fight. He checked his head for lumps, but he didn't find anything unusual.

"He's out," Roble said.

Odlon pried open and examined Riese's eyes. "He's been gassed."

Roble shook his head. "I didn't figure the Ratkin could've taken Riese down."

"Nor you and I together," Odlon said with a wry smile.

"Let's get him to a table in the tavern."

Odlon and Lehrling braced under Riese's enormous size and helped Roble lay the giant across a tabletop. Riese groaned and tilted his head to the side.

"Look," Lehrling said, pointing.

The last Ratkin's head was on the floor. It must be the one that had Shawndirea.

Roble's heart sank. Riese was unconscious and the Ratkin was dead. Neither had her. Where was she?

At the tavern door stood a man Lehrling immediately recognized. "Crukas."

"You know him?" Roble asked.

"Crukas?" Odlon said. "He's the greatest thief of all time. He's known throughout Aetheaon."

"I have what the Ratkins stole from you," Crukas said. "Do a favor for me, and she's yours."

Odlon brought up the crossbow and aimed. Crukas vanished and appeared on the other side of the bar. "That's a nasty way to begin negotiations."

"How'd you know she was with me?" Roble asked.

Crukas tightened the knot braiding his long black hair and smiled. "I followed them outside the tavern after the *lovely* brawl Riese stirred up. I watched them for several hours. Those filthy beasts gnawed their way through the rooftop. After you slew some of them, I followed the two that fled. Of course, I stopped following after they scampered into the sewer wastes. I have to draw the line somewhere."

"What's this favor you ask?" Lehrling asked.

"I need protection to get through the forests on the outskirts of Ironwood," Crukas said.

"Where is she?" Roble ignored the request and placed his hands on his knives.

"She's safe."

"Where?"

Crukas smiled and waved him to the bar. "Come see."

Roble took a step.

Crukas said, "Hands off the knives."

Roble held his empty hands out before him and walked to the bar. Shawndirea was trapped inside a large glass jar. She glared at Crukas with fiery indignation.

"Why do you need protection to bypass Ironwood," Roble said. "Looks more like you need protection from *her*. She's ready to cause you great harm."

Crukas laughed. "Yes. She might, but she's not as mad as those in Ironwood are. I'm a *very* wanted man there."

Riese rolled to his side and groaned. He squinted and tried to focus, but apparently the lingering drug strongly affected his vision. He lowered his head and closed his eyes.

Roble said, "I'd fear what Riese will do to you once he awakens."

Crukas grinned and offered a slight nod. "Yes, that's a greater concern. I need to leave Glacier Ridge immediately."

"Release her, and we'll get you past Ironwood safely," Odlon said.

Crukas looked untrusting.

"It's the best offer you'll get," Odlon said. "You have some magical abilities, but eventually its use weakens your energy. Besides, I don't tire easily when it comes to shooting. I like a good hunting challenge. Moving targets are nice practice."

Crukas motioned his open hand flamboyantly to the bottle and stepped away. "She's yours. I thought getting her for you was worth a favor. Nothing more."

Roble opened the wide-mouthed bottle and helped Shawndirea out. She raised her hands and her fingertips glowed. Roble shook his head. "No."

"Give me a reason why I shouldn't," she said angrily through clenched teeth.

Roble pointed to the Ratkin's head on the floor. "Because *that* was the one who took you. Crukas decapitated him."

Shawndirea glared. *"He placed me in a bottle!"*

"I'm sorry," Roble said.

"He owes me an apology. Not you."

"I understand your anger. I'd be infuriated, too. The good thing is you're safe with me again," Roble said. "I was afraid I'd lost you."

Sadness came to her eyes. "I feared the same about you."

"How close is Ironwood to your home?"

She took a deep breath and slowly exhaled. After some of her anger subsided, she said, "It's on the way. We must pass through it."

"We'll return the favor since Crukas killed the Ratkin and rescued you. Otherwise, we'd have had to travel to Icevale and hope to find you."

"Fine," she said. With a slight frown, she huffed. "What is it with you humans putting faeries in bottles?"

Crukas gave Shawndirea an apologetic smile. "My humblest apologies for placing you in the bottle. But would you have immediately believed I wasn't your captor?"

"Probably not."

"So will you forgive my transgression?"

Shawndirea crossed her arms. "I'll think about it."

Crukas met Roble's gaze. "So you'll help me?"

Before Roble replied, Lehrling tapped his shoulder.

"May I talk to you for a moment, Roble?" Lehrling asked. "In private?"

Roble nodded. He turned and left Shawndirea eyeing Crukas. Roble followed Lehrling to a table at the far side of the tavern.

"What is it?" Roble asked.

"Riese."

Roble glanced at the giant bearded stable master. He remained sprawled across the table, deep in sleep.

"What about him?"

"If we leave with Crukas, you'll lose all favor with Riese."

"Why? What are you talking about?"

Lehrling coughed, beat his chest with his fist, and cleared his throat. His reply was barely above a whisper. "While you were talking to Odlon,

239

Riese and I talked. He dislikes Crukas a *lot*. Perhaps even *hates* him. We cannot aid this thief in *any* way."

"Riese despises Crukas?" Roble asked.

Lehrling nodded. "In so many words, yes. He's already warned Crukas to never return to Glacier Ridge but he came anyway. When the fights started with Lord Waxxon's men, Crukas vanished."

"Where'd he go?"

Lehrling shrugged. "Who knows? He's the most infamous thief and the most wanted."

"Hmm."

"Crukas might've taken the opportunity to pick the locks to the sewers. You saw him vanish and reappear. Who knows what else he might've taken during the distractions?"

"You think he worked with the Ratkin?"

"It's possible. His table was beside theirs."

Roble frowned. "Then why not use the Ratkin to get him past Ironwood."

"Those rat vagrants would immediately draw the attention of the town's border guards. He needs a group like us to blend in and not draw suspicion."

"But if he had befriended the Ratkin, why'd he kill this one?"

"To keep the blame off himself maybe? Once he got what he needed, there's no reason to keep them. Thieves cannot be trusted, and they certainly don't trust one another."

Roble asked, "So you think Riese's distaste for Crukas is linked to why Crukas needs to bypass Ironwood?"

"Most definitely. I'm certain they want his head worse than Riese. Otherwise, he wouldn't have been so bold to allow Riese to see him last night. And then, he gassed Riese with something in order to overpower him? Roble think seriously on this before pledging an oath to assist him."

"So you won't go?"

"I'll go to aid you in getting Shawndirea home," Lehrling said. "I owe you that much. But you might target a bounty on our heads from Riese because he'll definitely feel betrayed and believe we're aligned with Crukas."

Roble stared at the floor and shook his head. "We can't have that."

"Not a way to build a healthy relationship with townships, especially if you're going to be a member of the Dragon Skull Order."

Roble said, "You're right. I'm not a member of your knights, so it's best I swap for other clothes."

"No," Lehrling said. "Don't be hasty. I never meant to imply you're an imposter. We need you. You're a man of nobility and that's rare in these lands."

Roble smiled. "I'm not a swordsman. I know which end to hold, but I'm not trained."

"I'll train you. I'm certain Odlon will, too."

"What makes you think I'm worthy to be one of your knights?"

"A lesser man would have left me to die," Lehrling said with a weak smile. His eyes grew misty. "Not you. You risked your life even though you had no idea what kind of person I am."

"Maybe I like to go against the odds."

"Aye, I know better than that."

"Okay, so what do I do now?" Roble asked. "I've sort of promised I'd help Crukas."

"We trick him and turn him over to Riese."

"Are you saying a man of nobility shouldn't keep his word?"

"Do you consider lying to a thief a great offense?"

Roble shook his head. "Well, no."

"Nor do I. After all, can you truly trust him?"

"Probably not."

"According to Riese, Crukas comes to Glacier Ridge to find thieves with high bounties, befriends them, and then he turns them over to authorities in neighboring towns and villages for the rewards."

"Really?"

"Aye."

"Never trust a thief," Roble said. "If I must be dishonest with him, I aim to make him believe my lies. Riese has done too much for us. I cannot ever make him think I'd double-cross him."

Lehrling grinned. "Since Crukas needs protection, it'll be easier to convince him he needs us than it is for us to believe anything he says."

"How long do you think Riese will be out?"

"Depends on what Crukas used."

Roble frowned. "Anything you know that could awaken him?"

"There are things I could try."

"Good. We'll leave you here with Riese and while we head to the stables, see if you can awaken him. Tell him where we are with Crukas."

Lehrling ran his hand through his beard and nodded. "Sure."

"I guess we should get started."

"Indeed," Lehrling said.

Roble approached Crukas. "What'd you use to knock Riese unconscious?"

"A mild vapor I've learned to concoct from a wizard."

"How long does its effect last?"

Crukas shrugged. "Not long, which is why we should hurry."

"Do you have an antidote?" Roble asked.

Odlon came closer with the crossbow trained on the thief.

"Sure, but if you give it to him, he'll kill me."

"Leave the antidote with Lehrling while we go to the stables."

Crukas looked startled. "Why should I do that?"

"Do you want our assistance or not?" Roble asked.

"Yes."

"Then leave the antidote with him. I'll explain on the way."

Crukas lifted a small corked vial filled with pale yellow liquid. He hesitated before he finally handed it to Lehrling.

CHAPTER 31

Outside Hobskin's Tavern, Odlon and Roble escorted Crukas to the stables. Shawndirea rested in Roble's shirt pocket where she was shielded from the harsh wind. The dark, gray sky made Roble wonder if the sun was ever visible in Glacier Ridge.

Roble and Odlon kept their torches, even though the morning had come. The wind flickered the flames.

"Crukas, that's the deal," Roble said.

Crukas shook his head. "You want me to *pretend* you're shackling me to turn me over to the officials at Ironwood?"

"Yes."

"Why should I do something so foolish?" Crukas said. "No one has *ever* had me in cuffs. With the reward on my head, the lot of you could be killed by bounty hunters already searching for me."

"Riese has been hospitable to us. We need to leave Glacier Ridge in good favor with him, especially after you drugged him."

"He won't know any better," Crukas said. "He didn't see me use it."

"His sons have our horses. They'll tell him. When they do, he'll send people after us. Possibly to kill us. I gather he's not fond of you anyway."

Crukas laughed. "No town leader ever is."

"Thieves' reputations aren't stellar, and since you're known border to border," Odlon said, "what do you expect?"

"I'm used to it. Trust isn't something I expect anyone to offer, which is why I scoff at your request."

"Let's put it this way," Roble said. "If you don't, by the time our horses are saddled and ready to go, Lehrling will be here with Riese. Riese's view toward you will be less hostile if he believes we're taking you to Ironwood than if you're not shackled."

Crukas remained silent and pondered the information for a few moments. Finally, he surrendered a sigh. "You'll remove the shackles after we've left Glacier Ridge?"

Roble nodded. "You have my word."

Crukas studied Roble's eyes. "Either you're an efficient liar, or you're the most honest person I've met."

"I realize you're taking a risk to trust me," Roble said.

"You've no idea. I seldom trust anyone, including myself."

At the stables, Roble hammered the closed door several times with his fist. After a minute, one of Riese's sons unlatched the inner lock bar and pulled it ajar.

"We're back for our horses," Odlon said.

The young man widened the door and looked out. "Where's my father?"

"With Lehrling at Hobskin's Tavern. They're on their way."

The young man nodded and opened the door wider. After everyone was indoors, he shut the door but didn't put the steel lock bar in place.

"We need a set of shackles," Roble said.

Riese's son frowned.

Odlon stood behind Crukas with the crossbow aimed at the thief's back.

Crukas played along and in rich proper accent, he said, "They're taking me to Ironwood to collect my bounty."

"Father has shackles over there," he replied, pointing at the wall where other odd and end tools rested.

Roble looked at the different sets of shackles and located one to hold Crukas securely without being too tight. He took these and returned to Crukas. Crukas reluctantly held out his hands. He stared intently into Roble's eyes, apparently studying Roble to discern a lie. Roble gave a slight nod and placed cuffs around Crukas' wrists. He tightened and locked them in place. The metal was heavy enough to lower Crukas' arms to his waist.

Crukas checked the strength of the shackles and became apprehensive.

"You vow to remove these once we get out of Glacier Ridge?" Crukas whispered.

Roble nodded. "Yes."

"I'll hold you to your word," Crukas said.

The stable door opened. A gush of bitter cold wind flowed through. Riese staggered through the door with Lehrling trying to support the near giant's weight. Roble shoved the door closed after they entered.

Riese's eyes were bloodshot and his face was beet red. Riese's anger shaded his face more than the harsh winter wind.

"Where is he?" Riese looked around until he located Crukas. Riese stormed across the stable floor and towered over the skinny thief. Riese's muscled hands wrapped around Crukas' throat, and he lifted him three feet in the air.

"Easy, Riese," Roble said. "He's shackled. He'll pay for his crimes and trespasses against you."

"How's that?" Riese asked.

"Lehrling didn't tell you?"

"Oh, he mumbled a lot of things I couldn't understand due to the wind and my throbbing head."

"We're taking Crukas to Ironwood and turning him in for the reward."

Riese chuckled and lowered Crukas to the floor. "I'll do you one better. *I'll* escort you to Ironwood myself."

Roble shook his head. "That's not necessary."

"I insist," Riese said. "I want to watch him dangle from the tree branch when he's hanged."

"You've no need to leave Glacier Ridge," Roble said.

"Either I witness his hanging or I gut him here and now," Riese said in a low, angry voice.

Chills ran down Roble's back and arms. The darkness in Riese's eyes revealed how intent he was to ensure Crukas died one way or the other. No mercy tinged his voice. No compassion softened his eyes.

Riese leveled his glare at Roble. "Which shall it be?"

"Ironwood." Roble hoped to buy enough time to keep his promise to Crukas. He turned and walked away.

Roble whispered to Lehrling in passing. "Damn."

Riese turned to his sons. "Marc! Jez! Hook up the wagon and lower an iron cage on the back."

"Yes, father."

Riese eyed Crukas. "I warned you never to return. Did I not?"

Crukas looked to the floor. His eyes revealed his sense of betrayal. "Yes."

"Yet, you defied my command."

"Yes."

"Any regrets?" Riese asked.

Crukas nodded and glanced at Roble. "More with each passing minute."

A HALF HOUR passed while Riese's sons saddled the horses for Odlon, Roble, and Lehrling. They rolled out an old, flatbed wagon and hitched two of Waxxon's massive horses to wagon's tongue. Riese slid a crate of smoked meat and jerky beneath the wagon seat. Marc placed a small keg of ale next to the crate.

Riese turned and smiled at Roble. "It's a long trip."

Marc and Jez lowered a large iron cage on the wagon bed. The cage was a long cylinder. It was barely tall and wide enough for Crukas to fit inside. The iron bands were far enough apart to keep Crukas vulnerable to the freezing, assaulting winds. The bands were too close together for someone as thin and agile as Crukas to squeeze through and escape. Odd symbols were welded on the iron bands.

"Isn't this a bit extreme for transport?" Roble asked.

"Not at all," Riese replied. "Exactly how'd *you* plan to carry him?"

Roble shrugged. "Put him in shackles and tether his horse behind us."

Riese chuckled. "For a thief who can vanish into thin air? That'd never have worked. You would've lost him once you reached the ice forest above Glacier Ridge."

"But isn't the cage excessive?"

"No. It's taking precautions." He placed his massive hand on Crukas' shoulder and forced the thief inside the narrow cage.

"Precautions?" Roble asked.

Riese slammed the iron cage door shut and locked it. "Iron neutralizes Crukas' magic. These runic symbols are an added assurance he cannot somehow bypass the metal cage with any spells. The runes counteract his incantations."

Crukas looked disgruntled and a bit worried. Not only was he caged, his hands remained shackled.

"Riese," Roble said. "You don't need to trouble yourself by accompanying us to Ironwood."

Riese frowned harsh and long at Roble. He seemed to dare Roble to question his motives again.

Roble nodded and stepped away.

Riese climbed on the driver seat and grabbed the reins. "We leave for Ironwood."

Marc opened the stable doors. Riese snapped the whip. The horses pulled the wagon from the heated stable into the blowing snow and cutting wind. Crukas stared at Roble with pleading eyes. Roble shrugged and winced with regret.

Lehrling brought a bay gelding to Roble and handed Roble the reins. "This was Bausch's horse. He's young and strong. Should make a great mount for you. Even if you decide not to help us find Lady Dawn, keep the horse. His name's Bleys."

"Thanks," Roble said.

Lehrling's eyes moistened with tears. He turned and got on his pale mare.

"Bleys." Roble looked at the horse's dark eyes. Shawndirea stretched her hands out and rubbed the white star patch on the horse's forehead. She giggled and kissed Bleys. The horse softly snorted.

"Best hurry, Roble," Odlon said. "Riese isn't waiting for us."

Roble swung on Bleys and glanced at Lehrling. "Lehrling, I didn't expect Riese to accompany us."

Lehrling laughed and shrugged. "Nor I. Hard justice comes in strange ways. I warned you about Riese's distaste for Crukas."

Roble nodded. "Worse than I imagined."

Odlon rode to the stable door and stopped. An emerald green shield, made from a large dragon scale, was strapped to the side of his saddle. On the outer side of the shield were sharpened spikes made from small dragon teeth.

Roble was intrigued, if not totally impressed, by how Odlon fashioned his armor and shield from the dragon that cursed him with non-healing blisters. Even though the dragon had attempted to kill Odlon, the elf was the victor. His armor and shield displayed his triumph.

Odlon addressed Lehrling and Roble. "What happens to a thief that should concern us, except he can no longer steal if the noose is his fate?"

"True, elf," Lehrling said. "But more dangers lurk in the dark forests. Especially if Crukas has partners lying in wait."

"Why would he?" Roble asked.

"Do you really believe he alone could bring several other thieves to collect bounties by himself?" Lehrling asked.

"I never really thought about it."

"Neither has Riese. It's best we keep our senses keen."

Odlon nodded. "You're right.

The three rode their horses into the frigid wind while heavy snow swirled around them. Jez and Marc closed the heavy stable doors. Heading up the slope leading out of Glacier Ridge, Riese cracked his whip. The two horses' hooves crunched through layers of hard, icy snow and gained traction to pull the heavy wagon uphill.

Shawndirea rested her folded arms on the rim of Roble's shirt pocket. With her hood pulled over her head, she seemed content watching the windblown snow filter through the leafless trees. Her eyes sparkled, and her smile never faded.

Roble chuckled. "You act as though you've never seen snow."

She looked at him. "I haven't. Well, nothing like this."

"What do you think?"

"It's beautiful and deadly."

"Deadly?" he asked.

She nodded. "Winter *is* death. The final season before spring renews life."

"Many view winter with symbolism. It's a postponement until the spring thaw," Roble said.

"Not here," she said softly. "Glacier Ridge knows no spring. Death always lingers over this ridge."

"What do you make of the ghost or banshee we saw on our way to Glacier Ridge? No one died."

"No one we *know* died," she replied. "Someone in the forest may have. Because we didn't witness it, doesn't mean it didn't happen."

"Should we be concerned?"

"You didn't hear her, so her cry wasn't for you."

Roble nodded. "I know. But something at the tavern still bothers me."

"What?" she asked.

"The barmaid serving our table looked exactly like the ghost."

"You noticed, too?" Lehrling rode up beside him.

"Yes."

Lehrling coughed violently and pounded his chest with his fist.

"Are you okay?" Roble asked. "Perhaps we should find a physician and have you checked."

Lehrling shook his head while coughing. Once he cleared the phlegm, he spat on the frozen ground. "It's the winter air. Makes it hard to breathe."

"It sounds worse than that," Roble replied.

"I'll be fine. Just an old man who can't handle the extreme weather elements anymore."

"So you noticed the barmaid resembled the ghost?" Roble asked. Although he and Lehrling had exchanged nervous glances about the barmaid's familiarity in the tavern, they never had a chance to discuss it.

"Yes. Worrisome, but she was still alive after the raucous fight," Lehrling replied. "She huddled behind the bar with the nervous barkeep."

Shawndirea's brow furrowed. "Then her death has yet to come. She'll probably die soon. I feel uneasy."

"Why?"

"The forest seems stranger this morning than when we first arrived."

"You indicated others might be in the forest," Roble said.

She nodded. "Travelers, mainly thieves and bondsmen, use this frozen path quite often. Waxxon's men did. So are we."

Roble glanced at the wagon as he, Lehrling, and Odlon rode closer. Crukas stood in the tight cage. His dark eyes bore into Roble's with an expression that declared he'd been betrayed. Even if Roble rode closer, Riese was too close for Roble to explain to Crukas that he never planned for Riese to escort them to Ironwood. He doubted Crukas would believe any explanation he offered.

Roble leaned closer to Lehrling and Odlon. "I gave him my word. I must honor it."

"Crukas is a con artist," Odlon said. "No matter what you promised, you need to understand. If the situation were reversed, he wouldn't bat an eye to betray you or us for better gain."

Roble clenched his jaw. "What do you think, Shawndirea?"

"He speaks the truth. A master thief's almost incapable of telling the truth. Their promises often are worthless."

"And Crukas'?"

"You cannot be a master of thieves and an honest person."

"You're right about that. But what if Odlon's correct?" Roble asked. "Crukas might have a group hiding in the forest to attack us."

She pursed her lips. "Be prepared to fight. Should any of his friends be waiting, it'll be difficult to hear their approach over the horses and wagon wheels. At least, it isn't totally dark."

"The clouds darken the forest."

"Yes, so watch for moving shadows."

The metal wagon wheels creaked and crunched the frozen road. The wind whistled and whipped through the icy-barked trees. The treetops were dark against the gray sky, and white fog billowed with frozen ice crystals. Locating shadows was nearly impossible. Roble shivered, more from nervousness than the cold. What hid within the fog and amongst the trees?

Shawndirea's uneasiness became his own. She was right. Hearing slight noises off the frozen path was also impossible. The wagon creaked loudly and gave away their presence to anyone or anything lying in wait.

They rounded the bend, and the road became more difficult to see. A heavy white veil of fog hung across their path. Roble looked from person to person. Odlon and Lehrling frowned while searching the area. They appeared on edge.

The horses backed their ears. Their eyes widened. The two horses pulling the wagon whinnied and reared slightly. Riese cracked the whip overhead, and they pulled forward. Their eyes remained wide. They flared their nostrils. Although frightened, they were more fearful of Riese than what was in the fog.

Riese stood at the front of the wagon and pulled back the reins. The horses stopped. They restlessly stepped side-to-side, bucked, and reared.

"Easy!" Riese commanded. He turned and motioned Roble and the others to stop. They stopped their horses on the frozen road.

Other than the horses panting and their nervous snorting, nothing else could be heard. At first. The wind abruptly calmed. In the swollen veil of fog, a large shadow appeared. Vague and shapeless. A constant creaking of ungreased hinges squeaked closer. The nearer the dark object came, the less obscured the fog made it.

A black carriage approached. Riese sat on his wagon seat, gripped his large hammer, and waited for the fog to peel away. The blackest horses Roble had ever seen pulled the carriage. Their dark eyes were odd with a fiery, red glow encircling them. The driver wore tattered black robes with a hood drooping over his brow. He had no facial hair, not even where his eyebrows should be.

The carriage slowed when it reached the side of Riese's wagon. The driver pulled back the reins and glanced at Riese. Shawndirea ducked deep inside Roble's pocket and hid. The sight of the man caused Roble to hold his breath and his hands tightened around Bleys' reins.

The driver stooped forward. He tightened the reins and tied them to the side of his seat. When he straightened, the hood eased back to reveal his face. The old man had paper-thin skin, dark large eyes, and narrow lips. His pale complexion held a slight blue tint, and he resembled a corpse.

"Ah, travelers," he said with a feeble voice. His thin lips barely moved while he spoke. "Where might the nearest town be?"

"Who are you?" Riese asked. His jaw tightened and his brow creased with an intent frown.

"I'm a weary old man in need of some food, strong drinks, and a warm place to stay for several days." Puffs of frosty breath drifted from his mouth. His withered, boney hands shook from the cold.

Riese rose and glanced at the back of the man's carriage. The windows were black with tattered cloth rolled down the outside of the glass.

"How many ride with you?" Riese asked with narrowed eyes.

"Only I."

Riese climbed down from the wagon with his hammer held tight. "Who are you? *What*'s your name?"

"Mors," he replied.

"Where's your homeland?" Riese asked.

"I drift from town to town and have done so my entire life."

"Mind if I check the carriage?" Riese asked.

"Help yourself," Mors replied with a crooked grin. Most of his teeth were missing, but the remaining ones were black and broken.

Roble slid his hand on his dagger, and Odlon's hands tightened on his crossbow. Riese walked to the side of the carriage and pulled the passenger door open. He leaned his head inside the compartment and looked around. A few seconds later, he shut the carriage door. He returned to the driver.

"See?" Mors said in a raspy, tired tone. He hugged himself and shivered. "I travel alone."

Riese nodded. "Follow the road. It dead ends in Glacier Ridge. There are taverns, inns, and a stable. I'm sure you'll find whatever you need."

Mors smiled. "Oh, I'm certain I will. Thank you. I was beginning to believe I'd die my death of cold out here. You've been most helpful."

Riese gave a slight nod and climbed on his wagon. Crukas looked at Roble and lifted his shackled hands while pleading with his eyes. All Roble could do was nod.

"Hope your journey's a prosperous one," Mors said to Riese. He untied the reins and snapped them across the black horses' backs. They jerked forward. Black smoke puffed from their nostrils.

Roble watched Mors' face as he rode past. His bulging eyes and eerie smile sent a chill through Roble.

The carriage rocked and creaked down the frozen road. When Roble glanced over his shoulder, the carriage vanished into the foggy mist and silenced.

"Onward," Riese said, snapping the whip.

Odlon slid the crossbow into a compartment on the side of his saddle.

Lehrling shook his head. "That's about the strangest sight ever."

"Why's that?" Roble asked.

"Why have a carriage with no passengers?"

Roble shrugged. "It's odd, but not the strangest thing I've seen."

Lehrling chuckled. "What's the strangest thing you've seen?"

"You wouldn't believe me if I told you," Roble replied.

CHAPTER 32

*A*n hour passed without anyone attacking them. Crukas didn't have a band of thieves. He was alone. And now, Crukas seemed destined to hang. Roble struggled with the thought because, even though Crukas wasn't an honest man, Roble had promised to help him. Instead, he was escorting the man to his death. Perhaps it was justice for some, but Roble didn't like the idea of Crukas dying and feeling complete betrayal. The thief had actually rescued Shawndirea. Had Crukas not intervened, Shawndirea would've been lost to Roble forever. The Ratkin could've taken her anywhere.

Farther down the road, the path was partially thawed. Slushy puddles and sticky mud lined the road. They entered a warmer climate. Yet, the fog became thicker. At least it *looked* like fog. Figures moved within the white haze, and Roble recognized them to be ghosts.

One spirit drifted to the side of the wagon and hovered alongside Riese. He yanked the reins. "Curses to the gods!"

In a panicked voice, a ghost said, "Father! Help us!"

Riese jumped from the wagon, unharnessed one of the massive horses, and climbed on it bareback. He tossed keys to Roble, kicked the horse's flanks, and galloped toward Glacier Ridge.

They sat on their horses and watched Riese ride furiously away. Dozens of ghosts appeared in the fog. Stunned, Roble recognized a lot of them. The barkeep, Riese's son Jez, and the barmaid the banshee had warned about. They were all drifting spirits. All dead.

"Should we help him?" Roble asked.

Odlon turned and was ready to head after Riese, but Crukas said, "No. There's no need."

Odlon frowned and looked at Crukas. "Why not?"

"The man on the carriage, Mors," Crukas said. "He's the Plague-bringer. Where he arrives, death follows."

"Why didn't you warn us?" Roble said.

Crukas shrugged and lifted his shackled hands. "Why should I? You betrayed me. Riese was delivering me to my death. I figure justice is served."

Angered, Roble said, "Riese's sons were innocent. You're a known thief!"

Crukas laughed. "They're not as innocent as you think. The entire town was filled with deceptive people."

Lehrling dismounted and marched to the wagon. His hands were balled into fists. "Seems you're only trying to eliminate your competition in any way possible."

Crukas grinned. "Such things are trivial. Besides, I didn't summon the Plague-bringer. He came on his own."

"But you knew who he is," Roble said.

"Their deaths aren't my fault. The Plague-bringer chooses his victims. Not all die when he appears."

"As badly as you wanted to flee Glacier Ridge," Roble said, "You seemed to have forewarning Mors *was* coming."

Crukas looked away. He shook his head back and forth to adjust his long black ponytail.

"Do you deny that?" Odlon asked Crukas.

"Yes. No mortal summons Mors. Besides, confronting him in any manner is instant death. You leaving Glacier Ridge with me as your prisoner is what spared your lives. Since Riese left, stick to our deal and release me from these shackles," Crukas said.

Roble climbed off Bleys and led the horse to the front of the wagon.

"What are you doing?" Crukas asked. "He gave you the keys. One of them unlocks this cage. So free me."

Roble shook his head. "Thievery I can handle, so long as it isn't me being robbed. However, you allowed Glacier Ridge's townspeople to die without giving Riese a chance to defend his own. You'll face whatever punishment Ironwood orders."

"Again, I had no foreknowledge of Mors' arrival." Crukas' tanned face paled with slight worry. "Please. I beg you to reconsider."

"I imagine so. But no, justice will be served. I'll drive the wagon to Ironwood to make certain your death's carried out."

Roble backed his horse to the wagon hitch. Lehrling helped fasten Bleys in place. Shawndirea climbed on Bleys' back and stretched out. She rubbed the horse's back with her hands. Once the horse was fastened alongside the larger horse, she stepped on Roble's shoulder.

Roble climbed on the wagon bench and looked at Lehrling. "Do you believe it's useless to help Riese?"

Lehrling nodded. "You witnessed the ghosts. There's nothing we can do."

"I'd almost rather take Crukas to Glacier Ridge and let Riese get his revenge."

Odlon shook his head. "No. If we return, we expose ourselves to whatever killed the townspeople. We continue to Ironwood."

"Agreed," Lehrling said.

Roble nodded, turned, and cracked the whip. The horses tugged forward and headed along the thawing road. At the bottom of the steep decline, sunlight brightened the path. The glare was almost blinding. Meadows came into view. The grass was brown, and the earth was muddy.

Riese held a handful of the horse's mane as he rode the large, thundering beast down the frozen path into Glacier Ridge. He gripped the heavy hammer in his right and looked for the wagon and its driver. He didn't see him or the carriage. But the carnage the withered, pale man left behind struck Riese's soul.

Several bodies lie on the street. Some slumped over rock fence posts. A dozen more were lifeless on the frozen, marketplace cobblestone. He kicked the horse's flanks and rode to the stable. His heart raced harder than the horse beneath him. His was from fear of what he'd find in his homestead.

He recognized Jez's spectral face and voice. What happened? Where'd the old man go?

A stable door was partway open. Riese swung off the panting horse. He hurried to the door and peered through the crack. No movement or dead bodies. Pulling the heavy door open, he entered and peered around.

Although probably useless, he called out for his sons. "Jez! Marc!"

His voice echoed throughout the forge room. No one replied. A metal object clanged on the floor from the other side of the heated forge. Riese's eyes narrowed. He cautiously stepped closer. Easing around the side of the forge, the movement of a shadow crossed from the tool bench to the anvil. Riese readied his hammer and brought it back to swing.

The figure stepped into the glow of the burning coals. He turned and faced Riese. In surprise, Riese lowered the hammer. His jaws tightened. He tried to swallow the lump rising in his throat.

"Jez?" Riese said, shaking his head.

Jez's eyes held a hollow, unblinking stare. His disfigured face was covered with swollen pocks of green pus. Buzzing flies swarmed around his son's head, in spite of the frigid cold.

"No," Riese said. "The gods be cursed! No!"

Jez hobbled at him. His mouth moved in biting movements. Strange groaning sounds escaped his lips, but no hint of words or recognition set in his son's eyes. Patches of skin flaked and peeled from Jez's face, arms, and hands. Black spots mottled his exposed flesh.

Riese brought the hammer back, reluctant to swing a deathblow, but at the same time, he realized his son was already dead. His body was controlled by another source or a curse. His son's voice had spoken to him in the frozen forest above Glacier Ridge. Jez's living corpse eased closer. Riese backed away and struggled against the thought of striking him.

"Forgive me, Jez," Riese said, with tears in his angered eyes.

Riese brought the hammer back, closed his eyes, and swung with all his strength. The blow crushed the left side of the corpse's face and pivoted the undead Jez backward. His lifeless body dropped to the floor. Though lifeless, the body didn't cease movement. Mors, Riese reasoned, wasn't a feeble old man. He was a necromancer.

Jez stirred and struggled to stand. He was undead.

With hot tears in Riese's eyes, anger flushed through him. He took Jez by the boots and dragged his body to the front of the forge. Careful not to touch any exposed, diseased skin, he tossed his son's living corpse through the fiery forge door.

Riese dropped to his knees and wailed. He shook his muscular fists at the ceiling and cursed. Furious, he stood and grabbed the hammer.

After he expelled his pent up anger and remorse, he wondered where Marc was. He searched all the rooms surrounding the forge. When he didn't find Marc, he went upstairs and checked each room. Nothing indicated Marc was alive.

He ran downstairs, opened the stable door, and rushed to the center of the marketplace.

"Where are you, old man?" Riese shouted. The question echoed throughout Glacier Ridge but no reply came.

Pellets of ice and large flakes of snow swirled around Riese. Steam rose from his body. He gripped the hammer tightly and went door to door looking for the wagon rider.

When he opened Hobskin's Tavern, the mass movement inside the bar shocked him. All the patrons were like Jez. Walking diseased corpses. They headed blindly toward the door. Riese yanked the door shut. He didn't wait to see if they could open the door. He ran through the cavern mouth into the marketplace. He searched for the carriage's tracks, but found none.

A small, dark creature darted from the side of the building across the path from Hobskin's Tavern. It moved swiftly. Its eyes glowed yellow. In seconds, it sought the dark shadowed areas behind the buildings, and Riese hurried after it. He'd never seen anything like it before, but it had to be a product of Mors. Perhaps by following the creature, he'd find the man who infested his town with disease and death.

When Riese crossed the icy path and stepped to the side of the building, the creature was gone. Old wooden crates and a couple of empty wine barrels was all he found. He moved crates aside and looked for the imp. Instead, he found a small hole into the building's cellar. Dropping to his knees, he peered through the hole. Without a torch or lantern, he didn't see anything. Even with a source of light, the hole was too small to put his head through. He almost turned to leave when a muffled voice struggled to cry out. Someone was gagged and fighting to break free and shout.

"Help," the strained voice finally said.

"Who is it?" Riese asked.

Then the voice returned to being nothing more wordless, stifled grunts and moans. The person's mouth was bound again.

Riese looked at the dark crevice in the cellar wall. The opening was large enough for the little imp to easily pass through. He didn't have time to find a torch and return. With disease consuming his town, the person in the cellar needed his help.

He swung his hammer against the rock foundation. The rock chipped and crumbled. He struck again and again. More chunks of stone broke free and the opening became larger. The whipping wind spiraled along the narrow alleyway and whistled through the cellar hole. The creatures hidden inside, stirred to life.

Hisses and wild chattering noises echoed in the dark cellar. His attention focused on discovering who was being held hostage. Riese hammered more rock and mortar from the foundation until a large section of the wall collapsed inward. The sounds in the cellars became more agitated, so Riese stepped back.

A black imp rushed through the large hole and lunged at Riese. Its high-pitched squeal rose into a fevered howl. It chattered and revealed its yellow teeth and fangs. It charged Riese fearlessly. Sharp claws lined its small fingers. It slashed at Riese's legs as he moved back and to the side.

Riese brought the hammer down to strike, but the nimble imp leapt backwards. The hammer struck the icy cobblestone and blasted chunks of rock and ice in the air like tiny pellets, which showered down around the hammer's head.

The imp bore its teeth, froth bubbled at the side of its mouth, and it charged again. Its rapid movement made it difficult to smash. Before

Riese lifted the hammer again, two more black imps emerged from the cellar.

"Father!" the voice in the cellar cried.

"Marc?"

"Help!"

Determination to save his surviving son surged through him. The town was doomed to whatever pestilence the old man had released. Perhaps Mors had summoned the imps, too. Whatever grip Death held over Glacier Ridge was more than Riese could fight alone. If he rescued his son, he wouldn't leave his town empty-handed.

The three imps separated and sought to encircle Riese. Once he noticed their intention, he edged his back against the wall. The imps leapt at him. He kicked the closest one. His boot caught its midsection and slung it through the air. It soared across the alley and struck a wall. He grabbed the next imp around the throat and squeezed until its eyes bulged and bones cracked in its neck. He tossed its lifeless body on the cobblestone and raised his hammer.

The third imp snarled with green spittle dripping from its mouth. Eying the hammer in Riese's hands, it backed out of range. The imp that struck the wall staggered toward Riese but with less enthusiasm.

"Come on!" Riese swung the hammer side to side in front of himself.

The imps narrowed their eyes and hissed.

"You filthy beasts! I'll kill all of you!"

Riese charged with his hammer and struck the weaker one in the head. It reeled in pain, spiraled around in the air, and landed facedown on the cold cobblestone. Riese jumped and planted his feet into the center of its back. Bones cracked and its insides squished out like a smashed grape.

He kept the dead imp pinned beneath his feet and swung the hammer around. The imp dodged the blow, kicked off the wall, and sprang in the air. It landed on Riese's chest and scrambled to bite his throat. Riese grabbed its feet, slammed its head against the street, and cracked its skull.

After the three were dead, he rushed to find Marc. Before he reached the hole in the cellar wall, an imp's head rolled out onto the cobblestone. Its eyes were wide in death, and its black tongue hung to the side.

Seconds later, Marc pulled himself through the hole and stood in the alleyway. He suffered bite marks on his hands and forearms. Other than appearing haggard, he seemed okay.

Riese asked, "Was that all of them?"

Marc nodded.

Riese embraced his son tightly.

"Jez didn't make it," Marc said softly, pulling away from his father's hold. "He was overcome by disease."

"I know," Riese replied. "Did you see the old man in a black carriage?"

Marc nodded.

"Where'd he go?"

"I'm not certain. He parked in the marketplace. Jez noticed his arrival and went to see if he needed to stable his horses," Marc said. He looked at the ground and wiped his eyes.

"What happened?"

Marc took a deep breath, closed his eyes. When he opened them, his son was no longer a young man. What he'd witnessed had stolen his innocence and forced him to be a man.

"It's okay," Riese said. "You need to tell me. We'll find and kill this man."

"That won't be easy."

"Why?"

"He and the carriage vanished not long after he handed Jez the burlap sack."

"What was in the bag?" Riese asked.

Marc swallowed hard. "The old man asked Jez if what was in the bag was payment enough. Jez opened the bag and a swarm of strange buzzing insects flew out. Some were dark flies. They flew in a greenish dust-like cloud. Others were beetles. Jez tried to close the bag, but the flies covered his face. He dropped the bag and swatted at the attacking flies. Scuttling beetles covered the ground by the hundreds. It had to be dark magic. The small bag couldn't have held that many insects. Even the flies on his face increased in number."

"Did you not help your brother?"

"I tried, but by the time I reached him, he turned and his face was covered with hideous sores with yellow pus oozing from them. He didn't respond to me. I pulled my sword and tried to get to the carriage driver, but he and the black carriage vanished."

Tears moistened Riese's eyes. "How'd you escape the swarm?"

"I ran to the stables. The flies came for me, but I reached the forge and pumped the bellows until the heat increased. When the flies neared, I stood as close to the flames as possible. The heat was too much for them. Hundreds of them dropped dead on the floor. The remainder of the swarm retreated from the stables. I don't know where they went."

"Hobskin's Tavern is filled with walking corpses."

Marc nodded. "I discovered that, too, which is how I ended up in the cellar. I went inside the main door. I barricaded it, but some of the townspeople beat against the door, so I ran to the cellar hoping I'd be safe. But, those imps were waiting down there.

"At first, I didn't see them. I heard you calling out, so I tried to go upstairs, but they attacked me."

Riese placed his hand on Marc's shoulder and squeezed. "You're safe now."

Marc looked from the alley at Hobskin's Tavern.

"You said some of the townspeople tried to get through the front of this building?" Riese asked.

Marc gave a slight nod while still watching the front of Hobskin's Tavern.

"Where'd they go?" Riese asked.

Marc's face paled. He raised his right hand and pointed. Riese turned. A dozen disease-ridden corpses staggered toward them. He and Marc couldn't get around them. Riese only had his hammer. Marc held his dagger. The undead townspeople marched forward. They blocked Riese and his son between the two buildings and cornered them against the ridge wall.

Riese looked at his son. "Be brave, even until the end."

CHAPTER 33

Queen Istrell placed her weary hands on the crystals to summon their power. A faint glow emitted from the stones, momentarily, but she failed to attain their full power. Her mirror remained dark. No matter how much she focused, no clear picture revealed Shawndirea's location. When she last saw Shawndirea, her daughter was in a frigid climate. The closest region with such icy temperatures was Glacier Ridge.

"Why?" she asked aloud. "Why would you venture there? No faery can withstand such frozen conditions."

After the human clothed her in the black cloth, Shawndirea was veiled beneath a different kind of magic.

"What did the human do?" She held the crystals tighter and hoped to learn Shawndirea's welfare. Instead, the crystals grew cold and no longer responded to her touch.

Frustrated, Istrell said, "I warned you about humans. As always, you stubbornly ignored my counsels."

Istrell left the small room and glided down the winding path until she reached the throne room. She plopped on her throne and released a long sigh. She covered her eyes with her right hand and tried not to cry.

"Your Highness," a dainty faery servant whispered.

Istrell opened weary eyes. "Yes, Feather?"

"I brought you honey wine," Feather said.

"You're always a dear one." Istrell patted Feather's hand and gave a tired smile.

Feather's black hair was long and curled. Her bright blue eyes sparkled like rare sapphires. Her flowing, pink gown matched the pinkish tint of her delicate wings.

Feather handed Istrell the golden goblet of wine, curtseyed, and glided backwards in respect of the throne. "What troubles my queen?"

Istrell downed the strong wine in one quick gulp. She set the goblet down. "Shawndirea."

Feather's eyes widened and she refilled the goblet. "Is she missing again?"

"Has such news roamed my kingdom?"

Istrell drank half the wine, licked her lips, and narrowed her eyes to focus on Feather.

Feather tucked her chin to her chest, looked at the floor, and shook her head. "No, Your Highness. But it seems a pattern with her."

"Yes." Istrell finished the wine, set down the goblet, and stood. With a slight woozy sway, she gripped the throne arm tightly. Once balanced, she staggered a step forward. "One builds hope in her heir to be the greatest queen this kingdom has ever had, and yet, Shawndirea disregards her destined responsibilities."

Feather extended her hand for Queen Istrell to grab. Istrell didn't hesitate to cling to it.

"Your Grace," Feather said softly. "Have you eaten?"

Istrell shook her head.

"When did you last eat?"

"I don't recall. Probably a couple days."

Feather extended her right arm. Queen Istrell looped her arm around Feather's. The dainty faery braced the queen. "Allow me to walk you to the Great Hall so you can eat."

The strong wine had taken effect quicker than normal. Istrell's words slurred. "She foolishly allowed a human to capture her."

"A human?" Feather gasped.

Istrell nodded. "Yes. Destroyed her magnificent wings."

"Oh my, not her glorious wings?"

Istrell closed her eyes and shook her head in disappointment. "Shredded. Absolutely shredded."

"Here, My Grace," Feather said, helping Istrell sit at the head of the long banquet table. "I'll see what the cook has prepared."

Istrell nodded sleepily. "Thank you, my dear one."

Seconds later, Istrell folded her arms on the table and rested her head. Her heavy eyelids slowly closed. She snored.

Feather shook her head. "Poor Queen Istrell."

"Has my aunt become such a lush?" the male faery said with laughter in his voice. He drifted along the top of the long table and hovered above Queen Istrell's head while she was lost in drunken slumber.

"Dirk?" Feather asked. "You've been eavesdropping?"

Dirk chuckled and flicked his long golden hair aside. It shook like fine threads of silk. "Knowledge is what I seek in order to claim the throne."

"Shawndirea's destined for the throne."

He shrugged. "She's never had the qualities of a true queen. She's too busy pursuing idle fantasies. She hasn't the discipline to reign over any kingdom."

"So you'll be our king?" Feather asked.

"I shall."

Dirk took her hand and pulled her close. He kissed her passionately and embraced her tightly. He backed away and looked in her eyes. "You, my love, will be my queen."

Feather grinned and squealed with delight.

"Keep milking her for information," Dirk said. "I need to know where Shawndirea is to prevent her from returning."

"As you wish," Feather replied.

"Istrell's in no state of mind to rule our kingdom. Especially not in her current condition."

CHAPTER 34

*R*iese heaved Marc upward at the side of the building. Marc grabbed the edge of the roof and held tightly. Riese placed his hands beneath his son's feet and shoved with enough power to get Marc securely on the roof.

Marc reached down his small hand. Riese shook his head. "I'm too heavy for you to lift."

"I can try!"

"No. Stay there. Don't move."

Riese swung the hammer and smashed the steel head through several walking corpses' heads. It parted the way enough for him to rush to the other side of the icy path.

"Father!" Marc shouted.

"Stay put!" Riese replied.

Two undead lie motionless on the cobblestone path. Blood oozed from the large dents in their skulls. The remaining undead corpses staggered in his direction. Pustules burst on their skin. Little green vapor clouds puffed from the lesions and leaked yellow ooze. Riese understood he mustn't touch any of their bodily fluids or the drifting green vapor. Otherwise, he'd become infected.

Their hollow dead eyes chilled him, but Marc was safe on the roof. Riese needed to destroy these creatures that were once his friends and

266

townspeople he held dear. Once they were immobilized, he and Marc could leave Glacier Ridge.

To Riese's advantage, the undead townspeople moved slowly. They no longer recognized him, but they were under Mors' control.

Riese tightened his grip on the hammer, shook his head with partial regret, and one by one, he brought the undead men and women to the last peace they'd ever know.

Tears heated his eyes. Broken bodies covered the icy cobblestone. Small green clouds of plague drifted over their pus-filled sores. He eased clear of the disease clouds and set the hammer against the side of the building to get his son down.

Marc embraced his father. "What about those inside Hobskin's Tavern?"

"Leave them be," Riese said. "I haven't the stomach to eliminate more."

"What do we do?"

"We pack up and leave this godless town."

"To where?"

Riese shrugged. "We must catch those that stayed last night."

"The ones with the thief?"

Riese nodded. "Yes. But first, we need to see if we can find the black carriage's tracks. I want to find that old man and make him suffer for what he did to Glacier Ridge. He will suffer dearly."

Marc and Riese studied the marketplace cobblestone. Only one place had a short path where the carriage wheels had pressed into the ice. The wagon had stopped at this spot the longest when Mors handed the bag to Jez. After that, the tracks disappeared.

"I see nothing else, father," Marc said.

"I know, son. These are the only marks left."

No tracks remained near the place Mors had asked Riese for directions, either. The man had magically disappeared.

Riese ran to catch his son. "Let's hurry, Marc."

"Can we ever return?"

Riese's jaw tightened. "Perhaps someday. For now, we concentrate on staying alive. You're all I have left in this world."

Marc didn't reply. He wiped tears away.

Riese placed a hand on his son's shoulder. "All will be fine. I was foolish to have left the town."

He and Marc returned to his stables, packed their best weapons, and slung the double-sided pack across the massive horse. He slid bags of gold and silver into several bags. The rest of his gold wealth he hid beneath floorboards in the back of his forge room and slid heavy crates over it. He didn't plan to leave Glacier Ridge forever. With what gold he carried, he could hire others to come back to eradicate the undead townspeople and reclaim his small town.

Riese saddled the horse and fastened a bridle in place. Marc did the same with his horse.

Riese opened the stable doors. Cold, rushing snow and wind dropped the forge room temperature quickly. When he turned around, Marc pulled his horse and Jez's horse behind him.

"What are you doing?" Riese asked.

"I can't leave Jez's mare behind, father. Jez would haunt me forever. What about all the horses we housed for the … our former patrons?"

Riese nodded. "We need to release them. Perhaps they'll follow us to the grasslands below Glacier Ridge."

They tethered Jez's mare behind Marc's horse and weighed the mare with weapons, food, and more supplies.

Riese and Marc opened dozens of stalls and led the horses out to the marketplace. They climbed on their horses and headed along the icy path. Eventually, the freed horses followed them up the hill, along the frozen mountain path, and down the next ridge line where fields of green grass bent beneath warmer breezes.

Marc remained silent during the long, cold ride. The loss of his brother weighed on him. They were close. The best of friends. Coldness set in Marc's eyes. Firmness hardened his jaw. Witnessing his son become a man should've been a blessing, a moment to celebrate, and under better circumstances. The way Marc reached that plateau was more costly than Riese wished to dwell on.

Riese's small town inside Glacier Ridge was dead. Nothing remained. His heart ached. Where the icy path thawed, he found wagon wheel tracks and hoof prints. If he hurried, he'd join Roble and his party as well as take delight in watching Crukas hang. Despite the deathly destruction in Glacier Ridge, Riese had something to look forward to.

CHAPTER 35

Marshall Jackson, an FBI agent in his mid-forties, sat across the table from Deiko in a mental hospital near Somerset, Kentucky. Marshall was a massive black man with broad shoulders, thick chest, huge arms, and massive hands. On the table before Marshall was an odd, leather-bound book, a yellow notepad, and a black ink pen. Marshall folded his hands together while he studied Deiko's demeanor. A young blonde nurse's aid stood on Deiko's side of the table.

Deiko's hands shook. His lips quivered. Whenever he dared a glance at Marshall, it was quick and without direct eye contact. Then, he stared at the table and mumbled.

"Mr. Deiko," Marshall said.

Deiko shuddered at the sound of Marshall's deep voice.

Marshall sat in his chair and made notes on his yellow notepad. "Mr. Deiko, what'd you see inside the cave?"

The nurse's aid shook her head. "He won't speak. We can't get him to say anything."

Marshall flicked his narrow gaze from Deiko to the young lady. "Ma'am, I wasn't speaking to *you*."

"I know," she replied nervously. "I was trying to be helpful."

"Well, *don't!*" Marshall slammed his fists on the table. "I'm a federal investigator. Should I *need* your opinion, trust me, I'll *ask* for it. Do you understand?"

"Yes, sir. I'm sorry."

Marshall shook his head and pointed at the door. "Why don't you busy yourself with some of your daily chores. I need to speak to Dr. Deiko. *Alone.*"

In near tears, she nodded and hurried out of the room.

Marshall waited until the door swung shut. After it closed, he smiled at Deiko.

"Mr. Deiko. Would you kindly tell me *what* you saw in the cave?"

Deiko's nervous eyes braved enough to meet Marshall's.

"It's okay, Mr. Deiko. I'm not here to hurt you. I'm here to help. I want to know about this Elias you encountered in the cave."

"El-El- Elias?" Deiko gnawed his fingernails.

"Yes. Elias. Do you know if his last name was Jackson?"

Deiko's haunted eyes looked away. He visibly shook.

"Mr. Deiko, I know you're frightened. I know. But believe me, I want to stop Elias from hurting anyone else. You understand what I'm saying, don't you? Tell me what I need to know, and I won't let the doctors and nurses know you're sane. You can stay in this facility as long as necessary. This place makes you think you're safe. Correct?"

Deiko snapped to attention and looked around. Apparently realizing he and Marshall were the only two in the room, his nervousness vanished. His voice became calm, collective. "How'd you know?"

Marshall shrugged. "A hunch. When people see something horrifying and without any rational explanation, they seek a place where security's higher than at home."

"What I saw? Was it real?" Deiko asked.

"What *did* you see?"

"A man ... he looked like a walking corpse. Old and rotten, but he walked, moved."

"In the cave?" Marshall asked.

"No. In my mind."

"This isn't a time for sarcasm, Mr. Deiko."

Deiko shook his head. "I'm not being sarcastic."

Marshall frowned. "Then explain."

"Elias took control of my mind and body. How's that possible?"

"Anything's possible when you're dealing with the paranormal."

Deiko shook his head. He glanced around the room, possibly checking to see if any doctors or nurses were secretly watching him.

Marshall smiled. "We're alone."

Paranoia gripped Deiko. He seemed relieved to confide in Marshall but feared Elias might also hear and return to kill him.

"Are you certain?" Deiko said.

Marshall nodded. "Yes. So he took control of your mind? Any idea for how long?"

"Not really. It occurred soon after my colleague captured a faery while collecting butterflies. I witnessed it through my binoculars."

"A faery?" Marshall's eyebrows rose. He looked at Deiko with intense speculation. "What medications do they have you on?"

Deiko chuckled. "Yes. I know it sounds crazy. You don't believe it. I swear, he caught one. After seeing the faery, a sudden urge to kill Ben and take the faery overcame me."

Marshall frowned and wrote on the yellow notepad. "Ben?"

"Dr. Ben Whytten. He's a zoologist at campus and a friend."

"He's your friend?"

Deiko nodded and sighed. "Yes. Well, probably not any more."

"So you tried to kill Ben to get the faery?"

"Something dark possessed me to get her at any cost. I remember looking in a mirror. My eyes were different."

"Different how?" Marshall jotted down notes.

"My eyes were black. And gray where the whites should be."

"Okay," Marshall said. "When did Elias release you and why?"

"I entered the cave and followed it for a ways. Ben's truck was parked at the road, so he was supposed to be in the cave, but I never found him. I had my gun. Had I encountered Ben, I'd have killed him. No doubt about it. But after I couldn't find him, Elias turned on me. He battered and forced me to leave the cave."

Deiko showed Marshall the scars on his arms and face. He lifted the back of his shirt and showed him more.

Marshall stood and walked around the table. He took Deiko's wrist and studied the marks carefully.

"Well, the good news is," Marshall said. "He didn't carve any symbols in your flesh."

Deiko stared at the marks and then at Marshall. "What does that mean?"

"He's no further purpose for you. If he'd cut symbols in your flesh, I'd worry. But he's done with you."

Deiko looked relieved. "So he won't be back?"

"Not for you."

"So I can leave the hospital?"

Marshall shrugged. "If you wish. Sure."

Deiko glanced around nervously. His eyes were timid like a frightened rabbit. His breathing increased. He shook his head. "No, I should wait a few more days. Okay?"

"Whatever makes you most comfortable," Marshall said in his deep voice.

"You won't tell them?"

Marshall took his notepad, shook his head, and headed to the door. He walked down the hall and stopped at the nurse's station. "I need the list of medications Isaac Deiko is being administrated ASAP."

The nurse looked up from her notes, unimpressed, and she cocked a brow. She seemed more lethargic than helpful.

Marshall slammed his badge on the countertop, frowned, and leaned over her. "That means *now!*"

His thunderous voice shook the woman. She searched through all the clipboards on the desk until she found Deiko's file. "One second, sir," she said. "I'll run off a copy for you."

MARSHALL RETURNED to his car and took the newspaper off the seat. He read the headline: "Strange Occurrences at Cider Knoll Cave." Deiko didn't have enough information to help Marshall find Elias.

He grabbed his radio receiver and contacted his secretary. "Ms. Banks, any new information?"

"We have something," she replied.

"What?" Marshall said impatiently.

"We tapped into a radio call from Sheriff Douglas to Deputy Higgins near where you are."

"What information did you get?"

"Sheriff Douglas called Higgins about a possible three homicide in a small mobile home at 1014 Maple Ridge Road in Cider Knoll. That's approximately a quarter mile from the cave where the boy was last seen."

"Thanks. Keep me posted if anything else comes up, Ms. Banks."

"Certainly, Agent Jackson."

Marshall drove from the mental hospital and headed to the rural area of Cider Knoll. A boy was missing. His friend was too much in shock to tell authorities what had happened. But he disappeared in the same cave where Deiko reported Elias had attacked him. Now, three more people were dead nearby. He needed to get to the crime scene before local authorities contaminated possible evidence or they accidentally stumbled into Elias. The officers had no idea how much jeopardy their lives were in, should they encounter Elias.

SHERIFF DOUGLAS LEANED against the front of his patrol car when Deputy Higgins turned in the short driveway. Douglas was a stocky man about five foot seven. His burred silver hair didn't cover his sunburned scalp. He crossed his arms and nodded at Higgins.

The old mobile home was tan, silver, and coated with rust.

Higgins parked his car and got out. "What happened?"

"I don't know how to explain it," Douglas said.

"How bad is it?"

"The worst thing I've ever seen."

Sheriff Douglas pulled his gloves on and opened the trailer door. He stepped aside and allowed Higgins to go up the stairs first. He entered the small living room with drab green carpet, a green sofa, and a glass-topped coffee table. He retreated a couple of steps and covered his nose and mouth with a handkerchief. Three dead bodies were positioned in odd forms. Blood was everywhere. Strange marks were carved in their skin, too.

A horrible odor permeated the air.

Higgins looked from the three bodies to Douglas. "How do you even begin to write up a crime scene like this?"

"It won't follow proper protocol."

"What kind of sick person does something like this?"

Douglas shook his head. "Hell, I don't know. Cult? Devil worshippers? I'm open to suggestions."

"I have none. Someone cut them up pretty badly. And those bloody sketches on the wall. What language is that?"

"Nothing I'd know."

Through his handkerchief, Higgins said, "That smell. Is it meth?"

Douglas nodded.

"How do you want this written up?" Higgins asked.

"I don't."

"What?"

"We write this report up like it is," Douglas said. "The FBI'll push us off the crime scene and treat us like we're too incompetent to be police officers. It won't make sense and might actually cost us our jobs."

Higgins frowned. "What should we do?"

"We rig this place to burn and blame the meth lab in the back room as the reason the trailer burned to the ground. The bloody paintings on the wall, the bizarre murders, everything—goes up in smoke," Douglas said with a devious smile.

"Sir, that's a bad idea. We need to know who's behind this hideous crime, don't we?"

Douglas nodded. "Of course. We'll keep looking, but we can't let the community know something this sick lurks among us. Think of the panic that'll cause. Hell, the old men that gossip at Harper's Grocery have already sent most of the county into an uproar over Donnie's disappearance. This area's too superstitious for something of this nature and magnitude to hit their rumor mill. We put an end to this before it gets further out of hand."

Higgins rested his hands on his hips and scanned the trailer. Two dead men and a woman lie in a sick, twisted display. His stomach soured. From his viewpoint, he couldn't figure out how they'd been killed. Two handguns, a knife, stacks of money and small bags of white powder were only a couple feet from their bodies. Whoever killed them wasn't interested in money or drugs. Just wanted them dead. This wasn't a typical murder, either. Far from it. "You know what? It won't hurt my feelings one bit for the Feds to take this one. Not one bit."

"You're talking BS, boy. Before you got here," Douglas said, "I drove out to the gas station and bought several gallons of gasoline. It's in the trunk. Help me get it and we'll prevent the county from going into further hysterics."

"Sheriff," Higgins said. "CSU needs to gather clues to discover who's behind this?"

Douglas turned and pushed Higgins against the trailer wall. He pressed his forearm across Higgins' throat. "Do you *want* to keep your job?"

Higgins nodded. "Of course."

"Then we dispose of what happened here. We investigate what happened without having our county folk constantly calling our office, talking to the media, and seeking to do their own investigations. You've no idea how crazy things will become once word of what happened here leaks out."

Douglas released the pressure from Higgins' throat, freed him, and slowly backed away. He allowed Higgins to walk to the door. Higgins rubbed his throat and took a deep breath.

Higgins pushed the screen door open. "Aren't you a bit frightened by what happened?"

"I'm scared shitless." The veins in Douglas' throat and forehead were swollen. He wiped sweat from his brow. "We're dealing with a maniac at best, but a crime scene this bad means we're facing something much worse. CSU can't make *that* any clearer."

"That's true, but—"

Sheriff Douglas frowned and pointed a firm finger. "Not another word. We get the gasoline and torch the place."

MARSHALL DROVE around a sharp curve in the narrow, two-lane road. Where the road straightened, two sheriff patrol cars headed toward him.

They passed at an incredibly high rate of speed for such a rural area. Their patrol lights were *not* on.

Once he found the small trailer at the edge of the road, he pulled his sedan in the drive. The edge of the driveway had grooves dug in the gravel where two different vehicles sped away. It didn't require a lot of deductive reasoning to know the tracks belonged to the patrol cars he'd just passed. Why had they fled from the place where three homicides had been reported?

Marshall got out of his car and left the door open. He walked across the driveway and peered through the living room window. The Venetian blinds were down, but a small, crumpled section didn't prevent anyone from seeing in or out. Three bodies lie in a bloody ritualistic murder scene, which was something he expected. Why had the officers left without doing a more thorough investigation?

He stepped up the rickety trailer steps and pulled open the screen door. He almost grabbed the doorknob when he stopped. He smelled gasoline and propane. He peered through the small window on the door and noticed the gas-stove door was all the way open.

"Damn!" Marshall leapt from the steps and ran for his car.

He was halfway across the drive when the trailer exploded into a giant ball of fire. The pressure of the explosion sent him through the air. He hit the gravel, rolled, and hurried behind the back of his car. He wiped dirt and grass from his suit jacket and watched the blazing fire through the windows of his car.

"Sons of bitches!" Marshall gritted his teeth.

He marched around the side of his car, got in, and slammed the door shut. He started the engine, backed up, and slung gravels as he exited the drive and sped down the county road. He glanced at the leather-bound book in the passenger seat. Sadly, he shook his head. The two officers needed to lose their jobs and be tried in court for destroying valuable crime scene evidence. But doing so wouldn't help his cause. He wanted to find Elias, but if Elias had made these ritual sacrifices and taken the boy, Elias wouldn't return for another twenty years.

"Dammit!" Marshall slapped the steering wheel. He placed his right hand on the leather journal. "I came so close to stopping you, Elias."

The next opportunity to destroy Elias and prevent the man from achieving immortality returned in twenty years. Wherever Elias hid in dormancy was a place Marshall might seek to find, but periodically. Marshall had hired several archaeologists to hunt for the man's tomb. No one had found his grave.

The leather-bound journal had once belonged to Elias. The book's passages vividly explained the wicked spells, rituals, and symbols necessary for Elias to gain immortality. However, nothing detailed where Elias remained dormant during each twenty year period. Marshall needed to find Elias and destroy him. Elias was Marshall's great-great grandfather, a voodoo Bokor, and a vicious murderer. In Marshall's opinion, Elias had tarnished the Jackson name. In twenty years, Marshall would return and be ready.

Marshall had no reason to stick around. Elias was done for the next twenty years. Marshall didn't need to make his presence known. At least not yet. However, he intended to have investigators remove Sheriff Douglas from office for destroying evidence and for not having enough backbone to do his job to protect his county.

CHAPTER 36

$\mathcal{A}$t the foot of Glacier Ridge, Roble stopped the wagon and horses at an open field. The air was much warmer. Sunlight not only brightened the horizon, it brightened their spirits with Crukas being the exception.

Roble always stood up for the underdog and helped those in need. He never backed down from a fight if the cause was worthy. Being in this realm, his outlook and attitude were changing. He was becoming harder and less affable. The rules in this realm were different and sometimes unclear. Fighting and killing the three demon-men that had held Lehrling prisoner proved that.

Crukas closed his eyes and allowed the sunlight to warm his face. He mouthed words without a sound, raised his shackled hands to the sky, and smiled.

Roble pulled the food crate from beneath the driver's seat. Inside the crate was dried meat, cheese, and stale bread loaves. Odlon and Lehrling took knives and cut off portions for themselves while Roble offered Crukas food.

"Why trouble yourself over me?" Crukas asked. "You're wasting food you and your friends need since I'll be hanged."

"You're not dead yet," Roble replied.

"I'd rather starve than hang. If I'm lucky, I'll be dead *before* we reach Ironwood."

Roble smiled and shook his head. "Perhaps you should've sought a different occupation."

Crukas' eyes narrowed.

"Don't taunt him," Shawndirea said.

"Does the faery harbor pity for me?" Crukas asked.

"No," she replied. "But I don't like caged animals being picked on."

Lehrling and Odlon laughed.

Crukas' face reddened. He placed his hands on the iron bars. "Riese knew exactly *how* to contain me. He went to the trouble of neutralizing my magical abilities with iron and engraved runes to counter my spells. Seems he knows quite a bit of magic himself."

Roble handed a large chunk of meat, cheese, and bread to Crukas. "Eat it or toss it. I don't care. No one suffers hunger on my watch."

"Yet, you'd see me hang?"

"For justice."

"Justice?" Crukas said with a wide smile. "What world do you live in? You're deranged if you believe such a concept exists. At best, fate sets things in motion. Sometimes, people pay their dues, but justice? Justice seldom prevails. People remove whatever they deem a thorn in their sides. Hangings aren't justice. They're entertainment. Nothing more. Adults and children flock to the square to spectate."

Roble shrugged. "Perhaps from your perspective it's entertainment. Not from mine. Especially when it pertains to you."

"What injustice did I bestow on you?" Crukas took a huge bite of bread and cheese.

"You allowed many in Glacier Ridge to die when you could've prevented it."

Crukas chewed the wad of food in his mouth, which muffled his words. "The Plague-bringer would've diseased us and continued to the next town if we'd attempted to stop him."

"You don't know that," Roble said.

Shawndirea nodded. "He's right."

"You agree with him?" Roble asked.

"He's correct," she said. "Confrontation with the Plague-bringer is death."

Odlon walked to the rear of the wagon. "No one has ever stopped the Plague-bringer. He's a worse sight to behold than one's own banshee spirit. Death follows him. Something else summons him."

"So Riese is dead?" Roble asked.

"It's hard to say," Shawndirea replied. "Depends on whether the Plague-bringer was finished and gone by the time Riese returned to Glacier Ridge."

"If you know so much about him, why didn't any of you say anything?" Roble asked.

Lehrling swallowed a bite of hard cheese. "Mors comes in many forms. No one knows for certain what form he may present. He was an old, feeble man today. Could be a rich knight tomorrow, or a female bard singing songs for money. A beggar. One never knows. Once he came as an elder priest and cursed the Temple of Bridgebarrow. Half the town died within a day. No one knows what he actually looks like."

"Crukas knew," Roble replied. "How's that?"

Crukas gave a firm nod. "He wore a golden ring on his right hand. The stone is a skull-shaped emerald with inserted ruby eyes."

Roble frowned. "How does this ring indicate who he is?"

"To be truthful, I wasn't certain it was he. However, a survivor said the Plague-bringer wore such a ring. The man survived the plague but his body and mind are forever scarred."

Lehrling looked at Roble and Odlon. "It's best we head south. We're in the open and need to reach Ironwood quickly."

"Indeed." Odlon nodded and scanned the meadow. "We're easy targets here."

"More bandits and thieves?" Roble asked.

Shawndirea said, "We travel the path leaving Glacier Ridge. Outside travelers don't know what's occurred there. News spreads slowly. Weeks might pass before thieves learn not to venture this route."

"That's true." Lehrling smiled. "We take advantage of the sunlight. Since it's not midmorning, we've a good five hours to travel."

"What awaits us between here and Ironwood?" Roble asked.

Odlon mounted his horse and looked at Roble. "Several small towns, trading posts, forests, and wilderness. Woodcrest is the first place we must pass through."

"Friendly town?" Roble asked.

Lehrling shrugged. "Sometimes. Sometimes not. Depends on what they lack in wares."

"Any trading posts along the way?"

"On occasion you pass them. However, there are small huts where thieves are disguised as traders. They lure travelers in to rob them," Lehrling said. "I'm guessing you don't travel much."

"Not in this region," Roble replied. "Sounds like folks are more hostile than friendly."

Shawndirea whispered, "Dangers are everywhere in Aetheaon. Never let down your guard."

Roble nodded. "You keep saying that."

"Because it's true. You don't take my warnings seriously."

"I've yet to see anything I view as exceedingly dangerous."

"Doesn't mean you won't encounter such."

"You're right," Roble said. "I should be more cautious, especially after nearly losing you and what the Plague-bringer did in Glacier Ridge."

Roble read her concern, which hinted her inner fears. He followed her gaze and looked beyond the grassy meadows to the shadowy woods shrouded within more mists and more mysteries.

Suddenly, he heeded her warnings with more concern. The abrupt pang in his stomach made him realize he'd been nervous all along their journey. Every odd situation—from the moment he almost fell into the River Styx, the intense encounter with the ghosts on Glacier Ridge, and then he almost lost Shawndirea—had increased his anxiety. His stomach acid was burning an ulcer in his gut.

Although Roble loved exploration and discovering new species and races he never knew existed, carelessness would end his life prematurely, if he weren't more cautious.

Shadows crept along the edge of the woods. The horses' ears backed, and they snorted.

Odlon stared at Roble and Lehrling. "Hide in the shelter of the trees, *now*."

CHAPTER 37

The Dark Chancellor stood before the violet crystal and focused until the crystal shimmered. He held his staff with the Sages of Vylan trapped inside.

"Botis," a low voice said. A dark image materialized inside the glowing crystal. "Why have you contacted me?"

"Lord Tyrann," Botis said with a bow. "Glacier Ridge has been stricken with the plague. The occupants now serve your dark commands. Other towns will follow."

"And Vylan? What news have you?"

Botis held up the ebony staff. The red eyes blinked. "The Sages of Vylan are now in *my* grasp. Their power's mine."

"Then Vylan's next to fall under my control," Tyrann said. Dark misty shadows swirled around Tyrann, which prevented Botis from seeing Tyrann's face.

"Yes. The neighboring forests the Ravenfolk occupy are yours for the taking."

"Good."

Botis smiled. "My Lord, the Black Chasm expands as your power increases."

"Indeed," Tyrann said. "Faithful servants, such as yourself, shall reap blessings and power as well."

"You're most gracious, my Lord."

"What of Elias? Did you strike him down?" Tyrann asked.

Botis stared at the cavern floor.

"He lives?" Tyrann said angrily.

"He's gone dormant again, but he won't succeed in gaining immortality. You've my word."

Through the swirling mists inside the hanging crystal, Tyrann's crimson eyes glowed. "You promised years ago to end his pursuit. He has only one more sacrifice before he's immortal. You've no idea the damage you'll cause should an Overlander become immortal."

Botis hissed. "I know."

"Why have you not stopped him? How has he eluded you all this time?"

"Elias is far more resourceful than expected. He's made certain to never step inside my magical circles."

"He detects the power of your magic?"

Botis said, "Unfortunately, yes."

"This is why magic should never be granted to those on the other side of the Underworld. They're beyond our grasp and control. Any sorcerer should understand the danger."

Botis bowed to Tyrann's harangue. "I deeply regret my mistake. I've no idea where his tomb is."

"He will rise in twenty Overland's years?"

Botis nodded. "Yes."

"How has his mortal body remained intact without succumbing to decay? He should be dust by now."

"He uses Overlanders' magic."

"What?"

Botis stepped back and bowed lower. "He's a master of black magic in his realm."

Tyrann raised his hands. Bluish fire shot from his hands through the crystal and propelled Botis through the air. Botis landed on his back. The ebony staff clacked and rolled across the floor. Soft laughter echoed from the staff. The glowing eyes of the Vylan Sages glared at Botis.

"I should destroy you right now," Tyrann said in a frightening low tone. "You've allowed a wizard from the Overlands access to our power? Should he succeed in gaining immortality, everything we possess is subjected to chaos and ruin. There'll be no stopping him, you fool!"

"Apologies, my Lord. Thousands upon thousands of apologies. I never knew his magical abilities until after he solicited me and made his first sacrifice."

"Destroy him when he resurrects or you'll be imprisoned worse than the Sages of Vylan."

Botis knelt and pressed his forehead against the cold, cavern floor. "Yes, my Lord. He shall die."

Tyrann broke their connection. The shimmering crystal went cold, dark. Botis waited several minutes before he stood and grabbed the ebony staff. Fear weighted his soul.

"You were warned," Staven hissed from the staff. "Is the sacrifice you made for the ebony staff still acceptable?"

Botis gripped the staff tightly, walked out of the crystal chamber, and shook his head.

"Well?" Staven said.

"Debatable," Botis replied.

"Your allegiance to Tyrann was a costly mistake. Not only will he destroy Vylan, he'll consume *you*. You may contain us within your staff, but you do *not* control our power. We'll resist your commands."

"Perhaps, for now," Botis said with amusement. "But soon, I'll feast off your power. You'll do my bidding."

"Even after Tyrann's chastising, you're willing to obey? You're much weaker than I imagined."

"It has nothing to do with weakness. It has everything to do with position."

Staven cackled. "No other throne within the Black Chasm houses the City of Mortel. Only Tyrann's. He won't share his power. His plan is to conquer Aetheaon beneath his dark power."

"I have my throne. I've no need to be seated within the Black Chasm."

"The Black Chasm is expanding. Eventually, it'll devour your cavern, your throne, and your soul."

Botis descended a winding, dark path. In the darkness a waterfall cascaded from an unseen ledge and splashed against the rocks. A mist saturated the cold cavern, and without light, Botis continued his walk unworried about stepping off the path.

"Your warning's more a vengeful desire than a concern for my well-being," Botis said.

All ten sages laughed.

After climbing a crude set of stairs in the dark cavern, Botis turned another sharp corner. Flickering sconces lit a large room. Small prison cages housed different races—elves, dwarves, Ratkins, and humans. The prisoners cringed, closed their eyes, and shielded their faces as the Dark Chancellor approached.

Each prisoner was missing appendages. Some more than others, but none were whole-bodied. A small altar stood at the center of the cages. A silver bowl and dagger rested atop the altar.

"What's this?" Staven asked.

"Where I make my sacrifices," Botis replied. "Dark magic requires sacrifices. The darker the magic, the more blood and flesh I must offer, which is why I use these in my stead."

"What spell do you seek?"

"To silence you and merge your wills to obey my commands. From this day forward, your voices are silenced and your magic's mine to direct."

CHAPTER 38

R oble and his party hid in the shadows of trees. During this half hour, nothing approached from the meadow or the roadway in either direction. They remounted and Roble drove the wagon along the road that cut through the forest.

The shadowy forest possessed an eerie atmosphere. The thick canopy blocked most of the sunlight. The road had become hard, compacted black soil from years of horse-pulled wagons traveling through. The forest floor, however, was deeply layered with leaves, briars, and thick underbrush. Traveling off the path would be challenging and time consuming, should they be forced to stay off the road.

Within the forest were broken, marble columns and moss-covered, headless statues of a fallen temple long forgotten.

Deeper in the shadows strange sounds echoed. Branches on the forest floor snapped and crackled. Roble wondered what the shadows moving along the outskirts of the forest had been. Now, he kept more alert than ever. At least out in the open they'd see any approaching attackers. In the dense forest, they'd never know until the moment they were attacked.

The rugged wagon creaked slowly down the black road. Shawndirea studied the narrow ditches. Crukas looked grim. He no longer stood but sat slouched at the base of the iron cage and hugged his knees. Occasional bursts of wind whistled through the woods, and quite often, Roble was certain voices traveled with the wind.

Midway through the dark forest, Roble said to Shawndirea, "How far until we get to your city?"

"Still several days."

Her soft voice soothed him. He wanted to do anything to take his mind off what the trees hid from their view. The deeper into the forest they rode, the more frightening the area became. Thick leafy vines clung to the highest branches and connected throughout the canopy. Occasionally, the overhead branches shook. Leaves swirled and drifted downward.

"No shortcuts?" he asked.

Her frightened eyes scanned the treetops. "What do you think this is?"

"I was hoping *this* was the long way."

"No."

A strange anguished cry echoed off the trail from something hiding in shadows.

"Ride!" Odlon raised his crossbow and fired into the dark forest.

Roble cracked the whip over the horses and alarmed them enough to yank the wagon forward and increase their speed. Odlon fired another bolt. Roble kept glancing over his shoulder to get a glimpse of what pursued them, but he never saw anything.

"Look out!" Crukas shouted. He crouched tightly into a ball at the bottom of the iron cage and closed his eyes.

Lehrling pulled his blade in almost the same moment the creature lunged from the tree branches and knocked him off his horse. His sword struck the road with a clang. Lehrling groaned in pain. The impact sent him rolling over and over on the harsh road. He finally stopped short of the thick, briary underbrush. The black furred, cat-faced humanoid bore teeth and sprang in the thicket before Odlon got a clear shot.

Though in obvious pain, Lehrling crawled several feet and reached for his sword. He grabbed the hilt of the blade. But when he pulled the short sword closer, he frowned. The blade wasn't his. His blade was several feet away.

Odlon kept his eye trained through the crossbow sight while he scanned the forest, but the creature seemed to have vanished. None of the underbrush rustled from its fleeing movement.

"What the Hell was that?" Roble pulled back the reins to stop the horses. Once they stopped, he tied the reins to the wagon seat and set the brake.

Shawndirea shook her head. "It's not a natural creature."

"Meaning?"

"A product of sorcery, possibly dark magic," she said.

Odlon rode his horse to the front of the wagon and eyed the forest. "You sensed it too?"

"Yes." She nodded.

"It's more than that, faery," Crukas said.

Shawndirea looked at the thief with worried eyes. "What do you mean?"

"It's sorcery, but the sorcerer behind the magic seeks to stop someone within our party."

Lehrling sat up, coughed, and wheezed. He could hardly get his breath. His face paled. Due to his age and weight, he had a difficult time trying to stand. Although he held the strange blade, his eyes searched the road for his weapon. Concern creased his brow. He seemed concerned the creature might return and finish him before he stood and defended himself.

Roble stepped down from the wagon. Shawndirea sat on his shoulder and held tightly to his collar.

"Keep going," Crukas said. "That beast will return."

"No, Lehrling needs our help and protection," Roble said. "He's obviously injured and can't defend himself against that beast. Besides, you don't give me orders."

"Being locked in this cage, I'm vulnerable," Crukas said. Still sitting on the hay, he gripped the bars and tugged.

"You're probably safer than the rest of us," Roble said. "You're caged because of your decisions. Should it return and kill you, you'd be one less problem to deal with."

Crukas feigned a hurt expression. "You'd allow a helpless prisoner to be ripped to shreds?"

Roble shook his head and refused to entertain Crukas with trivial banter. Instead, he ran until he reached Lehrling. The old man coughed, beat his chest with his fist, and spat bloody sputum on the ground. After Lehrling inhaled deeply and stopped wheezing long enough to catch his breath, Roble extended his hand and helped Lehrling stand.

"We need to get you to a physician," Roble said.

Lehrling shook his head. "No, I'm fine."

"No," Roble said, "you're not. You have pneumonia. If you don't get medicine, you're going to die."

Odlon sat on his horse and watched the dark area of the forest floor where the strange creature had disappeared. Wearing the green dragon scale armor, the elf looked more than regal. Faint light shimmered off the armor as though the dragon's magic clung to its scales. The glory shrouding the armor made Roble wish the dragon still lived, so he could see its true power.

The large shield hung across Odlon's back. His fierce eyes were alert and his finger rested against the crossbow trigger. It seemed the elf had the ability to see through shadows and detect what was hidden in those dark crevices. In that moment, Roble wondered if Odlon had inherited more than just the armor and somehow had taken the dragon's essence.

"Do you see the creature?" Roble asked while balancing Lehrling against him.

"No." Odlon shook his head. "Whatever it was, it's too fast."

"Or it turns invisible," Crukas said, slowly standing.

Roble brushed mud and dead leaf matter off Lehrling's back. "Other than your difficulty breathing, are you okay? No broken bones?"

A weak smile widened Lehrling's tired face. He clasped Roble's shoulder. Lehrling scratched his white beard. In a hoarse voice, he said, "Being an old man, my bruises and lumps will bother me soon enough. Nothing hurts worse than age sometimes. Or my bruised pride."

Roble smiled.

Lehrling held the blade out for Roble to examine. "This isn't my sword. Mine's over there."

"Then where'd this come from?" Roble picked up Lehrling's sword.

Lehrling shook his head and pointed at the edge of the thick, briary underbrush. "There's your answer."

In the crude ditch, almost hidden beneath the thorny branches, were two dead bodies. Their coat of arms was the same as the men who killed Bausch.

"More of Waxxon's demon-men," Roble said. He knelt and examined their wounds. The blood on their scratched faces was fresh. "They haven't been dead long."

"What killed them?" Odlon asked, riding closer.

"Apparently the creature," Shawndirea said. "They have claw marks on their faces and throats."

"It never attempted to claw me," Lehrling said.

"It could've easily killed you had it wanted," Roble said. "It definitely had the advantage."

"I know." Lehrling sheathed his sword and brushed debris from his pants. He and Roble walked to the wagon.

"We need to keep moving," Odlon said to Roble.

Crukas nodded. "Yes. The sooner the better."

Roble watched the trees. He expected to see the catlike creature again. When the total calm of the trees and underbrush convinced him the creature wasn't near, he said, "How far until we reach Woodcrest?"

"Shouldn't be much longer," Lehrling said. "Over the next rise."

"Can you ride?"

Lehrling smiled. "I told you I'm fine."

"I'm convinced otherwise." Roble braced Lehrling's shoulder to steady the old man. "You've had difficulty breathing since we met. We need to find a physician in Woodcrest."

"Good luck with that," Crukas said.

"Why?"

"At best you might find an herbalist," Crukas said.

Odlon shrugged. "That's good enough."

"Not in his present health," Roble said.

Shawndirea pursed her lips. "You cannot be too picky here, Roble. The luxuries in your world are scarce in ours. We accept what assistance we can. Whether it's good or not, it's all we have."

Roble climbed on the wagon seat and untied the reins. "The sooner we get to Woodcrest, the better. For Lehrling's sake."

Odlon nodded. "You see anything moving along the edge of the path, or elsewhere, let me know."

"I will," Roble said.

Lehrling struggled to mount his horse. Even though Roble didn't know Lehrling well, he felt close to the man, as he would a favorite uncle. The old man was sick and that concerned Roble.

As they rode, Roble whispered to Shawndirea, "Why would a sorcerer create a beast like that? Is it the same wizard that had the beast awaiting us in Devils Den?"

She shook her head. "No. The one in the cave protected the rift and tried to prevent me from returning to this realm."

"Why?"

"I honestly don't know. The catlike creature went for Lehrling though. Not me. However, its attack wasn't to kill, or it would've."

"So it seems, since it killed two of Waxxon's bounty hunters."

Shawndirea placed her hand to his cheek. "You're worried about Lehrling, aren't you?"

Roble nodded and smiled. "Of course."

"Yet, you barely know him."

"So?"

"Never lose that," she said softly.

"What?"

"Your compassion for others. Circumstances in my realm tend to harden men's hearts. No matter what you encounter, please never let your compassion die. That's what I love about you the most."

"Does my desire to see Crukas pay for his crimes alter how you view me?" Roble asked.

"Not at all, my love," she replied. "None in the least. He's guilty of many things, but not warning Riese about the Plague-bringer was sheer spite. He thought only of himself and not the lives of those in Glacier Ridge. Crukas is not a man with great qualities, and I, like you, believe justice exists. Crukas spoke some truth. Justice is limited here. Perhaps you can change that since you're a Dragon Skull knight."

"Only in attire," Roble said.

Shawndirea shook her head. "Also in virtue, kindness, and loyalty. You probably possess more high qualities than any other Dragon Skull Knight."

"Lehrling seems to possess those qualities."

"I agree, but he's older and not tarnished by greed like most men your age and younger. That's why I sought you. Darkness consumes our lands. The cat creature, the Plague-bringer, and Waxxon's henchmen forewarn of worse things to come."

Roble watched the road and the right edge of the forest while Odlon kept his focus on the left edge. The road became steeper and curved to the right.

Roble whispered, "Odlon mentioned the Black Chasm. What do you know of it?"

Her eyes widened slightly. "Dark things reside there. The growing mists hide what was once there."

"Which was?"

"The City of Mortel."

Roble frowned. "Who dwelt in the city?"

"Mainly humans. A few elves."

"Why does a black mist overshadow the place."

"We don't know," she replied. "The mystery's almost as unknown as the Plague-bringer."

"Do you think there's a connection between the chasm and the current unrest?" he asked.

"It's possible. Evil sweeps through the kingdoms. The fact Lady Dawn is alive and Waxxon seeks to find and kill her shows how evil seeks to strangle good. Queen Taube was the most honorable ruler in the kingdoms of Aetheaon. Her radiance brought so much hope."

Odlon beside Roble and pointed. "Woodcrest is ahead."

"I wouldn't advance any closer to Woodcrest if you wish to remain alive, elf." A man stepped from around a dark tree near the path ahead of them.

CHAPTER 39

Odlon turned and aimed his crossbow at the man dressed in a bluish-gray robe. His long flowing, black beard was peppered with strands of silver. He stared at the crossbow and his unusual, piercing eyes narrowed. His pupils were black dots inside silver irises. Meeting those eyes brought chills down Roble's back. He'd never seen any human eyes so eerie.

Zauber calmly leaned against his long staff. He wore a ruby ring on his right hand and a blood quartz ring on his left.

The tall, bearded man shook his head. "Odlon, I'm not here to harm you. I'm here to keep you alive."

Odlon frowned and lowered the crossbow. "How do you know me? Who are you?"

"Zauber, Wizard of the Misty Bogs." Zauber offered a slight bow. "I'm familiar with all of you."

"The Misty Bogs?" Roble looked at Odlon.

Zauber nodded. "Yes, it's well south of here."

"I thought it was a desolate swamp," Lehrling said hoarsely.

"Appearances can be deceiving," Zauber said with an even smile.

Odlon tapped his horse's flanks and eased closer. He hung the crossbow on his saddle horn. He looked down at the wizard. "Why's Woodcrest dangerous for us to enter?"

"Those two dead men at the edge of the road were scouts. Lord Waxxon, who should never hold such a title, has more men in Woodcrest. He's taken the town under his control."

Shawndirea stood on Roble's shoulder. "Did you slay those men?"

"Not directly, my dear faery. My cat did."

"The cat beast?" Crukas asked. "He's yours?"

"Yes, he's my familiar. My apologies, Lehrling, for the near attack. He mistook your party as another of Waxxon's group of plunderers. He's young, so if you'll pardon him."

Lehrling offered a weak smile and nodded. His pale face dripped with sweat. He coughed. "Some bumps and bruises is all."

"He's harmless unless he encounters Waxxon's soldiers," Zauber said. "Those two dead men passed less than an hour ago."

"I detected magic surrounding the cat," Shawndirea said. "I thought it was something much darker."

"That's my intention. He's veiled with a deceptive aura. His disguise makes it less likely for anyone to know I'm here."

"Why's that?" Roble asked.

"It's seldom I leave my tower. I'm stronger there," Zauber said.

"Most wizards are solitary," Shawndirea said.

Zauber smiled. Wisdom reflected in his light, silvery eyes. "Shawndirea, you've quite worried your mother. She sent search parties to find you."

Shawndirea gave an agitated sigh and frowned. "*That* doesn't surprise me in the least."

Zauber chuckled. "It's not the first time you've aged her with worry."

"The way she frets? It won't be the last, either. My arrival home will be much worse for her than my absence."

Zauber nodded and glanced at Roble. "Roble won't likely earn her blessings. Not at first."

"How do you know about us?" Roble asked.

"Ah, Overlander, more important tasks need discussed." Zauber smiled at Shawndirea. "For some odd reason, little faery, she's unable to see you. Where'd you get your dark clothes?"

"Roble cut a piece of cloth from his cloak to protect me from freezing," she replied.

Zauber studied her garments, boots, and the hood. Then he inspected Roble's clothing. "Where'd you get these clothes?"

"From my friend and comrade," Lehrling said. "Bausch was hanged. Roble—"

Roble said softly, "I had need of them."

Lehrling studied Roble for a moment. "Ah, it makes sense why you're unfamiliar with so many things. Zauber addressed you as an Overlander. Is that true?"

Roble nodded. "It is."

"An Overlander dares to pronounce his judgment on me?" Crukas shook the cage bars. "You've no right—"

"Silence!" Zauber waved his hand at the thief.

Crukas glared at the wizard. When he tried to speak, no sound came from his mouth. A horrified expression claimed his face. He motioned Zauber to come closer and with pleading hand signs, he pointed at his mouth. Apparently, Zauber had muted Crukas with a spell, and Crukas begged to have it undone.

Zauber shrugged and grinned. "That's much better."

"Roble, how'd you get to Glacier Ridge?" Lehrling asked.

"He can tell you about it later," Zauber said. "Lehrling, who crafted the Dragon Skull Order's armor?"

"No particular armorer. Mine were fashioned in Hoffnung. Bausch had his made in Woodnog."

Zauber held his right hand before Roble's chest and moved it right to left. He frowned. "These have been enchanted. Any odd occurrences, Roble, since you've been wearing them?"

Roble shrugged. "They adjust to the climate. When I was freezing cold in the forest overlooking Glacier Ridge, they immediately made me warmer and immune to the cold. After we left that climate, they've acclimated to keep me cooler."

"Same for me," Shawndirea said.

Lehrling rubbed his beard and smoothed it. He met Roble's eyes. "Now I understand why you've never been trained with swords. But, when you confronted Waxxon's three henchmen you showed no fear of them whatsoever. Why's that?"

"I honestly don't know. I don't remember what happened."

"Interesting," Zauber said.

"What?" Lehrling asked.

"Were the three men who held you prisoner the same men that hanged Bausch?"

Lehrling nodded. "Yes."

"Perhaps Bausch enchanted his own clothes," Zauber said.

"No," Lehrling replied, "He's not capable."

"Maybe not magically. But perhaps he placed a curse of vengeance before he died. And whoever took the clothes would kill the men and avenge Bausch's death."

"A vengeance curse?" Shawndirea nodded. "Roble went into a trance when the three men attacked. He showed no fear and killed them."

"Like I said," Roble said, "I don't remember what I did."

"So, Overlander," Zauber said, "You've been initiated into the Dragon Skull Order?"

"No."

Lehrling cleared his throat. "Not yet."

Zauber rubbed his hands together and smiled. "So much for you two to discuss."

"He's noble enough to join the Order," Lehrling said. "But no Overlander has ever been initiated. Certainly not someone untrained with a sword. What brought you to the Underworld?"

"Shawndirea," Roble said. "I promised to take her home."

Lehrling looked at the faery. "You went to the Overlands?"

"I've been several times."

Zauber shook his head. "Much to your mother's disapproval. Look at your wings."

"I know," she said sadly.

"That's my fault," Roble said. "It's why I insisted I'd get her home."

Zauber studied Roble. "Queen Istrell *won't* be receptive of your arrival."

"I expect not. But how do you know this?" Roble asked. "Why's our situation important to you?"

"We tend to other matters first, but I'm here to help. When my duty's done, finding me will be like one of those mysteries you enjoy solving.

Waxxon's soldiers are our concern at the present. The simple people of Woodcrest need our help."

"So you've been hiding in the forest and picking them off one by one?" Roble asked.

Zauber smiled. "Since I'm not a warrior, crashing the gates isn't an option in my favor."

"I suppose not." Lehrling adjusted his weight in the saddle. He bent forward and kept one hand pressed against his chest. "Any idea how many of Waxxon's men occupy Woodcrest?"

"Last count, before those two died, no less than a dozen more."

Stunned, Roble looked at Zauber. "Only a dozen soldiers took Woodcrest?"

"Woodcrest is a small town of mostly unarmed villagers," Zauber said. "Fear controls the town more than Waxxon's men."

"But still, even a small town should be able to prevent a dozen soldiers from taking over," Roble said.

"They're farmers with modest walls to protect them from wolves and bears at night. Waxxon's men attacked when they were working their fields outside Woodcrest's walls. Their gates were wide open. Even if they chose to fight, hoes and rakes are no match against swords and axes."

Odlon angered at the thought of Waxxon's men plundering a defenseless township. His emerald eyes narrowed. "'Tis true."

Roble studied Zauber's strange, silvery eyes. "How do you know only a dozen men occupy the town?"

Zauber pulled a glowing orb from inside his robe. It held an odd, vibrant, silver luminescence, similar to the wizard's eyes. Beneath the dense dark forest canopy, the orb shimmered brightly

"Look for yourselves," he replied with a broad grin. "I've watched where they wait, which is why my patience enabled me to eliminate them when they exit the gates."

Odlon, Roble, Lehrling, and Shawndirea peered into the glowing ball. The orb revealed the corner wall towers where several of Waxxon's archers stood guard. Swordsmen guarded both city gates. The poor townsfolk were dressed in tattered fur clothes. Their faces were dirty and their hair unkempt. Although they worked their normal menial tasks, their fearful eyes kept side-glancing their captors.

In the center of the town, two bodies hung from a tall tree. These unfortunate souls were better dressed than the survivors in Woodcrest, which meant they'd probably been members of the town council. Other dead bodies lie side-by-side in the street while flies and insects swarmed their decaying bodies.

Waxxon wanted to drive fear into the hearts of these farmers and hunters, and from their defeated facial expressions, he'd succeeded.

Tall, crudely cut timber walls fortified the small town. The thick surrounding forest added an additional deterrent that Waxxon's men oversaw. This averted any hope for neighboring farm villages to come to Woodcrest's aid.

While Roble and the others stared into the glowing orb, brittle dead leaves crunched softly on the forest floor. They stepped closer and closer to their vicinity. The small chorus of insects suddenly silenced. Several small sparrows chirped and flew deeper into the trees. The approaching steps were light, but not so soft that the leaves didn't emit a whisper with their breaking sounds. Their stalking movements crept closer and paused briefly at the edge of the thick brush.

Roble looked to the forest and pulled a throwing knife.

Zauber raised a hand and shook his head. "Easy, Overlander. It's only my pet."

From the thick bramble and thorns a black cat slinked on the dark road with its tail raised. A white star patch of fur splotched the center of its chest. Its emerald eyes studied the group before walking to Zauber and rubbing its head and body around the hem of his long robe.

"Surely this isn't the—" Roble began.

"The beast that killed Waxxon's men?" Zauber gave a firm nod and smiled while twirling a strand of his black beard with his finger. "Indeed, he is."

The black cat purred and leapt in Zauber's arms.

"The magic's worn off, so Phantom won't stop any more of Waxxon's men for a while." Zauber scratched between the cat's ears. Phantom closed his eyes and purred louder.

"If Woodcrest is occupied," Lehrling asked weakly, "how do we bypass it?"

Zauber smiled. "There are ways."

Odlon shook his head. "The forest growth is too thick to cut through. Returning to Glacier Ridge isn't an option."

Zauber approached the iron cage. "What of your loudmouthed thief, Crukas? I assume you're taking him to Ironwood?"

Roble explained the Plague-bringer, the crimes Crukas had committed, and that they were delivering him to Ironwood.

Thunderous hooves beat the road behind them. Roble turned. Riese and Marc galloped toward them at full speed. Riese's eyes were full of horror, hatred, and vengeance. Such a combination was deadly for foes or friends. As they neared the wagon, Riese pulled back so hard on the reins, his horse's eyes bulged. Its front hooves dug into the black road and slid across the hard surface. Before the horse fully stopped, Riese swung off the steed and ran along beside the horse. Froth dripped from the horse's mouth. It panted hard. Marc stopped his horse but didn't dismount. Instead his eyes focused on Zauber.

Riese held his hammer clenched tightly in his massive right hand. He bore his teeth and headed to the wagon. Crukas noticed the boiling hatred in Riese's eyes and wasn't certain what the giant blacksmith might do. Crukas lowered his head and held his hands over his head in a prayerful manner. No prayer would aid Crukas once Riese reached him.

"Riese," Roble said, stepping into the blacksmith's path. "Is everything—?"

Riese's huge left hand grabbed Roble's vest and heaved him aside much like a straw scarecrow. "Outta my way!"

Crukas opened his eyes enough to see Riese's approach, and then, he shut them tightly. Riese walked past the iron cage and climbed on the wagon seat. "Everyone, we ride!"

"Wait!" Roble said.

Riese turned and glared coldly at Roble.

Roble never broke their gaze in spite of Riese's massive size.

"Wait? For what?" Spittle flew from his mouth. "My son Jez is dead. The whole town's dead. I want to find Mors. He'll die for his pestilence!"

"We cannot head through Woodcrest," Roble said. "At least, not yet."

"Why not?"

"Waxxon's men now control it," Odlon said.

A mad grin spread across Riese's face. He growled deeply. "Then we take it from them."

"How?" Roble asked.

"Crash the gates."

Zauber shook his head. "We need a more subtle approach."

Riese glared at the wizard. "*Who* are you?"

In a soothing, almost hypnotic voice trickling like an invisible stream, Shawndirea said, "Zauber. He can get us through Woodcrest alive so we can find Mors, the Plague-bringer. No justice can be carried out if we're all dead."

Riese shook his head slightly. The lure of her voice sliced through his anger and found its way to where his pain festered. The hardness of his brow softened. Tears brimmed in his eyes. A couple of tears escaped and slid down his cheeks.

Riese wiped his face with the back of his left sleeve and looked at Zauber, quite angry with himself for shedding tears, and especially in front of Crukas. But even the tough blacksmith couldn't hide agony of loss.

Riese asked, "How?"

"We wait," Zauber replied.

"How long?"

"Until nightfall," Zauber said. "Then, Waxxon's men will fall."

CHAPTER 40

$\mathcal{A}$fter Mors had entered Hobskin's tavern and tossed his bag of disease carriers on the floor, Drucis—a dark-skinned dwarf—hid in a half empty barrel of dried nuts behind the bar. Having been a master explosive technician who worked deep in the Mines of Gordurth, Drucis had, at first, thought the bag contained a miner's bomb. He scrambled across the tavern, leapt, and rolled over the bar. He plunged into the barrel of unshelled nuts. Minutes later, when no raging explosion rocked the tavern, he peered through a knothole in the barrel's wall. Drucis feared little, but the bag's contents paralyzed him with horror.

The small, vibrating bag tipped to its side. Strange ticking sounds chattered inside the bag but nothing like the crude mechanisms Drucis used for countdown pieces. Through the bag's opening, a maddening swarm of black beetles scuttled across the floor and attacked those nearby.

His two comrades stomped and crushed dozens of the insects into puddles of green goo. The beetles' numbers increased at a magical rate. The bag held a never-ending supply. Moments later, the beetles climbed the dwarves' legs and covered their bodies. Though they screamed for help, dozens of thieves and rebellious rogues fought similar losing battles of their own. The biting insects overtook the half drunken patrons inside Hobskin's Tavern.

Shame overtook Drucis for his moments of cowardice. He struggled to find enough courage to leap from the barrel to help his comrades. In retrospect, he couldn't have save them. His fate would've been the same.

Draken and Sorgen, his thieving partners and close friends, dropped to the floor. They madly slapped and raked the beetles from their faces, their beards and long hair. The expanding swarm covered them. Draken and Sorgen hands stopped fighting. They dropped motionless on the floor.

Drucis ducked deeper inside the barrel. He worried the beetles would find him, but he'd rather take his chances in hiding than making a run for the door.

An hour passed, which seemed like days, before he braved enough to rise and look around the tavern.

Instead of his friends and patrons lying dead on the dirty floor, they staggered aimlessly. They were like the undead villagers in the Ruins of Sturn, where he, Draken, and Sorgen, had taken sport shooting the hobbling undead with arrows while standing atop the crumbling pillars. That had been fine entertainment on an otherwise boring day, until they discovered a wraith had summoned the undead for her use. Their sporting shots had almost turned her wrath on them. Never had his short, stubby legs run so fast to escape anyone's fury.

Wraiths weren't the source behind the sickening transformations inside the tavern, but he still faced the dilemma of escaping with his life. He wondered why the scuttling insects hadn't found and diseased him. None skittered across the floor. They'd disappeared, which relieved him, but he refused to lower his guard.

Twice the tavern door had opened, and twice it'd slammed shut. This attracted the undead's attention. Now, they lingered near the door. He took the opportunity to pull himself out of the barrel. Quietly, he set his heavy boots on the floor. Drucis shook the shelled nuts from his long, white, braided beard and flicked hull and skin pieces from his thick white ponytail.

Drucis' jewel-studded battle-axe was atop the table where he and his comrades had finished off two kegs before the sack of beetles ruined everything. Even with his axe, he didn't think he could get to the door without the undead mass surrounding him. Of course, he needed to *get* his axe first. He didn't see a possible way without alerting the undead patrons of his presence.

He edged around the side of the bar, grabbed a half-filled tankard of ale, and downed it. Then, he noticed the almost hidden door that led to the cellar storage room where kegs of ale and strong liquors were stored. He didn't set the tankard down. He kept it and snuck downstairs. A sly grin parted his thick, snowy white beard. His eyes widened at the intoxicating paradise now surrounding him. To a dwarf, this open-tab treasure was almost as valuable as gold.

Seeing the mouth-watering delights, he could think of no better way to spend his last moments before being turned or killed by the undead. Although he shared two kegs earlier with his two mates, he wasn't the slightest bit tipsy. Depending on the brew's strength he chose, he'd need to drink a half barrel more to feel a slight buzz. By then, he wouldn't have the clarity to worry about the undead attacking him. But, remembering the lost, undead look in his comrades' eyes—nah, he didn't want any clarity. He wanted to *forget*.

Drucis soured at the idea that came to him, which seemed the only way to escape the tavern alive. Searching through the storage shelves near the wooden kegs, he found a small mallet. He hurried to the kegs and smashed off the spigots of the aged whiskies, brandies, and rum. Before the kegs were completely emptied, he grabbed a small keg of ale and tucked it under his arm.

He took a lit oil lantern and smashed it against the wall. The leaking oil burst into flames, ran down the wall, and ignited the inch-deep liquor. Drucis ran farther into the icy cellar before the scorching flames swooshed and hissed into a towering wall of fire. Flames engulfed the barrels, the storage shelves, the side of the wall, and the bottom of the floor above. The heat filled the room and the wooden kegs crackled as the fire's intensity roared.

Drucis pulled the metal door closed, opened the small keg of ale, and sat to drink. He filled his tankard with the ale and smiled. The earthen ceiling overhead assured him that when the tavern burned and collapsed, the flaming embers wouldn't bury and consume him as well.

He raised his tankard to toast. "Aye, Sorgen and Draken, to your memories. We fought many battles and looted many treasures. I'll miss ya both. Nothin' worse than drinking alone."

Drucis sat with his back pressed against the metal door. The inferno on the other side gradually heated the door until he had to move to the colder side of the room. Several explosions quaked, which were sealed barrels of liquor treasures now forever lost. The raging fire had apparently burned through the floor overhead. Burning tavern tables and chairs plummeted through the weakened floor and crashed into the cellar. Horrendous wails shrilled from the burning undead outside the metal door.

He shook his head and poured another tankard. The metal door rattled from the flaming debris dropping against it. Had he foolishly barricaded himself inside his own tomb? The gray metal door brightened and turned yellow, orange, and red. The metal was far too hot to touch, and worse, the hinges were giving way. The door would soon collapse. The temperature inside the room became toasty warm.

While he doubted any of the undead had survived the fiery destruction, he worried about how long he'd have to wait for the heat to dissipate enough to trudge through the charred rubble and smoldering embers so he could leave Glacier Ridge forever.

Several hours passed. The buckled metal door cooled and activity on the other side diminished. He impatiently sighed. His breath was a visible puff of white. He set his empty tankard on the floor and walked to the door. With gloved hands he tugged the warped edge of the door. It stubbornly resisted. He pulled harder. The weakened rivets and bolts popped loose and the door widened.

A gush of smoke filtered into the room. He listened before peering out. Little of the tavern's remains were recognizable. Small flickering flames danced on the bar. Everything else was charred black with white ash running along the outer edges. An occasional burst of wind awakened red glowing embers, but none of the undead moved. Brittle skeletons smoldered in the rubble.

"At least you're at peace." Drucis kicked his way through the mess.

He kept his attention on the floor until he found his battle-axe. It was covered with soot, but the flames had not affected its soundness. The heat of the consuming blaze that destroyed the tavern paled in comparison to what a Dwarven forge produced. Even the welded runes and jewels along the blade's edge and the reinforced handle had not lost their polish. The runes didn't glow, which was a good sign. Otherwise, a sorcerer was nearby.

Drucis brushed the soot off his axe with thick fireproof gloves. Possessing his favorite weapon, his confidence increased. He marched through the black, smoldering remains of Hobskin's Tavern. The icy wind whipped through the narrow passageway that led to the marketplace. He bowed his head against the wind and stepped out onto the cobblestone street.

The square and the streets were eerily silent, other than the wailing, sharp-cutting wind and pellets of sleet plinking off the icy rooftops. The stable doors were wide open. Smoke exited the chimney, but he assumed those inside were cursed with the same disease as those in Hobskin's Tavern.

Hooves clopped along the cobblestone behind Drucis, and he turned with his battle-axe gripped in both hands. He sighed and lowered the axe. His small gray horse, Grey, walked to him. He rubbed its nose and patted the side of its face.

"How'd ya get out? Wouldn't leave me, eh?" Drucis smiled. "Let's find our saddle and get out of this frosty hellhole."

He walked to the open stable and searched until he found his saddle, the bridle, and a couple of saddlebags.

"Taint no one be needing these." He looked through the tools and weapons, and took different, necessary items for his solitary journey.

Before he bridled Grey, he led her to a trough and let her fill her belly with oats and sweet grains.

"Be a long journey to Gordurth, so eat up!"

Grey eagerly ate while Drucis watched the wide open doors and released a long sigh. He missed his friends. He wasn't certain if any undead villagers wandered the streets. Perhaps survivors like himself were trapped inside the buildings or their homes. A fortunate few might've been fortunate enough to leave Glacier Ridge before the pestilence had been released. He considered searching for survivors, but in doing so, he might open doors to masses of undead.

He shook his head. "Nah, best be moving on."

Drucis patted Grey's side and moved to her head. Gently, he slid the bridle in place and turned her toward the door. Movement caught his attention from the corner of his eye. A half dozen undead hobbled in his direction.

Drucis spat on the floor and cursed under his breath. He didn't know whether to mount Grey and gallop out or use his axe to dismember the strange, undead men and women. He had seconds to make such a decision. His life and Grey's depended on him making the right one.

CHAPTER 41

S moke rose over the horizon. Lehrling pointed.

"That's over Glacier Ridge, isn't it?" Roble asked.

Riese and Marc turned and looked. Both nodded.

"What's burning?" Odlon asked.

Riese shook his head. "No idea. We never set anything afire before we left."

"Survivors?" Roble asked.

"Maybe," Riese replied. "We didn't search through all the shops and homes."

"Why not?" Roble asked.

Riese swallowed hard. "After seeing what happened to Jez and the patrons inside Hobskin's Tavern, I didn't see the point. I figured everyone else had been diseased."

"Understandable," Lehrling said in a hoarse voice. He coughed until he couldn't catch his breath. His face flushed crimson red. He beat his chest with his fist several times. Finally, after the severe coughing fit passed, he spat a bloody wad on the black road. Sweat covered his brow, his eyes rolled back, and he dropped off his horse. He lie unconscious on the road.

Roble, Zauber, and Odlon rushed to him.

"He's in bad shape," Roble said.

"Riese," Odlon said. "Could you please get him to the wagon?"

Riese tied the reins to the seat and jumped off the wagon. He marched to where the rest of their party encircled Lehrling. Riese grabbed Lehrling, and effortlessly slung the rotund man over his shoulder. Riese carried him to the rear of the wagon and set Lehrling on the hay surrounding Crukas' iron cage.

To Shawndirea, Roble whispered, "Can you heal him?"

"I can try," she replied.

Zauber shook his head. "No, he needs herbs and rest. We can issue a spell to ease his pain and allow him to rest, but he needs medicine."

"But you're a wizard," Roble said, agitated.

Zauber nodded. "Yes, but magic *isn't* a cure all. Powers are attained differently for every caster. Mine are not aligned to restore health but to ward off evil."

Roble glanced at Shawndirea. She shook her head.

"But what you did," Roble said to her. "At my house. The dead butterflies and moths were reanimated."

"Yes, dear. I understand your frustration, but remember I'm the Butterfly Queen. My energy and magic are connected to the earth, and I bestow blessings and healing for them. Not humans."

Odlon glanced at Roble. "If Eyllisathem were closer, my sister has potions and salves to cure him. I'm sorry."

Lehrling lie unconscious on the bed of the wagon. His irregular breathing was consistent with people suffering from serious pneumonia. Roble swallowed hard.

"So he's going to die?" Roble asked.

Zauber frowned. "We'll do everything we can, but this matter isn't something we have power over."

Shawndirea kissed Roble's cheek. "I'm sorry."

Even though Roble hadn't known Lehrling more than a few days, he liked the man. Lehrling had survived the henchmen but now might die due to pneumonia. The situation angered him.

"What about Woodcrest?" Roble said. "Do you think someone there could help?" he asked.

"It's possible," Zauber replied. "If not, we need a priest. Priests have better effects with healing."

Frustrated, Roble said, "Any priests in Woodcrest?"

"Only if one traveled to the city before Waxxon's soldiers arrived. Woodcrest holds no allegiance to any deity."

Roble turned and walked away. "Luck couldn't be any worse."

"Don't give up hope," Shawndirea said.

"He's *dying*."

"I'm sorry."

"We must do something," Roble said, forming tight fists.

Zauber placed a hand on Roble's shoulder. Warmth rushed through Roble and eased his anger and frustration.

Zauber said, "Patience, Overlander. Nightfall's but a few hours away. When we get to Woodcrest, we should find what we need. They may not have priests or healers, but they're farmers and gatherers. They collect and store herbs."

"How do we get past the gates?" Roble asked.

"Still working on that," Zauber replied. "Should you approach during sunlight, the soldiers will immediately identify you and Lehrling as Dragon Skull Knights. At night, your armor's more difficult to see."

Roble ran his hands through his brown hair and sighed. He glanced at the dark forest surrounding them. The blue-tinted broken statues and pillars were the brightest objects amongst the thick vine and moss-covered trees. The dark forest seemed determined to subdue their brightness and hide them forever.

"What was this place?" Roble asked.

"The Ruins of Sturn?" Zauber said. "Once a great temple and monastery stood and thrived here before dark elves attacked and slaughtered the monks within."

"And Woodcrest?"

"Not settled and established for many years *after* this slaughter."

Roble walked to the edge of the road and studied the marble statues. All the heads and hands were broken away. The vandalism the dark elves had done was a testament against any follower of light and fore-warned travelers not to tarry long. The dark elves didn't fear followers of the light and viewed them as enemies.

Zauber slipped away from where Roble stood.

Alone with Shawndirea, Roble asked, "Do you trust Zauber?"

"He's not a stranger. My mother sought his council many times after my father died."

"So he can be trusted?"

"Of course."

Roble glanced at Lehrling. The old man's chest rose and fell slowly. His eyes remained closed. Zauber placed his left hand on Lehrling's chest and raised his staff with the right. After speaking some words, the wizard's blood quartz ring glowed and dimmed. Lehrling's body jerked, but his eyes didn't open. He rolled to his side into a more comfortable position.

Roble met Shawndirea's beautiful eyes. She smiled and blushed. "What if he tells your mother where you are? And about me … us?"

She shook her head slightly. "He won't."

"You're certain?"

"He'd rather I approach her without her patrols binding and returning me to Elvendale."

"They'd actually bind you?"

"Depends on the severity of her anger. She's threatened before, but never has. She has … *her moods*. She's insistent I take the throne, and soon. I don't want the responsibility. I've always been adamant about *never* assuming the throne."

"Zauber believes your mother won't accept me."

Shawndirea nodded. "She won't."

"You sought and chose me. Not out of spite, I hope."

Tears welled in her eyes. "Surely you don't believe—"

"I'm sorry. It sounded worse than I intended."

Shawndirea wiped tears from her eyes and her shoulders drooped. "So you still question *us*?"

"I'm sorry. No, I—"

She looked away. "Haven't I made my intentions clear? You don't believe I love you?"

Her tearful eyes, body gestures, and the hurt in her voice, caused him to grieve. Gently, he placed a finger beneath her chin and smiled. "I believe you. I don't want to be the reason you refuse the throne, though. No sense increasing animosity from the Fae than what I'll probably cause."

"No. You're *not* the reason. I've never wanted to be Queen of Elvendale. I'll always remain the Butterfly Queen because it's my birthright and calling. I refuse to assume the throne and marry whomever *they* believe's the best choice for our next king. What about you? Do you love me? You're human and most humans think love develops over time, but what are your true feelings?"

"Had we not gotten you from the Ratkins, I'd never stopped hunting until I found you. I love you. I was smitten before we began this journey, after you resurrected my collection.

"But when they took you—my heart was torn. Emptiness consumed me and determination pushed me to find you. I've never felt such an inner ache like the thought of losing you, or finding you dead. Mixed emotions overwhelmed me the second I saw you in the bottle. I was ecstatic you were alive, but angered you were placed inside the bottle."

"So you'll stay with me?" She studied his eyes intently.

"Of course."

Her eyes never left his gaze. Worry and hurt overshadowed her. "Won't you miss the Overlands?"

"No. I'm tired of the technology and its brainwashing effects on people. I'd prefer living a simpler life."

"Life in Aetheaon won't be easier."

"I expect it won't be," Roble replied. "I'm also tired of politics."

Shawndirea smiled. "You'll never escape politics. Politics abound wherever populations exist."

"True. But everything's more beautiful in your realm than my home."

"It's far more dangerous than you imagine. But, eventually, you'll return to the Overlands."

"I need to put things in order for closure. I don't want my sister, Lib, to think I'm dead. It's best she knows I'm alive."

"I agree. Will you tell her about Aetheaon?"

Roble shook his head. "No. I don't want her thinking I've gone insane, either."

She grinned. "Understandable."

"Although I might visit from time to time, I never want to return from where we exited. But I'm not certain how to get back home."

She said, "Many rifts exist throughout the plane, mostly in caves. Zauber could enchant an object to find your way home."

"Whenever I visit the Overlands, I'll always return quickly to you. That's a promise."

NIGHTFALL CAME. Darkness settled over the forest outside Woodcrest. Glowing eyes peered from the trees. Roble shivered from the eerie sensation. Strange bird and insect sounds echoed. The broken statues shimmered a murky, bluish tint in spite of the surrounding blackness. What else lurked in the shadowy trees?

Odlon stood beside Roble. "Are you ready to fight?"

"As I'll ever be."

"I've not had the chance to train you, but once we're settled somewhere safer, I will."

"I appreciate that."

Odlon smiled. "For what it's worth, your skill with knives is excellent."

"Thanks."

Roble followed Odlon to the rear of the wagon. Buried beneath straw and two sweaty, horse blankets, Lehrling lie unconscious. Sweat beaded his forehead. His staggered breathing was hampered by thick phlegm.

Shawndirea sat on the side of the wagon.

"He's getting worse," Roble said.

"I know."

Crukas sat and hugged his knees inside the cage. His eyes revealed his defeat. Zauber's silence spell prevented the thief from speaking his disdain or pleading for release.

Roble looked at Zauber. "How do we enter Woodcrest?"

"You won't like my suggestion," Zauber said.

Roble folded his arms across his chest. "At this point, I'm almost willing to try anything if it increases Lehrling's chances to survive."

"Crukas must be released for this to succeed," he said.

"What?" Roble and Odlon asked.

Riese raised his massive fists and rushed Zauber. The wizard's hand tightened around his staff. The crystal atop the staff glowed crimson. The sudden burst of light caused Riese to lower his hands and stop.

Through clenched teeth, Riese said, "He remains caged until we get to Ironwood."

"Very well," Zauber said. "We've no hope of passing through the forest tonight or tomorrow. Woodcrest is the only path to the other side. Unless you wish to leave your wagon, horses, and supplies behind while you cut your way through the ruins. Of course, to do that, Crukas can't remain in the cage."

The mention of freeing Crukas jolted the thief from his depression and he stood. He gently rattled the cage door and hoped to gain their attention and sympathy with his pleading eyes. Purposely, none of the party regarded him.

"What do you propose?" Roble asked.

"Crukas stays with you, me, Odlon, and the faery," Zauber said. "Riese drives the wagon to the gate."

Riese shook his head. "Crukas can vanish and reappear elsewhere. You release him, and we'll never see him again."

"Should he escape without aiding us," Zauber said. "He'll never speak again. Only I can reverse my spell."

"It's too risky," Riese replied. "He could panhandle as a mute beggar in Hoffnung or any other grand city. People pity folks like that. He'd probably earn more gold begging than he does as a thief."

Insulted, Crukas glared.

Zauber looked at Crukas. "Will you help us in order to speak again?"

Crukas nodded.

"Of course he's going to agree," Riese said.

Roble asked, "What does Crukas need to do?"

"Unlock the gate."

Odlon shook his head. "They'll kill him before he reaches the gate."

Riese smiled broadly, and Crukas' hopeful smile faded.

"Riese is our distraction," Zauber said.

Riese's smile vanished. Confusion tightened his brow. "What?"

Zauber said, "You're the same bloodline as Waxxon's henchmen, so you can drive to the gate without them killing you."

"I'm *not* one of them."

"I won't argue your heritage," Zauber said. "But we need you to distract them long enough for us to kill the men at the gate towers. Once we do, Crukas unlocks the gate and you drive the wagon inside."

Riese looked at Crukas. Crukas smiled sheepishly.

"I don't like this idea," Riese said.

"Noted, "Odlon said. "But there's always the chance Crukas dies."

Crukas stopped smiling.

"Can you guarantee that?" Riese asked.

Roble frowned. "Why do you want Crukas dead?"

Riese's jaw tightened. "He turned on his fellow thieves and collected their bounties. That's a direct violation of Glacier Ridge's rules. All bounty hunters are turned away. I already forbade Crukas from returning, but he did anyway."

"None of us will ever return there," Roble said. "Glacier Ridge is gone."

Fury rushed through Riese. "For now. But I'll reclaim it."

Crukas waved his hands and shook his head vigorously.

"What's wrong?" Roble asked.

Crukas motioned at Riese and shook his head again.

"You deny Riese's charges?"

Crukas crossed his arms and nodded.

Riese growled. "Do you trust a thief to tell you the truth?"

"Right now, it's difficult to decipher what he's saying," Roble said. "Perhaps, he should be given the opportunity to speak his side?"

Crukas nodded.

Zauber said. "After he proves his trust and aids us, we'll hear his side."

Frustrated, Riese glared at Crukas.

"Here." Zauber handed Riese the leather armor from one of Waxxon's dead Vyking soldiers. "Wear these. It'll lessen the chance for them to think you're *not* one of them."

Riese took the armor and opened his mouth to speak but the wizard cut him off.

"No arguments," Zauber said, "Unless you want to spend the night in this darkened forest where the roaming, angry spirits of murdered monks and priests abound."

Riese's eyes peered at the dark forest trees. Riese was beyond brave fighting physical beings. But spirits could only be defeated through arcane magic. Riese somewhat feared magic, so the subtle threat of ghosts lessened his stubbornness to cooperate.

"Unlock his cage," Zauber said.

Riese grumbled and took his key ring from Roble. He placed the key into the cage lock and met Zauber's eyes. "Trusting him's a mistake. He uses magic to vanish."

Roble nodded. "I've seen him."

"He may flee." Riese turned the key.

The lock clicked loudly.

Zauber smiled. "If he flees, he won't get far. Another spell hangs over him. Should he run, he goes blind. Permanently."

"Ah, well. Blind and mute?" Riese said with a broad smile. He swung open the whining cage door. "In that case, by all means thief, step out."

Crukas hesitated. His nervous eyes glanced from Riese to Roble and to Zauber before he stepped out. He held his cuffed hands to Riese. Riese grunted and unlocked the cuffs.

The cuffs dropped to the hay beside Lehrling, and Crukas rubbed his wrists. He humbly bowed to Riese and then to Zauber. Riese grabbed the leather armor, turned, and headed to the front of the wagon to change.

After Riese changed armor, he sat on the wagon seat. "Are we ready?"

"Not quite yet," Zauber replied.

Zauber motioned Odlon, Roble, and Crukas to stand in the center of the road with him. Shawndirea stood on Roble's shoulder.

Zauber looked at Odlon. "Be ready to use your crossbow immediately. Just in case."

Odlon gave a firm nod.

"Faery," Zauber said. "Draw upon your power while I use my own."

Shawndirea closed her eyes, raised her hands, and her fingertips glowed. Zauber stood in the center of them and drove the tip of his staff firmly into the road. Red swirls of light formed a large, glowing red circle that wrapped around them. Wind whistled, and in an instant, they were gone.

Seconds later, they stood in Woodcrest's center square near a well.

"What the Hell?" Roble grabbed a wooden post to keep from falling. "How?"

"Translocation spell," Odlon said with a wide grin.

"We're in Woodcrest?"

Odlon place his forefinger to his lips and nodded. He motioned Roble to move behind a wagon filled with cut wheat stalks. Roble obliged while the elf moved into the shadows of the town hall and disappeared. Zauber headed the opposite direction, and he too, vanished.

Crukas was gone before Roble thought to look for him. Roble understood why Crukas was renowned for his thievery skills, but he realized *why* Riese feared the thief would leave the party without aiding them.

"What do I do?" Roble asked Shawndirea.

"Keep your eyes open and watch for any patrols."

"The town's too quiet," he said.

She nodded. "Curfew. Waxxon's men have it under their control. The townspeople are too afraid to move about."

Roble regarded the two hanged bodies on a tree near the center of Woodcrest.

"What does Waxxon gain by occupying this tiny town? The buildings are poorly constructed. They can't possibly gain riches from these people."

Shawndirea shrugged. "Woodcrest sets in the direct crossroads that leads to Glacier Ridge. Many thieves travel this direction, and some, as you've well seen, are willing to kidnap for ransom."

"So I hide in the shadows?" Roble asked. "That seems cowardly."

She shook her head. "Odlon will take out the men on the gate towers. Crukas will pick the gate lock to let Riese pass through. You're an extra preventative should any guard pass this direction."

Roble placed his hands on the daggers tucked inside his belt and waited. The quiet town slept, but soon, it'd awaken to the tragedies of unexpected living nightmares.

CHAPTER 42

*R*iese's teenage son hid beneath the wagon seat before he reached Woodcrest's gates. He packed hay around Marc to make certain he wasn't visible. While they might accept Riese as one of their brethren, which was true, but never something he'd confess, his son didn't favor his bloodline. He was like his mother, who wasn't of Vyking descent.

Dressed like Waxxon's soldiers, Riese's conscience struggled with pretending to be one of the bloodthirsty bastards. He detested his race that much.

Riese's appearance was as foreboding as theirs. His anger and hatred toward his bloodline ran deep because of how they'd betrayed him and their offenses against Riese and his family. He'd never forgive their transgressions and vowed to avenge his losses with their blood.

Jez and Marc were twins, born to Riese from Odrissus—a half elf— and the love of his life. Her heritage was why his sons were nowhere near his size and appearance. They favored her size and possessed her gentle mannerisms. His heart ached at losing her. Her death was why he hated the Vyking Lords.

Before he renounced his allegiance to the Vykings, he served King Obed on the Isles of Welkstone, and paid homage to their God, Reus. While pillaging and plundering a small port, he found Odrissus frightened and pleading for her life from three of his comrades. They sought to do her great harm in unspeakable ways *before* they killed her. No amount of begging and pleading would've dissuaded their minds. They surrounded her in her bedroom. Their lust prevented them from seeing Riese slip up behind them with his battle-axe.

After ripping her blouse open, they laughed at her helplessness. She covered her breasts with her long braided red hair, scooted across the hardwood floor, and crouched in a corner. Her fearful blue eyes pleaded, but the three grinning men circled her. They stood seven feet tall, were dark skinned and had long, thick beards. Tattooed runes covered their arms and bare chests. They roared with deep laughter as she squirmed on the floor. The more she fretted, the more pleasure they took.

Riese beheaded two of his comrades before the third even reached for his sword.

He faced Riese. "Brother, what've you done? We take what we want during our raids, especially the women."

"Not her, Tryke," Riese said.

"The king'll have your head for killing two of your brethren," Tryke said.

Riese spat on the floor. "Make it three. To the abyss with King Obed!"

"Traitor!" Tryke said.

Tryke's eyes narrowed. He gnashed his teeth with fury, but it was his last living act. The sharp battle-axe blade separated his head from his shoulders. Tryke dropped in death like his two comrades.

Riese turned to the redheaded maiden and extended his hand. She flinched and covered her face. Moments later, she peered through her fingers. "Please, don't hurt me."

"I won't hurt you. Take my hand."

Timidly, she reached for his hand. When she placed her tiny hand into his, he pulled her to her feet.

"What's your name?" he asked.

"Odrissus."

"I'm Riese."

Her soft blue eyes stared into his. She read he meant her no harm. She could trust him. Her fear faded and her breathing relaxed.

"Quick," Riese said, "Get dressed. Others will be along soon."

Odrissus grabbed a blouse and pulled it over her head. "Why are you helping me?"

"Hurry," he whispered. Outside, horses galloped past. He pulled open the door slightly. More Vyking soldiers rode past. Smoke billowed from the burning huts. Swords clashed and people screamed in anguish.

She hurried to the door and stood beside him. She was half his height. Her ears were pointed, similar to an elf's but slightly different.

"My horse is by the fence," he said. "My people are too busy to notice us, but we must be quick and not draw attention to ourselves. Understand?"

Odrissus looked up at him and nodded. "I run fast."

"Good."

Riese pulled open the door. They sprinted across the compacted dirt field until they reached his horse. He swung on the horse in one smooth movement and extended his hand to her. She grabbed it and pulled herself behind him on the saddle. He tugged the reins to the right and kicked the horse's flanks.

"Riese!"

Riese glanced over his shoulder. His general sat atop a magnificent steed and glared at him. Two soldiers exited Odrissus' hut with their swords drawn and reported the three headless Vykings.

"Don't let him escape!" General Yerdrick shouted.

The two men drew their swords and rushed across the path while three horsemen circled around and headed toward Riese and Odrissus.

"Hang on," Riese told her.

The two swordsmen moved quickly. Riese believed he had a better chance rushing them than being encircled by the three horsemen. His horse thundered across the barren field. Riese brought his axe around and caught one man in the gut with the blade. The axe sliced through the man's armor, his midsection, and protruded through the man's back. The momentum propelled the man upward, and Riese yanked the blade free. The man rolled in the dirt several times, and once he stopped, he never moved again.

The second swordsman rushed. Riese kicked him in the face and knocked the man off balance. Riese's horse charged past without injury. Once the horse got to full gait, no man on foot could catch him. Riese tapped the horse's flanks harder. He glanced back long enough to see the three horsemen in pursuit.

Although the Vykings were seamen at heart, they were also experienced horsemen. Riese had to be crafty to lose them. As good as he was with his axe, he realized fighting three of his angered brethren at once lessened his odds of successful victory.

Waves of smoke drifted in dark sheets across the small village. Thatched roofs blazed. Huts engulfed with raging fire crackled. Other than the three men pursuing him, the rest of the pillagers were too busy looting to notice his betrayal to King Obed and his fellow comrades.

Riese rode a side path leading away from the port village and up the side of the mountain. The three horsemen pursued.

Once Riese reached the top of the ridge, they rode into a dense forest. Riese hoped he'd lose the men or they'd turn back. They didn't. Their determination to capture him was as dedicated as he was to escape.

Odrissus wrapped her arms tightly around his waist and pressed the side of her face against his shirtless back. As the horse galloped through the darkening forest, he held the battle-axe firmly in his right hand. Drying blood dripped from the silvery axe blade.

None of his Vyking brethren were archers, which spared him from being killed from a distance. All Vykings preferred heavy axes or swords because such meant strength and power. Plus, they loved hand-to-hand combat because they witnessed the life drain from their enemies' eyes after they ran swords through them.

Riese glanced back. His three pursuers slowed their approach. Their horses were as tired as his, but why were they slowing down? Ahead, he noticed why. He tightened the reins to slow his mount.

Over fifty men stood on the path. Farmers. They wore modest fur jackets and ragged, leather pants. They carried various crude weapons, mostly farming tools and hatchets. When they saw Riese, they charged him like raging fools.

"What is this?" Riese asked.

"A neighboring village."

Riese shook his head. "What do they plan to do?"

"Help protect my village. When your ships docked, our leader sent a rider into the neighboring town for help. Leave me with them, if you truly wish to rescue me."

"No, I can't leave you. They're not contenders against my people, in spite of their foolish bravery. These men will be slaughtered. If you remain with them, you'll die."

Riese turned the horse, tapped its sides, and headed through the forest. Rather than pursue him, the three Vykings turned and headed for the port village. He figured they'd tell the other warriors of the approaching villagers. They'd kill these simple men in less than an hour. It was what Vykings thrived on. Lust for loot and bloodshed.

He halfway expected her to protest, but she held tightly. The horse galloped around trees, down rugged rocky slopes, and farther from the easier path. Not familiar with this terrain, Riese had no idea where he was headed, nor did he actually care. The seaman life he'd always known was over. He'd find a place far inland where he could live. Perhaps raise a family. He'd never deal with his people again. Or so he hoped. But in spite of wherever he chose to settle, he was marked. King Obed would never rest until someone brought the king Riese's head.

After several days of riding during the day and camping at night, Riese found a small, quiet place nestled in a wooded area near a clear spring and a wide creek where he could fish. They stayed sheltered beneath a rocky shelf against the ridge while he built a small hut with a thatched roof.

The second morning he awoke, Odrissus sat at the edge of the creek watching darting minnows along the water's edge. Her bright blue eyes met with his brown eyes. He smiled. She returned the simple greeting.

"Odrissus," Riese said. "You may take the horse and return to your people if you choose. I won't keep you against your will. You're free to go."

"I don't wish to leave," she replied. "Even if I could find my way, it's doubtful my village survived. Isn't that what you told me?"

Riese looked away and nodded. "Aye. It is."

"Would you mind if I live with you?"

The warmth inside her gaze and voice let him know he was more than a plundering murderer that ransacked harbor towns. She smiled and stood.

"I'd like that very much," he said softly.

Odrissus pulled back her hair and revealed her elven ears. "As you see, the village wasn't my true home. I was a servant traded to them when I was a little girl. I can be your servant, if you'd like."

Riese shook his head. "Nonsense. You'll be no such thing. I'd have you be my wife, if that pleases you?"

Her eyes widened with surprise. "You wish that of me?"

"Yes."

"I've known nothing except being a servant. Never had I thought I'd be a wife."

Riese smiled. "From today forward, you serve no one."

Tears moistened her eyes. She rushed and embraced him tightly. When she glanced up at him, he leaned and kissed her lips. He placed his arms around her. She leapt and wrapped her legs around his waist. He carried her to where they slept and held her close and kissed her for hours.

ver several weeks, Riese constructed a large, secure house for he and Odrissus to live comfortably. About a year after they settled, she gave birth to twin boys: Jez and Marc.

The twins were so small Riese feared his huge hands would crush them. Odrissus laughed when he expressed his fears, but she coaxed him into holding his boys, one in each hand.

"You'll make the greatest father," she said with a smile.

Riese had never known such pride—a beautiful dainty wife and two sons—and what he felt inside outweighed any sensation he'd ever experienced before. The boys favored her in size and appearance, and they grew quickly.

Before Riese realized it, they'd lived at the edge of the wooded creek for six years. He marveled at how fast time passed. His boys were fast, rambunctious, and quick learners. They learned to fish, track game animals, and climbed trees swifter than squirrels.

Few people traveled along the creek, so trading goods with travelers was impossible. From time to time he loaded dried fish, animal furs, and jerky, and carried them two days to the closest town. He traded his supplies for weapons, so he could train his boys how to effectively use them if ever the occasion occurred. Eventually it did.

During his final trip to the town, a faded flyer written in his language caught his attention. A substantial reward was offered for him, dead or alive. The crudely drawn poster didn't quite resemble him. The image could be almost any bearded, dark-haired man. However, the description detailed Riese perfectly but he doubted any locals could've translated the words.

The townspeople apparently couldn't read the language, as they didn't pay him any more attention than they would an ordinary trader. Yet, fear nipped at his soul. His brethren had tacked the poster, which meant they'd been within two days of his homestead. His wife and two sons were home without him. He packed his wares and placed his axe over his shoulder. He hurried through the trading square, down a short cobblestone street that exited the town, and headed into the wilderness. Once the town was out of view, he ran through fields and forests, and cut his journey's time by almost a full day.

Out of breath and weak from overexerting himself, Riese stopped long enough to eat berries, dried jerky, and drink water. He took to running again. When he reached his home, he splashed and sloshed across the creek.

The rear door of their home was wide open. A Vyking lie facedown in the dirt. A sword protruded from the man's back. He immediately recognized Jez's blade.

Riese turned the Vyking over. The man's tattoos were the same as his. King Obed's coat of arms was sewn to his leather chest piece. His brethren had found his home.

"Odrissus!" Riese shouted frantically. "Jez! Marc!"

No answer.

His heart thundered in his ears. Sickness turned his stomach, and for a moment, drawing his next breath seemed impossible.

"Odrissus!" Riese tracked footprints leading away from the hut.

Two sets of footprints were too large to be his wife's or sons'. They were similar to his own. The twins were too light to leave impressions in the soil. But he made out Odrissus' barefoot outlines where her toes had dug into the ground while she fled.

While Riese ran from his home to the thick brambles, he came upon another dead Vyking. The Vyking's throat had been sliced so deeply, Riese was surprised the man's head had not been completely removed.

"Jez! Odrissus! Marc!"

He didn't care about shouting and giving away his whereabouts. He actually *hoped* the remaining man would face him. Riese needed to know his family was safe, and he wanted to kill the man for invading his home.

Deeper in the forest, Odrissus screamed.

Riese sprinted through the trees until he located her. Her long, red hair flowed behind her as she fled from the large man.

Where were his sons? He rushed through the forest.

The man grabbed Odrissus' red locks and yanked her down. She struggled and kicked. Her tiny hands clawed the man's face. He lifted her off the ground and growled.

"Odrissus!" Riese ran faster. He was less than ten yards from where she struggled to break free from the Vyking's grasp.

Breathing heavily and exhausted, Riese ran on adrenaline. He rushed the man, but before Riese reached him, the man thrust a dagger into Odrissus' side. The man yanked out the bloody blade and shoved her to the ground. She clutched her ribs and curled into a fetal position.

"You bastard!" Riese sprinted at the man.

Before the Vyking brought the dagger around to defend Riese's attack, Riese thrust the palm of his hand against the man's leather chest piece. The devastating blow brought the man off his feet and flung him backwards. The man's sternum cracked and the sound echoed through the forest. His dagger dropped in the loose leaves. The man's eyes widened with pain and surprise. The harsh landing took his breath.

The Vyking writhed on the ground and gripped his sternum. Riese stood over him and recognized the man. General Yerdrick.

Yerdrick blinked in surprise, more from Riese's strength than from recognition. Blood coated the general's teeth. He coughed. More blood bubbled from his lips. He forced a smile.

"Ah," Yerdrick said. "You spoiled the surprise."

Riese's eyes narrowed. He tossed his sword aside, reached down, and grabbed the general by the throat with one hand and heaved him to his feet. He squeezed until Yerdrick's eyes bulged, his face purpled, and seconds before the man lost consciousness, he loosened his hold.

Riese released the general's throat. Yerdrick could barely hold himself upright. With a huge open hand, Riese smacked the side of Yerdrick's face so hard the man spun around and dropped to his knees.

Though weak, Yerdrick laughed. "You picked a feisty one. She was full of spirit like yourself."

"You'll die slowly for this," Riese said. "Painfully slow."

"Kill me, Riese. End me now. But know, my brother Quenid knows I came to kill you. He'll continue the search, as will others. You'll never find peace in this world."

"Let him come. He'll meet you at the River Styx!"

Riese glared with a murderous stare. A purple handprint pulsed on the general's cheek where Riese had struck him. Blood leaked from Yerdrick's nose and mouth. He chuckled. "Good thing she only had two swords. She'd probably have killed me, too."

Anger and rage rushed through Riese. His huge fist struck Yerdrick in the face—cracking his nose and shattering his teeth. After the general collapsed, Riese leaned over him and pounded his face until the man didn't move. Most of the man's facial bones were sunken, crushed. He was no longer recognizable and no longer breathing. Even though his former general was dead, Riese regretted killing him too quickly.

Riese spat on the man and stood. He wiped blood from his bruised fist. He hurried to Odrissus and dropped beside her. He rolled her slightly and rested her head on his lap. Her blue eyes stared at him. A weak smile formed on her lips. She panted and winced.

"Odrissus," Riese said. Tears formed in his eyes, and he brushed her long red hair with his fingers. "Don't die, my love and my lady."

She looked at him with sad eyes. "I love you. Take care of our sons."

"Where are they?"

"In the cellar. They're safe."

Riese's voice shook. "I'm sorry I wasn't here."

"It's not your fault. I almost killed them all."

"You did well, my wife."

Her breathing slowed. He brushed her red hair from her face. Her cheeks grew colder. He leaned and kissed her bluish lips. She smiled and her eyes went distant. Her breathing stopped.

Riese wailed. His voice echoed through the forest. Birds and animals fled deeper into the trees. Silence fell. He clenched his fists and shook them at the heavens. Veins popped up on his arms and forehead as his entire body flexed in rage. At that moment, his fury was enough to kill a bear with his bare hands. He growled like a mad animal until his vision darkened, and he collapsed beside Odrissus.

When he awakened, he closed her eyes, leaned over, and pressed his cheek against hers. Tears flowed, wetting her hair, and he wrapped his arms around her lifeless body and held her. His heart was torn. He was empty inside.

Riese walked through the forest until he found his blade and returned to Yerdrick's body. He swung the blade overhead, hacked downward, and decapitated the general he hated.

Riese returned to Odrissus, picked her up, and marched through the forest until he came to his house. Before he got his sons, he placed Odrissus on their bed. He gently fixed her hair and crossed her arms over her chest. He wrapped the blanket she'd made over her body, and one last time, he kissed her cheek, which was colder than marble. He left her, went to the cellar, and found his boys sitting in the corner playing with the wooden animals he had carved for them.

"Come Jez and Marc." Riese fought to keep his voice from quaking. "It's time to go."

Riese saddled his old horse, which he'd retired from long trips and only used to plow their small garden. He placed the twins on the saddle, returned to the house, and gathered the best weapons and tools they had. After he placed these inside the saddlebags, he returned to the cellar, took several oil lanterns, lit them, and tossed them down the stairs where they shattered. The flames ignited the oil. He hurried to his horse and his sons, and led the horse by the bridle reins.

Before he went down the next ridge, he turned. The small hut engulfed in flames. Although he no longer claimed the traditions of his brethren and ancestors, he wanted to guarantee that Odrissus entered the heavenly afterlife. The general and his two soldiers, on the other hand, were left for the crows and wolves where he hoped their unburned bodies awakened and suffered their rightful torment in the depths of the hottest Hell.

CHAPTER 44

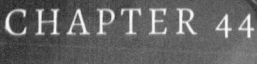

Riese drove the wagon to Woodcrest's gates. The memories of loss burned renewed rage through Riese. Losing his wife and son fueled his anger. The combination of his anger and rage ignited a need to kill Waxxon's henchmen. He despised them, but to keep his sons safe, he never openly engaged in attacks against them in Glacier Ridge.

But secretly, whenever they stabled their horses with him, Riese sabotaged their riding equipment. He weakened saddle straps, bridle bits, and embedded sharp burrs in their saddle blankets. While such small things weren't actual assaults for the former brethren he despised, it was a small thorn in their side. He considered the actions subtle forewarnings of the stormy attack he'd eventually pursue.

Whenever any Vyking entered Glacier Ridge, they thought he was a cordial stable master. What they didn't know was how much he cursed them under his breath. He longed for the day when he could slaughter them like they had his fair Odrissus. Now, that day had arrived.

Torches blazed on the stone pillars at each side of the gate. Massive oaks towered near the watchtowers. The massive trees allowed the guards shade during the daylight and camouflaged hiding places after sunset. Watchmen above stood near torches while others positioned themselves higher in the tree branches; invisible only when they didn't move.

When the horse was within a few yards of Woodcrest's gate, a deep raspy voice beckoned from the tower. "That's close enough! Come no closer."

Riese pulled back the reins.

The watchman shouted, "Who goes there?"

"You don't recognize one of your own?" Riese shouted. He held a lit torch near his bearded face.

The man above leaned near the edge and looked down.

"What brings you out in the dead of night?"

"Delivery for Lord Waxxon," Riese replied.

"Oh? And what might that be?"

"Quite the trophy," Riese said. "I deliver a Dragon Skull Knight."

Suddenly, more curious guards surrounded the man in the tower, and although surprised, Riese never expressed it. However, he counted a dozen men between the two gate towers, which meant Zauber either underestimated the true number of Waxxon's guards, or he'd deceived them.

To make matters worse, several men that stepped into the light of the tower torches were archers. The Vykings didn't have archers. But Riese recognized these archers' armor and helms. He had, on occasion, repaired this type of armor in his blacksmith shop. These archers were dark elves, which meant his party faced greater odds than the wizard had led them to believe.

"Where's this man you speak of?" the guard asked.

"In the wagon bed."

"Dead?"

Riese shook his head. "Not quite. He's alive, but not in good health."

"So he can be interrogated?"

"When he awakens, yes."

A long rope ladder lowered from the watchtower. Seconds later, one of Waxxon's guards climbed down while the archers guarded him. He approached the driver's seat, took Riese's torch, and walked to the rear of the wagon. Riese's gaze went to the towers. The archers aimed their arrows at him.

The guard brought the torch over Lehrling's face. He felt for a pulse and gave a slight nod. He ran his finger over the Dragon Skull pendant.

He raised the torch with a broad grin. "He speaks the truth!"

The man held the torch and searched the wagon. He stopped beside Riese again. "What's the cage for?"

"The prisoner, of course."

"Why isn't he in it?" the guard asked.

Riese smiled evenly. "He's a bit large fit inside, don't you think? After he lost consciousness, I took him out to ensure he stayed alive. After all, dead men don't talk."

The Waxxon guard grinned. "They don't, do they? What's wrong with him?"

Riese laughed. "I'm not a physician. I seek my compensation in gold from Lord Waxxon for finding him."

"Compensation, you say?" the man asked curiously.

Riese nodded.

"No one asks Lord Waxxon for compensation for our sworn duties."

"What?" Riese said angrily. He pointed at the golden button on the guard's shoulder pad. "What do you call that?"

"It's a medal of honor," the man replied.

"Isn't that compensation enough?" Riese asked with a harsh frown.

"My apologies, brother. I thought you meant gold *pieces*. Of course, there are medals."

Riese nodded. "That's all I ask."

Waxxon's soldier peered closer to Riese and his eyes widened with recognition. "Say, don't I know you?"

Riese studied the man's face. He shook his head. "You don't look familiar to me."

"Which of Waxxon's bands are you with?"

Riese replied, "I'm the last of mine."

The man studied Riese's eyes suspiciously. Riese never flinched or looked away. He handed the torch to Riese and motioned for the gate to be opened.

Where's Crukas? Riese wondered.

The gears of the wooden gate cranked and slowly opened inward. Something wasn't right, but Riese had no choice but to go forward.

Outnumbered possibly twenty to one, whatever resided on the other side of those walls could lead to their demise.

LIGHT POLES LIT Woodcrest's modest intersecting streets. Atop the poles, housed in glass, were yellow, glowing crystals. Elven stones. They prevented the town from being completely shrouded in darkness at night. On occasion, lighted candles flickered when nervous townspeople dared a peek through their windows.

Roble hid in the shadows behind a trader's wagon containing tanned hides. Shawndirea stood on a metal wagon wheel near him. The market square was divided by the intersection of two compacted roads. Although Woodcrest was small, it was a hardy trading town. Stringed dried fish dangled from the sloped roofs of small wagons. Small traders' huts lined the corners of the intersection but were boarded up for the night. Loaded wagons of grains, produce, and dried fish lined the streets. Apparently since Waxxon's men had taken over, the trading routes were closed. Woodcrest was prohibited from sending their goods to the neighboring towns and villages and vice versa.

Woodcrest supplied Glacier Ridge with breads, flours, and ale they made from their farmed grains.

The smell of fresh bread and beer lingered in the still, night air. Roble's stomach growled, but he ignored his hunger.

Riese's loud voice soon drown the sound of Roble's growling stomach. They listened intently to the gate guard questioning the stable master's arrival.

A white marble statue of a new nude maiden gleamed beneath the closest light pole. At the base of the statue was a marble altar. A water dish rested atop the altar. Shawndirea gasped.

"What?" he asked.

She whispered, "The statue. It's a tribute to Aerlene."

"Who?"

"One of my mother's sisters long believed dead. They seem to worship her as a guardian to bless their crops and harvests."

"Zauber said they didn't pay homage to any deity."

"Apparently, they do for her," she replied.

Heavy iron clanked and groaned. Chain links clattered from the far end of the street to their left.

"The gates are opening," Roble said. "But did you hear what Riese said?"

She nodded.

"He offered Lehrling up. That's not part of the plan."

"Riese had to give reason for coming to the gate," she said. "Otherwise the guards might kill him. Few people, except bandits and rogues, travel the roads late at night."

"You don't think he'd hand Lehrling over?"

"Why would he?" she asked. "You don't trust many people."

"That was your advice."

"I know."

"Besides," Roble nodded. "I'm skeptical by nature. It's how you survive."

"Has Riese given you any reason not to trust him?" she asked.

"No, but we've given him reason to turn on us. As much as he hates Crukas, we freed the thief. If Riese chose to exact revenge, now's the best chance to get even."

"I doubt that's his choice, but the offer *got* the gates opened."

Roble nodded. "Crukas was supposed to open the gates. So where is he?"

Shawndirea's brow furrowed. "That's a good question."

ODLON FOLLOWED the edge of the shadowed buildings along the wooden town wall until he neared the two guard towers at the gate. He favored the darkest crevices of the buildings outside the yellow lanterns' glow.

Crouching low, he edged to the side wooden wall and rose. He placed a bolt on the crossbow and and locked it in place. Scanning the tower wall, there were far more men guarding the gate than what Zauber had told them. And worse, posted with Waxxon's guards were dark elves, which were his mortal enemies.

He counted four dark elf archers and eight Waxxon Guards. At the gates, four more guards stood at ground level.

"Dammit," Odlon whispered.

Why were dark elves in league with Waxxon?

Odlon was fast with any type of bow. If he faced only swordsmen, he could overpower these men in a matter of minutes. However, four dark elf archers weighted the scale in their favor, not his.

While Odlon's green dragon armor could possibly thwart any arrows the dark elves possessed, they were the most accurate archers in Aetheaon. Since he didn't wear a helm, a quick headshot from a dark elf marksman would be his demise. Their eyesight was keen, and more so after sunset.

Oldon slinked farther into the shadows and went to find Roble. He turned when Riese offered Lehrling to Waxxon's guards. He paused and listened to the ongoing conversation until the guards began winding the wheel to open the gate. Odlon sprinted through the dark town. They needed a better plan to save Lehrling and set Woodcrest free. Since they'd entered the center of Woodcrest by the wizard's spell, they were trapped inside and greatly outnumbered.

CRUKAS TRIED to use his invisibility spell but couldn't since he was unable to verbally cast the incantation. He didn't possess the power to mentally will himself invisible. After all, he was a novice in the use of magic. The best he could do was hide behind a covered wagon where the townspeople hung herbs to dry.

His resentment for being ordered to open the gate made him want to retreat and find alternate route out of Woodcrest. However, doing so meant losing his sight, and what good was a blind and mute thief? Besides, not helping Roble and the others possibly meant his own death by Waxxon's men for trespassing in their newly acquired town.

Crukas squatted lower when he noticed movement along the top of the gate wall. He rolled under the wagon and crawled between the front metal wheels where he peered out to see the wall. He hoped they couldn't see him.

CHAPTER 45

*C*rukas' life as a thief had given luxuries he'd never have owned otherwise. His notoriety became his honor. People whispered his name in taverns, towns, and even sang about him in bards' tales. Disadvantages came with his reputation. Being a famous thief warned all vendors and wealthy travelers to keep a constant watch on him whenever he entered a town or city. So he hired knowledgeable sorcerers and apprentice wizards to teach him magic spells to vanish and escape in a crowd.

Crukas' childhood in Hoffnung began as one filled with poverty and hunger. He was an orphan but never housed in an orphanage. He learned to steal food in order to stay alive. He explored the sewers and other hidden passageways beneath the otherwise glorious City of Hoffnung. Once he learned the ease of slipping through iron grates, smelly drains, and dark trashy tunnels, he chose more expensive items to loot.

News soon caught the attention of guards about a young thief no one could catch. His wanted poster intrigued someone else, too. Agretor—the leader of a thief guild in Hoffnung—found Crukas in the sewers soon after the boy had stolen rare jewelry from a city magistrate's wife.

Crukas tried to escape, but six other thieves appeared from the shadows and surrounded him. Frightened, like any teenage boy when confronted by a group of scarred, weapon-carrying thieves dressed in black hooded robes, Crukas cowered in a corner.

"What do you want?" Crukas asked, looking around at the cloaked figures. They tightened their circle around him to prevent him from fleeing.

Agretor lowered the hood on his tight robe. He was a gray-haired man, thin, and muscular. Although elderly, he appeared agile and quick for his age. His bright, blue eyes studied Crukas before he offered a slight smile. "You've not gone unnoticed, boy."

"For what? What have I done?"

Agretor laughed heartily and the rest of his guild members did as well.

"Your thievery," Agretor said. "Although you're quite resourceful, you've drawn the attention of the city guards. Because of their determination to catch you, it's made it more difficult for us to do our labors. You're good, but you need improvement. A great thief never allows himself to be seen."

The critique offended Crukas. Unable to contain his anger, he revealed the ruby and diamond jeweled necklace. The large jewels glinted great radiance even in the dim torchlight. "How can you improve on *this*? Have any of *you* ever stolen anything this valuable?"

Crukas studied the thieves' eyes. Immediately he realized the revelation had been a horrible mistake. They couldn't hide their lust for the necklace. Several minutes passed before Agretor spoke. "A great thief steals without notice, often creating distractions and misdirection so the victim's not aware a theft has occurred."

"I'm getting better," Crukas replied.

"How long before a guard nabs you? They know what you look like." Agretor unrolled a tattered wanted poster with Crukas' image. "It's a spitting image of you. Every detail is vivid. Did you stop and *pose* for the artist?"

The other thieves chuckled, but their attention remained on the necklace clutched tightly in the young man's filthy fingers.

Crukas frowned at the bitter ridicule and their laughter.

But in a soothing tone, much like a father might offer corrective advice to a son, Agretor said, "Eventually, they'll catch you. A rat-infested prison isn't where you *want* to live your life, is it?"

Crukas took careful thought and shook his head.

Agretor smiled. "My guild can train you to be one of the best, only quicker and without stumbling through all the trial and error."

Crukas frowned and studied the men. "Why would you do that for me?"

Another within the thief party lowered her hood. Crukas was stunned. She was a young elven thief with coal black hair. She sighed and shook her head. "Agretor's inviting you to join our guild. We can help you polish your skills so you won't need to scrounge for your next meal."

Crukas smiled. He glanced from the girl to Agretor. The old man nodded. "Darrath speaks the truth. Accept our invitation."

"And if I don't?"

Agretor shrugged. "We'll turn you over to the authorities. Where you have continually escaped them, you won't us. An unruly thief won't tarnish our reputations. Rumors spread. An inexperienced thief like you might be falsely accused of being one of ours. I won't tolerate such shame cast upon my guild."

The thieves drew their daggers. Their eyes and intent focused on him.

The blood drained from Crukas' face. He recalled that moment of decision with clarity. Although he wasn't given any other choice but to join them, he never regretted siding with the guild in his early years. Food and a place to sleep were difficult to attain. Besides, no one is his or her own master.

Darrath smiled at Crukas. "I was about your age when they invited me. We never hunger or thirst. We have the finest of all things, but we don't announce our presence when we steal treasures. We strive to become invisible."

"She's right," Agretor said. "Our reputation's so well known that knights and noblemen have hired us to steal for them."

"Okay," Crukas said, nodding. He mimicked the importance of their guild. "I'd be honored to become a member of your society."

"Good," Agretor said, extending his hand to Crukas.

Crukas offered his small hand to shake, but Agretor shook his head.

"The necklace," Agretor said. "That's your contribution to join us."

Crukas was stunned. His stomach sickened at the thought of parting with his most recent prize, but the lust and greed in the thieves' eyes was alarming. None had sheathed their daggers, even after he accepted their invitation. They stepped closer and pressed him into the corner to prevent any attempt to escape. Their hardened gazes indicated they'd kill him for the necklace and toss his body in the rat-infested sewers. No one would ever miss or look for an orphan. He'd be forgotten. Forever.

Reluctantly, he handed the necklace to Agretor.

"Now," Agretor said. "Your training begins."

Crukas spent seven years in their guild. He learned their tactics and secrets that eventually made him a better thief than they. After Agretor's death, due to old age, the guild disbanded to join rival guilds in various cities, but not before Crukas stole his necklace from the treasure vault and fled Hoffnung. Knowing they would pursue him for robbing the guild vault, Crukas moved through forests and from village to village, town to town, and city to city. Ever on the move, he kept them guessing where he was. Of course, he added more stolen trophies to his list as well. That is, until he ventured to Glacier Ridge for the first time and stumbled into Darrath outside Hobskin's Tavern.

Her fury set harsh in her elven, green eyes. She wanted the necklace for herself. Had Crukas kept the necklace on him, she'd have slit his throat in an alley and taken it, regardless of Glacier Ridge's ordinances. After she'd patted him down and discovered he didn't have it, he convinced her to release him unharmed and he'd take her to where the necklace was stashed.

Darrath lowered the blade and agreed. But instead, when they arrived at Ironwood, he turned her over to the authorities, collected the bounty, and rode away a hero. He only did this with each ex-guild member he came across. Not for the reward, as Riese insisted, but because these thieves were his enemies and vowed to kill Crukas on sight. And unlike Crukas, his ex-guild members did more than steal. They often murdered their victims. Crukas had never injured anyone he'd stolen from.

Glacier Ridge was the best place to wait because eventually the most successful thieves gathered to boast about their greatest thefts. The only disadvantage was Crukas never realized Riese was watching and studying his ill-gotten deeds in a town where thieves roamed freely and without any fear of being apprehended.

Thinking on his previous actions, Crukas didn't feel much remorse for the murdering thieves. Without the former guild members, Crukas could enter any town without the fear of being revealed to guards or competing thieves. Wanted posters might give a depiction of his likeness, but Crukas learned to adapt and disguise himself. The last thing he expected was becoming Riese's enemy and being handed over to the Ironwood's town council to be hanged. And even more unexpected was being forced to *help* Riese, the man who wanted Crukas to swing at the bottom of a rope more than anyone else.

Fate was funny like that sometimes.

CHAPTER 46

*R*oble scanned the town. The rhythm of steady footsteps echoed on the other side of the lined merchant wagons near the intersection. Not certain who or how many approached, he rested his hands on the hilts of two throwing knives.

A lantern swayed. The Waxxon guard walked past.

Roble held his breath. "Patrols?"

"Patrols," Shawndirea whispered.

Roble's heart hammered. Shawndirea gave a half smile and a slight shrug, but her eyes revealed her nervousness as well.

Seconds later, Odlon stood beside them.

Roble almost jumped in surprise at Odlon's stealth.

Odlon whispered, "Zauber lied to us."

Roble turned and frowned at the disturbing news. "What?"

Odlon nodded.

"What'd he lie about?" Shawndirea asked.

"How many of Waxxon's men are here."

Stunned, Roble said, "You're certain?"

"Yes. More than a dozen Vykings are at the gate Riese entered," Odlon said. "To make matters worse, dark elf archers are here, too."

Shawndirea gasped.

Roble glanced at her. "That's bad?"

"Worse than you understand," she replied.

Odlon said, "Where'd Zauber go? We need to leave."

Roble shook his head. "Zauber went in the opposite direction you took. What about Crukas? Did you see him near the gate?"

"No sign of him."

"You said Zauber's trustworthy," Roble said.

Shawndirea nodded. "He is."

"Looks like he set us up," Roble said.

"Why would he do that?" She planted her hands on her hips.

"You tell me."

"Shh," Odlon said. "We don't have time for arguments."

Roble nodded. "I agree."

A flash of blue light caught Roble's attention. It vanished as quickly as it gleamed. Then it shone brightly for several seconds and faded.

"Did you see it?" Roble asked.

Both Shawndirea and Odlon shook their heads.

"See what?" she asked.

"Come with me," Roble said.

Roble placed her on his shoulder. He slipped farther from the lighted intersection and into a shaded area of the town. An old hut with a thatched roof was half hidden in the trees. Strange vines surrounded it. The blue light flashed again.

Odlon loaded the crossbow. They crept from the side of the road to the dark building. Roble kept his hands near his knives. When they came closer, the light gleamed. The odd light was a reflection off the hut's crude window.

Roble turned. The light emitted from the base of a building on the other side of the intersection.

"What is it?" Roble asked.

Odlon shook his head. "No idea."

"You?" Roble asked Shawndirea.

"Not certain."

Roble pulled his throwing knives. "Let's find out."

They slowed near the intersection. Odlon glanced down the streets. When he was certain no guards were headed their direction, they sprinted to the building.

The blue light glinted from a cellar door window. Roble and Shawndirea descended the steps. Before they could peer through the window, the door slowly creaked open.

"Careful." Odlon readied his bow and slipped past Roble.

"No weapons," an old woman said with a harsh, raspy voice. "We're peace-seekers here."

Roble sheathed his knives. He placed his hand on Odlon's forearm and lowered the crossbow. Odlon looked at Roble with a confused expression.

"Our enemies are along the gates and the wall," Roble said. "We need assistance from anyone who can help us."

Odlon nodded and placed the bolt in its quiver.

"Come inside and shut the door," the old woman said, "before the bastard patrols see you."

They stepped inside and quietly shut the door. Once the door closed, they were engulfed in near darkness. The only light came from the faint, crackling fire in her fireplace. The dim cellar was dank. Its aroma was blended herbs, earth, incense, and oddly, the pleasantry of homemade stew—reminding Roble of his grandmother's house on family weekends.

Near where she spoke, something raspy and feathery rustled in the corner.

"That's better," the woman said. A bluish light shimmered and made her visible.

She sat in a wooden rocker constructed from dried willow saplings. In her lap, a lantern contained a blue, glowing crystal, which made her features eerier to behold. At first glance, she appeared every bit like the evil crone images most people in the Overlands associated with a witch. Her wide eyes bulged and sent chills down Roble's back.

Her wrinkled, thin face and long, flowing hair seemed strange in the blue light. She struck a match on her rocker's armrest and lit a candle beside her black crystal ball. Tapping the glass box on her lap, the blue crystal dimmed and went cold. The candle flame rose and revealed shelves filled with bottled herbs, potions, and various animal skulls, claws, and bones. More shelves were lined with thick, aged books. Scrolls were tucked above and around various books as well.

On a perch behind her rocker was a white crow with deep blue eyes;

identical to those near Bausch's hanging body. On the floor a midsized gray kitten played with a dehydrated crimson newt.

Once the candlelight increased to full flame, the old woman became less frightening. Her wrinkles weren't nearly as etched, her hair was smooth silver, but her aura remained mysterious. She was blind in her left eye, and her right eye was milky white. Her few teeth and chin were soiled brown from snuff. Her nose whistled slightly when she breathed.

Roble didn't want to offend her, so he asked, "What's your name, my lady?"

She cackled wildly and waved her hands in the air. "Dispense with such nonsensical words and manners, Roble. We're simple folk, not aristocrats."

Astounded, Roble started to speak, but she held up a boney finger and shook her head. She studied him carefully. Brown drool leaked from the side of her mouth. He found it difficult to maintain eye contact but forced himself to be polite.

"No need for questions, Overlander. You aren't of the Dragon Skull Order, but yet, you wear their emblem and armor. Do those with you know you're an imposter?"

Roble sighed. "Yes, I wear the emblem. But, I'm not an imposter. My comrade, Lehrling, knows, as do the rest in my party. We came to restore order to Woodcrest."

She spat brown juice on the floor near other similar, drying stains. The little gray cat wrinkled its nose. It smacked the dried newt away from the rocker and scampered after it, quite possibly seeking refuge outside her spitting range.

Across the room, a small fire crackled beneath a large black, iron pot. The stew in the kettle bubbled. The aroma permeated the room. He realized how hungry he was. He'd worried about so many other things that he'd given little thought to eating. What little they'd eaten from Riese's rations had been hours earlier.

"Ah, nice gesture you offer, but Woodcrest's invaders hanged two of your order in the center of town yesterday. They killed some of the town council members, too."

"Ma'am," Roble said softly.

"Haigla," she replied.

"Two Dragon Skull Knights were killed?"

"Aye."

Roble shook his head. Although he didn't know others in the Order, he grieved. Their numbers dwindled on the side of order while Waxxon's number and chaos increased. If others within the Dragon Skull Order were as noble and caring as Lehrling was, they somehow needed to be preserved.

"The dark elves?" Shawndirea asked. "Why are they here?"

"In time, little faery."

"Haigla," Roble said. "We were summoned into Woodcrest by a wizard."

Odlon stepped beside Roble. "Yes. Do you know where he might be?"

She smiled and revealed a mouth with few brown-stained teeth. "I suspect he's nearby."

"But—"

"By listening you learn much more than speaking," she said. "You see, Woodcrest's a town of farmers, hunters, and gatherers. We're neither servers of the Light or Darkness. We pledge our devotion and allegiance to Aerlene. She blesses our harvest. While you say you're here to aid us and possibly set us free, you should know why the greedy bastards are here in the first place."

"To find Lady Dawn," Roble said.

Haigla waved her index finger back and forth and placed it to her lips.

"Now," she said in a rough voice that creaked painfully as she spoke. "You overstep your thoughts, and doing so distorts the true nature of events, making you blind to understand the truth. There's more to this maddening occupation than Lady Dawn. They overtook this town, not in hopes of gaining her, but in expectation of finding another."

"Who?" Shawndirea asked.

"One in your party, my dear."

Odlon and Roble exchanged glances.

"Who?"

"Crukas," Haigla said.

"Why do they want him?" Roble asked with sudden surprise.

"Only he can answer that. Why else would Waxxon's bastards overtake the only town that trades with Glacier Ridge, a town that houses and entertains despicable thieves? It's a far impossibility Lady Dawn would ever pass this direction. There is, or shall I say, *was* no hope or harbor for innocents in Glacier Ridge. They do *not* seek her here."

"Perhaps this is why Riese wants to deliver Crukas to Ironwood himself," Roble thought aloud.

"Ironwood?" Haigla asked.

Roble nodded. "They want Crukas hanged for his crimes. Riese assumes Crukas has betrayed his own. He tricks other thieves into joining him to steal treasures, but turns them in for their rewards."

"Thieves are cunning," she said. "Difficult to trust."

Odlon nodded. "He never reached the gates like he agreed."

"Could be the dark elves," Shawndirea said.

"You defend him?" Odlon asked.

"No," she said. "But *what* turned you back?"

The elf's jaw tightened, but he gave no reply. He looked at Haigla.

Roble squeezed Odlon's shoulder. "You know, she's probably right. But worse, Riese entered the gate with Lehrling ailing. They're no match for the guard or the dark elves."

"Those defiled, unholy dark elves," Haigla said with rage rising in her voice. "Despicable excuse for wasted air breathed."

Odlon whispered to Roble, "Exactly how I define their existence."

"Why are they here?" Shawndirea eyes were filled with worry.

"For various reasons. They attempted to take the area soon after they destroyed the monastery, but another intervened. I assume their loyalty to the Vykings is temporary. Once the Vykings leave, the dark elves will claim Woodcrest for their own."

"So they're after Crukas as well?" she whispered.

"Aye," Haigla said. "Woodcrest's greatest disadvantage is not having a holy priest or wizard. Otherwise, the dark elves would never set their attention on us. What say you, Odlon, Dragon-slayer of Eyllisathem?"

"I'm nothing more than an archer."

Shawndirea frowned at Haigla. "You practice magic and healing, why have the dark elves *not* set their attention on you?"

She cackled. "They think me daft and harmless."

The daft Roble could envision, but harmless? Hardly. The woman had more power than she wished to reveal, even to them.

Haigla kept her attention on Odlon for a moment longer. "Your armor came from a dragon with magic of its own. Surely some magic in the armor protects you."

He nodded. "Yes, but for my own health. Nothing more."

Haigla shrugged. She studied Roble and tilted her head to the side. "You're touched by magic, Overlander, and not by your faery. It's not magic I've sensed before. Who enchanted something for you?"

Roble shrugged. "I've seen no one, but Zauber believes this armor was blessed by an enchanter."

"Or cursed," she said in a near mumble. Her lower jaw trembled. Taking her twisted cane, she rose from her chair and hobbled in a stooped position toward him. The ice crow stretched its white wings, flapped, and flew to perch on her shoulder. Its blue piercing eyes watched Roble and Shawndirea with keen interest. She passed them to reach the bubbling pot of stew.

Roble said, "Are you a healer?"

Haigla stopped walking. "I've learned the ways of old remedies, if that's what you ask."

"Lehrling suffers from an infection deep inside his chest," Roble said. "Do you have something to cure him?"

"Lehrling's a Dragon Skull Knight, is he not?"

"Yes."

"And he's on the wagon with Riese?"

"Yes."

"His dangers are not with the infection, Overlander," she said, "But with surviving the hands of Waxxon's bastards."

Haigla made her way to the boiling pot, reached above the mantle, and took a stack of clay bowls. "Come, come. Fill your bellies."

"We must help Riese and Lehrling," Roble protested, but his stomach sided with her offer. The food looked appetizing and warm.

"Hunger' a distraction, Overlander. Eat. Time's still on our side. Besides, I'm an old woman. Feeding visitors is deeply-rooted within me."

She handed Odlon and Roble a clay bowl, and then she took a

wooden dipper and filled their bowls with steamy soup. She pointed to a small table in the corner of the room away from the door's window. As they seated themselves, she brought a wooden thimble of soup for Shawndirea.

"Sit, eat, and wait. The night's truly about to become interesting, if not entirely troublesome."

CHAPTER 47

*R*iese stepped down from the wagon. His heavy boots thudded along the street while he walked. He gripped his hammer tightly. Without making obvious surveillance of the wall guards, he counted four dark elves, a race he loathed because they often lived in dark caverns and ransacked villages during the night. These elves trained their bows on him. If he made any sudden movements, they'd fire without hesitation.

In Glacier Ridge he'd encountered a few dark elves, but most didn't explore the colder regions like he and his Vyking race preferred. The dark elves thirsted to kill and shed blood more than his Vyking brethren.

Two Vykings wound the gears to close the gates while two headed to the wagon bed to get Lehrling. Ever mindful of the dark elves, Riese hung his heavy hammer on his belt loop. They eased back on their bowstrings.

Lehrling coughed when the men heaved him into a seated position on the wagon. His eyes parted slightly, but then his head lulled to the side. He remained unconscious.

"What's wrong with him?" One guard asked.

"Not sure," Riese replied. "He's been that way for most of the trip. I wouldn't get too close to his face if I were you. You might catch what-ever he has."

Lehrling coughed and both guards cringed.

The two Vykings looped their arms around Lehrling and carried his dead weight.

"Where are you taking him?" Riese asked.

"The old town council where our general awaits. You should come. He'll want to speak with you."

Riese nodded while wondering how he could avoid meeting the general.

Another Vyking circled from behind Riese. His greedy eyes stared at the wagon bed. "What wares have you stored in there?"

"Just weapons I've crafted," Riese replied.

"Ooh, may I?" the man asked. Although of Vyking blood, he seemed different, or perhaps something was wrong with him. Excitement was something his race seldom expressed. Any passion Riese ever possessed died after Odrissus' death.

The older Vyking searched through the many blades, axes, and swords Riese had setting on the wagon bed. "You made these?"

Riese's eyes narrowed, and he nodded.

"You're a masterful smith."

"Thanks."

The old man brushed his gray beard with his fingers. He looked at a short sword, lifted it, admired the blade, and set it down. Then he grabbed another and repeated the process.

"Oh, so nice. Such quality. What be your name?" he asked.

"Riese," he replied without thinking. "And you?"

"Nordell."

Returning to his trader mentality he exhibited so well in Glacier Ridge, Riese smiled at the old man. "Great to make your acquaintance."

"Aye, same to you." The man kept his attention on the blades. His mind raced while he touched each one. He shook his head. "Such admirable quality."

Riese crossed his arms and studied the old man. In many ways, the man acted like a small child searching through toys in a shop but didn't have enough gold to make a purchase.

"Nordell?" Riese asked.

Nordell's timid eyes glanced from the weapons to Riese. He wrung his nervous fingers together. "Yes?"

"Pick any weapon. Any one at all, and it's yours."

"Free?" he asked with wide eyes. "No gold?"

Riese nodded. "Free. My gift to you."

Nordell nervously shook his head. "Ah, no. No, no, no. Can't. Wouldn't be right."

"Go on," Riese said. "Otherwise, you'll hurt my feelings."

The old man straightened his beard with his hands, over and over, and looked at the weapons. He gave a shy look at Riese. "Any one?"

"Any one," Riese agreed.

"I like this one." Nordell picked up a short sword. A few seconds later, he put it down and grabbed another. "No, this one. This one's better."

"Is that your choice?" Riese asked.

Nordell studied the broad bladed Vyking sword. He nodded.

Riese smiled. "It's yours."

Tears moistened the old man's eyes.

In a hearty, deep voice, Riese said, "Nordell, you're a strong warrior. The blade will exact justice in your hand."

The old man smiled with satisfaction and pride.

"What are you doing?" another Vyking said to Nordell. He took the blade and set it in the wagon. "Leave it be!"

Angered, Riese stepped to the guard.

"You keep out of this," the man said.

"I gave Nordell the sword. It's his."

"Nordell can't have a sword," the man said.

"Who are you to make that decision?" Riese asked.

"Name's Verlon. Everyone knows Nordell is *touched*. He cannot be trusted with a blade."

Sadness filled Nordell's eyes. His shoulders slumped, and he stared at his feet.

"Why's that?" Riese asked.

"Are ye deaf?" Verlon tapped the side of his own head. "He's touched. Not stable."

"Has he ever hurt anyone with a blade?"

Verlon nodded. "Once. Long ago."

While Riese kept Verlon's attention, Nordell held up a short dagger for Riese to see. Nordell grinned and nodded. He pointed at the dagger and then at himself, seeming to ask for it instead. Riese gave a quick nod. Nordell slid the dagger behind his belt and adjusted his vest to cover the dagger's hilt.

Once the old man hid the dagger, Riese waved his hands in feigned surrender. "I'm sorry, brother. I didn't realize. But if he's unstable, why does he journey with you?"

Verlon's nose crinkled with disgust. "He's King Obed's nephew."

"I see," Riese said.

"Come Nordell," Verlon said, "We'll watch the Dragon Skull Knight's interrogation. As will you, blacksmith."

The man looked at Riese and the blacksmith nodded. He allowed the two men to get a few yards beyond the wagon and paused near the wagon seat. To Marc, he whispered, "Stay still. Sorry to keep you hidden, but if you move, those archers will kill you. I'll be back soon."

He waited for his son to reply, but no words came. Only light snoring.

Riese hurried to catch the others. He didn't want them to interrogate Lehrling. He knew what his people did to make men talk. The obese old man would die for certain, if his disease didn't kill him first.

CHAPTER 48

Roble and Odlon each ate three bowls of the warm, savory stew. Revived energy pulsed through them and eased their tensions and fatigue. Shawndirea drank half the thimble of soup but declined more after Haigla brought her a thimble filled with honey ale. She drank it merrily. While they ate and drank, the old woman busied herself by placing herbs in another boiling pot. She read various scrolls, and softly chanted in a language unfamiliar to Roble.

The old lady didn't offer much more information while they ate. Her attention and devotion lie elsewhere. Roble thought it odd she never questioned why a wingless faery was accompanying the elf and he. Although she insinuated the faery was his, and this time, Shawndirea didn't protest such a directed conclusion. Perhaps Haigla had already spoken with Zauber and learned of their arrival and quest, or it could well be the news of their journey had already spread throughout the land.

Although Crukas had killed the Ratkin to free Shawndirea, it was possible dozens of Ratkin had escaped Glacier Ridge before the Plague-bringer arrived. For reasons he didn't truly understand, he believed the Ratkin thrived in large groups. Perhaps it was due to his knowledge of rats and their social inclinations, so he concluded the Ratkin were similarly society minded.

A couple more thoughts came to Roble. Why had the Ratkin so desperately sought to take Shawndirea? What was their purpose? Rats spread diseases and plagues. Was there a direct correlation between the Ratkin in Glacier Ridge and the Plague-bringer following soon after?

The gray kitten leapt to an empty chair and watched Shawndirea drink from the tiny thimble. Crouching low, the kitten rested its chin on its forepaws, shook its hindquarters, and sprang into the air to capture her.

Shawndirea rolled, shot a ball of green energy from her fingertips, and knocked the kitten off balance. When it landed on the floor, its fur was frizzled and puffed. The wide-eyed gray kitten hissed and ran across the room to hide under the rocking chair.

The white crow squawked with what seemed amused approval.

A horn blared at the center of Woodcrest's intersection. Odlon stood and hurried to the window. The horn sounded three more times.

Near the intersection, a crowd of Vykings gathered. Riese stood with them. Lehrling, still limp and motionless, was draped between two Vykings. More Vykings came and placed Lehrling's wrists inside metal cuffs welded to long iron chains. After securing Lehrling's wrists, they pulled the chains and raised his arms above his head. The tension hoisted him upward, but his head remained slumped forward.

Riese showed no emotion.

The horn sounded again.

Odlon reached for the doorknob.

"Not yet," Haigla said. "Not ... yet."

Roble hurried to the window. The urge to help Lehrling overcame him. A Vyking with a thick leather whip walked to Lehrling.

Roble grabbed the doorknob and twisted. The door came ajar for a brief second, and then something more powerful slammed it shut.

"I said, 'not yet!'"

Roble and Odlon faced her. Strange electrical energy flowed from her hands. She touched her black crystal ball. Colors swirled inside the dark globe.

"Come watch and learn," she said.

Roble tried the door again. He tugged furiously with both hands, but the door didn't budge. They were sealed inside.

In spite of their frustration, Roble and Odlon walked to the crystal ball. Images of Lehrling came in view. The muscled man with the whip drew back, ready to strike. Sadly, all Roble and Odlon could do was watch.

~

THE VYKING BROUGHT BACK the whip. Bloodlust gleamed in his comrades' eyes.

"Wait!" Riese shouted and stepped forward.

Verlon frowned with fury. "How dare *you* interrupt the interrogation? You brought him here!"

Verlon stepped to Riese with his sword drawn.

Riese pointed. "He'll never survive such torture, especially if you want answers."

"One lash should spring 'em awake," Verlon said.

Riese shook his head. "One lash will kill him."

From the dark street, another voice called, "What's the ruckus? Carry on, Verlon!"

"Sorry, General Quenid," Verlon said. Spittle frothed the sides of his mouth, and he pointed at Riese. "He delays the interrogation."

Riese's stomach tightened. Yerdrick had threatened his brother would avenge his death. However, recalling Odrissus' murder allowed Riese's fury to overtake his nerves and readied Riese to seek vengeance of his own.

General Quenid stepped forward. The Vykings behind Riese dropped to one knee and bowed. Even Verlon dropped and bowed, but Riese turned and faced the man with evident spite.

"You should know your place," General Quenid said. He was heavily armored and wore his metal helm with pride. His long, sandy brown hair spilled flowed from beneath the helm. He was muscled, stood six inches taller than Riese, and was fifty pounds heavier. He carried a large round shield in his left hand. In his right was a great sword, which was nicked and scarred from many battles. If Riese accurately guessed, based on a general's reputation, the sword had beheaded many prisoners.

The Quenid's long beard hung past his belt but was deftly braided every ten inches. His piercing eyes narrowed when he met Riese's defiant gaze. "What? You *refuse* to bow? You'll learn the price for defying me, dog."

Riese spat at the man's feet. Quenid's eyes widened and then narrowed with fury. The surrounding Vykings gasped and fell strangely quiet.

"What's your name? I should know before I send you to the River Styx?"

"Guess," Riese replied.

The general huffed. His nose flared. He eyed Riese with a murderous glare. "You're not in my band of warriors, but your face is familiar. I can't place you, but I don't tolerate defiance. Your traitorous words have announced your death sentence. I'll cut your tongue from your head."

Riese grinned. "I'd like to see that."

Quenid paced back and forth to size Riese up. Perhaps he wondered why Riese, who was dressed in leather armor and carried a heavy, black-smith hammer, dared to challenge a general dressed in his warrior armor. Riese maintained his smug-filled glare without fear. Quenid addressed his men. "Who knows this fool?"

"Riese," Verlon said without glancing up.

"Come again?"

Verlon dared to look up and spoke louder. "His name's Riese."

The name rocked Quenid. His eyes widened with immediate recognition. He faced Riese yet again.

"Now, I remember you," he hissed and spittle flew from his mouth. Quenid's eyes grew darker than coal. "You killed my brother."

"You shall join him soon," Riese said.

Quenid laughed heartily. "Hear how this defiant traitor speaks to your General? This man murdered General Yerdrick."

"He's dead because he killed my wife in cold blood," Riese said.

The kneeling Vykings shifted. Some stood and grabbed their blades. Verlon stood with his blade drawn.

"Your wife? She was the harlot from the bay where you killed three of your blood brothers to win her. That's what their deaths were for?" Quenid's face flushed red. Veins in his forehead and throat bulged.

"Today vengeance for Yerdrick's death and your brothers comes with your blood!"

"No," Riese replied, "Today, you meet your brother in death. If the fires of the eternal abyss exist, it heartens me to hope you suffer forever."

Riese yanked his heavy hammer from the belt loop and caught the edge of Quenid's blade mere inches from his face. Metal clashed and sparks flew. The general's strength matched the his muscular size. He was a strong opponent, which clearly gave him the upper hand. Both sought vengeance. Such desire increased their strength, however, Riese's had the added measure of love lost, which was a greater reason to kill than Quenid's brotherly oath. Riese had held Odrissus, witnessed the fleeting love and life vanish in her eyes, felt her body grow cold, and listened to her last breath before she left him forever. That weighed more in Riese's favor than the report of Yerdrick's death had to Quenid.

Quenid tapped his sword against the side of his round shield to set the challenge for Riese to take his best shot. Riese grinned. All he was equipped with was his hammer. Was the general worried Riese might actually overtake him? Clearly, Quenid's men could see the unbalanced nature of the fight, which at best proved Riese's bravery far exceeded their general's.

Riese had not fought combat style since his days under Yerdrick's command, except when he killed Yerdrick. But Riese thrived on challenges. He'd often fought several men at once during his raiding days. He wondered how rusty his skills might prove now, but armor-wise, he was at a disadvantage. Only one thing increased the odds. Sharp wit.

Riese rushed Quenid with his hammer raised high, which was the needed distraction he hoped. Quenid brought the shield around to block the attack, but Riese leapt upward and kicked Quenid's round shield full force with both feet. The weighted impact knocked the general backwards. Using the momentum of the kickback, Riese spun and brought the hammer around, striking Verlon in the side of the head. The hammer made Verlon's helmet ring. Verlon groaned and toppled, and landed on his back. The jarring pain rattled the sword from his hand. Verlon winced and clutched the sides of his head with his hands.

Riese tossed his hammer to his left hand, rolled, grabbed Verlon's loose sword, and found footing on the other side of the road beneath a light pole. Quenid, although huge, moved swiftly. He rushed Riese, striking hard and fast, but Riese parried the blows with the sword, and then battered Quenid's round shield with his smith hammer.

Back and forth, they swung at one another, rage burning in their eyes. Each sought to draw blood, but the other blocked each attempt. The surrounding Vykings cheered at the vicious battle, but Riese ignored their shouts, jeers, and praise.

Being a sword-maker, Riese identified the weaknesses in the general's blade. Several deep grooves were in great need of repair, but those notches often were considered marks of triumph in battles where the blade had drawn life's blood. Those nicks Riese kept his attention on.

Quenid brought his sword overhead and downward into a harsh sideswipe, hoping to catch Riese off-guard, but Riese countered and easily deflected the blade. Perhaps the general's heavy armor weighed him. The huge man was losing stamina fast. His breathing was labored, heavy. Sweat beaded from beneath his helm and dripped down his face.

Riese remained agile. His light armor allowed him to dodge side to side with ease. Using his quickness, Riese infuriated Quenid. Where Quenid expected Riese to be when he lunged, Riese was not. The more he missed his mark, the more Riese taunted the general. Riese discovered Verlon's lighter broad sword was more effective for quick assaults than most Riese had used in battle before.

Riese's newfound blade was solid with few dents, which indicated Verlon had not fought with the sword often. Or, the blade was recently crafted for him. Whichever the case, Riese capitalized on the weak points in Quenid's blade.

Quenid huffed deeply and brought the sword downward. Riese noticed a wide notch in the blade, spun to add momentum, and connected a direct strike at the weakest point in the general's blade. The blade shattered. Quenid's eyes widened. The rattling sensation jarred the hilt from his hand. He winced ever so slightly but enough that Riese predicted their battle to end soon.

Normally, an automatic defeat landed to the man whose weapon broke as this meant the man was defenseless, but this wasn't a duel, it was a death match. Honor meant everything to his brethren, so Riese didn't worried about another warrior interceding. From the disappointed looks on their faces, they seemed ashamed of Quenid's performance.

Riese came at the general and swung the sword hard. He connected with the round, metal-framed wooden shield, and when he brought back the sword, he countered with the hammer, and battered the shield. Over and over, he smashed with everything he had. Fear overcame the general. He backed his way to the intersection in retreat. His act of cowardice brought jeers from his followers.

Riese didn't let up, but at the same time, Verlon rose to his feet behind him. Verlon shook his head and blinked several times. When he no longer staggered, he pulled a long dagger from a sheath on his belt and crept slowly behind Riese.

CHAPTER 49

*O*dlon, Roble, and Shawndirea peered into the crystal ball. Nosiness got the best of the gray kitten. It watched the activity within the tiny globe but remained leery of getting close to the faery.

When the Vyking approached Lehrling with the whip, Shawndirea cringed. Roble and Odlon turned to the door with their hands on their weapons.

"Wait," Haigla said.

Roble turned with frustration. "They're going to kill him."

The old woman shook her head. "Look."

Inside the ball, Riese stepped between the Vyking and Lehrling.

"See?" Shawndirea said. "I told you Riese was offering Lehrling to the guards in order to get past the gates."

Roble smiled with a bit of relief.

When Quenid stepped into the town crossroads, Roble and Odlon exchanged worried glances.

"We have to get out there," Roble said.

Odlon nodded.

Haigla shook her head. "If you go out there, they'll kill you without hesitation. Riese is one of theirs. The Vykings respect him, but you, an elf and human? No. They'll take pleasure in cleaving you to bits with their axes. Let's see what your comrade is capable of."

∽

RIESE LUNGED FORWARD with the sword. He hoped to swoop the hammer in low when Quenid blocked, but the general guessed Riese's strategy and flung the shield into Riese's chin. Blood flew from his busted lips and the impact of the blow spun Riese around. Bright lights danced behind his closed eyes. He hit the ground, narrowly missing Verlon's blade, and rolled to stand.

Dazed, Riese blinked and shook his head. The world was black for several moments. His vision blurred. He staggered and wobbled but kept his balance. While Riese tried to compose himself and kept enough restraint to prevent passing out, Verlon circled behind Riese again, and like a coward, he sought to stab Riese in the back.

Quenid grinned, roared, and rushed Riese. The general lifted the round shield high overhead to batter Riese senseless. Riese spun and brought his hammer into Quenid's metal breastplate. The plate dented and knocked Quenid breathless. The shield slid along the hard road while Quenid bent forward and clutched his ribs. He wheezed.

Riese braced against his hammer to catch his breath. He wiped blood from his mouth and chin. The taste of iron coated his tongue. His ears rang and his vision came and went. Gazing at the surrounding Vykings, he was thankful none intervened. Disappointment and disapproval reigned in their eyes. He supposed it was because their general had retreated rather than stand and fight or face death bravely.

Verlon eased closer, ready to stab Riese's right kidney. He drew back to shove the blade, but Verlon screamed in pain and cursed. His dagger dropped to the ground. Verlon fell face first on the road, writhed, and tried to pull the steel dagger from his back. In a matter of minutes blood pooled in a large circle beneath him. His fingers twitched slightly.

Alarmed, Riese glanced around. Nordell stood over Verlon and spat on him. His crazed eyes met Riese's, and Nordell grinned. Riese nodded his gratitude. Nordell placed his foot against Verlon's back and yanked his dagger free. He wiped away the blood with his tunic and admired the blade with an odd, hypnotic stare.

Verlon's backstabbing attempt had gotten him what he deserved.

Riese had never fought alongside a Vyking that lacked the fortitude to attack an enemy head on. Verlon was more cowardly than Quenid.

Riese took a deep breath, stood, and arched his back. Quenid turned, picked up the shield, and took several steps to stand in the intersection with Riese. Although Quenid stood there, his confidence had faded. He'd underestimated Riese, and now, he no longer felt superior to the blacksmith. Yet, the challenge to the death remained. He slipped his arm through the loop and secured his grip on the shield. He nodded.

Riese took his hammer and swung. The blow splintered the front of the shield and the *thwack* echoed throughout Woodcrest. He drew back again, and Quenid squinted. The hammer cracked the shield with enough force the wood planks broke free of the iron bands and dropped to the ground.

Quenid flung the metal frame to the road. He placed his hands to his sides and nodded for Riese to finish him. Before Riese moved, a Vyking tossed Quenid a dagger, hilt first. Quenid caught and readied it. He grinned.

Riese looked at the blade and immediately his mind carried him to Odrissus' final moments. The dagger was exactly like the one Yerdrick had used to kill her. Rage surged through Riese.

He no longer saw Quenid before him. Yerdrick's face replaced Quenid's features. The accurate resemblance left no doubt they were blood brothers, but to Riese, the two men were one in the same. Odrissus being stabbed by the blade took place again. In his fury, rage, and loss, Riese charged Quenid full force.

Riese swung the sword, but Quenid deflected it with the dagger, which proved the general's skill, but without a shield, Quenid wasn't fast enough to stop the hammer. The hammer clanged harshly against the general's right pauldron. The strike crushed his shoulder, broke bones, and several ribs.

General Quenid gnashed his teeth and released a seething growl of pain. Before the man opened his eyes, Riese slashed Quenid's throat with the blade. The general's eyes widened. He clutched his throat with bloody hands and dropped to his knees.

Riese whispered in Quenid's ear, "Never forget my name and tell your brother I sent you to him."

He spat in the general's face before driving the killing blow through the dented breastplate and into the man's heart. He yanked the blade free. Quenid's lifeless body dropped. The leaves above rustled. A harsh wind blew through Woodcrest.

Riese lowered his weapons. Heat rose off his tired, aching muscles. A sensation of momentary victory rushed through him. He gazed around the crowd of those he once considered his brethren. Even now, if they welcomed him, he'd never rejoin their plundering ways. His life had changed into what he hoped was for the better.

The Vykings drew their weapons and shields and circled around him.

CHAPTER 50

Zauber crept behind the herbalist's storage shed, which was located beneath Woodcrest's darkest trees. He took his staff and outlined a large circle in the soft earth. Within the circle, he etched symbols and runic letters with his finger.

He pulled his wizard dagger, Meoriki, from its sheath and pricked the tip of his left index finger. He squeezed two blood droplets in the circle's center and softly chanted a spell long rehearsed but seldom used.

The wind increased, tree branches shook in mad swirling motions, and his long black beard curled. His robes ruffled. With his eyes closed, he didn't sense these changes. In his right hand, he rotated his black wand in a counterclockwise motion. The howling wind intensified. From his robe pocket, he took a glowing, yellow orb. It tinted his face an eerie yellow.

Thick leafy branches swayed and cracked in the oak canopy, but he focused on the bright orb. Seconds later, the orb changed. Queen Istrell's furrowed face appeared in the crystal. Her sorrow, heartache, and fading rage weighted her expressions.

Zauber whispered a soft message through the orb. "Istrell. Shawndirea's safe. She's journeying home to you. Be at peace. She'll return."

Although Istrell couldn't see Zauber through the crystal orb, her mind, soul, and heart jumped at his words. She peered at the colorful crystals in her tree. Her eyes brightened. A slight smile curled her aged lips. She glowed and her facial muscles eased. She didn't look as aged.

"Hope," Zauber whispered with a smile, "can turn back time."

RIESE HELD his weapons and studied the crowd around him. With only ten or so warriors standing with their weapons in hand, he calculated his attacks and how he could drop several before they eventually over-powered and killed him. Sacrificing himself, however, offered no benefit for his son or Lehrling, for that matter.

His eyes were drawn to the buildings and huts farther behind where the Vykings stood circled. The citizens of Woodcrest had stepped outside their homes to watch the battle. Their frightened eyes held little hope. Riese captured the gazes of the angered circle of Vykings, and they pressed closer. The closer they came, the less room he had to counter their attacks. Besides, he was exhausted. He tossed his weapons to the ground.

The thought occurred to him that his former brethren had not killed all the townspeople like they often did in plundering raids. The Vykings didn't plan to keep Woodcrest for an indefinite post. They were here for something else. *What exactly?*

"You fought more noble than either of them," the eldest Vyking said, pointing at Quenid's and Verlon's corpses. He motioned the circling Vykings to lower their axes and swords. They did without question or protest. "You've no fear of death, but a haunting rage to contend with."

"General Yerdrick killed my wife. We had two small boys at the time. My rage will never end."

The old man nodded. His eyes testified to his own losses. "That's understandable and justified."

His saddened blue eyes looked into Riese's. The rugged old man wore scars of battle on his wrinkled face, his arms, and he was missing several fingers. His long, gray hair was pulled in a ponytail. His frazzled beard was long but clean.

"I did this," Riese said, "for her."

"I heard," the old man said. "It's why we won't kill you unless forced.

But since you have a bounty on your head, we're required to present you before King Obed after our mission's completed. You could argue your case before him. Will you come peacefully?"

"I will, but under one condition," Riese said.

"What's that?"

Riese pointed at Lehrling. "You spare him."

The old man frowned. "Are you in allegiance with the Dragon Skull Order?"

Riese shook his head. "No."

"Why's his life important to you?"

"He's a noble man. He's committed no crime."

"He's an enemy of Lord Waxxon. An enemy of Waxxon is an enemy of our king."

"You are?" Riese asked.

"Hordus."

"So answer this for me. What has the Dragon Skull Order done to deserve being tracked down and killed like wild dogs?"

Hordus said, "Lord Waxxon's orders."

"And the cause?"

Hordus shrugged. "Never gave one."

Angered, Riese said, "Since when have our brethren laid down our allegiance for another man? How's Lord Waxxon tied to King Obed?"

"That's an answer only the king can give. But be forewarned, asking such questions will get your head removed before you plead your case."

Riese eyed his weapons on the ground. He could easily get the hammer before Hordus or any Vyking attacked. But these men weren't his real enemies. They were like he'd once been. Men followed the orders of a king they believed in. Riese no longer possessed such allegiance.

The old man took a set of iron shackles and locked them around Riese's wrists.

Hordus said, "It pains me to do this, but only the king can pardon you."

Riese didn't resist. As a prisoner, he stood a better chance getting close enough to kill King Obed than leading a raid against his throne.

"I won't offer a fight if you release the knight," Riese said.

"Might I consider your request overnight?"

"Do you assume Quenid's position?"

Hordus nodded. "For now, we've no assigned frontrunner. I'm the eldest, so until King Obed appoints a new leader, the decisions fall to me."

"If your wisdom's as great as your years, you've enough knowledge to know Lehrling's not your enemy."

An aged smile creased Hordus' face. "When the sun rises, you'll have an answer."

Hordus led Riese to another set of posts near Lehrling. They hooked chains to Riese's shackles and hoisted them tightly. They pulled Riese's hands high over his head until Riese was forced to stand on his tiptoes.

Once they locked the chains tightly, Hordus tugged the chains with all his strength. They offered no slack.

"Even in the might of your rage, Riese," Hordus said, "These restraints won't yield. Again, I wish I didn't have to chain you like an animal. Perhaps I, in your very situation, would've done the same. May King Obed have mercy on your soul."

"It's not my soul he should pity," Riese said. "But his own."

The entire band of Vykings separated and returned to the gates or wherever else they'd chosen to house themselves overnight.

Riese gazed at Lehrling. The round old man had not awakened. His attention turned to his brethren disappearing into the shadowy trees and buildings. He thought of Hordus' last words.

Obed had no more mercy for Riese than Riese did for the king. Death would come, but it wouldn't be his own. He thought of his son sleeping in the wagon. He still had something to worry about. He yanked the chains. Hordus was right. The chains were secured. He needed to get to Marc before the guards found him. He wasn't certain how much mercy Hordus had if he discovered Marc.

"Now?" Roble headed to the door with Shawndirea on his shoulder.

"Yes."

The door unlatched and swung inward. A strong breeze flowed

through the cellar and blew several tattered scrolls off the table. Leaves, dirt, and small twig debris swirled inside her cellar. She mumbled curses. Roble swore Zauber's name was mentioned in the middle of her obscenities.

Odlon, Roble, and Shawndirea crept from the cellar and moved along the shadows lining the buildings but stopped when a pair of patrols walked the street nearby.

Odlon fired two quick headshots and dropped the Vyking plunderers on the road. Roble was stunned at his cold, calculated assassinations.

"Remember," Odlon said. "These are murdering raiders. They killed Woodcrest's leaders and might kill Riese and Lehrling if we don't free them from their restraints."

Roble helped Odlon drag the heavy Vykings off the trail and hide their bodies behind thorny shrubs.

"*Kill or be killed,*" Roble reminded himself. A worrisome change for his conscience in a world filled with different rules, laws, and power struggles. And while he sought peace about what lie ahead and what he must do to take Shawndirea home, he couldn't ignore the truth that reigned deep inside his soul. Life was life, precious to anyone good or evil. To rid any world of evil through murder tainted oneself with evil as well, didn't it?

Shawndirea caught the troubled look on his face. "Should you stay in our world, you'll see far worse as time passes."

"I'll adjust, but it won't be easy."

"To survive, your wits must react before you think your actions through. Sometimes your decisions will be in error, but never underestimate an enemy. Most won't give you time to weigh your odds. Most don't care."

Roble nodded. How'd one determine who was a friend or foe? In the Overlands he wanted to trust everyone, but Deiko tainted that ambition. The only ones he truly connected with were his students because of his passion to teach. Here? He was the student searching for the correct answers in order to keep his head on his shoulders. At least, he was quick to learn.

CHAPTER 51

*C*rukas watched the majority of the combat between Riese and General Quenid. He was surprised Riese had taken out a man much larger than himself. The bravery and combat skills Riese displayed were something he now admired about the man he'd come to despise. The entire ordeal occurred because Riese defended Lehrling. Now, Riese hung in chains beside Lehrling, even though Lehrling might not be released the next day.

After the guards passed to return to their posts, Crukas crawled beneath a wagon. Staying low and in the shadows, he scurried from wagon to wagon.

He lie on his stomach, watched, and listened. No footsteps approached from any direction. The dead of night had settled over Woodcrest. The only activity remained at the gates. Believing the path to Riese was clear and without opposition, Crukas left his hiding place and sprinted through the intersection until he reached Riese and Lehrling.

~

RIESE LOOKED surprised when Crukas stepped into the open. All smart thieves sought to remain hidden. They worked best in the shadows.

Why was Crukas coming to him? To mock him? The thief had every reason to begrudge him since Riese wanted Crukas hanged for blatantly disregarding Glacier Ridge's mandate against bounty hunters. Thieves could come and go freely, provided they never stole from one another or the traders in the marketplace.

Riese narrowed his eyes at Crukas. "Our tables have turned, thief. Here to find your amusement?"

Crukas shook his head and placed his finger to his lips. He reached in his pocket and removed his lock-picking tools. He grinned and his eyebrows rose.

Perhaps *redemption*? Riese wondered.

"I thought you abandoned us," Riese said, "or you made a run for it?"

Crukas shook his head.

"Oh, that's right. You cannot speak."

With a shrug and sad face, Crukas studied the cuffs, but due to Riese being almost twice the height of Crukas, the thief had no way to reach the locks over Riese's head.

Riese's eyes widened. "Crukas, look out!"

Crukas turned. A crazed Vyking rushed Crukas with a bloody dagger.

"Nordell, no!" Riese said.

Crukas tried to move, but Nordell raised the dagger overhead, growled, and swiftly brought down the blade. Crukas' mouth opened to scream, but no sound came.

ODLON FIRED a bolt before Nordell would've killed Crukas. The tip went through Nordell's back and lodged in his heart. He arched backwards before he fell forward on the road.

Crukas sat on the ground beneath Riese, closed his eyes, and shook his head. He took a deep breath and sighed.

Odlon, Roble, and Shawndirea hurried to Riese and Lehrling. Roble patted Lehrling's cheek, but the old man's eyes remained closed. He placed his ear to Lehrling's chest. The man's breathing was hampered.

Hoisted in this position wasn't favorable and was making his pneumonia even worse.

"We have to get him down," Roble said.

"Help Crukas free me first. I can get Lehrling down," Riese said.

Odlon and Roble cupped their hands together to give Crukas foot supports. They held Crukas high enough to pick the locks. In seconds, the thief used his picks, and to Roble's surprise, Riese lowered his hands and rubbed his wrists.

Riese stepped behind Lehrling. After Crukas unlocked Lehrling's cuffs, Lehrling dropped in Riese's arms. He prevented the heavy man from collapsing to the ground.

While Riese supported Lehrling's weight, Zauber walked to them.

"Good to find you all together," he said.

"Where've you been?" Roble asked. "You brought us here and abandoned us. Why'd you deceive us?"

Zauber raised his hand. "Careful. Our enemies abound. We must remain discreet."

Roble ignored his answer. "You deserted us once we got to the center of town. Why?"

Riese carried Lehrling to the nearest wagon and laid him gently on the bed.

Zauber looked at Roble and gazed to each of the others. "You must keep unity in your party. Do you understand?"

Roble crossed his arms but didn't reply. Odlon seemed as upset as Roble, especially at the underestimated numbers of the Vykings and learning about the dark elves. Shawndirea watched with slight amusement, indicating she knew Zauber's ways.

Zauber focused his attention on Crukas and waved his hand. "Crukas, The silence spell has been removed. Riese needs to hear and respect your voice."

"Thanks." Crukas cleared his throat.

Riese rested his hands on his hips and nodded. "He's proven himself to me. He risked his life to free me."

"Riese," Zauber said. "Your inner rage will burn forever after your loss of Odrissus, but that's *not* Crukas' fault. It's those your bloodline is drawn from. Crukas has secrets of his own he'll reveal to you in time. But he's *not* your enemy."

"I know," Riese replied.

"He is, however," Zauber said, "a resourceful key to your group's success."

"So you won't hand me to Ironwood's magistrate?" Crukas asked Riese.

"No."

A great ease settled over Crukas' face. He gave a slight bow. "Thank you."

Odlon said, "To take Shawndirea to Elvendale we must pass through Ironwood. There's no other route."

"First," Riese said. "We must rid Woodcrest of the Vykings imprisoning them."

"What about the dark elves?" Shawndirea asked.

Odlon's nervous eyes glanced from person to person. What power did the dark elves hold over him to cause him such fear?

Haigla walked past with a bottle of orange potion and made her way to the alabaster faery statue. "Leave the dark elves to me."

Zauber stared at Shawndirea questioningly. Shawndirea shrugged and shook her head.

Riese watched the old woman with curiosity.

Roble looked at Riese. "What are your plans?"

"You're placing *me* in charge?"

Roble shrugged. "You're the largest in our party. You've fought with them before, correct?"

In a deep voice, he whispered, "Yes, long ago."

"You know their tactics and how best to approach. Besides, with your immense size, I'd never consider giving you orders. I trust your decisions."

"We kill them all," Riese said. "Except for the old man, Hordus. Keep him alive. The dark elves are our biggest concern. Archers at a high position hold the advantage. How does the old lady plan to take care of the dark elves before we reach the gates? Marc's still in the wagon. Protect him at all costs."

"You got it," Roble replied.

Odlon nodded.

Riese met Haigla at the statue. The rest of the group stood behind him. The old woman knelt before the statue with her eyes closed. She poured the concoction on the faery's feet and chanted.

Glittering lights flickered in the oak branches. From the trees near the gates, anguished screams wailed and stopped seconds later.

"The dark elves are no more," Haigla said with a near toothless smile. "Take out the Vykings and our town's free once more."

THE DARK ELVES stood watch in the tree branches along the gateways. Four per gate and each favored a tree of his own. One by one, a slight giggle echoed from the tree branches where the dark elves positioned themselves. While searching for what produced the luring laughter, the dark elves climbed the branches and followed. Nothing was visible, but the giggles taunted them.

Without warning, camouflaged dryads within the trees' patterns reached out from their hiding places and yanked the dark elves into the bark. The bark solidified and paralyzed the elves with agonizing deaths.

The dark elves' high-pitched screams caused the Vykings to look to the trees, where they witnessed several of the dark elves' demise.

"What strange magic is this?" A Vyking guard drew his blade.

"Spirits of those we slaughtered," another suggested. "They've come for vengeance, Dougan."

They eyed one another, stood back to back, and moved slowly away from the gate.

"Dreygurs?" Dougan whispered.

"Possibly."

"Or the trees are enchanted, Wylis," Dougan said.

Wylis gripped his sword tighter. His eyes widened. He faced Dougan. "Perhaps, the Dragon Skull Knights we killed?"

Dougan shared his worry. He nodded. "Another entered this town. Their spirits have come to protect him."

They watched the light poles and the faint lighted areas beneath the trees. They sought the eyeless ghosts of the town council members they'd killed. Nothing slinked within the shadows, but they couldn't shake the possibility of vengeful spirits stalking them.

"Head to the center of the town," Dougan whispered. "Where there are fewer trees."

Before they reached the center of Woodcrest, Odlon shot and dropped the men with his crossbow.

CHAPTER 52

*D*rucis rode Ol' Grey along the dark forest path outside Woodcrest. His eyes shifted each time a twig snapped, a strange bird cried, or something rustled overhead. Normally such things didn't disturb him, but after escaping the undead of Glacier Ridge and riding through a band of drifting ghosts, he was certain the entire region was haunted. What else had the Plague-bringer left behind?

The luminous bluish, broken and decapitated statues didn't bother him. With suspicion, he looked for any dark moving objects around the statues. His hand rested on the handle of his battle-axe. Strange screams echoed through the tree and he pulled the axe. He recognized the cries.

Dark elves.

Grey's ears backed and the horse whinnied slightly. Drucis tugged the reins. His eyes searched the ruins and statues because he remembered the area's history and how the dark elves had slaughtered all the monks and priests in the towering temple that no longer existed.

Had they returned?

Several more anguished screams rose and silenced in sudden death.

"No," Drucis whispered, looking around the forest. "They're not here. Come now, Grey, let's get on to Woodcrest. Seems they may be needing me axe to aid them."

~

THE DYING shrieks of the dark elves wreaked havoc on the Vykings' superstitious nature. With haunted expressions, they fled the trees near the gates and headed to the center of Woodcrest. Odlon waited with his readied crossbow. He dropped most before they turned and noticed him.

Hordus dropped his weapons and shield when his comrades dropped dead on the road.

Riese brought the wristband shackles and locked them around the old man's wrists.

"Why spare me?" Hordus asked. "I'm old and of little use in battles anymore. Is it because I spared your life?"

Riese gave a slight nod and shrugged. "That's part of it, but I've a mission for you."

Hordus chuckled. "A mission? For me?"

Riese nodded. "Yes. Once we reach the other side of Ironwood, I'm releasing you. Return to the Isles of Welkstone and tell Obed I'm alive. I plan to remove his head for joining Lord Waxxon."

"You're a fool. Why not release me, and I tell him you're dead? Live the rest of your years in peace. He doesn't need to know you're alive."

"I'll never find peace, Hordus. What was taken from me can never be replaced. Nothing repairs a broken heart and mind."

A sad expression crossed Hordus' face. When he looked at Riese, tears brimmed his eyes. "I understand. I do. I lost my wife after many years, but not as you. She died from sickness. Had what happened to your dear wife happened to mine, I'd share your fury. In some ways, I do."

Riese clasped his huge hand on Hordus' shoulder. "In better times, we'd have a lot of stories to share. As long as you journey with us, I promise no harm comes to you."

Hordus smiled. "I never saw you fight on the battlefield, but the stories about your courage are often told around the nightly campfires. Many fell to your blades before you *lost your way*, as they say. But you didn't lose your way. You're a better man because you found love, which is a far, rarer thing than most consider in this life. As far as telling stories, it's still quite a journey we must take. Plenty of time to tell tales."

While Riese engaged Hordus in conversation, Odlon circled around Woodcrest and dropped any remaining Vykings.

The townspeople left their homes and hiding places to drag the dead bodies to the edge of the intersecting roads. Like scavengers, the men, women, and children pilfered whatever caught their eyes. Most though only took gold, silver, or copper coins they found in small pouches and pockets.

When the townspeople lined the bodies, Riese walked alongside Hordus, and they counted the number of the dead.

"Twenty-two," Riese said. "Was this your entire band?"

"Yes," Hordus replied.

"Good," Riese said. He glanced at Odlon and Roble. "Woodcrest is free!"

Haigla did a little jig while singing in a strange language. She grinned.

Wiping the sleep from his eyes, Marc staggered across the street and stood beside his father.

"It's over," Roble said to Shawndirea. "We go to Ironwood and then onward to Elvendale."

Shawndirea kissed Roble's cheek.

"Shawndirea?" a female voice asked. The voice was sweet, soft, and almost seductive. A voice any man would love to hear call his name.

Shawndirea turned and was startled. Hovering behind her was a faery with strawberry blonde hair and bright blue eyes. "Aerlene?"

"Yes! Child, it *is* you!" Aerlene said.

"Yes."

She took Shawndirea's hands and whisked her away. Roble's eyes widened. Shawndirea blew him a kiss and hoped the action let him know she was safe and not being snatched from him again.

Aerlene landed on a high branch near the top of a massive oak. She held Shawndirea's hands. The setting moon on the horizon was spectacular. Stars glittered the darkening sky. She realized exactly how much she missed her wings and her ability to fly. From the towering height, she viewed lights from small bonfires, which dotted the landscape and detailed the locations of the neighboring farmsteads. The cool air was fragrant and magical.

Aerlene gasped. Her eyes widened. "Your precious wings. My dear, what happened?"

Shawndirea shook her head. "It's a terribly long story. One that would most certainly bore you."

"Don't be silly, child. We've much to discuss."

Shawndirea smiled and hugged her aunt. "Another time, maybe, about my wings. Seeing you's a grand relief. I thought you were dead."

Aerlene shook her head and giggled. "Dead? No. I'm very much alive. That's the rumor circulating Elvendale? Your mother's been busy spreading misinformation again."

"The rumor's one my mother insists is true," she replied. "I was convinced and everyone else is, too."

Arlene shook her head. "Tsk tsk. Of course, she did. Your mother's too bullheaded for her own good. I'm surprised we came from the same parents. If you offer even the slightest difference of opinion, she goes to no end with bitterness and hateful harangues, trying to change what you believe. And if she cannot, she'll carry the grudge until the end of Hell. So I told her I'd had enough of her nonsense, and I left Elvendale for good."

"So that's what happened? A goblin didn't capture and eat you?"

"A goblin?" Aerlene cackled. "Only in her *maddest* dream, my dear. Certainly, she's *hoped* that."

Shawndirea hugged Aerlene and smiled. "I'm grateful you're living and well."

"Just before I darted off with you, did you kiss that human on the cheek?" Aerlene asked.

"Yes, that's Roble."

"Why are you with him?"

"I'm in love with him," Shawndirea said with a bright smile. Her eyes lit up and she squeezed her aunt's hand. "*And* he loves me."

"Does Istrell know?"

"Not yet. He's taking me to Elvendale so I can get my wings healed."

"She doesn't know you're bringing him?"

"No."

Aerlene beamed. "You *have* to let me be there when you tell her the news."

"You'd like that, wouldn't you?"

"Oh, *every* second of it."

"I don't look forward to going home, but being up here makes me want my wings restored more than ever. I *must* go home."

Aerlene nodded. "I'd die without my ability to fly. There's so much liberation soaring on the wind and flying with the songbirds."

"It's frightening not having my wings. If not for Roble's help, I'd have died by now." She chose to protect his reputation instead of revealing he'd shredded them.

"Bringing Roble to the High Court will send your mother into a horrible tirade," Aerlene said.

"I expect so."

"She'll threaten your right to the throne."

Shawndirea smiled. "It's fine if she does. I hope she denies my right to the throne."

"Does she know this?" Aerlene frowned, but a smile tugged her lips.

"I've told her often."

Shawndirea watched the fleeting moonlight. Soon darkness would blanket the night for a couple hours before the sunrise. The stars' magnificent radiance would be mesmerizing.

"Which kingdom does Roble call home?" Aerlene asked.

Shawndirea smiled. "The Overlands."

Aerlene feigned a gasp before bursting into a fit of laughter. "*No!* I've always known you held a rebellious streak, my dear. Regardless of what your mother insists, you always choose a different path."

Shawndirea gave a sneaky smile.

"Oh, I'd love to see her expression when you tell her! Ple-e-ease, let me witness the moment. Roble from the Overlands? Wow, you're going for the kill, eh?"

"No. I'm certain she'll take it that way, but honestly, what I feel for

Roble is genuine. I'd never choose a human within our realm, or a faery either, for that matter."

"I'm afraid we have few noble choices, so I can't blame you for being resourceful and exploring better options."

Shawndirea curtsied.

Aerlene shook her head at her niece's playful gesture. "In spite of your choice, Istrell will do everything to persuade you to assume the throne."

Shawndirea nodded modestly. "I know. If I don't take it, I'll solicit her to let Dirk reign in my stead."

"Dirk?" Aerlene shook her head. "No. I love Dirk, but he isn't suited to sit on *any* throne."

"He's your son. You don't want him over Elvendale?"

"No."

"Why not?" Shawndirea asked.

"He's a tyrant. He's ruthless, self-centered, and cold-blooded. He's the last person I, or anyone, should want on the throne."

Shawndirea was stunned.

"That surprises you?" Aerlene asked.

She nodded.

"It shouldn't," Aerlene said. "When you two were children, I cannot count the times you complained about how unfair he played *any* game. He cheated no matter what you played."

"We were children."

"Well, my dear, he's never outgrown it. In fact, he's matured into something far worse. Power is his wealth."

"He thinks you're dead, too," Shawndirea said.

"Good," she said bluntly. "I intend to keep it that way."

Changing the subject, Shawndirea asked, "How'd you end up in Woodcrest?"

"Opportunity arose. I accepted it," she said with a firm nod.

"The people worship you?"

"Some do."

"They've built a statue and altar in your honor. Some I've heard pray to you. Why?"

Aerlene smiled. "I protect them. They rely on the earth to survive, and I bless their crops and watch over them."

"The Vykings killed their leaders, but you didn't stop them."

She shrugged. "They *weren't* believers."

"You mean you could've prevented their deaths?"

Aerlene nodded. "Yes."

"Then *why* didn't you?"

"Several reasons actually. It wasn't because they didn't believe in me. Now, others in Woodcrest view their nonbelief as the reason I didn't defend them. It'll increase their faith and allegiance. However, the biggest issue was how many dark elves might arrive. They wish to control these forests and they believe some dark relic remains hidden where the old monastery and temple were. They've never found it, nor will they. Once they sided with the Vykings, I allowed ample time to see if more dark elf reinforcements came. They didn't, so I took action."

Shawndirea looked at Aerlene with deep concern.

"What is it, child?" her aunt asked.

"You call Dirk a tyrant?"

Aerlene's eyes narrowed and glowed. "Careful, niece."

"You're *not* a goddess. They owe you no allegiance."

Aerlene took a quick breath and sighed. "I know, but they don't."

Shawndirea shook her head. "That's not the point. What if Haigla discovers you're a faery with limited powers?"

Aerlene smiled. "The old woman? Ah, she's a dear. Her devotion to me is greater than all of Woodcrest combined."

"That's the danger, aunt," Shawndirea replied. "If she discovers you're not as powerful as she, she could bind and place you in restraints. Or much worse, use your blood in potions to increase *her* power."

"She's merely an herbalist who's learned a few spells here and there," Aerlene said, without worry.

"You're mistaken," Shawndirea said. "Have you not watched her? Have you not seen what she can do?"

The questions drained the anger and confidence from Aerlene's face. Her troubled eyes searched Woodcrest for Haigla. She pursed her lips. "What have you seen?"

Shawndirea mentioned some of the things she, Roble, and Odlon had watched in her dark cellar. The small library of spell books and scrolls indicated she performed magic, and she possessed the power to move inanimate objects at will.

Aerlene grew more concerned.

"She used a potion when she summoned you at the statue," Shawndirea said.

"I hadn't noticed."

Shawndirea nodded. "Whatever spell she used, the dark elves died soon after."

"Yes, the dryads killed them."

"They've sided with you?"

"Not directly. They protect the trees they're attached to. The dark elves were a threat, so they snared and killed them."

Shawndirea shook her head, and gently placed her hand on her aunt's arm. "No. Haigla made a potion, she chanted her spell, and seconds later the dryads did *her* bidding. *She* controls them, not you."

Aerlene swallowed hard. "That *is* alarming."

"Did you communicate with the dryads near the gates right before they attacked the dark elves?"

"No."

"Then she controls them. Perhaps she has control on you as well?"

Aerlene shook her head. "No. I detect nothing magical holding me here."

"You're still in Woodcrest. Fly beyond the town walls and see."

Nervousness claimed Aerlene's eyes. She hesitated to attempt Shawndirea's challenge.

"You're afraid I'm right, aren't you? Shawndirea asked.

Aerlene didn't reply. She shot into the air and flew toward the nearest gate. Right as she reached the guard tower, a flashing yellow light radiated like lightning. Aerlene shrieked, lost her flight balance, and spun helplessly to the ground.

Shawndirea gasped. "Aerlene?"

Without her wings, Shawndirea was stuck at the top of the tree. She couldn't help her aunt. Getting to Roble and the others was almost as troubling.

CHAPTER 53

The sudden, ghastly shrieks abruptly silencing near Woodcrest's gates caught Drucis' attention. Grey's restless ears backed and the horse's eyes widened with terror.

"Easy, boy," Drucis said. "Don't be thinking we're next, cause we ain't."

Drucis held the battle-axe handle tightly. His eyes narrowed. His bushy eyebrows made it look like he'd closed his eyes. However, they were deceptively alert with keener vision than a hawk with the sun directly overhead.

After the pain-filled cries silenced, the forest surrounding the road became oddly quiet. The only sounds were his and Grey's breathing.

Drucis looked to the faint blue statue outlines again. He expected spirits to glide past, but nothing stirred. The night birds and insects hushed as though the death of winter had claimed them.

An occasional wind gust rustled leaves high in the treetops.

Grey whinnied.

"Easy, now. We be getting out of these blasted woods soon enough."

He tapped Grey's flanks and coaxed the horse to steadily move to Woodcrest. Near the gates, Grey became more uncomfortable and set his hooves solidly on the paved road. An odd smell hung in the air, which reminded Drucis of the deathly decay in Glacier Ridge when the undead creatures came for him.

But it was more than that. The looming, acrid smell resulted from painful, sudden deaths dealt by magical beings. The exact kind of magical creatures he didn't know, but he was more leery than before. He had sensitivity to magic, and since this had occurred recently, the power lingered with the night breeze. The runic markings on his axe glowed and dimmed, which indicated his suspicion of magic was correct.

The hairs on his arms stiffened. Chills ran down his back. He shuddered even though he wasn't cold. He missed his Dwarven comrades, Sorgen and Draken. They, like him, thrived with delight whenever they encountered possible skirmishes, especially against those who wielded magical powers because it made such fights more challenging. They watched one another's back, but now, he was alone.

The flickering torches burning atop the Woodcrest gates lighted the top section of the walls. When Drucis noticed a dark elf's mangled armor burrowed partway into the side of a massive oak, he pulled the reins and directed the horse to the side of the road near the trees. He hefted the axe and swung off Grey, half expecting an arrow to slice through the night air and strike him or his old horse. When the elf didn't move, Drucis was more curious than concerned. Had the townsfolk of Woodcrest made some type of scarecrow from dark elf armor to frighten away night travelers? Doubtful, but a possibility nonetheless.

"Stay steady now," Drucis told Grey.

Hiding in the dark shadows at the edge of the grove, Drucis watched for the slightest movement along the wall. Other than the dancing sconce flames, nothing else moved. He wondered why the dark elf didn't move and why it was there in the first place. When he'd passed through Woodcrest with his two companions, the gates were open. The guards along the wall were a couple of townsfolk. Nothing more.

"What's a goin' on 'ere?" Drucis asked softly.

A rope ladder hung down the side of the wall on the other side of the path. He smiled with amusement. "What fool be leaving dat hanging o'er the wall?"

He ran for the ladder. He'd almost reached the ladder when a growl

383

rose behind him. Drucis turned. A massive Vyking rushed him with his two-handed sword drawn.

"What the—?"

The Vyking guard gnashed his teeth. "Little man, you *did* this?"

Drucis brought up his axe a second before the sword would've made him a head shorter. Sparks flashed.

"Did *what*, you ol' filthy ogre?"

"You killed the dark elves," the Vyking said evenly, readying his next attack. He brought the sword overhead with both hands and came at Drucis with a downward slash. Drucis swung his axe and caught the blade with the curve of the handle and blade, twisted and yanked. The giant almost dropped his blade.

"If only I would 'ave," Drucis said with a grin. "My day would've ended on a better note. However, killing you will amend what I've lacked on such an otherwise sorrowful day."

"Bring your best, little toadstool."

Drucis' eyes narrowed. "I always *do*, you oaf!"

The Vyking stood nearly three times Drucis' height, but the size difference didn't deter the dwarf. He loved challenges and the bigger, the better.

He eyed the giant Vyking. "Wouldn't you have been safer on the *other* side of the wall? It be a bit dangerous out here for the likes of ya."

The angry Vyking swung his sword. Drucis parried the strike with ease, spun, and slashed the giant's thigh. Blood spilled from the gash. The Vyking groaned, growled, and spat on the ground.

"I kill gutter rats like you all the day long," the Vyking replied.

"You be a bit outmatched this day."

The Vyking growled and charged. The dwarf stepped aside and darted between his opponent's legs. He could've easily hacked one of the Vyking's legs, but he wished to toy with him a bit longer. He'd encountered several of Waxxon's recruits over the past few weeks and observed how they bullied townspeople in different villages. Now he had an opportunity to humiliate one. Only then could his opponent know the Vykings weren't superior to everyone else.

Drucis turned behind the giant and smacked the Vyking's backside with the flat side of his axe blade, which angered the man even more.

The Vyking turned, leaned forward, and rushed again. Drucis flipped his axe and used the handle to strike the man's left shin. He roared in pain and dropped to the ground. Drucis swung to decapitate his newfound enemy, but the blade dug into the dirt.

The Vyking rolled, held his knee, and shoved himself to his feet. He hobbled on his good leg. Blood seeped from the gash, but the bleeding seemed to be slowing. Drucis pried the axe from the ground, but before he could swing again, the giant man's fist caught Drucis' jaw and sent him sprawling backwards.

He held fast to the axe, but the man pursued with his sword.

"Aye," Drucis laughed. "If it be fists you wish to exchange?"

"Nay, lil' imp!" The man brought his sword high overhead.

Before the preemptive strike, Drucis used the axe head to block the downward blow, pivoted the sword to the side, and kicked the man's right shin. Before the man reached for his injured shin, Drucis ducked low and caught the man around the knees, lifted him off the ground, and pushed him backwards. With both shins aching and his balance toppling, the Vyking dropped hard and landed on his back.

Drucis didn't allow him time to struggle and get to his feet. He straddled the man's chest and pummeled the man's face with stubby thick fists. He hit and hit, not easing his blows or slowing until the Vyking lie unconscious.

Sweat beaded from beneath Drucis' helm. He huffed. The only thing he regretted was Grey was the only witness to the duel. Grey wasn't going to expound praise anyone.

Drucis returned to Grey, grabbed rope from his saddlebag, and he led the horse to the Vyking. The dwarf tied the man's hands and feet in tight knots. Once he was certain the man couldn't free himself when he awakened, Drucis climbed the rope ladder.

At the top of the wall, he examined the dark elf. He was stunned. The tree bark had engulfed the elf's head and neck. He tapped the side of the tree near the elf's chest. Solid. The bark wasn't splintered, and the elf was cold to the touch.

"How?" Drucis said.

Little chuckles grew into hysterical laughter on the higher branches. He pointed the tip of his axe to where the laughter faded.

"Aye. Show yourselves. Your laughter will cease."

With a fast swing of the axe, he removed the dead elf's body from the tree. The limp, headless corpse landed on the rampart at Drucis' feet. He rolled the body over, removed the elf's daggers, his boots, and two small pouches filled with silver coins.

"Ya won't be needing these," he said with a broad smile.

Drucis hoisted the ladder up to the platform. Then, he descended the crude stairs to Woodcrest's grounds. Before he opened the gates to get Grey, he decided to scout around to make certain no Vykings were posted inside.

Commotion stirred farther inside the town. He held his axe tightly and smiled.

"Aye, a skirmish. Just what I be needing!"

Drucis sprinted toward the bickering voices.

CHAPTER 54

*R*oble searched for Shawndirea in the dark tree branches. The thick leafy canopy was impossible to see through. He didn't want to think she was in danger, but he wasn't certain. She seemed to know the faery.

"Where are you?" Roble whispered.

"What happened?" Odlon asked. "Where's Shawndirea?"

"Another faery took her."

Riese walked to them. "We should sleep here today. Once the sun rises the following day, we head out. Roble, I'll escort you, Odlon, and Shawndirea past Ironwood, but after that, I've other endeavors to attend."

"Fair enough," Roble said. He stared at the tree limbs and hoped Shawndirea presented herself.

Odlon said, "Get some sleep. Later I'll teach you basic swordsman-ship skills. It won't be a lot though for what little time we have."

"Every bit helps. Whatever you teach me, I'll practice at great lengths every chance I get."

"After you and Shawndirea reach Elvendale, and her wings are restored, meet me in Woodnog for more training. I'll find some trainees for you to spar with."

Roble nodded his appreciation. "I look forward to it."

Roble and Odlon followed Riese to the wagon. Lehrling lie unconscious. Haigla placed her wrinkled hand to Lehrling's sweaty forehead
and checked his eyes. She put her ear to his chest and listened. Her good
eye widened with intent interest. Seconds later, she rose and shook her
head.

"How bad is he?" Roble asked.

"Too bad to travel. Leave him with me," she replied. "He's very
weak."

"You have a remedy?"

She cocked her head and gave a faint, snuff-coated grin. "I've lots of
things that may work. But if he leaves in this condition, he'll die. He's
too sick."

Roble couldn't argue about Lehrling's condition. The rocking and
jostling wagon would worsen his health. He'd die. Roble was leery,
though. He wasn't sure Haigla was trustworthy.

Roble shot Odlon a questionable stare. Odlon shrugged and nodded
his agreement.

"We'll leave his horse and belongings in your care," Roble said to
Haigla. "I hope to find him in the near future."

Odlon nodded. "As do I. Roble, after Ironwood, my journey detours
to the Woodnog swamps."

Roble worried about being left on his own with Shawndirea. He'd
somehow survived the journey through Hell with her, but he'd grown
comfortable with his new friends in an unfamiliar world. A part of him
grieved, but another part looked forward to learning more about
Shawndirea. Too much had happened and prevented them from having
intimate time to talk. He wanted to learn what she envisioned their
future together to be.

Odlon clasped Roble's shoulder. "You'll have only a day's journey left.
Of course, there's Crukas. I doubt he'll stay anywhere near Ironwood,
but he could be persuaded to follow you."

Roble shook his head. "Crukas is a thief, not a warrior. He'd rather
move in the shadows than take up a sword to fight."

Odlon smiled. "You learn quickly, which benefits you greatly. But
he'll follow you for part of the journey I'm quite certain."

"Why?"

"Roads are the safest paths to travel between towns. Shortcuts through forests can be deadly. I suggest you take this to heart."

Roble nodded.

"Roble!" Shawndirea shouted from the tree canopy.

He looked for Shawndirea but couldn't find her. "Where are you?"

"I'm stuck in the tree," she replied.

"She left you up there?"

"Not intentionally, but I need to get down."

"How?"

"Catch me!" she yelled.

"Wait. Don't jump!"

SHAWNDIREA DOVE from the tree branch. Her light weight prevented her from dropping too fast. Near a lower branch, she grabbed a thick leaf, snapped it loose, and glided between the branches. She moved slowly, so she didn't need to worry about getting bruised should she collide with twigs or branches.

Roble lifted his hands when she came into view, and Odlon did the same. She pulled both sides of the leaf tighter and bowed the shape to catch the wind and change direction. A gentle breeze caught her leaf and spiraled her toward Roble. When she drifted directly over his hands, she released the leaf and dropped.

"What happened?" Roble held his hands steadily so she could stand. "Why'd she leave you?"

"It's not what you think. Now hurry." She pointed in the direction Aerlene had flown. "My aunt needs help."

Roble carried Shawndirea and Odlon followed.

"Your aunt? Is she okay?"

"I don't know." The fear in her voice beckoned Roble to move faster. "Be careful. She's on the ground. *Don't* step on her."

A faint, pink glow emitted in a thick patch of grass beneath an oak tree. Aerlene lie on her back and squinted while they stood over her.

Shawndirea leapt from Roble's hand and ran to her aunt.

"Are you okay, Aerlene?" she asked.

Aerlene shook her head and blinked hard several times. She frowned. "A bit taken off guard is all."

"She cast a spell on you," Shawndirea said.

"Yes, that nasty witch," Aerlene seethed. Her tiny hands balled into fists. She started to stand.

"Stay still."

Roble frowned. "Whom is she talking about?"

"Haigla," Shawndirea said. "She bound Aerlene to Woodcrest, which prevents her from leaving."

"Why'd she do that?" he asked.

"Control and power," Aerlene said, rubbing her temples. "Perhaps a bit of revenge as well."

Odlon knelt near Aerlene. "Haigla helped us regain control of Woodcrest."

"No," Shawndirea said. "She used a potion to get the dark elves killed. The potion controlled the dryads. Right after she used it, the dryads had no choice but to obey her command."

Odlon frowned. "Without the dryads' assistance, we'd still be trying to figure out how to stop the dark elves."

"True," Shawndirea said. "But she's no reason to control my aunt."

"Of course not," Roble said.

"You don't understand," Aerlene said. "If she already had power over the dryads, she could've commanded them at any time. Instead, she allowed the town council leaders to be killed by the Vykings and the dark elves. She could've summoned the dryads to kill the dark elves without the leaders dying."

Shawndirea nodded. "Now, the townsfolk believe she's their savior and will allow her to rule them."

"Surely, they're not that blind," Roble said. "We should tell them what happened."

"No," Aerlene said. "These people are simple folks. They're workers and abhor violence. They refuse to take up arms against others. Partly because they're raised to follow the monk virtues that existed before the dark elves destroyed the monastery. These virtues they learned from old scrolls."

Roble said, "They'd remain under the dark elves control even though these elves were the ones who destroyed their ancestors? That'd difficult to believe. Why would they subject themselves to the dark elves?"

Aerlene groaned and sat up. "Fate."

"What?" Roble asked.

"They attribute it to fate, thinking the gods are punishing them for some ill deed."

"If the gods have a hand in their bondage, why would they suddenly follow Haigla and do her biddings?" Odlon asked. "That contradicts any means of faith."

Aerlene smiled. "You underestimate the power of magic. The towns-folk in Woodcrest fear magicians, sorcerers, and Haigla for being a witch. Their fear gives her prominence. She'll do whatever she wants. None will oppose her."

"So she's a tyrant?" Roble asked.

"Yes," Aerlene replied. "Her goal is to overtake the town."

"Nothing less," Shawndirea said.

Roble looked in Aerlene's eyes. "Why'd they build a monument to you? Aren't you somewhat to blame for what's happening?"

Aerlene looked away. She swallowed hard, brushed herself off, and slowly stood. "I made an innocent mistake."

"I wouldn't call it 'innocent,'" Roble said. "Perhaps *vain*."

Aerlene's eyes narrowed. Her jaw tightened.

"He's right, Auntie," Shawndirea said. "You know he is."

Aerlene huffed. "Perhaps. The truth's hard to accept. She tricked me into believing she and the others worshipped me by building the statue as a tribute to me. But she magically bound me to the statue to control my magic."

Shawndirea said. "That makes perfect sense."

"However, due to my lack of judgment, it's not right for me to be tied to Woodcrest."

"No, it isn't," Odlon said.

"Perhaps Zauber can free you," Roble said.

"It's possible," Shawndirea said, "but only if he's still here."

"You think he'd leave?" Roble asked.

"He's no reason to stay. The Vykings and dark elves no longer control Woodcrest. Besides, he and Haigla are *not* friends."

Odlon whispered, "I doubt she has friends."

"She's definitely an outcast of any social circle," Aerlene said. "That may explain why she bound me. Using my charisma, she could subtly make others like her."

"How do we break the spell?" Roble asked Shawndirea. "Especially if your aunt no longer has magical powers."

"I have magic," Aerlene insisted. "But it's limited."

"Destroy the statue." Shawndirea's face beamed. "She bound you to it. Destroying it should break her control over you."

"That might work," Aerlene replied. "But only if she isn't anywhere near it."

Roble searched but didn't see Haigla nearby. "What would that matter?"

"Again, *the magic.*" Aerlene rolled her eyes. She sighed and shot Shawndirea a glance. "Tell me *why* you chose *this* human?"

"Now, don't," Shawndirea said. "Remember where he's from. He doesn't have much knowledge about magic. He's learning though."

"Sorry." Aerlene looked at Roble and waved her hands in slight surrender. "My head's still spinning over the abrupt shot of electricity that dropped me. And besides, my anger grows with the things I like to *do* to the old hag."

Odlon extended his hand for Aerlene to step upon. "My lady."

Aerlene glowed a radiant, flattered smile and stepped on his palm.

"Find Riese," Shawndirea said.

"Why?" Roble asked.

She smiled. "He could use his hammer to destroy the statue. With his powerful strength, he shouldn't fail."

Roble and Odlon carried the faeries to the intersection. Riese stood talking to his son and Hordus. Although only Hordus' hands were restrained, the elder Vyking didn't attempt to flee. He seemed to respect Riese's authority.

"Riese," Roble said. "We need your help."

Riese frowned. "What do you need me to do?"

Roble explained their situation, but the mention of Haigla's power made Riese uncomfortable.

"You want me to break the statue?" Riese asked.

Roble nodded.

"What prevents her from attacking me after I've done so?" Riese's eyes hinted his uncertainty.

"For one thing," Aerlene said. "Destroy the statue and you greatly weaken her power. Shawndirea and I are strong enough to counter any vengeful attacks she might attempt."

"Once the dryads discover her spell over them, they'll assist us," Shawndirea said.

Riese walked to the statue and gripped his heavy hammer tightly.

"Stop!" Haigla stepped out from behind the water trough near the town council building.

Riese met her wicked gaze. He swallowed hard and narrowed his eyes.

"Take heed, Vyking." She raised her hand and pointed her wand in his direction. "Don't touch my statue."

Odlon set Aerlene at his feet, pulled his crossbow, and loaded it. He aimed at the old woman. Shawndirea stood on Roble's shoulder. He pulled two weighted throwing knives from his belt.

Haigla waved her hands. A strong breeze flowed past. Seconds later, the doors to houses, huts, and even the town hall opened. People stepped into the street and crowded the statue of Aerlene.

Roble wondered if she controlled these people or were they curious about what was happening? Their odd gazes indicated the former.

"Elf," she said. "Put down the crossbow."

Odlon chuckled. "No. You may have power, but you can't stop all of us."

"I won't have to." She nodded at the gathering crowd. "They'll do it for me."

Riese glanced at Odlon. The elf nodded and smiled. Odlon boldly stepped forward and aimed at Haigla's head. She readied her wand and faced him. When she did, Riese flung his hammer hard. Before the hammer struck the statue, a townsman flung himself into the hammer's path. The hammer struck the man's head and killed him instantly.

The rest of the people faced Riese, Roble, and Odlon. Their expressionless faces let Roble understand the strength of Haigla's control.

They didn't worship her. She controlled their minds with such force they'd die before any harm to came to her or the statue.

"Put your weapons away," Haigla said.

Odlon's jaw tightened. He closed his left eye, aimed, and placed his finger on the trigger.

"Wait," Roble placed his hand on the elf's elbow.

"Why?" Odlon asked. "She's in my sight. I can kill her."

"I know."

"Then what's the problem?"

"What if her mind control remains after she dies? We'll have to kill our way out of Woodcrest. These people aren't acting on their own free will. She's forcing them to obey."

Odlon eased the tension on the trigger and glanced at the increasing mob. The men and women stepped closer, their girth tightening as they approached. With slight agitation, Odlon lowered the crossbow. His shared sympathy was for the crowd, not Haigla.

"That's better. I showed you folks hospitality. Nice hot soup to fill your bellies," she said in her raspy voice, "and then you turn on me."

"What you're doing isn't right," Roble said.

"Nothing usually is," Haigla replied. "All the years I've lived here with such scrutiny and being shunned like a plague by those I've helped. Anytime someone became ill, they sought my help. Not once did I turn them away. When all is well, they want me to remain hidden like an outcast because they don't want to look at me. There's never been any real appreciation."

She aimed her wand at Roble and Odlon. The tip of her wand glowed. Riese's face tightened with anger. He stood weaponless. Shawndirea and Aerlene aimed their glowing fingers at Haigla, ready to counter any spell she might cast.

From the middle of the crowd, Drucis shouted, "Aye! I believe you dropped this!"

The dwarf tossed the hammer over the townsfolk heads. Riese caught it and smiled. Without a hesitation, he threw the hammer at the statue with all his might.

The hammer struck the head of Aerlene's marble statue. The entire head shattered. Marble fragments exploded and showered over the hypnotized crowded.

Haigla wailed and dropped to her knees. Rage changed her facial features into that of a hideous demon. Her voice deepened.

Aerlene and Shawndirea combined their powers and directed their magic at the old woman. Haigla shuddered, covered her face, and pressed her forehead to the ground and wept.

The townspeople shook their heads and awakened from their strange trances. Roble suspected Haigla had aligned with the dark elves more than she'd let on. She destroyed them after they'd ensured the town council members were dead.

Aerlene flew to her headless statue and looked down at the townsfolk.

"You're free now," Aerlene said. "Haigla's the one responsible for your leaders' deaths. She tricked me and used my powers to entice you into believing she was the one who saved you. Not only did she charm you, she wanted you to kill the ones that killed the Vykings. She must be punished."

"How should she be punished?" a woman asked.

"Yes," a man said. "What can we do?"

"Drive her from your town," Aerlene said. "Make certain she never returns."

Haigla lie prostrate on the ground and sobbed. She received no pity. Aerlene's magic had been ripped from the old woman. When Haigla fell, her withered wand fell far outside her reach.

Crukas appeared from the shadows, grabbed the wand, and hurried to Roble and the others. A young girl ran to Crukas and extended her hand for the wand. He studied her eyes for a moment before handing it to her. She smiled, waved the wand and pranced around. Two men grabbed Haigla and helped her stand. Then they bound her hands behind her back and led her to Woodcrest's intersection.

Tears streamed from her good eye. Her milky white eye increased its darkness until it was blacker than obsidian.

"Take her far from here," one man said, looking at Riese.

Riese gave a nod. "We can do that."

"No," Haigla said. "I can't survive outside Woodcrest."

"What about Lehrling?" Roble asked.

"Yes!" Haigla's face brightened with hope. "I *must* stay to heal him. Don't send me out, or he'll surely die."

A middle-aged woman approached and smiled. "I'll tend to him until he has recovered."

"You know how to treat his illness?" Shawndirea asked.

The woman nodded.

"Good." Roble smiled. "Thanks. He'll die if he travels with us."

"I'll make certain he's well taken care of."

"I've no words to express my gratitude," Roble said.

"None are needed," she replied.

The sun peaked over the horizon. Men and women gathered their wagons, garden tools, harnessed mules to the plows, and headed along the roads to the opening gates for the first time since Waxxon's recruits had taken over the town.

While Riese checked his horse, several women brought cloth-covered goods—cheese, bread, honey, and skins filled with wine—to the wagon.

"In our appreciation," a lady said. She placed the food on the wagon seat. Marc nodded and placed the goods beneath the seat.

Two men brought large sacks of oats and grains for their horses. After they set the bags in the wagon bed, Drucis rode up on Grey.

"Be room for one more along your journey, ya old ogre?" he asked Riese.

Riese turned and smiled. "Drucis, I must've *overlooked* your arrival."

The dwarf's eyes narrowed. "Don't be *overstepping* your boundaries!"

Riese chuckled. "Can always use you along the way. The first stop is Ironwood. After that, we part ways. I don't quite know where we'll be going."

"Anywhere's fine. Sorry about Hobskin's Tavern," Drucis said.

Riese's eyes widened. "No others survived?"

Sadness claimed Drucis' eyes and his facial expressions. "No."

"How did *you*?"

"Twern't easy."

The dwarf explained how the Plague-bringer came into the bar and everything that transpired soon thereafter. When he mentioned the loss of his two comrades, his voice weakened and his eyes softened.

"Again," he said. "I'm sorry about the tavern. Setting it ablaze was the only way I could survive."

Riese shook his head. "To have you alive, old friend, burning the entire town down is worth it."

"Aww, don't be getting all misty on me now. Tears rust your weapons and armor."

"Look who's talking."

A half hour passed and everyone was set to depart Woodcrest. Roble glanced at the gates one last time as they rode around the bend. He hoped it wouldn't be the last time he saw Lehrling.

CHAPTER 55

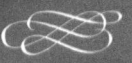

*C*rukas walked alongside the wagon. Amusement curled his lips when he stared at Haigla locked inside the old iron cage on the wagon bed. The bitter old woman stood stooped and held the bars tightly in her wrinkled hands. She studied the bars, the welded runic symbols, and sighed. Hordus sat on the back of the wagon bed. His feet dangled a couple inches above the road as the wagon moved. His cuffed hands were tethered to a lower bar on the cage.

"Who constructed this cage?" she asked.

"Riese," Crukas said.

Haigla turned in the cell and looked at Riese. "Who taught you these symbols? Most Vykings shun any sort of magic. You've hung a spell to neutralize the powers of the occupant. How'd you know to do this?"

Without facing her, Riese replied, "My wife."

"Not a Vyking, I'm guessing."

"No."

"Then how?"

"Enough about her," he said, bluntly.

Haigla's eyes glanced from Riese to his son. She studied his freckled complexion, red hair, and how dainty his body was compared to Riese.

"Part elf?" she said.

Riese handed the reins to Marc, turned, and pointed his hammer at her. His eyes were mean, cold, and determined. "One more word."

The old woman's face paled. No one with common sense would question the meaning of Riese's harsh gaze and intent. Another word and the blacksmith would kill her. Haigla chose silence. She turned and faced the road behind them. Apparently, she wanted to live even if it were outside Woodcrest.

Crukas grinned. He was relieved Riese's anger was directed elsewhere.

A CRUDE WOODEN sign with a carved arrow pointed to Ironwood. Crukas was apprehensive after they passed the sign. The road nestled along the side of a steep ridge on the right hand side. On the left, the drop-off was dangerously deep and filled with large jagged rocks and trees. Water from a narrow stream splashed on the rocks below.

A foggy mist drifted in the cool, morning air. What should've been a pleasant morning for walking and meditating was anything except. Despair and anxiety settled over Crukas like a black miserable cloud. He didn't want to travel any closer to Ironwood, but he couldn't retreat. Otherwise, he feared, Odlon or Roble might kill him.

Moving forward was a death sentence anyway. Although Roble and the others promised to keep him safe, he didn't think they'd ever get past Ironwood. *They* might, but Ironwood's town council wanted him dead at all costs. He wondered why.

Each time Crukas had collected the bounty on an ex-guild member, the town's council threw a large banquet and celebration. The tables were covered with roasted pork, venison, game fowls, fish, and more breads and desserts than he'd seen at most royal gatherings in Hoffnung. The townsfolk ate and drank heartily. Most danced while quartets played stringed instruments. Bards told tales. Magicians performed fascinating tricks. Skilled men and women challenged one another in competitions with axes, bows, and knives. During all of this, people approached Crukas with gifts or handshakes. Beautiful women danced with him. Others offered more, and after a day of celebration, he left the town feeling like a hero. Though, he was *not*. He never wished to associated with the title.

Having chosen the life of a solitary thief, these celebrations went against his code and placed him in the open view of the city's council. Perhaps, this was intentional? Even though they relished his presence, several times he was certain the show was a facade. While he couldn't trust a thief, he trusted politicians even less.

Ironwood's council's attitude abruptly changed during his last venture through the city. Crukas didn't bring another wanted thief or burglar. He sought to pass through unnoticed.

He entered the gate at sunrise, before the vendors began their morning tasks. A guard recognized him and shouted for his surrender.

Crukas regarded the request as a joke. He turned and smiled at the guard. To his surprise, the guard drew his sword and rushed him. Crukas ran.

Midway through town, the guard blew his horn to alert other patrols. Clattering swords and creaking, leather armor informed Crukas they were in fast pursuit.

Crukas, a master at vanishing, hid behind a barrel of dried fish. While he crouched low, the light morning breeze rustled the edges of a yellowed, tattered piece of parchment nailed to the corner post of the trader's tent. His eyes widened. The wanted poster had his image sketched on it.

Two guards rushed past his position. He stood, yanked and folded the poster, and tucked it inside his tunic. More horns sounded. Shrilling whistles awakened the townsfolk.

Crukas ducked, crawled from behind the barrel, and slid beneath a trader's table. He watched the street for approaching patrols. Between two poles on opposing sides of the cobblestone street, a thin rope held tanned hides, which he used like a partial wall to conceal himself and cross the street. Once there, the chainmail of armored guards rattled in his direction but the guards sprinted past.

He hurried down a side alley, farther from the market square, and found a small opening in the wall. The acrid scent drifting from the hole was familiar. The sewers. Years had passed since he endured such squalor. With his accumulated wealth, he ate and dressed like an aristocrat, except when he sought to steal valuables. Never had he considered the possibility of crawling through the sewers like a wet rat again.

Not certain why the town council turned against him or what his outcome was, should he be captured, he squeezed his thin body through the opening. The round enclosure was similar to a water well except nothing was drawn from the hole. Waste and garbage were tossed inside, and left to rot.

He gagged from the horrid smell, but balanced between the grimy, ooze-covered rocks. The roaring guards sounding alerts near the market square left Crukas no choice. He went deeper into the sewers and hoped he found the flow leading outside Ironwood. The filth smudged his face, his hands and arms, and ruined his silk shirt.

Pressing his fingers in the narrow grooves between the blocks for leverage, he climbed downward and deeper in the darkness. The air became toxic. The gaseous methane nauseated him and he neared unconsciousness. If he failed to find a source of fresh air, the gas would kill him.

His slick, filthy fingertips clung to the blocks. His head spun. He coughed and lost his grip. His back struck the opposite wall. He flung his arms helplessly and dropped to the bottom of the garbage pit. His fall ended with a tremendous splash in a deep pool of cold, stinking water. The frigid water snapped him awake. He swam upward and broke through the water's surface. A thick layer of floating waste prevented him from going back under. The smell was terrible but at least he was below the gaseous layer.

Water dripped from the walls. His heavy breathing escaped in choking gasps. Surrounded by filth and darkness, he contemplated which direction to swim. No torches lit the passage, which was a blessing. A torch would ignite the gas and incinerate him.

This gutter lacked any system of proper management. Unlike the elegant sewers in Hoffnung, which he thought odd to think in such terms, but it was true. The City of Hoffnung had been well kept with properly dug sewer channels that dipped at the appropriate angle to ensure the waste flowed *out* of the city. Unlike Ironwood's, which was a nonmoving, stagnant channel with piling, rotten dung. Hoffnung's channels were lined with torches and walkways so the city maintenance crews could prevent the waste from getting blocked.

Crukas used a pillow of solid waste to keep afloat while kicking his feet. He rounded a few twists and turns in the long sewer tunnel. At the far end of the channel, light brightened the path slightly. Water trickled and cascaded through a metal grate with enough force that a slight undertow tugged him toward the grate.

He kicked his feet harder and pushed his way through the garbage until he reached the iron barred grate. He clung to the bars and glanced out. The sewer waste spilled through the opening and splattered on rocks a hundred feet below. From his viewpoint, the trees indicated he was on the southeastern part of Ironwood. He squeezed through the grate bars with great ease. He'd never known a fat thief, and that day he understood why. To survive the life as a thief, one had to be quick, nimble, and fit through tight places.

A half day passed before he reached the rock ledge to the flowing river below. Instead of heading southward, Crukas returned to Glacier Ridge. That decision led to him joining Roble's party without any way to bypass Ironwood.

Crukas shook his head.

He wished he'd headed south, perhaps even to the Woodnog swamps on the outskirts of the City of Woodnog. Should he survive passing through Ironwood this time, he planned never to head north again.

Crukas glanced at Haigla. Her good eye was trained on him. Her blind eye resembled a shiny orb of black obsidian. Her near toothless mouth hung partly open.

"You do know you will die on this journey, don't you?" Haigla said. The words weren't audible but whispered in his mind.

He frowned at her with curiosity.

She smiled. "You want to know how I speak to you, eh?"

Her laughter rang inside his mind. He nodded.

"Go on," she said. "Reply in your mind. I can hear you. We can talk."

Crukas projected his thoughts. "The cage stops magic. How can you speak in my head?"

She cackled. "That's not magic, thief. It's something I've always been able to do."

"Can you read others' thoughts?"

"At times. But getting inside *your* head to *steal* your thoughts is more amusing than any of the others."

"Why?"

"You're a thief unable to lock the treasures inside your own mind. You worry about what happens when you return to Ironwood, but do know, you'll be betrayed when you reach that town."

"By whom?"

"The only way you'll be safe is to release me. We can flee together."

Crukas' eyes narrowed. He turned his attention to the road ahead. Although he refused to look at her, she didn't cease speaking to his mind. He trained his thoughts to other activities like lock picking, boring things, anything to ignore her words. He wanted to keep mundane thoughts so she'd grow weary of reading his mind. After fifteen minutes, it must've worked. She sat in the cage and closed her eyes.

He worried about who would betray him. He didn't doubt her prediction. If she could read his mind, she'd read the mind of which person sought betrayal. When he reached Ironwood, he'd discover who it was. He hoped to escape with his life.

CHAPTER 56

*D*rucis rode Grey alongside Bleys. The dwarf gave Roble a quick nod. "Roble, is it?"

Roble nodded. "Yes."

"Drucis," he replied. "Nice to meet ya."

"Likewise."

He studied Roble for several minutes, almost like he was sizing Roble up for a duel. Finally, he shook his head. "I don't recall seeing ya in these parts."

"That's because it's my first time traveling here."

Drucis frowned with keen interest. "How can dat be? The only way to Glacier Ridge is through this pass unless, of course you be from the frost plains and the highlands, but they're fair skinned with white hair. No, you're not from there."

Roble shook his head. "No, I'm not."

"You don't favor the folks from the southern kingdoms, either."

With a slight smile, Roble said, "I imagine not."

"Well, lad, no other roads lead ya to Glacier Ridge."

"There's a pass through the mountain on the other side of Glacier Ridge."

"Don't be kiddin' wit me, lad. There be no other way."

Roble laughed.

"Something funny?" Drucis said with a harsh glare. Aggravation set in his stern tone and matched the frustration narrowing his eyes.

"Nothing that concerns you."

"Aye. Tell me why a faery rides with you?"

"We're escorting her home, so she can get her wings repaired."

Drucis frowned. "They can do dat?"

"We're hopeful."

"Should we 'appen upon any unruly rogues or bandits. Be swinging me axe, I will."

"Does such a possibility exist for where we're headed?" Roble asked.

Drucis studied Roble for a few moments. A thin grin parted his white beard. "You really don't know the area, do you?"

Roble shook his head. "No."

"Well, this pass cuts into Corwin's Pass. A far more treacherous path. Makes it difficult for armies to invade any towns out this way. The road's too narrow to march in large groups."

Ahead, down the sloping road, two figures approached. The one in the front walked on foot. The second rode on horseback. He wore the armor of Waxxon's men.

"What we be having here?" Drucis asked with excitement growing in his voice. His hand slid to his axe. "The day may not be a total loss."

Riese pulled back the reins and stopped the wagon. He glanced over his shoulder at Odlon, Roble, and Drucis. Crukas slinked between the wagon and the ridge wall to become inconspicuous.

"Be ready, lad," Drucis said to Roble.

The man on the horse had blonde hair and brilliant blue eyes. His shoulders were broad, his chest thick, and he possessed a steel shield and a sheathed long sword. His Vyking armor was overly loose and he looked too small to wear it. He obviously wasn't a Vyking.

The boy in front wore ragged clothes. His hair was cropped short and his face was covered with grime. The rider raised both hands above his head as he and the boy on foot approached.

"We want no trouble," he said.

"Who are you?" Riese stood on the wagon with his hammer in hand.

"Caen."

"You wear Vyking armor," Riese stated. "But you *aren't* of Welkstone blood."

Caen studied each of Roble's group before returning his gaze to Riese. He acquiesced a nod. "Your observation's correct."

"You travel alone?" Odlon raised his crossbow.

"Just me and my squire," Caen replied. "We're headed to the next town for supplies, nothing more. Let us pass without incident, and all is well."

"An odd request for someone under Waxxon's command," Odlon said.

"We hold no reverence for Waxxon," he replied with an even grin.

The squire's brow narrowed with anger at the mention of Waxxon's name. His hands tightened on his halberd. Although a teen, the young squire kept an intimidating posture. Roble wondered how difficult it'd be to disarm him.

"Again," Caen said, "let us pass and there'll be no bloodshed."

Riese shook his head. "You dare make a boastful challenge before us?"

"Let me at him," Drucis said, dismounting.

"Apologies," Caen said. "I should've phrased that differently. There's no need for attack from either side. You hold the advantage over us. I'm *not* seeking any violent skirmish between us."

Riese lowered his hammer. "Very well. Pass in peace."

Drucis grumbled. "Dammit."

"In exchange," Caen said, looking at Roble. "I offer you this. Iron-wood has guards dressed like myself. They'll not be kind to you as I've been. In fact, since you're a Dragon Skull Knight, they'll not hesitate in trying to kill you."

Goosebumps ran up Roble's arms. The hairs on the back of his neck stiffened.

Caen gave a slight nod to Roble as he and the squire passed. Roble glanced at Caen's icy blue gaze. Roble didn't detect the hardness and hatred he'd witnessed in the others who wore Vyking armor.

"Are you fleeing Waxxon's service?" Roble asked.

Caen's tugged the reins tightly and the horse stopped. Without looking back, Caen said, "What makes you draw such a conclusion?"

"Several reasons, actually," Roble replied. "Your armor doesn't fit. It's too loose around your chest, and your leggings are much too long. As Riese mentioned, you aren't of Welkstone blood. Plus, Waxxon never sends a guard out alone. They travel in pairs, and sometimes in greater numbers."

"All I'll say is Waxxon's guards await at Ironwood. A half dozen, but they're well armed. You've been warned."

Drucis laughed heartily.

Caen turned and narrowed his gaze. "You find the situation funny?"

Drucis shook his head. "Nah. Sounds like you're inviting us to turn around and join ya. This pass leads directly to Ironwood. There's no alternative route."

"At least you've the knowledge they're there." Caen turned and tapped his horse's flanks.

"Dat we 'ave," Drucis said with a broad grin. "By sundown, less of your comrades will roam the lands."

Caen didn't reply, nor did he bother looking back.

"Peace be to you then, soldier," Drucis said in a mocking tone.

Caen looked over his shoulder. "The witch you hold prisoner ... it'd serve you best to kill her *before* you release her."

Riese looked at Haigla and then to Caen. "Why?"

"She's controlled by a greater darkness than you know," Caen replied. "Her power's similar to what reigns in the Black Chasm. The closer you transport her to the chasm, the greater power you allow her. Lighten your load now, for the sake of your group."

Roble and Crukas stared at the old witch. Her face lightened with scorn. Worry claimed her good eye and she warily glanced at each of her captors. Roble, Odlon, and the others studied her with renewed suspicion.

"He prattles nonsense," Haigla said.

Shawndirea said, "He tells the truth. Otherwise, you'd not fear his words."

"It's not his words I fear," Haigla said. "It's your *belief* in his words I fear."

Caen and the squire continued traveling farther down the road. Riese jumped off the wagon and headed to the rear where Odlon,

Drucis, and Roble remained on their horses. "Do you believe what he said?"

"Oh, he speaks the truth," Shawndirea said.

"How do you know?" Roble asked.

"Her aura's quite dark. It's grown darker since we left Woodcrest. The cage neutralizes her powers while she's in it, but she's absorbing power from another source, just like Caen said."

"Not true," Haigla insisted. Her hands gripped the iron bars fiercely. Veins swelled up her thin arms like snaky ribbons. Smoke streamed from between her fingers and the iron. She reeled back and screamed. Blisters puffed on her hands where she had held the bars.

Odlon raised the crossbow and aimed at her head.

"No!" Roble said.

"Now's not the time for mercy," Riese said to Roble. "You see what she becomes."

"He's right," Shawndirea said.

"How can she become stronger if the runes in the iron bars prevent her from using magic?" Roble asked.

Drucis shook his head. "You've a lot to learn, lad. Her magic's not growing. Something entered her."

Odlon nodded. "A demon."

Froth foamed from Haigla's mouth. Her dead eye turned from opaque to fiery red. Strange guttural sounds rumbled inside her throat. Claws sprouted on her fingertips.

"Kill her!" Riese said.

"Why not turn her over at Ironwood?" Roble asked.

"The bars won't contain what possesses her," Shawndirea said. "What's inside her will rip through the cage door long before we reach Ironwood."

Remorse coursed through Roble. He'd hoped to spare the old woman because of her kindness when they arrived in Woodcrest. She acted grandmotherly and decent. However, the revelations about her lust for power and authority over Woodcrest exposed how nasty her true countenance was. Roble hoped they could remove her from the town and take her elsewhere to lessen the possible dangers she might unleash. Now, witnessing her odd transformation, it was no longer an option.

Odlon aimed the crossbow, fired, and the bolt sunk deep in Haigla's forehead. She dropped hard in a bent position to the floor of the cage, but her breathing didn't stop. She panted like she'd sprinted for miles. The claws in her hands tore through the ends of her fingers. Her skin split up her arms. Beneath the human flesh was crimson, reptilian skin. She wasn't human. Had she ever been?

Odlon fired another bolt through Haigla's heart. Whatever moved inside her ceased breathing. He swung off his horse and pulled a blade from his belt. Riese opened the cage door, and Odlon slit the creature's throat. Black oozing blood leaked from the cut.

"What's that?" Roble asked.

Odlon kneeled over the creature. "I'm not certain, but it's not Haigla. Perhaps she was already dead when this thing captured her image so it could snare us?"

Shawndirea nodded. "That's possible. Or she's hiding somewhere in Woodcrest. It appears to be a form-taker type of demon. It took her appearance."

Drucis and Odlon exchanged worried expressions.

Drucis dropped off the side of his horse with his axe in hand. "Dat Black Chasm causes chaos throughout Aetheaon. Since its formation, odd creatures are popping up all over. Pull dat beast out on the ground."

Riese and Odlon each grabbed a leg and yanked the odd creature off the wagon and it dropped on the dark road. A dark trail of blood leaked as they moved it. Drucis took his axe blade and tapped the creature's skull. More human flesh peeled away like brittle plaster, exposing its hideous lizard-like face.

Roble moved closer. "Remarkable."

Odlon shot him a perplexed glance.

Roble gave a slight shrug. "I've *never* seen anything like it."

Drucis laughed. "Only say dat when it's a dead one. Never marvel over a live one or it be de last thing you witness before death."

"No doubt," Roble said. "So what is it?"

"Ain't seen anything like it, so I don't rightly know," Drucis replied. He heaved his axe above his head, and in one swift downward swing, he decapitated it.

"How'd Caen *know*?" Roble asked.

"That's a good question," Shawndirea replied.

A horrid stench rose from the beast's black blood. Drucis glanced at the others. "What do we do with it?"

Riese said, "Leave it for the crows."

Caen and the squire had disappeared out of view.

Roble said, "How does this change our plans?"

"What do ya mean?" Drucis asked.

"The townsfolk of Ironwood want Crukas. Not sure if it's dead *or* alive, but before we can even negotiate for his freedom, we have to rid the town of Waxxon's men."

"Only a half dozen," Drucis said. "Nothing to be alarmed over."

Odlon nodded. "I agree."

"Perhaps so," Roble said, "But this creature has been with us the entire journey. Should it have any connection to Waxxon's men, they'll know we're coming."

"Aye, dat will be a better challenge," Drucis said.

Roble looked at Odlon. "Zauber misinformed us of the numbers at Woodcrest."

Odlon replied, "That's true."

"It might not have been purposely," Shawndirea said.

"What do you mean?"

She said, "Perhaps some were cloaked with invisibility."

Drucis rubbed his thick white beard. "Aye, dat could well be."

Crukas stepped closer. "We can always turn back."

Roble shook his head. "No. That's not an option. So what's the bounty on your head?"

"Not sure the amount. The reward tends to increase daily," the thief replied. He brushed the jet-black hair from his dark eyes.

"Don't short sale yourself," Odlon said.

Drucis frowned at the remark.

"What's that supposed to mean?" Crukas asked.

Odlon said, "You're the master thief of Aetheaon. Your worth far exceeds what they offer."

Drucis' eyebrows rose when he recognized Crukas. "Aye, he's right, lad. You're much more valuable alive and to us. Ya never know when ya need a good thief. We be protecting ya with all we got."

Crukas smiled with relief.

"What are the chances that this reptilian demon might have connections with Waxxon's men?" Roble asked.

Odlon frowned. "Do you mean like a spy and magically links his information to them?"

"Yes. Exactly like that."

"We'll approach Woodcrest more cautiously now," Drucis said, returning to his horse. "But I've my doubts dat Waxxon's men would have anything to do with the likes of this creature."

Odlon nodded. "I have to agree with you."

"Dat is rarer than most treasures I seek," Drucis said with a broad grin.

Odlon laughed. "Indeed."

An hour later they came to the long wooden bridge that crossed Icethaw River. Fog mists drifted above the river several hundred feet below. The temperature dropped thirty degrees on the bridge. Horse hooves thudded and rattled the sagging planks.

Roble peered over the bridge's edge. The thick, white fog hid the rushing river. He sighed a stream of white, frosty puffs of air.

"Won't be much longer to Ironwood," Drucis said. "About three hours or less."

"Not bad," Roble replied.

"Over two days journey to Elvendale though," Shawndirea said. "No telling how long we'll be hindered in Ironwood."

Drucis smiled. "Not long if I've me way about it."

Near the center of the bridge, the temperature plummeted even more. Roble enjoyed the sudden coolness. The rushing, splashing river was soothing. The gap between the two ridges was about a quarter mile, but due to the rising fog, visibility was less than fifteen yards. He worried what they might encounter on the bridge.

Occasionally, he checked to see if Caen had circled back to attack from the rear, but he hadn't. The man's warning revealed his sincerity. However, he wasn't exactly certain what Caen's true intention was. An air of mystery shrouded the man. The farther south Roble and his group traveled, the more he doubted their paths would cross again.

Riding into the thick fog made Roble wonder if Caen was a leading decoy and behind him, hidden on the shrouded bridge, Waxxon's riders were waiting with weapons drawn.

Sounds echoed below with the rushing waters. The cries were odd, not human, and if they came from beasts, the deep volume of their voices brought chills to Roble. The loudness reminded him of a lion's roar mixed with an angered ape. Although beasts, they seemed to speak in sentences to one another.

DRUCIS NOTICED the worried expression on Roble's face. "Dat be bothering ya?"

"Not sure. Should it?"

Drucis released a hearty chuckle. "Nothin' to be alarmed about from way up 'ere."

"Okay ... then what are they?" Roble asked.

"Dat be ice trolls, lad. They're big, burly, and stupid, but they never leave the caves or the edges of Ice Thaw River. They probably be spearing fish along the banks. That's about all the smarts they 'ave."

Roble said, "You ever see one?"

Drucis winced. "No sane person travels Ice Thaw River."

"Which is why I asked *you*," Roble said with a grin.

"Oh, jest now, will ya?"

"Sorry, couldn't resist."

Drucis chuckled. "No problem, lad. At least your remark can't be taken as a *low* blow or a cheap shot about me height. Now, had the *ogre* driving the wagon said dat, we'd 'ave different problems."

"Pipe down, Drucis," Riese said without looking back.

Drucis faced Roble and whispered, "He hears a bit too well for his old age."

"You ramble endlessly with your remarks," Riese replied.

"*See?*" Drucis said with a broad grin and his eyebrows raised.

Near the end of the bridge, Drucis' hand tightened on the heel of his axe, which alerted Roble to take precaution. Roble placed his hands near his throwing daggers hidden on his belt. Drucis tapped his horse's flanks and moved ahead of Roble.

Shawndirea sat on Roble's shoulder. She leaned closer to his ear. "The dwarf seems entertained by you."

"That's good I suppose," Roble said.

"It is. You make friends quite easily, which is also a good thing. However, other than those in this party, you need to be more wary. You can't be overly trusting."

"I know. I've been fortunate so far."

She nodded. "Yes. Once we get to Ironwood, be prepared. The townspeople are from various races, half-breeds, renegades, and tyrants."

Roble frowned. "I wonder why they've turned on Crukas?"

"We may never know."

"He doesn't seem to know, either."

"I know, and the closer we get to Ironwood, the more nervous he's become."

Roble nodded. "I noticed."

No other riders or travelers crossed the bridge, which relieved Roble. He thought about Caen and the mystery shrouding him. The man knew more than he wished to reveal.

At the end of the bridge, giant images stood on both sides of the road. After the fog thinned, they turned out to be carved statues. The one on the left was an armored dwarf, and the one on the right was a regal elf with her sword drawn and shield raised.

Roble's tension lessened, and so did Drucis'. Once they left the bridge, the fog vanished and the temperature returned to the post-spring warmth. The dark road ahead remained narrow. The black forest branches were webbed with white silky mesh, which was inviting in one aspect, but ominous in others. The biggest concern was discovering *what* had knitted the expansive web.

Little sunlight seeped through the thick branches. The deep, elongating shadows loomed. The wind whispered through the forest while various insects hummed and chirped from their hiding places. Tacked to a tree was a sign indicating the distance to Ironwood.

Drucis smiled. "Not much farther."

CHAPTER 57

*I*ronwood was centered inside a massive grove of giant trees with smooth, rust-colored bark that looked like aged iron. The corner wall posts were living trees. Carved, stone blocks were stacked to form impressive walls between the thick, tree trunks.

Felled trees were stacked along the road. The massive stumps stood a head taller than Riese and two wagons could set end to end atop the stumps with room to spare.

Platforms and plank bridges were high in the trees. Some connected from tree to tree. Intersecting roadways led to shops, inns, and houses for the elite. No one entered Ironwood's gates unseen, and perhaps even now, Roble reasoned, they were being watched.

He couldn't explain it, but he felt eyes watching them.

Near the gates several riders entered and disappeared from view. Roble and his party watched the activity at the gate of this trading town. None of Waxxon's men were present, but Caen's warning wasn't necessarily false. These henchmen might be inside the gates or high above with keener vantage points. Waxxon's scouts hadn't taken over Ironwood like they had Woodcrest.

Woodcrest was a town of farmers who sought peace and lived modestly. Ironwood was filled with various classes and ruled by corrupt council members. Crukas' feared returning, and the situation confused

Roble. Why would they have paid bounties for the wanted thieves Crukas had delivered, but now they sought to punish him in the same manner? This meant the council did what favored themselves and no one else. Any authority acting in this manner couldn't be trusted.

"What's the best way to enter?" Roble asked Crukas.

"I'd say we skip the town altogether, but the forest isn't any safer," he replied.

"Why isn't it safe?"

"Poisonous vines, dark elves, and the bear traps set by poachers." Crukas pointed at wooden signs posted on both sides of the road: **STAY ON THE ROAD**. "Their warnings can't be clearer."

"They held you prisoner?"

Crukas said, "No. They *attempted* to take me into custody."

"How'd you escape?" Roble asked.

"The sewers."

Drucis shook his head with disgust. "I say we barge in headfirst! I'm not taking the sewers like some ol' damned rat."

Riese smiled. "Three of us cannot enter for obvious reasons."

Shawndirea frowned.

Riese said, "Crukas is the one they want. Roble will attract Waxxon's men since he wears Dragon Skull armor. The rest of us can go inside and scout. My son can accompany us, but Hordus must remain here."

"I won't betray you," Hordus said.

"Perhaps not," Riese said. "But the Vykings will recognize and ask you questions."

"Very well," Hordus said with disappointment in his voice. His eyes reflected his hurt that Riese didn't trust him.

"Your idea's not a bad one, Riese," Odlon said. "We could enter and look around."

"Won't it be a bit odd? What will they think if they see a dwarf and a pale elf traveling around with a big ol' ogre?" Drucis asked. His tone was serious and didn't imply any jest.

Riese towered over Drucis. "We don't have to enter together, shoe-scum."

"Easy there," Drucis replied. "Didn't mean anything bad by it. Just an observation *they* might assume. Dwarves and elves ain't exactly chummy friends, ya know? Not even after one or the other is half drunk."

Riese sneered and chuckled.

Crukas brushed his dark hair from his eyes. He didn't like being right outside Ironwood at all.

Riese pointed his long finger at Drucis and Odlon. "Saddle up. We three ride in together. If it draws attention, all the better. The sooner we find Waxxon's men, the quicker we move past Ironwood."

"Waxxon's men may not be what we need to fear the most," Roble said.

Riese turned sharply with a frown. "What then?"

"Crukas was befriended by the council for turning over thieves. Then without notice their attention focused on taking him into custody. Someone else, possibly a council member or merchant discovered who Crukas really is," Roble said. He looked at Crukas and asked, "Did you steal from any merchants in Ironwood after you turned over the thieves?"

Crukas shook his head. "No. With the high reward they paid, I had no reason."

"Ah, be honest now," Drucis said with scorn. "A thief's a thief, through and through. Always be a temptation to see what one can take without getting caught. Isn't that type of excitement worth more than gold?"

"That's true," Crukas said. "But I never took anything while I was in Ironwood, in spite of obvious treasures I could've taken during their banquets."

Drucis and Riese stared in the thief's eyes. He didn't flinch or look away.

"Aye, he be telling the truth," Drucis said. "I don't say dat lightly, 'cause I don't trust a thief."

Riese nodded. "I agree."

Nothing about Crukas revealed he was lying. Roble said, "Can you think of *any* reason they'd turn on you?"

Crukas shook his head. "Nothing, I swear."

"You stay with them," Riese said to Roble. "Let us scout around."

CHAPTER 58

"*W*here am I?" Haigla peered through the open doorway into the grand alchemy room. Zauber glanced up from his studies.

"Spellhaven," Zauber replied.

"How'd I get here?"

"It was necessary."

Her brow furrowed. Her one good eye studied the dark bearded wizard with interest. "*Why* am I here?"

Zauber twisted a long strand of his beard, "If I hadn't taken you from Woodcrest, you'd be dead."

"What alerted you to my danger?" she asked.

"Whispers in the wind, the swaying grasses, and the dryads inside Woodcrest called to me. Strange things keep arising ever since the Black Chasm formed."

"I know, but why take me from my home?" she asked warily.

Zauber stared out his tower window. Haigla rose from the wooden chair in his alchemist lab and met him at the window. Looking out from the top balcony, she studied the marshy terrain below. The tower stood in a thick cypress grove. The river flowing from the north branched into two smaller rivers and provided a water barrier on each side of his tower, which was a great deterrent to unwanted visitors and allowed him complete privacy.

He placed a spell to enshroud a constant, misty haze above the two flowing rivers to conceal his tower from adventurers. Seldom did an unfortunate explorer cross to his peninsula.

Black crows perched on thick-needled pine branches. Their attention focused on Zauber's rock-walled tower. Their harsh caws echoed with the sound of the two rushing rivers.

"I don't *recall* leaving Woodcrest. What happened? Why am I here?"

Zauber smiled. His eyes sparkled with energy. "You remember the guests you fed?"

"The elf, and a human with a faery?" she asked.

"Yes."

"Of course. What about them?"

"The man, Roble. Did you detect anything different about him?"

Haigla thought for a moment. She nodded. "He seemed different."

"He's from the Overlands," Zauber said. "Did you know?"

"Of course. There's no denying that. He's unlike the humans on our side of the rift."

"But something's different about him and I don't understand what it is."

Haigla thought for a moment. "Perhaps he came because of the Black Chasm?"

"No," Zauber replied. "Nothing like that. What concerns me is how Shawndirea travels through the veil joining our realms. It's dangerous. One day she might allow something worse to enter our realm or his."

Haigla chuckled, hacked a bit, and then wiped brown snuff juice from her chin. "I don't think she will. She's content with her human. Now that she has him, she shouldn't have a need to return to the Overlands again."

Zauber pulled the glowing yellow orb from his robe pocket and watched it flicker. He nodded. "She has an obsession for Roble."

"Almost a deep love and devotion."

"That may be. But he won't stop whatever the Black Chasm is. Although, he'll be a factor in destroying the powers that brought the chasm alive."

"How so?"

Zauber stared intently at the orb. He frowned. Shapes and shadows twisted and turned inside the small globe. He winced. "That, my dear witch, I don't know. At least not yet. Time will tell."

"How long must I *endure* your hospitality?" she asked.

Zauber laughed softly. "My accommodations aren't to your liking?"

"Are anyone else's ever enough for those who practice magic?"

"No, dear lady. No. They're never the same as the home we hold sacred."

Haigla smiled a near toothless smile. "Our powers are always the most powerful where our source of energy flows."

"You can root yourself elsewhere."

Her brow furrowed. "You're not letting me go back to Woodcrest?"

"I won't stop you, if that's your choice, but Woodcrest is no longer safe for you."

"Why?"

Zauber sighed. "Perhaps it's best I show you. Come with me."

Haigla turned from the open window and followed him across the polished marble floor to his crude work table with various bubbling potions, open spell books, and dried herbs.

The wizard lifted a black cloth and revealed his black crystal ball. It glistened in the glowing candlelight. With a gentle wave of his hand, the ball came to life, revealing swirling shadows that soon materialized into an overhead view of Woodcrest. The night sky was filled with a twinkling array of stars. An ice crow cawed, and they witnessed the inside of Haigla's shack from the bird's point of view.

Haigla shivered with concern and partial rage. "How often have you witnessed what I've done?"

"Only when necessary," he replied.

"*How* was this night necessary?" she asked. "Or *any* night?"

"Don't view me as your enemy, Haigla. Had I not seen what was to occur that night, you'd be dead."

"What warning did you have? What right have you to enter my house and spy on me?"

Zauber waved his weary hand and calmly shook his head. "Spying is a bit harsh."

She pointed at the crystal ball. "Harsh? What do you call *that?*"

"Saving your life."

She scowled.

"Now wait, dear witch," he said. "Watch."

Haigla leaned closer. Zauber pointed his bony, long finger.

Something moved in the shadows behind her spell library. It moved so subtly that had she not looked when he pointed, she'd have missed it entirely. Neither her cat nor the snow raven had noticed its presence.

"What is it?"

"An imp."

The witch glanced from the crystal ball to him. Startled concern creased her brow. "An imp? In my cellar? What was it doing there?"

"Making certain to alert its master when the opportunity arose."

"Opportunity for what?"

"A shape-shifting demon lurked outside your home that night. Its intent was to kill and replace you, thus taking over the town. But after you fed Roble, Odlon, and Shawndirea, I intervened."

Inside the ball, the little imp leapt from the bookshelf. It stretched its scrawny arms and flailed long fingernails that resembled razor-edged knives. A second before the imp struck, Haigla disappeared. The imp's mouth opened to shriek, but hit the small boiling cauldron where Haigla had been mixing her concoction. The bubbling liquid flamed orange for a brief moment before the imp melted into the soupy mixture.

"That's when I took you," Zauber said.

"I gathered *that* much. Why don't I remember it?"

Zauber shrugged. "Body transportation spells sometimes render a daze effect when one's snatched so quickly without the participant's foreknowledge. On the plus side, you slept well for the past few days."

"Days?"

"Unfortunately, yes. But at least you're alive."

"True." She shook her head. Her good eye darted back and forth. She struggled to remember what had occurred. Her dead eye remained glazed over with a milky-white film. "But what about my belongings? My spell books and ingredients? My pets?"

"You rambunctious kitten and obnoxious snow raven are on the floor below. As for the rest of your essentials, we'll have them brought here."

She shook her head. "No. I don't want to live in your tower."

"I didn't mean *here* exactly. But choose another town or forest grove or wherever, and I'll make certain your belongings get to you."

"My wand!" she gasped. "You didn't take it from me, did you?"

"No," Zauber said.

"It's still in Woodcrest then. I must return and retrieve it."

"I'm afraid that isn't possible."

Haigla shook her head and in a pitiful, whining voice, she said, "Why can't I go back to Woodcrest?"

Zauber had her watch the rest of the events in the crystal ball. When the townsfolk turned on her doppelgänger and took it into custody, she cringed.

"I'd never have betrayed those people like that."

"While that may be true, nothing you say could ever convince them otherwise."

"What about—"

"I'm afraid they won't be persuaded by me, either."

She sulked.

"Aetheaon's filled with wonderful places to make a new homestead. Somewhere with more privacy, if that's what you'd like."

Haigla wiped brown drool from her chin and nodded. "I like your suggestion. More isolation. Less people. Woodcrest was nice, but the folks shunned me unless they needed my magic."

"Simple folk fear the works of magic. Most people fear what they don't understand, so I wouldn't take it personal."

"Wouldn't you?"

"No."

She frowned. "So why are you in the middle of the wilderness where no one else lives?"

Zauber ignored her question and unrolled a yellowed parchment. He used bottles to weight the corners. "Here's a map. Study it and seek wisdom. A place will beckon you. When you choose where you wish to reside, I'll send someone to get your wares."

"I need my wand," Haigla insisted.

"Choose a place in Aetheaon to call your new home. You can make a new wand from a tree, which will give you a higher affinity and attune you with nature's power. Draw off the power where you settle because your surroundings will accept you as part of it. That's why I reside in Spellhaven where magical mists protect me and my tower."

"I guess a new home isn't all that bad."

"Home's where your magic is strongest. You said so. Woodcrest was sapping you. Find a new home. You'll be stronger."

CHAPTER 59

*R*iese rode into Ironwood on the massive stallion that had pulled the wagon. Odlon and Drucis rode slightly behind him. Contrary to what Drucis feared, none of the townsfolk paid them attention. Instead, desperate traders and vendors shouted their specials. They pleaded for the trio to stop and buy wares. The three ignored the vendors' pleas.

The path was named Cheapskate's Way because these vendors sold poorly made items or peddled wilted produce, soured milk, and moldy cheeses. Others tried to sell deformed chickens, ducks, or runt piglets. The better goods were farther in town, near the taverns and brothels within the Redlamp Borough, where travelers spent more gold than they had god-given sense.

"Buy this?" A toothless old man held up a stained silk bundle. "Or this—"

Drucis chuckled slightly. "He has some fine things to make an elf proud."

Odlon said, "Looks like old Dwarven undergarments to me. Smelly and discolored like your hand-me-downs."

"Oh! You wait!" Drucis tightened a fist and grinned.

Odlon laughed. "All seems well here. No sign of Waxxon's men."

"Nah. Too much harassment 'ere. Waxxon's goons are probably near the town's center," Drucis said.

Riese kept his gaze on the rope-plank bridge overhead that crossed from one side of the town to the other. Two women cautiously walked across the bridge carrying heavy baskets of linens. Not far behind them, two Ironwood archers paused to study the streets. Other sky-bridges detoured from the main overhead bridge, which was where the richer folk in Ironwood lived. Archers patrolled all the intersecting bridges.

Riese whispered, "It's best we start no brawls in the open."

Odlon and Drucis followed his gaze.

"You be right with dat," Drucis said. "But still, Waxxon's men aren't along the streets. Most likely, they be in the darker sections of Ironwood."

"You know a place?" Odlon asked.

"Aye. Need ye ask?" Drucis replied. "That be the Redlamp Borough where all the trouble-seekers hide."

Riese said, "Lead the way."

"With pleasure."

Drucis tapped Grey's flanks and moved past Riese. They left Cheapskate's Way and turned right at Slatter's Row, which headed down a cobblestoned slope. Once the path leveled, the sounds from the upper town level grew silent.

Blazing lampposts flickered and prevented the streets from being swallowed in complete darkness. More vendors were here, but they weren't boisterous like those on the street above. Of course, their goods weren't simpler wares.

Fluttering bats swooped and dove at swarming insects around the blazing lights. Rats darted from the main street into tiny crevices along the building edges or behind empty barrels. Horses were tied outside taverns or houses of mysteries. Masters of various magic and healing powers had shops where, for a price, they sold spells to those with enough gold to pay.

Mercenaries lurked in the shadows to sell their services should someone need an unwanted foe or family member taken out. Others sold swords and daggers they'd taken off their victims or from slain bodies found in recent battlefields.

Several people dressed in dark robes and hoods slinked past in the shadows. Although partially visible, their mysterious movements from building to building were cause for most visitors to be alarmed. They were beastmen.

"Watch your gold pouches," Drucis whispered. "Crukas probably knows this area quite well. Thieves scurry like rats in the bottom of a ship."

The horses' shoes clacked on the cobblestone. Eyes from the shadows watched the trio pass various lodges, taverns, and brothels. Drucis pulled the reins when they reached the Murky Flask Cellar.

"Here be strong drinks!" Drucis swung off Grey and tied the horse to a post near a water trough.

Odlon rolled his eyes.

"Keep your wits, Drucis," Riese said in a low tone. "This isn't the time to swim in liquors."

"Aye, I know. But Murky Flask's the best tavern 'ere. Bound to be the place for finding what we came for."

Riese and Odlon dismounted and tied their horses to the post outside the tavern. Drucis handed a stable master several gold coins to watch their horses. The old man nodded modestly and bowed his appreciation. He was armored with tarnished chain and two short swords hung on his belt. In the faint light, the man appeared old and feeble, but his eyes revealed a rugged nature keen on fighting. He was no stranger to murder.

Drucis pushed open the heavy wooden door. It creaked as the gap widened. The smell of rum, ale, and burnt oak hung in the humid air. Drucis took a deep breath and smiled.

"Now, we got something," Drucis said.

The dimly lit tavern bustled with drinking patrons. Barmaids brought tall flasks to and from the tables. Candelabras hung over each crudely carved table and kept the room modestly lit. Drucis headed to the nearest available table and sat. A wide smile parted his white beard.

Odlon and Riese joined him, but not with the same enthusiasm. Riese looked uneasy.

"What is it?" Odlon asked.

Riese shook his head. "Ah, this reminds me of Hobskin's Tavern."

Drucis said, "At least what it *used* to be."

"And what it will be once again," Riese said.

"You plan to rebuild?" Drucis asked.

Riese nodded. "After I destroy all the undead creatures roaming Glacier Ridge."

"Need an extra axe, let me know."

A barmaid came to their table. "What will ya have to drink?"

Drucis and Odlon ordered strong ales, but when the maiden turned to get Riese's order, her eyes widened, and she became uneasy.

"Is there a problem?" Riese asked.

She shook her head. "No. I'm not in trouble, am I?"

A frown creased Riese's thick brow. "For what?"

She studied Riese for a few moments. "You're not with them, are you?"

"Who?"

She nodded toward the back of the room. Riese followed her direction. Four of Waxxon's recruits were seated at a table. They laughed heartily after one slapped a barmaid's ass. They were drunk. The patrons at neighboring tables didn't dare glance in their direction.

"No. I'm *not*." Riese ran his hand down his long beard and watched the Vykings a moment longer.

She breathed a sigh of relief. "What do you wish to drink?"

"Cider. Nothing stronger," Riese replied.

Drucis' mouth gaped.

She nodded and smiled. "I'll be back quickly."

"Teetotaler? Bah, what's with you?" Drucis asked.

"One of us needs to keep our senses sharp."

Odlon shook his head. "One drink's my limit, and that's not serious drinking for me."

Drucis laughed. "A whole barrel wouldn't dent me senses! Makes 'em keener, I say!"

The barmaid returned and set the flasks on the table before them. As she turned to leave, Riese asked, "Why are you fearful of those men?"

Her eyes widened. "They have Duke Q'aran's protection, which means they can have their way with anything or *anyone*."

"Q'aran? Isn't he the son of King Offaerius of Legelarid?" Drucis asked.

"Yes," she whispered. "This town has headed for ruin every since Q'aran was deeded the title to Ironwood."

She lowered her gaze and quietly slipped away from the table.

Drucis gave Odlon a serious stare. "Why would Q'aran let these renegades take charge of Ironwood? Offaerius has more strength than Lord Waxxon."

Odlon nodded. "I agree. There's more to it than what we know."

"It could be," Drucis said, pausing to take a swig from the flask, "Q'aran seeks to be a fist for Waxxon, using this town as a tariff haven for any traveling to the North."

"Possibly," Odlon said. "But what could he gain from it? His father has the largest armies in Aetheaon. He could shred Ironwood to sawdust if he chose."

"Aye. But why waste the time or energy. Nothing here's worth King Offaerius to wipe his nose or royal ass with. He'd think his son a brat like any other, and those type of children, royal or otherwise, usually don't live long."

"That's true."

Riese kept a harsh gaze at the four drunken guards. One grabbed a barmaid, wrapped his arms around her, and forced her sit on his lap. She struggled to free herself, but the man was too strong. Her eyes widened, and she tugged desperately to yank loose of his hold. The man roared with laughter, as did his three comrades.

"There's one way to find out." Riese stood with his hammer in hand.

"What happened to keeping a low profile?" Drucis asked.

"I'd say you have a head start on that," Riese replied with a wry smile.

The dwarf frowned, took a big gulp from the flask, and stood. "Well, if it be an all out brawl—"

"Not yet," Riese said, "but if they attack, and I expect they will, you two be ready."

Drucis sat, lifted his flask at the barmaid, and said, "Another!"

Riese crossed the tavern floor in a few long strides. The various races seated at different tables regarded Riese with the same nervousness they did Waxxon's men. Riese was comfortable none of these would rise to defend the Vykings seated at the far corner table. Should worse come to worse, he hoped they'd ally with him.

Riese towered over the man seated with the maiden in his lap. "Let her go."

The man's wide grin narrowed when he looked into Riese's harsh stare. His smile soon returned when he noticed Riese was of Vyking blood.

"What's with your peasant-like clothes?" the man asked. "You need to dress as King Obed has commanded."

"I don't follow Obed's commands," Riese replied.

The other three men partway rose from their chairs and placed their hands on the hilts of their swords. Before they stood, Riese brought his heavy hammer down on the center of the table. The wood splintered, and the table collapsed. All the seated men looked up with wide eyes.

He turned to the Vyking with the barmaid. "Let her go."

The man's hold lessened. The barmaid screeched and ran from the table. The seated man brushed back his long wavy hair, straightened his belt, and ran his hand through his short brown beard.

"I don't know *who* you are," the man said, crossing his arms. "But you've one Hell of a nerve to challenge me in front of my men."

"You may pick on a lass because she's not strong enough to fend you off, but I'm *more* than your equal."

"*More*? How do you come to such a conclusion without first knowing my name?"

"A name holds no strength." Riese smiled and softly chuckled with chiding mockery. "You can't be too powerful since you yield yourself to another's command. I rule my life and bow to no man."

"Nor do I."

"You're nothing less than a dog on Waxxon's leash and wag your tail at his barking orders. You'd hump an Orc if he commanded."

The three Vykings snickered but covered their mouths when their leader glared at them.

"Careful," the man said. His fierce eyes narrowed. "Or I'll be forced to put you into your place."

"I've no fear of you."

The man studied Riese's eyes intently. Riese didn't blink and held the man's gaze with overbearing confidence and challenge.

He said, "Then perhaps I should offer my name since you can't bring yourself to ask."

"Names have no importance to me, other than my own," Riese replied.

"I'm Prince Manfrid, second son of King Obed."

Riese shrugged.

"Now would be a good time to bow." Manfrid stood and grinned.

"Perhaps you didn't hear me," Riese said. "I bow to no one."

"I heard," Manfrid replied without blinking, "but I wanted to at least give you one opportunity."

The three men seated in the corner stood to draw their swords. Before they drew them, a bolt pierced through one's right shoulder. He clutched the bolt, spun around, and growled in pain. His sword clattered on the floor.

Riese swung his hammer and smashed through Manfrid's closest guard. The hammer caved the guard's chest piece and shattered the man's sternum and ribcage. The Vyking's feet lifted inches off the floor, and he dropped lifeless in his chair.

Drucis rushed across the hardwood floor. His feet thudded. He leapt, ran across a table, and then dove. He caught the last of the three men behind the table by wrapping his thick muscled arms around him and tackling him. Drucis pounded his thick fist into the Vyking's face over and over, until the man lie unconscious beneath an oak table. The Vyking Odlon shot through the shoulder tugged to pull out the bolt. Drucis turned, grabbed the bolt and twisted. The Vyking roared in pain, clutched Drucis' throat, and hefted the stubby dwarf in the air.

Drucis snapped the bolt shaft, drew back and drove the splintered shaft deep into the Vyking's right eye. The tight grip around Drucis' throat lessened. The man toppled backwards, and the dwarf fell with the giant man.

Odlon edged around the table with his crossbow trained on Manfrid's face. Drucis grabbed his axe and stood directly behind Manfrid. Manfrid held his hands away from his sword and daggers.

Manfrid shook his head. "Didn't expect that."

"What? That I came alone?"

"Well, that, plus I never expected you to be teamed with an elf *and* a dwarf," Manfrid said. "Odd combination, don't you think?"

Drucis smiled. "Odd, but effective."

Manfrid shook his head. With a proper royal accent, he asked, "Why a blacksmith hammer? Why not a sword or axe?"

Riese smiled. "It has a comfortable feel in my hand. I know how to use it, and it's never failed me."

"Very well," Manfrid replied.

"You have two other guards in Ironwood. Where are they?" Riese asked.

Manfrid ignored the question. "How is it that you know so much about me and my party when I know absolutely nothing about you."

"Oh, but you *do* know me," Riese said. "I'm Riese."

Manfrid's brow rose with sudden interest. "All legends I hear of you have never been pleasant. You're a traitor, and betrayed my father's throne by killing General Yerdrick."

"And Yerkrick's brother."

Manfrid winced at the news. "Adding more to your list of crimes, I see."

"Your death would be worth more than all combined. That'd strike deeper pain for Obed, which will satisfy me until I watch his last fleeting breath."

Manfrid laughed and waved his right hand elegantly in the air. Though surrounded by Riese, Odlon, and Drucis, Manfrid held his arrogance and dismissed any possible dangers. He acted as if the tavern was his throne room and court, and these weapons held on him were nothing.

Manfrid seated himself, brushed away table splinters from his elegant jerkin, and sighed. "If only that were true, Riese. My father despises me, which is why he sent me on the excursion with the incompetent Waxxon that praises himself as a Lord. Pity. The bastard knows nothing about fighting, swords, or how to overtake a town, which is why he requested my father's aid in taking Hoffnung. Now we scour the lands looking for some little cur that poses a threat to the throne if we don't find and kill her. She's of no importance, but Waxxon's a fool. He's too paranoid to forget about the girl and we're chasing rumors of where she's been or going."

Riese leaned closer to Manfrid. "And yet, *you* follow *him*."

"Why not kill Waxxon?" Drucis leveled his broad axe at Manfrid.

"I have my reasons."

"Such as?" Odlon aimed the crossbow between the prince's eyes.

Manfrid looked around. Most of the patrons had returned to drinking and swapping tales while the others positioned themselves farther from the Vyking skirmish. Even the bartender ignored the brawl, not looking their direction while he talked to two of Ironwood's drunken guards.

Manfrid lowered his voice to a near whisper. "With Waxxon to blame for Queen Taube's death and overtaking Hoffnung, he's the prime enemy in all the land. He's hated more than any man. Once he's established his kingdom, and I kill him, who do you think will be their hero?"

Riese nodded while thinking the suggestion through. "That'd work, but you failed to consider one thing."

"What's that?"

"You need to be alive to fulfill such ambitions."

Before Manfrid could reply, Riese struck the prince in the face with the hammer's head and knocked him unconscious. He collapsed and fell forward on the broken table.

"Bind him," Riese said.

"Why?" Drucis asked. "What you got in mind?"

"You'll see soon enough," Riese replied. Looking at Odlon, he said, "Go to the others, bind Crukas, and enter Ironwood. Make certain Hordus is with you, too."

Odlon frowned. "What? Why?"

"It's time to discover the truth of what's really going on in Ironwood."

CHAPTER 60

Odlon met Roble, Shawndirea, and Crukas on the road in Ironwood Forest. He explained Riese's plan.

Crukas paled. "They'll kill me."

Odlon shook his head. "We'll protect you. As long as you're in shackles, they've no need to kill you. At worst they'll attempt to take you into custody, but we won't allow it."

"Q'aran won't hesitate to kill me," Crukas said.

"He has to have a reason," Odlon replied.

"Any idea why he wants you dead?" Roble asked.

Exasperated, Crukas said, "No. I told you I don't know."

Odlon smiled. "There's a reward for you, right?"

"A substantial one."

"They'll want a trial," Roble said.

Crukas laughed. "A trial? You can't be serious."

Odlon dismounted and walked to Hordus.

"What do you need me to do?" Hordus asked.

Odlon removed the shackles from Hordus and asked Crukas to hold his hands at his waist. With a reluctant sigh, Crukas did. Odlon locked the shackles.

"You have a pick to unlock these?" Odlon asked.

Crukas nodded and smiled. "Of course."

"Good. Have it ready. Once inside Ironwood, I'll signal you to unlock them."

"What about me?" Hordus asked.

"Riese asked for you to join us."

Roble said, "Where do we meet him?"

"Murky Flask Cellar."

"Where?"

"It's a tavern. Just follow me."

WHEN ROBLE ENTERED the Murky Flask Cellar with Odlon and the others, Riese sat beside the bound Prince Manfrid. The prince's nose was slightly twisted and obviously broken. Dried blood covered his mouth and partway coated his short beard. He looked more frustrated than angry and seemed to realize he wasn't in charge.

Shawndirea sat on Roble's shoulder and quietly studied the tavern.

"What are we doing?" Roble asked.

Crukas' eyes darted back and forth. He expected to be attacked at any moment.

Riese whispered, "I wanted Crukas brought here, so we'll discover *why* they want him."

Roble said. "In a tavern? Those who want him are the ruler or the magistrate."

"Crukas is a master thief. The Redlamp Borough is where thieves tend to hide."

"So?" Roble asked.

"Patience," Riese said. "Whomever actually wants Crukas knows he's in Ironwood. They'll expect us to collect the bounty from the magistrate, but since we're here, they'll come to us."

Crukas swallowed hard. His eyes reflected his uneasiness. Roble noticed the lock pick between Crukas' fingers. He was ready to release himself and dart into the shadows. Roble wondered if the thief was fast enough.

Odlon said to Riese, "You have suspicions?"

Riese nodded. "I find it odd there's a reward offered for the master thief when other thieves roam throughout the borough. They prey on travelers and drunks without persecution."

Drucis weighed the information. "Makes sense."

"So you don't believe the magistrate wants Crukas?" Roble asked.

"He might have a hand in it, but someone else has a greater desire to get Crukas." Riese looked at Manfrid.

"I've no part in this," Manfrid said. "All this over a thief? It's not even *my* jurisdiction."

Riese smiled. "No, what's about to take place has nothing to do with you. I've other plans for you."

"If it be my death," Manfrid said, "that'll be your loss. My father won't shed a tear. He won't grieve or miss me."

Riese chuckled. "You're his son. A prince. You announced it a half hour ago."

Manfrid offered an embarrassed shrug. "So I did, but the part I intentionally left out was the part of me being his *bastard* son."

"I'd like to believe you," Riese said. "But—"

Hordus cleared his throat. "He speaks the truth. King Obed doesn't favor him at all."

"You see, dear Riese," Manfrid said, "I'm worth far more to you alive than dead. My father resents me, as does his wife, the queen. Both would have me dead and lost in order to prevent me from tarnishing his image. Why else would a prince be riding with a dimwit like Waxxon in the first place?"

"Good point," Riese said. "So where's Waxxon?"

"Not in Ironwood. Yesterday, he took a band of warriors north to Hoffnung and left me to scout for the little cur should she happen into town." Manfrid touched his broken nose and winced. "Gods, Riese, did you have to strike my nose?"

Riese shrugged. "Gives you character. But until the swelling goes down, don't pose for any busts or coin images."

Manfrid shook his head and sighed. "Again, you *overestimate* my worth."

The tavern door burst open. Several town guards entered with a band of hooded thieves. Riese and the others turned. At the rear of the guards and thieves stood a short stocky man wearing a crown and a flowing crimson cape. He held a short sword and his gaze passed across all the tables.

Riese glanced at Manfrid questioningly.

"Q'aran," Manfrid said softly.

"Ahh." Riese faced the man and frowned. His even grin warned the Duke to keep his distance.

Crukas moved behind Riese and Manfrid to hide in the tavern shadows. Although Crukas' pace was fast, Q'aran noticed him.

"Crukas!" A hooded, shorter figure standing beside Q'aran shouted. "Show yourself!"

Half drunken patrons rushed past the guards and hooded thieves and ran out the door. The bartender and barmaids followed, leaving Q'aran and his men alone with Riese and his party.

"If you want out of here," Manfrid said, "use me as a body shield."

"Why?" Riese asked.

"I've convinced him my father will savage the town and behead him should any harm come to me."

"He believes you?" Roble asked.

Manfrid gave a sheepish grin and shrugged. "Hold a blade to my throat, and he'll make certain you're released."

"Gladly." Drucis pressed his sharp axe blade to the prince's throat.

Manfrid's throat tightened. His eyes widened with genuine fear. He whispered, "You don't have to be overly enthusiastic about it."

Drucis grinned and winked. "Gotta make it *look* realistic."

"Crukas!" The hooded figure said. The voice was rugged but feminine. She pointed. "There, in the corner, behind those men."

"Guards," Q'aran said and pointed. "Take him. Kill anyone who stands in your way."

"Aye," Drucis said. His hands tightened on the axe handle. "I wouldn't be doing dat."

Manfrid raised his hands. "They're serious, Duke Q'aran. They'll kill me."

"Crukas is with us," Riese said. "He leaves with us as well."

Q'aran motioned his men back. He stared nervously at Riese, Roble, Odlon, and Drucis. "What are you doing in Ironwood?"

"Passing through," Roble said. He stepped forward with his hands on the hilts of his throwing daggers. Odlon stepped beside him with the crossbow trained on the Duke.

"Passing through?" Q'aran said. "With the most wanted thief in Ironwood? That's unbelievable. Surely you're here to collect his bounty?"

Riese shook his head. "No. Your gold's worthless."

"Then what?"

"Crukas hired us to get him past Ironwood, so *why* do you want him?"

"He's a thief. That's reason enough," Duke Q'aran said.

Riese grunted a laugh. "Then arrest those beside you, and the thieves slinking through the borough alleys and streets."

"You dare instruct me on how to perform my duties?" Q'aran asked.

"Only because your double-standard belittles your ability to rule," Riese replied.

The small hooded female looked at Q'aran. "Arrest Crukas!"

Riese smiled. "Ah. The wench has a hold over you. She's the reason you wish to kill Crukas."

Q'aran's face flushed red.

Angered, the small hooded woman faced the Duke. "We had a deal. Kill them and take him."

Q'aran looked at Odlon's crossbow, which was aimed at the Duke. Q'aran's uncertain glance studied Manfrid and his captors.

"Perhaps you should've brought more men," Riese said.

The Duke spat on the floor and looked at the female thief. "If you want Crukas, *you* take him." To his guards, he said, "Let's go."

Q'aran and his men exited the tavern, but the hooded woman and her two companions remained.

"You've taken something I want, Crukas," the small female thief said. "If you don't surrender it to me, I'll track you until I get it."

Crukas frowned and stepped around Riese. "Darrath?"

She yanked her dark hood back. Her jet-black hair and pointed ears caught his attention.

Crukas gasped. It was she.

Drucis nudged Odlon's ribs with his elbow and grinned. "Don't be losing your focus. The elf's a thief. Better elven women reside in Faybourne. Fairer ones that are honest and true."

Odlon gave Drucis an even frown.

Crukas' facial expressions were hard to read. For a few moments he struggled between attraction, sympathy, and fear in regard to the dark-haired, elf thief.

"Surprised to see me alive, aren't ya? I imagine so since *you* turned me in for my bounty. But, they didn't kill me." She seethed. Her chest swelled, and so did her anger. "The things I had to do to get Q'aran to spare me. And now he betrayed me by not taking you."

"What does she want?" Roble asked Crukas.

Darrath didn't allow Crukas to answer. "What he took from our thief guild treasury."

Crukas crossed his arms and glared. "The necklace was *mine* before I joined the guild."

"It became *ours* when you joined. Everything has a price, and the necklace was your dues."

"Agretor died. The guild disbanded," Crukas said. "I had the right to take back my offering."

"The guild should've voted on it," Darrath replied. "The necklace was the most expensive item ever looted in Hoffnung. We should've taken a vote."

"No," Crukas said. "Agretor and the elder thieves *stole* it from me. Had I not handed it over, they would've killed me for it. There's no question of their greed when they beheld my treasure. They were jealous I had stolen something they couldn't. And, as you bear witness, they never stole anything worth its value afterwards."

"But you gave it."

"I was a child, unable to defend myself."

Darrath frowned. Her eyes blazed with anger. "You weren't a child when you betrayed and handed me over to Duke Q'aran for my bounty."

"You tried to kill me in Glacier Ridge. If I'd had the necklace in my possession that night, you would've killed me."

Darrath smiled. "You don't know that."

"Pressing a knife to my throat is a pretty clear indication you planned to carry it out."

With a shrewd grin, Drucis said, "At least it wasn't an axe, lad."

Odlon glanced at the dwarf and shook his head.

"Could be she was teasing?" Drucis whispered. Sweat beaded on Manfrid's brow.

Drucis slowly lowered the blade.

With a relieved expression, Manfrid rubbed the axe indention on his throat.

"The sad part, Crukas," Darrath said in a softer tone. "I secretly held affection for you the entire time we were in the guild."

Drucis rolled his eyes. "Oh, 'ere we go."

Crukas unlocked the shackles and let them drop to the floor. He studied her for a several moments. "I didn't know."

Drucis shook his head. "Ah, don't be falling for dat, lad."

Darrath glared at the dwarf, but Crukas ignored him, and took a few steps toward her. He searched her dark eyes. They'd been cold so long, he couldn't detect any sincerity. Did she even possess a conscience? "I never had any idea."

She shrugged and crossed her arms. "What's it matter now? You *betrayed* me. You're my sworn enemy. I'll hunt you down and carve your heart from your chest."

Darrath turned and strode to the door. Her two companions followed close behind. She reached for the door handle and paused. "Take him!"

The three scattered like swift, moving shadows. One of the men turned. A blast of blue light flowed from his fingertips. The energy burst like a ball of lightning aimed at Roble.

Shawndirea was quicker. She cast a green energy shield around her and Roble. The blue light shimmered, crackled, and disintegrated. She'd neutralized the attack.

Odlon fired a bolt at the robed wizard. With an erratic wave of the wizard's hand, he sent the bolt's trajectory sharply to the left. His nervousness spared his life but still proved a grave mistake in his judgment. The bolt plunged into the gut of the wizard's companion. The other wizard's eyes widened. He clutched the bolt buried in his stomach and dropped to his knees. Dark blood oozed and coated his fingers. He gasped a few times and the light in his surprised eyes dimmed.

Darrath gnashed her teeth and rushed Riese. She pulled two daggers and dove forward like a leaping mountain lion. Riese positioned himself to parry her attack while Crukas hurried to get behind Riese.

Riese deflected both blades with his hammer, which was Darrath's intention. When he prepared his counterattack, she changed direction. She rolled on the dusty hardwood floor and came up on the other side of Riese. She slashed her blades at Crukas' throat. He mumbled. Before her razor-edged knives sliced his flesh, Crukas transported to the other side of the room. She growled curses. She pivoted forward, off balance for a moment, and right as she turned, Odlon raised his crossbow.

Instead of slowing her pace, Darrath ran to the wall. Odlon fired. A second before the bolt would've pierced her back, she jumped, kicked off the wall, and back-flipped over the bolt. The bolt struck the wall with a dull thud.

Landing on her feet, Darrath rushed Crukas at the far end of the tavern. Roble stood in her path, turned. and faced her. He flung two daggers. She moved remarkably fast. Darrath slid, knocked Roble's feet out from under him, and nimbly twisted into a sprint before Roble collapsed. Shawndirea leapt from Roble's shoulder to prevent getting crushed beneath his weight. Roble winced and immediately regretted he'd thrown the knives.

Shawndirea stood on Roble's chest. Angered at the female rogue's blatant arrogance and attack, Shawndirea fired two greenish orbs at the thief and struck Darrath in the back.

Darrath groaned and sharply took a deep breath. She toppled forward, lost her balance, and crashed on an empty table. Tankards and flasks slid off the table with her and smashed into jagged shards. She fought to stand. Splinters of thick glass dug into her leather armor. Dazed, she winced in pain but shoved herself to stand. She brushed away the looser shards and pieces of glass tinkled on the floor. The larger pieces appeared to have pierced the armor into her flesh.

Crukas ran for the bar before she targeted him again. He dove behind it where the weaponless Hordus was crouched and hiding. They regarded one another with a nod.

Darrath's wizard companion's eyes widened. His hands rose and bluish sparks flowed. She turned to see an bolt slicing through the air and headed straight for her heart. The bolt went off course and stuck in the far wall. The shaft wobbled madly. Darrath turned to run to the door. The wizard turned to follow, but Riese's hammer struck the back of the wizard's head. He dropped lifelessly to the hardwood floor and his robes fanned delicately, outlining his thin body.

"Mark my words. I'll find you Crukas!" Darrath darted through the door and vanished into the borough.

Riese extended his hand and helped Roble stand. Crukas was pale and visibly shaking. Hordus stood from behind the bar and helped the thief stand. Crukas peered around the tavern, hesitant to leave his place of protection. Almost reluctantly, he braved the steps to join Roble near the fallen wizard.

"She's injured," Roble said.

"Aye," Drucis said.

Crukas gathered with their circle. "Thanks for keeping me alive. I'm indebted to you."

"WHAT'D you steal that she wants so badly?" Roble asked.

"A necklace from a high official's wife in Hoffnung. It's so expensive and well known, I could never sell it."

"Why not give it back?"

Crukas shrugged. "Pride? Notoriety? With Waxxon's men now in control of Hoffnung, I doubt the woman's still alive. Even if she is, she probably no longer holds a position of power."

Drucis nodded. "Probably true."

Manfrid walked to the two dead robed men. Near the wizard's smashed skull, Riese picked up his heavy hammer from the growing pool of blood.

Manfrid looked at Riese with great admiration. "Indeed the hammer's your weapon of choice."

Riese turned the dead wizard over.

"Careful," Manfrid said. "His magic may still linger to protect his corpse."

"It can do that?" Roble asked.

Odlon nodded. "The mysteries of magic are never-ending. Well, at least to those of us who don't wield it."

"Too much to learn," Roble sighed.

"You could live ten lifetimes in our realm and never know the fullness of all there is to know," the elf replied.

With caution, Riese pulled back the man's hood. He was human. Strange, blue tattoos covered his bald head.

"He's a worshipper of Lez'minx." Manfrid stepped back. "The elf thief has powerful allies."

Roble gave a confused glance at Shawndirea. She said, "A reptilian god worshipped by a sect deep in the Woodnog swamps."

"Does he exist or is he a myth?" Roble asked softly.

Shawndirea opened her mouth to reply, but their attention quickly returned to the corpse.

Blue flames flickered on the dead wizard's fingers. Riese stepped back. The intense flames rose higher. The candles throughout the tavern flickered. The wizard's dead eyes opened. His eyes blazed bluer than the flames. His lips suddenly moved.

"Don't challenge me, Overlander," a deep voice said from the dead man.

Drucis readied his axe and looked at Roble. "Does dat answer your question?"

Roble took a deep breath, slightly shuttered, but no words came. He nodded. The room chilled.

"My power has protected you," Lez'minx said.

Roble cleared his throat. His eyebrows rose in question. "In what way?"

"The blessing on your armor has protected you thus far, has it not?"

Riese and the others stared at Roble with keen interest. Drucis held his axe, and for a few moments, he looked like he might decapitate the dead wizard. But instead, he lowered the axe. His interest was more in what else the god might reveal.

Uncomfortable to see a dead man speak, Roble swallowed hard. "Yes."

"Seek me out, Overlander, and see what other gifts I bestow on those who worship me."

Something about the deep voice disturbed Roble. Although frightening in tone, it held a subtle seductiveness that made him want to listen.

"Do you fear me, Overlander?" Lez'minx asked.

"I don't know you well enough to fear you," Roble replied.

Lez'minx softly chuckled. Roble's armor moved as though it breathed within the god's presence.

"You've a lot to learn, Roble," he continued. "Take the wizard's rings. These I've blessed like I have your armor, only with different attributes. In this dark world, you'll need additional help, at least until you've grown wiser."

Roble stared at the dead wizard's rings—one held a large ruby and the other, a topaz. He was never a man to wear rings, not even a class ring, but these lured and made him lust to possess them.

"Seek me out in Woodnog swamps." The blue energy surging through the wizard's dead body vanished.

A chill shot through Roble. He shivered. Looking at the corpse, he said, "So odd."

"Be wary," Shawndirea whispered.

Odlon stepped closer. "That's not an invitation you should take alone."

"I've no plans to find him," Roble replied.

Drucis cocked a brow. "Aye, but *he's* found you. He won't rest until you seek him out."

Roble kneeled beside the wizard's corpse. He reached for the topaz ring.

"No!" Shawndirea gasped.

"Why not?" Roble asked. "He offered them to me."

"To be his slave? His servant? Is that what you wish to become?" she asked.

Roble removed the ring. "No. I won't wear them."

"Then why take them?"

"Do you not think others in Ironwood won't steal these for themselves, or far worse, use their power to harm others?" Roble asked.

Drucis nodded. "He's right. The first lowlife dat enters the tavern will loot anything of value these two have. He might as well take them."

Roble slid the wizard's rings off while Drucis took the dead men's gold pouches, an amulet, and a small spell book.

Manfrid watched Roble with new interest and smiled. "Overlander? Interesting. What brings you here? How'd you become a member of the Dragon Skull Order?"

"It's a long story," he replied.

Manfrid raised his shackled hands. "I've plenty of time."

Riese shook his head. "Not as much as you might imagine."

Drucis' brow furrowed. He glanced around the tavern and realized they were the only ones inside. None of the barmaids or the barkeep had returned. A smile crossed his face. Drucis nodded at Odlon and Roble. "Bar's open! Let's help ourselves!"

Roble and Odlon followed him to the bar. Crukas walked behind the bar and placed several corked bottles of strong liquor on the counter. Shawndirea stepped on the bar and requested honey ale. Crukas searched the bottles until he found some. He poured her a small amount in a silver spoon.

Manfrid appeared hurt by Riese's statement. "If your grudge is truly against my father, keeping me alive and joining me is the best way we can dethrone him. Consider it a chance for your redemption."

Tired, Riese walked to the nearest table and sat with a serious frown on his face. He looked in Manfrid's eyes. "I don't seek redemption. I'm not ashamed of anything I've done or the Vyking lives I've taken. I've not killed the innocent as King Obed and his men have done."

"Help me take my father's throne," Manfrid said. "You'll be a man of great power."

"Not interested," Riese said bluntly.

"Then perhaps I could join your mission to stop Waxxon and his men?"

"I've no interest in pursuing Waxxon. I seek to remove your father's head and end his reign. Nothing else will satisfy me."

"Don't be a fool," Manfrid said. "Without me, you'll never succeed."

"I've done well thus far."

In his stately voice, Manfrid said, "You're on the outskirts of the outskirts. Thousands of Vykings stand between you and where my father reigns. Thousands. One man cannot charge the throne and take my father down. He's too powerful."

Hordus pulled his long silver hair behind his head and tied it. "Riese, Manfrid's correct. You could use us and our knowledge to get to Obed."

"I can gather troops," Manfrid said. "Most of those under my charge agree with you. My father's a tyrant and lost his way. All secretly despise his queen."

"I don't trust you," Riese said. "No more than you trust me. Besides, you're willing to make any deal to get free of your death sentence."

"I understand you don't trust me. How can I prove myself?" Manfrid asked.

Slightly angered, Hordus said, "Why kill a bastard prince? What glory is that, Riese? Even if you killed Obed, the throne won't fall to Manfrid. You spared me in Woodcrest, and for that, I yield my life to you. You're a man of honor, and I understand your rage. I'm in your service."

Hordus took a knee before Riese.

Riese studied Hordus' face for a long while. The old Vyking's words held great wisdom and logic. "Basically, you're indicating I should help Manfrid take his father's throne?"

Hordus gave a solemn nod.

"What's to say that Manfrid won't have me beheaded after he assumes the throne? Or he'll kill me during our journey?"

"I'm in your service as well," Manfrid said. He, too, took a knee. He slid his signet ring from his finger and handed it to Riese. "I swear to you on my grandfather's grave I won't betray you. I will, however, richly reward you when our deed is done."

"I'm not interested—"

"In riches," Manfrid interrupted. "I respect that, but once the battle's over, you'll need a place to retire. I can give you that."

"*Why* would a prince yield himself to a common blacksmith?"

"You're much more than a blacksmith, Riese," Manfrid replied. "You're a better warrior than most of the men I've led. Proof lies at the table. You're even better than myself, and that's not a compliment I'd normally give."

"You know I don't trust you," Riese replied. "I'll always look at you with scrutiny."

"I understand, but I'm your best way to leave Ironwood alive," Manfrid said. "Q'aran will have dozens of men waiting for us to leave the tavern? He knows I'm here with you. Keeping me alive is in his best interest."

"He may well attack with you in our custody anyway."

Manfrid gnawed at his lower lip for a moment. "Possibly, but there's another way out of Ironwood."

"The sewers?" Riese asked.

"Okay," Manfrid said, "Then I know *two* other ways."

"What's the other?"

"For that, we have to come to some agreement on how we join forces."

"I'll have to think about that."

"You have my ring, which states my authority. That token shows I've placed complete trust in you."

"Others may think I forced you to give it up."

Manfrid smiled and shook his head. "Not without the removal of my finger, they wouldn't. Even you know that."

Riese looked at the signet ring and thought. "Let me think about it."

"I wouldn't waste much time," he replied. "They could corner us in this borough the longer we wait."

CHAPTER 61

Running through the dark alleyway, Darrath clutched her chest. Warm blood dripped from where large shards of glass remained embedded. She staggered, nearing unconsciousness, and placed her hand against the corner of a building to steady herself.

Pain rippled through her. She gasped. Death wasn't something she welcomed. Not yet. She wanted revenge, to kill Crukas and take the necklace for her own, but she grew weaker by the minute. Her bloody fingers touched the jagged tip of glass sticking out of her leather vest. A gentle tug brought intense pain. Removing the glass meant immediate death. She needed help, fast.

Darrath took two steps and stood outside another tavern where two Ironwood guards stood. Weakly, she said, "Take me to Q'aran now."

She dropped to her knees. The two men caught and helped her stand between them.

One guard said, "Q'aran's outside Redlamp Borough."

"Get me to him, but fast," she said in a near whisper.

They hoisted her between them and hurried up the dark winding, cobblestone pathway. Two lines of armored guards stood with their swords drawn on the upper roadway. Q'aran was seated on his mount at the rear.

The guards carried Darrath to Q'aran.

Q'aran looked at her. "Darrath? What happened?"

"I need a healer," she said weakly.

"When they emerge from the Murky Flask, they're dead," he said sternly.

Darrath shook her head. "No. Let them leave."

"What? They nearly killed you. They have Manfrid."

"Manfrid's not your concern," she said. "Let them leave Ironwood unharmed. Have a scout follow them. But don't kill them. When I've regained my strength, I'll find Crukas myself."

"Why? I can end them here."

"True, but doing so will cost you a great fortune."

"I don't understand," Q'aran said.

"If you kill Crukas and the others, what he stole is gone forever."

"And what exactly does he have that is so valuable?"

"I cannot tell you. But help me with this, and I promise to make you an even wealthier Duke."

Q'aran studied her eyes for several minutes. "Very well."

Darrath coughed and warm blood coated her teeth. "Get me to a healer before it's too late. If I die, my secrets die with me."

Q'aran waved his hands to the two guards, and they hurried away.

DRUCIS DOWNED another flask of strong wine. "Ahh! Dat's more than plenty."

Odlon smiled in agreement. Crukas sipped from his wine flask, and then he corked all the half empty bottles.

Riese explained what Manfrid's plan was to get out of Ironwood.

Roble said, "Can we trust him?"

Drucis slid his axe off the bar. "He best not betray us."

Manfrid said, "Like before, keep a blade on me. But, less forceful this time, if you don't mind."

"If you be misleading us—" Drucis said.

"You'll kill me," Manfrid said. "It's not a difficult decision. I know. Since I wish to overthrow my father and have my life spared, I won't betray you."

"Good." Drucis gave a firm nod but his narrowed gaze didn't lessen.

Riese said, "It's time for us to leave." He glanced at Manfrid. "Which direction?"

"We stick to the back alleys of the borough and head to the sewers," Manfrid replied.

"The sewers?" Drucis asked with a harsh frown.

Roble shook his head. "I'm not leaving without my horse."

"Nor I," said Drucis. "Ol' Grey's too old to abandon. Besides, I'd rather fight to the death than crawl through the stinking sewers like a grubby ol' maggot."

AT DRUCIS' insistence, Riese, Roble, and the others mounted to ride to the upper road and confront whatever resistance Q'aran might've positioned.

Manfrid was seated on Bleys with Roble while Roble kept a dagger pressed to the Vyking prince's throat. Odlon held his crossbow aimed at Manfrid. To their surprise, the cobblestone street leading out of the Redlamp Borough was deserted. No patrons, workers, or guards were seen.

"Something's amiss," Drucis said.

"I have to admit," Manfrid said, "this is suspicious to me, too."

Riese eyed the upper bridge-ways of Ironwood, and although guards marched across the planked walkways, none paid them any mind.

They continued through the Cheapskate Way to the front gates where Roble was certain confrontation awaited.

Again, nothing. Even the poor traders and merchants had vacated. Most left their wagons and unsold goods.

"Never seen Ironwood so ... empty," Drucis said.

Odlon shook his head. "No."

Riese kept his attention on the higher roofs, the balconies, and the overhead bridges.

Shawndirea balled a small green orb between her hands.

"What are you doing?" Roble asked.

"Detecting magic."

"Find anything?"

"Other than my own? No. Even the rings in your pocket from the wizard have grown cold."

"You think Q'aran's just going to let us leave?" Roble asked.

Drucis cleared his throat. "Appears dat way."

"Makes no sense," Roble said, shaking his head.

"Are ye looking for a fight?" Drucis said with a broad grin.

"No. But with his numbers, he has a superior advantage and yet, he seems afraid of us."

Odlon shifted in his saddle, keeping the crossbow aimed at Manfrid. "Q'aran didn't act like he wanted Crukas anyway. Darrath thought she had a hold over the duke but learned differently. Q'aran holds position in title only. The less trouble he involves himself with, the longer he'll live."

"That's true, I suppose," Roble said. "If most of the town feels the same toward Q'aran as the barmaids do, it's doubtful he has many willing to die for him."

"Few deal with the politics and allegiance in a town like Ironwood," Manfrid said. "Most are too preoccupied keeping food and shelter to worry about who presides over whom. Unless, of course, the ruler's a tyrant like my father."

"Thousands follow him," Drucis said.

"Only by fear," Manfrid replied.

Drucis scoffed. "Your kind's known for plundering the shorelines."

"Ask Riese why."

Drucis looked at Riese.

"We're taught at a young age to obey whatever our king demands without question," Riese said, deep in thought. "Otherwise, painful death is warranted. As children we're forced to watch captured turncoats be burned alive to spare their souls. Some were beheaded. The only true honorable death came from dying on the battlefield by serving our king and our gods."

They passed through the gates and into the towering rust-colored giant trees. No guards awaited, so Roble removed his dagger from Manfrid's throat and Odlon lowered his crossbow.

Through the thick forest they traveled several hours before the forest darkened with twisted trees forking their spindled branches toward the dark overcast sky. They didn't pass any riders in their journey farther away from Ironwood, which brought a brief sense of relief for all of them. That is, until Manfrid caught sight of the single scout riding at the farthest edge of the path.

"We're not alone," Manfrid said.

Drucis and Odlon turned in their saddles and peered back.

Drucis smiled. "Appears someone's following us."

Odlon nodded and pointed at the darkest part of the path. The path forked at the foothill of a great mountain rise. "Ahead, he'll become confused."

Roble looked at the elf. "Why's that?"

Odlon grinned. "That's where we part ways. You take Shawndirea to Elvendale and the rest of us travel to Woodnog."

Shawndirea kissed Roble's cheek. Excitement shot through her. "I'm almost home!"

Roble was filled with mixed emotions. He was happy Shawndirea was close to her kingdom where she could get her wings restored, but he'd miss Drucis, Odlon, and Riese. Crukas wasn't as much a loss, but lacking a circle of friends, Roble felt less protected.

The slope of the mountain ridge blocked the sun. The trees at the fork in the road were thicker and kept the shadows deep and the ground moist. Strange insects buzzed. Birds quieted as their party separated into two groups.

"Roble, blessings to you in your journey to Elvendale," Odlon said.

Roble nodded. "And to you."

"Once you're done in Elvendale, meet us in Woodnog."

"I look forward to it," Roble said with a slight grin.

"Shawndirea knows how to find us," Odlon replied.

Roble peered at the steep mountain ridge. "This place's shrouded in shadow."

Drucis said, "Aye. The Black Chasm's nestled on the other side of this mountain range. But don't worry, it's not like you'll fall into it."

Roble became uneasy.

"It's difficult to reach," Odlon said. "Simply keep to the path to Elvendale, and you won't go near it."

"But be wary of what may come *out* of it." Drucis ran his hand through his white beard.

Shawndirea bowed to them. "Many thanks for your help."

Crukas stayed with Roble and Shawndirea. He decided to go to the Kingdom of Legelarid where he'd be farther from Riese. Although Riese had mellowed and no longer desired to see Crukas hang, Crukas wished to be in a place where recognition wasn't likely. Legelarid hosted the largest city population in Aetheaon, which made it easier to vanish into the crowds.

Odlon, Drucis, Manfrid, Riese, and Riese's son headed to Woodnog where they planned to gather warriors and Dragon Skull Knights to find Lady Dawn while killing Waxxon's men along the way.

CHAPTER 62

Roble stopped Bleys outside the gates of Elvendale. Shawndirea sat on his shoulder. Crukas kept walking.

"Aren't you staying the night?" Roble asked.

Crukas shook his head. "No. I need to reach Legelarid before midnight. Besides, I'm not fond of the tricks Fae play on humans."

Shawndirea giggled.

"Is he serious?" Roble asked.

She nodded. "Of course."

Crukas turned to walk on. "You'll see soon enough."

"Be safe, Crukas," Roble said.

Without turning back, the thief said, "Thanks for honoring your word, Overlander. I had my doubts about you at first, but you've proven yourself to be a man of honor. I hope your time in this realm never tarnishes that."

"*Me, too,*" Roble thought. Aloud, he said, "May our paths cross again."

"Eventually all paths do," Crukas replied.

He watched until Crukas rounded the next bend on foot. He glanced at Shawndirea and smiled.

"What?" she asked.

"I kept my word to you as well."

She kissed his cheek. "I never doubted you."

"Even in the beginning?"

Shawndirea made a near pinch with her index finger and thumb. "Well, maybe a smidgen. But you did what you promised. Now you can return home and leave me here."

"Why would I do that? You said we're meant to be."

She smiled. "You've yet to enter Elvendale, so you have time to turn back, if you harbor any doubts about us or living in my realm."

Roble shook his head. "I've no doubts. I've nothing left, if I don't have you."

"I feel the same. But once you cross into my kingdom, you're sealed with me."

"How? You promised never to cast a spell on me."

She shook her head. "I won't. That's not what I mean."

"Then what do you mean?"

"Before I left Elvendale on my quest to find my husband, I swore never to enter Elvendale until I found him ... you. No spell has been placed on you, nor have I ever bewitched you. But with you entering with me, you're letting my goddess know you've pledged to live your life with me. Is this what you truly want?"

Roble studied her emerald eyes, her nervously shy glance, and the perfect pout on her lips. "Of course, you are *who* I want to share my life with."

Flattered, her beautiful smile brightened her face. She waved her hand with a gesture to move forward. "Then so be it."

He nudged the horse's flanks. Bleys stepped from the path into Elvendale. A heavenly fragrance permeated the air and for the moment, all his stress vanished.

Down the sloping grassy path, the meadows blossomed with pastel-toned flowers. Thousands of butterflies drifted from flower to flower with the gentle breeze carrying them. He marveled at the splendid perfection of a place he often dreamed of discovering. His heart raced at the vast differences in the butterflies. Unlike when he collected in the Overlands, where butterflies were categorized into various species based on their colors, shapes, and sizes, these were unique creatures.

Roble tugged the reins slightly, and Bleys stopped.

"This is my home," Shawndirea said.

"Spectacular."

She kissed his cheek hard. "Thank you for bringing me home."

"Where can I tie Bleys?"

"Let him roam," Shawndirea replied.

"I don't want him to damage the flowers or butterflies."

"They'll be fine."

Roble dismounted and patted Bleys' face. The horse snorted and lowered its head to graze.

"Where do I take you?" Roble asked.

"That depends," she said.

"On what?"

Shawndirea smiled and slightly blushed. Her eyes held a bit of fear and she struggled to find the proper words.

Roble read her confusion. "What?"

"You have a decision to make." She took a deep breath. "Do you wish to remain with me awhile longer before I introduce you to my mother?"

"Certainly," he replied. "I'd love to see Elvendale. This is far more beautiful than I imagined."

"Will you ever desire to return to the Overlands?" she asked.

He looked in her sparkling green eyes. Her eyes pleaded for an answer. She held her breath while awaiting his reply.

"Other than returning to tell my sister I'm fine and not to worry, I'll stay with you."

Tears moistened her eyes. "I'm glad you feel that way, but are you certain?"

He nodded. "I've no doubts."

"We'll be happy together."

"Where should I take you?"

She pointed to a small grove of trees. "There."

"Why there?"

"To make you my size."

Roble chuckled. "Why don't you become my height?"

"In time. But in order to introduce you to the Courts and my mother, you must be my height to enter."

"I see. Do you think she'll accept me?"

Shawndirea said, "Doubtful, but don't take it personally."

"Then why have me enter the Courts anyway?"

"To follow royal procedure. Since I'm destined to one day assume the throne, I'm to bring my prospective husband before the courts."

"And if she rejects me?"

Shawndirea shrugged. "I'll forfeit my right to the throne."

"Don't do that."

"Roble, I've never desired the throne."

At the center of the grove was a circle of scarlet mushrooms.

"Step in the center, and set me at your feet," she said.

Roble did what she requested. She spoke several words. A turquoise hummingbird zipped through the forest, slowed and hovered an inch from her. She took what looked like a slender twig. After she held the object, the hummingbird zipped away. In her hands, the tip of the twig glowed bright green.

"What's that?" he asked.

"My scepter. I never leave this realm with it. It's too risky. I'm in my kingdom now, so its power is at strongest. Are you ready?"

He nodded.

Shawndirea closed her eyes and raised her hands. The ground around her feet shimmered and glowed. The emerald scepter glowed brighter. Other Fae came from their hiding places and joined her.

A rush of warmth and power surged through Roble's body. The power overwhelmed him. He tried to keep his eyes open, but a blinding light stung them. He felt dizzy. His stomach became nauseous. When the power increased to its next level of intensity, he lost consciousness.

He awakened two hours later and opened his eyes. Everything was blurry. His head rested in Shawndirea's lap. She gently stroked his hair and face. Her radiant smile and her eyes were the first things he saw.

The sun sank on the horizon. Dusk was less than a couple hours away.

"How do you feel?" she asked.

"Light-headed but okay."

He pushed himself into a seated position.

"Careful," she said.

"Yeah, I won't rush myself. How far are we from the Courts?"

"Not far," she replied. "I've arranged for transportation. We'd never reach the halls before dark."

"Transportation?"

She nodded and pointed at a massive moth resting on a scarlet mushroom.

"Wow."

"I hope you're not afraid of heights."

"Never really thought about that, until now."

THE MOTH LANDED OUTSIDE THE COURTS' grand doors. She escorted Roble up a side flight of stairs and down a long gloriously jeweled hallway. She opened a side door and led him inside.

"Where are we?" he asked.

"You need suitable clothes before you enter the Courts. This is where my father's belongings are stored. Let me find you something. After searching through the closet, she returned with a silk shirt and pants. He hurried and changed clothes.

After a half hour, Shawndirea led him downstairs and hurried to the tall doors of the Courts. Various gems glittered from their insets on the golden doors. Two guards raised their halberds defensively until they recognized Shawndirea. They lowered their weapons and bowed slightly.

"Young Queen," one said. "What brings you to the Courts?"

"I came to announce my engagement to my mother."

The elf guards' eyes widened. They stared at Roble in question.

"Yes," Shawndirea said. "This is my husband to be."

The guard swallowed hard, turned, and pushed the door inward. "One second, your grace. I will break the um ... news."

He left the door slightly ajar. A few seconds later, a high-pitched shriek echoed from the chambers.

"A human? Send them in!"

CHAPTER 63

Queen Istrell's face darkened with anger, spite, and disapproval. She glared at Roble and then shifted her heated gaze at Shawndirea. The darkness in her eyes didn't lessen.

"You're abandoning your rightful place on the throne to marry *him*? A human?" Istrell fumed. Her severely harsh tone dripped with bitterness and distaste. Her lips quivered like a child's after tasting something vile. She fought her urge to spit on the floor. She forced her next words. "Really, child? Explain yourself!"

"I love him." Shawndirea crossed her arms and lifted her nose in defiance.

Istrell's prune-wrinkled face shriveled worse. She seethed. "You love him? After he destroyed your magnificent wings? Child, surely you've more self-respect than that?"

"What happened to my wings was accidental, but risking his life to bring me to Elvendale was intentional," she replied.

She flared her gaze at Shawndirea while giving Roble a harsh side-glance. "As well he should since he destroyed your beauty."

"An *accident*, Mother! He's more than compensated for his mistake. You've no idea what dangers he put himself through to ensure our arrival."

Istrell wrung her withered hands and shook her head. "With humans

458

it's always *an accident*. Humans never respect what nature offers. They dig deeper, either mining or destroying whatever lies in their way to find more gold."

"Not *all* humans, mother."

"Does this human *love* you?" Istrell asked.

"I do," Roble replied.

Istrell's nostrils flared. Her eyes widened. "Did I *ask* you to speak? Keep your silence until you've *my* permission to speak in *my* court."

Roble offered a slight bow to signal apology.

"He loves me." Shawndirea frowned. "It's not *his* fault your heart has grown cold and bitter after the loss of your husband, my father."

"How dare you!" Istrell's anger boiled. "You best mind your tongue, my child! I won't tolerate your insolence."

"If you forbid me to marry him, you've lost a daughter."

Istrell gasped and fanned her face with such a feign gesture anyone could recognize the queen was openly mocking Shawndirea.

"Really, mother?" Shawndirea's hands balled into tight fists. A tinge of green glowed around them. "Think of how long I was gone. I almost chose *not* to return to your halls."

Istrell smirked. "Then *why* did you, child?"

"To be healed. To have my wings whole again."

"I won't grant you that, not if you choose to be a human."

"I don't *need* you to grant this."

Istrell's eyes narrowed. "Oh? How do you expect such a blessing?"

"The power lies within me."

Istrell chuckled. "If that's true, why haven't you healed yourself?"

"Because seeking your blessing for my marriage *seemed* more important at the time."

Istrell swallowed hard and thought on how best to reply. Her eyes softened, but only for a moment. She cleared her throat and glared at Roble.

"You love my daughter?" Istrell said.

Roble nodded.

"My question indicates I expect you to answer," she said.

"Yes," Roble said. "With all my heart."

Another smirk curled the queen's lips. "Those words are *so* easy for a human to say. Love is carelessly used to express feelings for almost anything. True love often comes with pain and sorrow. An ache so deep, you can't mine deep enough to soothe it. Care to put some action or risk behind your words?"

"You're challenging me? My word's not enough?"

"Humans are filthy, untrustworthy individuals, prone to say anything to gain what they desire. My daughter deserves to marry someone brave, daring. I need to know she hasn't foolishly chosen someone incapable of protecting her."

"I'm willing to prove myself," Roble said.

"Don't," Shawndirea said. "It's a trick."

"No," Roble said. "Name the challenge. What does it take to prove my love for your daughter to *you*? Odd, you need proof for something she already feels."

"Very well," Istrell said with amusement in her eyes and a devious smile on her lips. "This is what I require. We have a situation growing in our world. I'm certain you've heard of the Black Chasm by now?"

"Mother," Shawndirea said.

"Hold your tongue, child."

Roble nodded. "Yes. I have. What do you ask?"

"A party of warriors is gathering to ride into the strange dark misty fog engulfing the chasm. You lead their charge. Report to me what lies inside the fog, and I'll grant you liberty to marry my daughter. What say you?"

"That's suicide!" Shawndirea shouted. Her voice rang throughout the palace rafters.

"The choice is his," Istrell said. "Be he a man of bravery and integrity or is he a *coward*?"

"I'll do it." Anger rose in Roble's tone. His eyes narrowed at Istrell to which she seemed greatly amused.

"Do you swear it?" the Queen asked.

"Roble," Shawndirea said. "*No.*"

"I swear it."

Istrell studied Roble's eyes but found no dishonesty. He never broke their gaze or flinched. His breath didn't quicken. He remained calm in spite of Shawndirea's adamant protests. A flicker of fear arose in Istrell.

She'd never seen such boldness in a human. She worried about having Roble's anger turned against her.

Istrell smiled. "Perhaps she judges character better than I. Time will tell."

In fury, Shawndirea squeezed her fists tightly. "I'll not allow you to do this, mother. What you're asking is for his death!"

"He swore an oath to me, child. To break that oath *is* death."

"To honor it is death! Mother, I swear if he dies because of this, you're *dead* to me. Dead! Do you hear me?"

Istrell ignored Shawndirea's outbursts. "Roble, tomorrow morning you'll be escorted to a neighboring town where you'll join the group. The Black Chasm is a day's journey. Rest well and say your goodbyes in the morning."

Roble bowed. "Your Highness."

He took Shawndirea's hand and turned to walk away.

"You can't do this," Shawndirea whispered. Tears flowed down her cheeks. Hurt possessed her. "You can't. You'll die."

"I've no choice, dear," Roble said. "I want to gain her blessing. Otherwise, she'll always detest our marriage. Besides, I love exploration."

The pleading in her voice was desperate. "You don't know her. I do. Even if you succeed with this *exploration*, as you call it, she'll never grant you her blessing. She hates humans."

"I'll prove myself to her."

Shawndirea tried to speak, but her voice broke into heavier sobs. She held his hand tightly and covered her eyes with her other hand. She wiped away tears and flung herself against his chest and sobbed.

"You did so much to get me here," she whispered. "You've nothing to prove. I love you so, but I can't bear this pain inside."

Roble wrapped his arms around her and kissed the top of her head.

His silken shirt was soaked with her tears. Seeing her in this state, indicated how deep her love was for him. He ached at her tears and pain.

"I'll be okay," he said softly. "I promise. Don't worry. I love you."

She peered at him with sad eyes. "This isn't a game. Most who've ventured into the chasm have died. Anyone that survived was never the same. They were different, mindless creatures. Darkness surges within those shadows known as the Black Chasm. The force controlling the area terrifies everyone, even my mother. Please reconsider your oath."

"Any ideas for what caused this chasm to appear?" He wiped tears from her eyes.

"The City of Mortel's ruins are possibly still there."

"There's a city?"

Shawndirea sighed, still trying to calm herself. "One prince of King Offaerius was granted the land for hunting grounds, nothing more. Instead, his son, Tyrann, hired an architect and workers to build his castle. When Offaerius learned of this, he was outraged and insisted Tyrann stop the construction."

"Why?"

"Offaerius believed this was a threat to the Kingdom of Legelarid, even though Tyrann held no armies, no loyal allegiances to other cities in Aetheaon or any other continents."

"There must be more to it than that?" Roble asked.

"Perhaps. Tyrann's mother had been of the Shi'marush clan from the Isles of Bloodmoore, deep in the South Seas. According to bard's tales, this region is where a strange race of people reside. They're considered people of the night. Their isles are shrouded with misty darkness, much like the Black Chasm."

Roble ran his hand through his short beard. "So his queen is from Bloodmore?"

"No. His mother was the daughter of Bloodmoore's matriarch and became Offaerius' mistress when she visited his kingdom. The queen never knew of the affair until a year after Jez'baal returned to Bloodmoore. A ship docked and with the cargo a midwife delivered Offaerius his illegitimate son, Tyrann."

"Not a present he quite expected, I suppose."

"No, but he received his wife's resentment. However, he treated Tyrann as a prince, favored amongst his own children even though he was different."

"Different? In what way?"

"He favored Jez'baal. Dark eyes, pale skin, and coal black hair. But he had other differences, too."

"Like what?"

"A keen understanding of the occult. Dark magics. Animals and demons communicate with him. The queen was terrified of him and, according to the tales, tried—unsuccessfully—to kill him several times during his youth. After her third attempt, she died from a mysterious plague."

"So he lives in the Black Chasm?"

"Not quite," Shawndirea replied.

"What do you mean?"

"After his castle was completed, Offaerius sent several knights to inspect Tyrann's new home. Only when they arrived, they discovered an entire city surrounded the castle. No citizens resided there. But the magnitude of what he had crafted, some suspect through his magic or demonic connections, appeared to be ready to establish a civilization loyal to Tyrann.

"The City of Mortel contained a temple with Tyrann's image on a huge tapestry above an ebony altar. When Offaerius received news of this, he was further outraged. He sent dozens of knights to Mortel. Two knights confronted Tyrann in the temple and sought to bind and return him to Legelarid. He refused. The knights killed Tyrann inside his temple on the ebony altar. Or so they thought."

"So he's alive?"

Shawndirea nodded. "He set them up. By killing him inside his temple, on the altar where his followers would worship, he became immortal. After the knight had run his sword through Tyrann and pulled it out, Tyrann rose. He cast a curse on the men. All except one, died. He survived only long enough to return to Offaerius and tell the tale. That knight became like those left with Tyrann. None of Offaerius' knights could kill him. He returned to Mortel and joined the others, so the tale goes. They became Tyrann's first knights."

"Is there any proof?" Roble asked.

"Sadly, bards sing these tales and legends in the taverns. All legends contain some truth, but how much? We're uncertain. That's why I'm begging you not to go. We don't know what's there or the strength of Tyrann's power. Again, any who've returned from the chasm, *never* returned the same way. I love you for who you are now. Please, don't go."

"I'll be okay, Shawndirea," Roble said, changing the subject, to ease her mind without dismissing the subject entirely. Although the information made him more apprehensive than before. "How about you show me your kingdom? But first, how do you heal your wings? Before I journey into the Black Chasm, I want to see you in your full beauty. I have to know, if nothing else, our journey to your homeland was successful."

She glanced at the rugged frame of what had been her glorious wings. She nodded. "Thank you for everything you sacrificed to get me here. Picking you was not a foolish choice, but your decision to accept my mother's challenge *is* foolish. I'd sacrifice my wings to be with you."

"I'm not worth that," he replied.

"To me, you are. Entering the Black Chasm is too risky. My mother chose such a thing because she doesn't want you to marry me. Your death ensures we won't be together."

"I'm not dead yet," Roble replied. "Nor do I intend to die anytime soon."

"We're not masters of our fate," she said, taking his hand. "Come see the glories of my kingdom."

Shawndirea strolled through the kingdom and showed him the fountains, the pools, the extravagant flower gardens filled with hundreds of spectacular butterflies. She explained the history behind each monument and statue of those who had reigned over her kingdom long before she was born.

Roble squeezed her hand when she showed the statue of her father, the former king. "Be honest with me, dear. Don't you want your name and likeness to follow in your father's lineage?"

"My father was an honorable person. He possessed no vileness or resentment like my bitter mother. He'd have been proud to see us married."

"You mentioned her resentment came because he died while in the company of humans. Does she use her hatred to bury her pain?"

Shawndirea shook her head. Her eyes remained saddened. "No. My father took such quests and traveled to far away lands to get away from her. He filled his life with adventure, which isn't something a king does often.

"My mother's always been filled with malice. She rules in a cynical nature. It doesn't matter if someone has dreams. She'll do everything possible to destroy them. Aerlene is her sister. For years, my mother's spread the rumor that my aunt was dead."

"Dead?"

Shawndirea nodded. "Yes. I thought Aerlene was until we saw her in Woodcrest."

"Why lie about such a thing?"

"Because she wishes death upon Aerlene. They had a dispute and Aerlene left Elvendale vowing never to return. My mother's anger was so bad she told the Courts Aerlene had been killed by a goblin."

Roble shook his head. "I often wished I'd come from a large family. My sister, Lib, is my only sibling. In ways, seeing all the turmoil and politics that run through competitive siblings is enough to make me thankful she's the only one I have. We've always been the best of friends, and we'd never turn on one another."

Shawndirea smiled. "But you're not of royalty, love. Such blood's often tainted with jealousy, lies, and backstabbing. That's another reason I abhor the thought of taking the throne. I want a loving husband and wonderful children to rear." She crinkled her nose and pointed a playful finger at him. "That's why you best not get killed."

Roble smiled. "I've no plans to die."

"No one ever does."

Roble nodded. "She never said how far into the chasm we had to travel. She asked for an investigation. That's all she'll receive."

"You're right! She didn't say how far."

"See? All's not lost."

She faced him with a broad smile, studied his face, and her smile slowly faded.

"What's wrong?" Roble asked.

"It won't happen like that though, will it?"

"What do you mean?"

"No. It won't. Even though we've not been together long, I understand you better than you think."

He frowned. "I don't understand."

Shawndirea pursed her lips. "You're a scientist. You love to explore and discover new things. You'll attempt to view as much of the Black Chasm as possible. No amount of persuasion from me or anyone else will deter your lust to discover something new."

"I never hinted anything of the sort," Roble said.

"You don't need to. It's instilled inside you. It's who you are. No matter. Let's not discuss it for now. Come." She took his hand. "Let's restore my wings."

Roble took her hand, but his heart ached. Was he destined to do exactly what she insisted? Of course, being a scientist made him search for new discoveries and information. He thrived on it. But he didn't have his heart set on fulfilling this journey. He didn't want to leave Shawndirea, but his pledge bound him to the task. He only planned to enter a short distance and turn back, but the more he thought about her prediction, the more her instincts were probably correct. He feared he'd keep exploring the chasm until he knew everything about it and why it originated where it had.

Since the chasm evolved at the City of Mortel, all they had were the legends and tales. No real reason. He might look until he found the truth since no one else ever had.

Roble followed her down a long, winding set of ivory stairs. Flowering vines and shrubs lined both sides. The intoxicating mixture of jasmine, vanilla, and citrus scented the air. Butterflies, damselflies, and little dragon sprites drifted from flower to flower. They stepped off the last step and into a vast field filled with thousands of pastel-colored flowers. A miraculous event unfolded right before Roble's eyes. Micro butterflies swarmed her with little kisses and mournful fluttering at the sight of her damaged wings. These butterflies were too tiny for him to see at his normal height.

Without warning, the iridescent blanket of swarming butterflies gathered on the stubs of her broken wings. Green light shone around Shawndirea's feet. Light illuminated around her like a glowing bubble and blasted with such radiance that Roble covered his eyes. After the light faded, he looked at her. Her wings glittered in the greenish-turquoise like they had on the day they'd first met. Tears filled his eyes.

Shawndirea flexed her shimmering wings. Such spectacular colors twinkled from being kissed by the sunlight. She smiled in spite of her mournful tears.

"You're the most beautiful sight I've ever seen," Roble said.

The butterfly swarm drifted upward and scattered. They returned unharmed by the light to drink nectar from the flowers. Her wings didn't quite resemble the colors he'd seen on the day he captured her with the butterfly net. But being her height allowed him to get the full glory of her true colors.

"How?" he asked.

"I'm the Butterfly Queen. They saw my injuries and in their own kindness donated part of their wing scales to me. Their compassion, joined with my magic, rebuilt my wings."

Shawndirea ran to Roble and grabbed his hands. He pulled her close and kissed her. When he looked in her eyes, he read so many emotions, but the greatest thing he sensed was the bond of love between them.

She said, "Come with me."

"Where?"

"The spell allowing you to be my height won't last until morning. If the possibility exists that this might be our last night together, I would have this night with you in my chambers."

"Without her blessing?"

She crinkled her nose and kissed him firmly. "We're adults. With the circumstances as they are, I would *without* her blessing. Besides, she has no say in the matter."

Roble smiled.

Shawndirea took his hand and led him across the fields of flowers filled with flittering butterflies until they came to a large oak. She spoke words in her native language and a door materialized on the wide tree trunk. She opened it and led him inside. When the sun rose the next morning neither had slept.

CHAPTER 64

$\mathcal{E}$xhausted, Roble exited the invisible door and stepped on the flowery field. Since he planned to scout the Black Chasm territory, he wore the Dragon Skull Knight armor. The enchanted armor had protected him during the harsh, frigid temperatures in Glacier Ridge. He hoped it was enchanted with other attributes to protect him inside the Black Chasm.

The moment sunlight touched him, he returned to his normal size. The spell had dissolved. He knelt to pick Shawndirea up.

She laughed, ascended into graceful flight, and glided before his face in all her regal splendor.

"I don't like our size difference. I want to return to your size," he said.

"When you return from the Black Chasm, I'll be your height," she replied.

"Don't you mean *if*?"

Shawndirea frowned and playfully shook her finger. "If you can be optimistic, so shall I."

"By becoming my height, doesn't that mean you're giving away your right to the throne?"

She smiled and nodded.

"Why?" he asked.

"It's not worth the agony to oversee a kingdom's problems. Besides, Dirk loves controversy and control. He's better suited for assuming the kingdom."

"That doesn't bother you? He'll have authority over you and others?"

"Not at all."

"His reign, should he take power, could be far worse than you think."

Shawndirea shrugged. "Perhaps, but I'll chance it. Once we're wed, none of the Fae will accept you as a king."

"If you're certain this is what you want."

"Of course. I've explained my reasoning multiple times. Let's not discuss the matter again. Okay?"

He nodded.

"I've something to give you," she said.

"What?"

She handed him a folded square of cloth about the size of a handkerchief. He unfolded it.

"What is this?" he asked.

"Some enchanted cloth. It never hurts to have some added protection, much like your armor."

Roble smiled and tucked the cloth inside his vest.

A male faery dressed in a thin layer of fancy armor drifted through the air and hovered before them. On his belt he wore a sheathed dagger and sword.

"Roble?" the male faery asked.

"Yes?"

"I'm to escort you to Westwyrm to meet your squad outside the Black Chasm."

"You are?" Roble asked.

"Cildaer. If we hurry, we can be there before midday."

"Okay."

"Do you think you can keep up with me?"

Shawndirea frowned. "Cildaer. No pranks and *no* hide-and-seek. Always stay within Roble's view, or you'll have *me* to contend with later."

Cildaer blushed and tugged the collar of his fancy armor. He sighed and motioned Roble with his tiny hand. "Come on."

Shawndirea hovered before Roble and kissed his lips. Trying not to cry, she said, "Return to me, my love."

"I will. I promise."

Roble climbed on Bleys, gently tapped the horse's flanks, and followed Cildaer from the flowery paradise into the evergreen forest filled with mossy rocks and gentle flowing brooks.

THE JOURNEY from Elvendale to Westwyrm wasn't a rugged journey. While riding through the beautiful trees, Roble thought of Shawndirea, her fears, and their future together. He didn't want to disregard her worries as unimportant because she continually warned he needed to take stronger precautions.

The closer he rode to Westwyrm, the darker the skies became. A warm breeze rustled the treetops, but the wind didn't hint of a thunderstorm or even a drop of rain. The warmth was more like summer near a beach.

He couldn't help but think about what lie within the Black Chasm. Since he met Shawndirea, she'd never expressed such emotional worry and absolute fear. Part of him wondered why he had decided gaining Queen Istrell's approval meant more to him than what it should have. He understood why Shawndirea didn't have or ever would have a close relationship with her mother. He had gained an immediate distaste for Istrell's attitude and how she tried to exert dominance over her stubborn, resistant daughter. Perhaps that was the problem. They were too much alike.

No. He shook his head. Shawndirea was much stronger than her mother credited her.

Istrell wanted to usurp her power and position over her own daughter. When that failed, she tried to guilt her daughter into becoming the next queen, even though Shawndirea opposed.

Cildaer glided ahead of the horse. The faery looked bored and sighed. Then, he said, "Westwyrm once was a more fearful place."

"Why?" Roble asked.

"Two dragons discouraged travelers from venturing here. They

weren't monstrosities, but pesky nonetheless. Stealing sheep from shep-
herds for food. Occasionally, they flew over small villages and set roofs
on fire to appear more intimidating than they actually were. They never
went full onslaught and wiped out a town. They only wanted to be
appear menacing."

"Odlon told me there weren't any dragons anymore."

"None have been seen in years. Those two are now dead."

Roble felt saddened he'd never see a dragon.

"What happened to them?"

"Politics," Cildaer replied.

"Politics?"

Cildaer nodded. "King Offaerius offered the hand of his daughter to
any prince that brought the dragons' heads to him. Many kings
throughout the land lost sons due to this challenge and were angered at
their losses of future heirs. However, Prince Bhelgan of Nagdor
survived the challenge and returned to Offaerius' throne with the heads.
It was laughable, to say the least."

"Why?" Roble asked.

"You aren't familiar with our cities and kingdoms, are you?"

"No, but I'm learning."

Cildaer sighed and rolled his eyes. "Bhelgan's a dwarf, and Offaerius
is an elf. Not exactly a match made by the gods, is it?"

Roble grinned. "I imagine not."

"Indeed," the faery said.

"Did King Offaerius honor the reward?"

"To a dwarf?" Cildaer's eyes widened. "How absurd! Bhelgan refused
the marriage. Offaerius was happy to oblige, size not being the culprit
here, but their religious clashes, cultural differences, etc. No, neither
would have it, but Offaerius paid a hefty bit of gold for Bhelgan's troubles. A few barrels of ale to boot as well. He was *really* happy about the
exchange then."

Roble chuckled. The dragons died for gold. A sport. Dismayed, he
shook his head.

The narrow road through the trees arched along a winding tree-
lined ridge. Where the road curved sharply to the left, the Black Chasm
was visible. The purple-black mists swirled with flickering electrical

surges that resembled strange lightning. No rumbling sounds echoed in the small canyon below.

"What do you know about the warriors I'm meeting at Westwyrm?" Roble asked.

Cildaer shook his head. "No one's given me any information."

Roble glanced at the Black Chasm. He envisioned the best of the best warriors risking their lives with him to discover what lie beyond the eerie, purplish-black veil. So many sought fighting as a means to prove their strength, which generally brought the most intimidating people he'd seen. Riese was a prime example. A dozen or so men like him, and Roble didn't have much to fear. Most trophies were in titles more so than gold.

Even though Odlon had given him some practice with the sword, Roble wasn't comfortable using one in combat. He packed his best knives and even stashed knives in his saddlebags, his boots, and his belt. The worst thing about using throwing knives for weapons was a knife could only be thrown once, unless he was fortunate enough to retrieve it. So he needed to hit each mark accurately.

When the narrow road wound around the ridge, he studied the Black Chasm one last time. If a city existed within, the swirling mists prevented him from seeing them. He didn't have any idea how many troops were there, either. Yet, the sense of something watching him increased.

"Not much farther," Cildaer said.

"What's at stake for Queen Istrell?" Roble asked.

"What do you mean?"

"According to her, this mission was of the utmost importance," Roble said.

"In a lot of ways, it is. Even though some kingdoms have sent warriors into the chasm, none have discovered the true nature of this chasm or the source behind its power. None have returned alive or in their right mind, either."

He thought about what Shawndirea had told him. "Does Queen Istrell not know the tales?"

Cildaer laughed with great amusement. "Only fools believe drunken tales."

"So the queen believes this group can succeed where others have not?"

"Again," Cildaer said. "No further information was given to me. I'm only an escort. Sorry."

Cildaer led Roble into the tiny settlement of Westwyrm and introduced him to the eight men he'd lead into the Black Chasm. Not only was he disappointed with their number, he couldn't believe the group standing before him. All were human.

Dread shot through Roble's mind. He looked at the ragtag squad of human warriors gathered together. What Shawndirea had expressed to her mother was correct. This *was* a suicide mission. She'd deliberately set him up to fail. And if they all died, nine less humans existed, much to her satisfaction.

This poor excuse of a squadron was merely a group of unknown misfits no one would miss. Roble missed Odlon and Lehrling. Had they accompanied him to Elvendale, they probably would've swayed him to not accept the challenge. Indeed, the queen didn't want him to survive. Killing him prevented her daughter from marrying a human. Her hatred toward humans was so strong she didn't care if Roble died proving his honor and love for Shawndirea. If he died, he was out of the picture. Forever.

Realizing he'd been set up, anger rose inside Roble. Beneath his breath he swore if he survived the Black Chasm, he'd find a way to turn the tables on Istrell whenever the opportunity arose.

None of the squadron before him had a full set of gear. They were malnourished, weak, battle rejects, if such a rank existed. Their dull, shoddy weapons were rusted or cracked. Few possessed shield. Those who did, had battered ones that might survive a solid blow before falling apart. The horses' hooves were split, untrimmed, and unshod. Two rode lame mules and another one rode a fat, bloated pony. Despite their disadvantage, these men's eyes gleamed with flickering hope.

"This is it?" Roble asked the faery.

Cildaer said, "Afraid so. Good luck."

Before Roble could reply or ask for further directions or instructions, the faery darted through the trees and disappeared.

Roble faced the men. "What prompted you to join this mission?"

"Gold," one said.

"Treasures," said another.

A tall slender human said, "Land grants."

Puzzled, Roble frowned and looked at the eagerness on these men's grimy faces. None seemed alarmed about *what* the Black Chasm was or what awaited them once they entered. They'd all been misinformed and apparently on purpose. The offer of great riches overrode desperation. These men probably journeyed from town to town searching for handouts.

"By whom?" Roble asked. "Who told you such things would be awarded to you for venturing into the chasm?"

The slender man reached inside his vest and pulled out a rolled up piece of yellowed paper. He unrolled and tapped the paper with his filthy index finger.

"Here, see?" He pointed. "This is the meeting point."

Roble nodded. "You're to meet the leader here."

"That's you, isn't it?"

"I guess so."

The flyer offered the promises these men sought, but none of the real dangers were listed, which might not have deterred them anyway. These men didn't have anything valuable to lose. Their lives weren't worth much if they didn't find treasure, so they gambled everything. Sadly, even a hundred men like these weren't worth a lot should a battle ensue inside the chasm.

"I suppose we should enter the chasm," Roble said without enthusiasm. He wondered if Shawndirea was right about just abandoning the journey and heading back. But, he couldn't. He had given his word to prove his love for Shawndirea, even though she didn't need further proof. Besides, a part of him wanted to succeed to spite Queen Istrell. After all, Shawndirea would've done the same.

CHAPTER 65

The swirling black, purplish mists shrouding the Black Chasm reminded Roble of a massive tornado but without the roaring winds. The eerie silence intimidated him. The mists held a hypnotic, drawing power.

Even without Queen Istrell's challenge, his curiosity would've eventually drawn him into entering the chasm. Being a scientist, this was his nature. His innate need to find the answers to satisfy his curiosity caused him to overturn every stone to see what lie beneath them. This chasm's mysteries lured him. Though he tried to deny these urges, Shawndirea recognized his blatant need to seek answers in the most dangerous places like Devils Den and now the Black Chasm.

A smile crossed his lips. She knew his nature, which flattered him but frustrated her. Their differences would probably always remain, provided he survived this exploration.

Roble studied the ragtag treasure hunters. Their facial features formerly etched by greed succumbed to their sudden fear of the unknown.

"We can turn back," Roble said.

Their fear faded, replaced with quick, seething anger. They gripped their crude weapons in a blink. A toothless man said, "Are you reneging on the campaign?"

"No," Roble replied.

"Because if you are—" Another drew his rusted sword.

"It's only a suggestion, in case you have second thoughts."

They shook their heads.

Roble sighed. "Prepare yourselves for whatever awaits on the other side."

"What'eva it be, will taste death before I do."

Roble shook his head. The towering misty wall defied all logic. Greed often was stronger than fear. Not always, but when people lacked essentials but didn't surrender, they did foolish things. No words could dissuade these men into turning back. They'd die before admitting their defeat. None of these men could survive living with the questions of what wealth they'd forfeited by turning away. Not knowing would gnaw at them for the rest of their meager lives.

When he suggested turning back, their fierce glares were frightening. Roble understood what caused mutinies on ships at sea. Greed for greater wealth was the ultimate blindness that caused men to cheat, kill, or destroy.

Roble led them to the Black Chasm wall. He expected, and *hoped*, the wall to be impenetrable but no resistance met them. They passed through easily. Entering was *too* easy. He wondered what traps and possible ambush awaited them. But far worse than he ever imagined lingered within the shadowy mists. Without intervention, their quest for discovery was dead before they began.

QUEEN ISTRELL STOOD at her magical summoning crystals. She couldn't believe Shawndirea's contempt, in the High Court, of all places. In the past, her daughter deliberately disobeyed her, more often than not. Now, as an adult, Shawndirea needed punished for her actions.

She took the black mirror and focused until the silvery glass shimmered. Shawndirea's image materialized. Her daughter sat on her bed in her chambers. She wept and wiped tears with a cloth. Little butterflies flittered around the room, landed on her face, licked her tears, and tried to soothe her.

Part of Istrell's heart swelled at her daughter's agony. After all, her unruly daughter had challenged her in the courts.

"How dare you bring a human into my courts." Istrell watched her daughter heave and sob.

Roble standing in the court left a horrid taste in Istrell's mouth. Shawndirea's nerve to even *entertain* the idea of tarnishing her future bloodline was intolerable.

Istrell set the mirror down and placed her hands on the crystals. Power shimmered through them and radiated up her skinny, wrinkled arms. Her eyes turned back in her head. Roble had moved inside the Black Chasm. She'd never gazed beyond its veil. Why had the veil suddenly allowed her sight to move past the swirling mists?

Roble rode his horse while the others followed behind. All of them covered their mouths and noses with cloth. Thick smoke billowed from small holes along the gray rocky path they followed. One rider collapsed off his horse. His limp body sprawled on the path. He wasn't breathing. Roble shook his head. He clamped the enchanted cloth tight to his face and leaned lower. None of the others bothered to check their fallen comrade. They looked weakened—perhaps poisoned—and perhaps dying.

The horses faltered, stumbled, but kept fighting to move forward.

A smile curled Istrell's lips. For as long as the chasm had been in the vale, she wanted to know what was inside. Now she witnessed what had eluded her for so long.

Skeletons of dwarves, humans, and elves were scattered along the path. These were the remains of former explorers. A couple of horse skeletons were crumpled across the dark ground. Skulls were placed on tall skewer poles, which stood like a foreboding forest. This was a clear warning for whomever entered the Black Chasm. Their fates would be the same.

The rocky path resembled volcanic rock, black and sooty. Vapors and dust rose with each step the horses took. No grass grew inside the chasm. Strange gray briars and weeds were scattered in small clumps. The path ascended slightly and leveled at a short bridge. Beyond Roble stood pillars made from the same stone that composed the road. Roble's horse stopped outside a massive double set of sealed, castle doors. An oozing channel of black fluid flowed and bubbled like thick tar around the outer edge of the castle walls. Lavender gases rose from the moat in a mist.

No one stood above the tower gates.

Odd, she thought.

Roble turned his horse, left the gate, and started around the edge of the black moat. The remaining seven men followed. Two more horses collapsed. The two riders swung off before they would've been pinned. Roble's horse stumbled, and he dismounted. He took his face cloth and placed it over the horse's nose while he led the horse by the bridle. He rubbed the side of its nose.

Two men dropped on the sparsely vegetated ground. They gasped for several seconds before their bodies seized with tight spasms. They moved no more.

Poison?

"How far will you venture, human?" Istrell whispered while watching with keen interest. She wanted to know what else was in the chasm, but if he continued much farther, he'd die, and then she no longer needed to worry about her daughter's ridiculous wedding plans. Shawndirea would have to take the throne, despite her rebellious objections.

Another man fell and died seconds later.

No sentries guarded the castle. With the poisonous air, an army wasn't necessary.

The veins in Istrell's arms swelled. Sweat streamed down her face. The overpowering flow of energy from the crystals surged through her. Never had she been connected to such power. The magical conduit alarmed her. She feared she'd lose consciousness before she discovered what else occupied the Black Chasm.

Roble held the cloth over his horse's mouth and nose. His face reddened while he apparently held his breath to protect the horse from the poisonous gases. He heaved, coughed, and almost choked. He placed the cloth over his face for several seconds before covering the horse's again. She realized what the cloth was and who had given it to him.

The enchanted cloth was Shawndirea's and given to her by Zauber for when she ventured into dark caverns that housed poisonous mushrooms, which Shawndirea gathered to trade for other herbs. The cloth resisted most all poisons but didn't seem to completely aid Roble inside the chasm.

A few minutes after the group entered the chasm, Roble was the only one still alive. Instead of leaving, he headed deeper into the misty fog. A large, strange shadow lengthened from something she was unable to see.

For no explanation, her contact was cut off.

Istrell dropped to her knees, gasped for air, and was soaked with sweat. Her heart hammered. What blocked her view? Why was her connection severed? She leaned forward on her hands and knees, and panted. Her mouth was dry. Darkness clouded her vision, but she fought keep consciousness. Roble was braver than she credited, and now, she wanted to know if he survived.

Nauseated and fatigued, she reached and grabbed the crystals. She pulled herself to her feet and caught her breath.

Istrell called on the power of the crystals, but they remained cold. No magic flickered. No pulse or twinkle. Nothing.

Still breathing heavily, Istrell remembered her daughter's words. "Mother, I swear to you if he dies because of this, you're *dead* to me. Dead! Do you hear me?"

Queen Istrell's hands shook with fear. Shawndirea's words were a solemn threat and not uttered lightly. Her daughter's rebellion was mellow compared to the endless grudge her daughter would carry out. Somehow, Istrell needed to help Roble, but how?

She summoned the crystals again, but they remained cold. She grabbed the mirror and held her focus, but the glass didn't shimmer. Both refused to acknowledge and obey her power.

With everything she had, she commanded, and then pleaded but the power was gone. She dropped to her knees and sobbed. Her magic was somehow gone.

ROBLE STOOD ALONE BESIDE BLEYS. The horse trembled but understood the danger they were both in. Bleys took turns breathing through the cloth with Roble. The odd thing was, the horse held its breath until Roble placed the cloth back over its nose. Bleys knew the air was poisonous. Near the corner of the castle wall was another set of dark pillars. Something large with massive wings moved between two pillars.

Roble readied a knife in his left hand and waited. He wasn't certain what had passed by. He might get at least one knife throw before the gases claimed his life like it had the rest of the ragtag treasure hunters.

He hated having led the group to their deaths, but they were probably better off not struggling with their day-by-day begging existence. Their reward was death, the absence of hunger, thirst, and pain. Did he feel guilty for their deaths? No. He offered to turn back, but they insisted with unspoken threats to proceed.

The winged creature stood between the two pillars. It was, as best he could describe, a demon of some sort, but bigger than any he'd seen along the River Styx. Black veined wings unfolded and the beast filled the gaps between the pillars. It had hulking arms, chest, and legs. Thick claws protruded from its fingertips.

More wings shifted and moved behind it.

Even if his dagger could penetrate this beast's skin, which he doubted, this demon wasn't alone.

The demon roared with a wide mouth and revealed rows of jagged, yellow teeth. Others roared in the shadows. A dozen or so mounted knights lined the center of the pillared garden. Their vivid, blue eyes glowed through the eye slots of their skull-faced helms. Were these the knights Tyrann had cursed? Their black armor glistened like wet onyx.

Roble looked toward the path where he'd entered. The dead treasure-seekers' bodies twitched. The men were coming to life. They tilted their heads and glanced at him. Their radiant blue eyes were like the mounted knights beyond the gates. He shook his head. For a moment, he wondered if the poison was affecting his mind. Perhaps.

Roble thought of Shawndirea. Tears moistened his eyes. She had warned and pleaded with him, but he stubbornly decided to honor his oath to her vile mother. He shook his head in regret. He could never reach the chasm's veil in time. The large black demons took flight and fluttered toward him. His knives weren't enough to kill them.

To Bleys, Roble whispered, "What's your preferable choice of death?"

The horse whinnied and nudged his hand.

"Yeah, me too," Roble said. He folded the cloth and tucked it into a pocket. "Poison's the least painful route."

He inhaled one deep breath, choked on the air, and sputtered. He and Bleys dropped to the ground. Fiery pain radiated through his lungs. If one could breath liquid flame, this was how it felt. His vision dimmed, but he kept his attention on the three large, approaching demons. The undead men on the path behind him staggered to their feet.

Roble reached and patted Bleys' nose.

A shimmering blue light exploded in front of him. The demons shrieked with bone-chilling cries. Their wings buzzed like giant locusts and they retreated to the walls. The shimmering light prevented him from seeing anything. Fingers wrapped around both wrists and dragged him into the light. Seconds later, he lost consciousness.

CHAPTER 66

Q ueen Istrell rested on her knees and hung her head at the base of the crystals. She sobbed.

"I'm so sorry, Shawndirea," she whispered. "I hope one day you'll forgive me for my foolishness."

Covered with sweat, she didn't have the energy to stand. She lie down and drifted to sleep.

TWO DAYS LATER, Roble awakened in a bed. He slowly opened his eyes but didn't recognize his surroundings.

He rolled over and gazed into the wide eyes of an elderly woman seated at the side of his bed.

"Where am I?" Roble asked.

"Easy." The woman smiled, stood, and headed to the door. "Wait here."

"Who are you?"

"Timirius."

The woman hurried from the room and returned a few minutes later. Behind her, standing in the door, was Shawndirea. She stood about five-foot six inches by his estimate, *or* he'd shrank to her size again. She smiled in spite of the tears flowing down her cheeks.

"You're awake." Shawndirea crossed the floor in hurried steps. Tears spilled from her eyes, as she sat on the bed's edge and took his hand in hers.

"Where am I?"

"In a cottage on the outside of Elvendale," Shawndirea replied.

"How'd I get here?"

She shook her head. "We're not certain. You were found on Corwin's Pass."

"Corwin's Pass?"

"Yes. You were barely breathing."

"Without the enchanted cloth you gave me, I'd be dead. The fog surrounding the Black Chasm is poisonous."

Shawndirea smiled. "The cloth probably helped, but your armor protected you far more than the cloth."

Roble touched his chest. He was wearing a sleeping gown. "Where's my armor?"

Timirius pointed across the room. The armor hung on a rack.

Shawndirea placed her hand to his cheek, leaned, and kissed him. "When I got here, I feared you'd die. Your breathing was so shallow."

"That close, eh?"

She wiped tears. "Yes. What do you remember inside the chasm?"

"I'll tell you after I feel better."

She nodded. "We'll have a scribe write your report and send it to my mother. Neither of us shall enter her Courts for a *very* long time."

"That's good. A report should suffice."

"It'll do."

"What about Bleys?"

"He's at the stables. He's healing and should recover fully."

"Great."

"What happened to the troops that ventured with you?" she asked.

"All dead." Roble shook his head. "They died before the poison affected me. But you were right."

"About what?"

"Your mother intended for this mission to fail."

Shawndirea nodded. "I warned you."

He sighed. "I know. None of those men had adequate armor or weapons. None had any more combat training than I. They wouldn't survive fighting chickens."

"That bad?"

He nodded. "Worse, but they refused to run."

"So they had some bravery?"

"No, greed. That's why they came."

She squeezed his hand. "Greed?"

"Yes. One showed me a map where they could mine or hunt for treasures. Another thought land would be deeded to him."

Shawndirea pursed her lips. "My mother—"

"Now what do we do?" he asked.

"We find a home to settle and a priest to wed us."

Roble smiled. "You have a place in mind for us to live?"

"Lots of them."

He brought her hand to his lips and kissed it. "Am I your size or are you now mine?"

"Yours, of course."

Roble eased into a seated position. His vision blurred and the room spun. The elderly lady brought a pot of tea, some bread, and honey.

"How long have I been here?" he asked.

Timirius replied, "Two days."

He shook his head. "Two days?"

She nodded. "Do you remember how you escaped the Black Chasm?"

Roble closed his eyes and frowned. "Vaguely. The last thing I remember was … Black flying demons targeted and flew toward me. I collapsed. A shimmering portal or *something* appeared on the ground beside me. Before I lost consciousness, someone grabbed and pulled me through. They must've somehow taken Bleys through, too."

"Who?"

Roble shook his head. "No idea. I never saw a face. But isn't Corwin's Pass a good distance away?"

"There's a rough mountain ridge between the chasm and where you were found. Someone must've used a magical teleportation spell, which requires a lot of power and drains one's energy severely."

"Who'd do that?"

"Your guess is as good as mine."

Roble chuckled. "Doubtful. You know far more people capable of that than I."

"True. But who else knew you were there? Or why they'd deplete their energy to save you? I'm thankful they did."

"Me, too. Who found me on Corwin's Pass?"

Shawndirea spread honey across a rough slice of bread and handed it to Roble. "A traveling peddler on his way to the Kingdom of Legelarid found you. This was the first cottage he came to, so he left you here."

Roble chewed the bread slowly. "He give a name?"

"He never said."

"He should be rewarded."

Shawndirea nodded. "I'll send word to Legelarid for him to be found so we learn his identity. Then we'll give him gold for his aid."

"How'd you find out I was here?"

"A blue raven brought me the message. A small scroll tied to its leg informed me. I came immediately."

Roble frowned, rubbed his eyes, and then looked into hers. "You think the peddler sent the note?"

"Not likely."

"Then who?"

Shawndirea smiled. "The mysteries continue to increase, my love. My guess is a wizard since a raven message is a calling card. But I don't know a wizard who owns a blue raven. I don't think such a raven exists in the wild."

She reached in her pocket and pulled out another note. This one was still sealed. She handed it to Roble. "This one arrived for you yesterday."

Roble took the note, broke the seal on the back of the folded parchment, and unfolded it. He read the message and looked at her.

"What does it say?" she asked.

"Odlon requests I journey to Woodnog to train and discuss a possible search mission to help him form a group to find Lady Dawn. Apparently Lehrling's well enough to travel and is heading to Woodnog."

"Not before our wedding, dear," she said softly. "Besides, you need a few more days to recuperate."

He rubbed his temples. "I'm not ready to ride to Woodnog. Bleys would probably protest, too."

Shawndirea stood beside Roble inside a white marble temple hall. A priest dressed in white robes stood before them as they exchanged their vows. Thousands of butterflies flittered around the hall. She and Roble kissed one another passionately, and then they went outside the temple. The massive cloud of butterflies followed them.

He helped Shawndirea get on her horse before mounting Bleys. They rode half a day until they came to a ridge of dense trees. She stopped her horse and pointed.

"*This* is where we'll live," she said.

Roble eyed the place suspiciously. The trees were tall and massive with thick underbrush. He didn't see anywhere to build a cottage.

"Here?"

She nodded. "There's more than meets the eye."

Shawndirea chanted a series of words in a language he didn't understand but hoped she'd teach him. On the front of the largest tree trunk, a door appeared. His eyes widened, and she smiled with amusement.

"How?" he asked.

"I've spent years building this house. It's camouflaged so we'll always be safe from intruders. Some dryad kin also protect the trees. Unwanted visitors won't venture here long and certainly without notice."

She opened the door. "Come inside. Let me show you around."

"What about the horses?" he asked.

Shawndirea whistled. Nearby a servant stepped from the thick ivy vines, took the horses by their bridles, and led them through a curtain of oddly cloaked vines.

After they disappeared, she looked at Roble. "We have stables. When you're ready to travel to Woodnog, I'll show you."

"I look forward to it."

Shawndirea smiled, winked, and took his hand in hers. "Good. Now, let me show you our home."

THE END

The End

AUTHOR'S NOTE:

Thanks for purchasing a copy of *Shawndirea*. I hope you enjoyed your first journey in Aetheaon. Please take the time to write a review to let others know as well. Every little bit helps. Thanks, again, and the journey continues with *Lady Squire*. My best to you.

ABOUT THE AUTHOR

Leonard D. Hilley II grew up a quiet, shy kid with an inquisitive mind. Learning to read at an early age, he fell in love with books. He read every book he could get his hands on and stacks of dark comics about ghosts, monsters, and creepy things that stalk the night.

Like a lot of boys, he caught beetles, wooly bears, butterflies, and had an ant farm. When he was ten, his interests in science increased even more after seeing a professor's insect collection. Soon he set out on his quest to build his own collection. He also learned to rear butterflies and moths to obtain perfect specimens. He learned botany, gardening, and set his goal to become an entomologist.

At eleven, he watched Star Wars on the big screen. His imagination soared. Soon after, he discovered Roger Zelazny's Chronicles of Amber. Six months later, he had written the first draft of a novel. A novel he later discarded, but the characters stuck with him. Years later, these characters came to life in Shawndirea, which Hilley intended to be a novella for Devils Den. The characters, however, refused to be ignored and took the opportunity to unveil Aetheaon in their first epic fantasy. Lady Squire: Dawn's Ascension was quick to follow.

Shawndirea was Hilley's farewell to butterfly collecting, and those who have read the novel understand why. He has taken Ray Bradbury's advice to heart: "Follow the characters." He does. He follows, listens, and take notes—often never knowing where they're going to take him, but he's never been disappointed in the results.

Hilley earned a B.S. in Biology and an MFA in Creative Writing to combine his love of science and writing.

Sci-fi Titles: Predators of Darkness: Aftermath, Beyond the Darkness, The Game of Pawns, Death's Valley, The Deimos Virus.

Epic Fantasy: Shawndirea (Aetheaon Chronicles: Book One), Lady Squire (Aetheaon Chronicles: Book Two), Frosthammer (Aetheaon Chronicles: Book Three), Shadowfae (Aetheaon Chronicles: Book Four), and Devils Den.

UF/PR: Succubus: Shadows of the Beast (Nocturnal Trinity Series: Book One), Raven (Nocturnal Trinity Series: Book Two), A Touch of the Familiar

YA UF/Paranormal: Forrest Wollinsky Vampire Hunter; Forrest Wollinsky: Blood Mists of London; Forrest Wollinsky: Predestined Crossroads.

www.ingramcontent.com/pod-product-compliance
Lightning Source LLC
Chambersburg PA
CBHW030541020726
47494CB00005B/1447